Dickeyville

Joe Abbott's essays and stories have appeared in literary and academic publications. He teaches language arts at Butte College in northern California, where his office overlooks a complex of Pleistocene lava domes considered the world's smallest mountain range. He has been a ship's mate and has worked for the Humboldt/Del Norte County Public Health Department and Public Guardian's Office, the Northcoast Environmental Center and the Año Nuevo Interpretive Association. He once wrestled lumber in redwood mills and farmed in northern California's "emerald triangle", where income is not of a taxable variety. He has a BA from the University of Wisconsin at Madison and an MA from University of California at Davis. His wife is a physician; they have two sons.

DICKEYVILLE

a novel

by Joe Abbott

For Margot,
A beautiful lady always
Best,

Starhaven

©Joe Abbott 2012
ISBN 0-936315-35-0

STARHAVEN, 42 Frognal, London NW3 6AG
in U.S., c/o Box 2573, La Jolla, CA 92038
books@starhaven.org.uk
www.starhaven.org.uk

Typeset in Berthold Baskerville by John Mallinson

for Annie, for Robin and JT

1

Bundled in heavy coats against Iowa's killing winter, bus passengers not sleeping at this predawn hour were mindful of a dozing young man. He obviously wasn't one of them.

Twenty something, dressed in a black tee-shirt and linen Hugo Boss suit, he wore canvas loafers without socks – in Iowa the clothing of an insane man. Proof of this status was his seeming indifference to the frigid air currents sweeping the floor, the icy leakage from every seam in the lurching bus. When he'd climbed aboard the previous night, he'd seen that most male passengers wore woolen stocking caps. In L.A., home to this young man, only bank robbers and gang-bangers wore stocking caps, while the occasional psychopath might wear one lined with tinfoil to protect his skull from CIA transmissions.

Handsome, with shoulder-length blond hair and an ocean tan, the Californian looked like a king among the dour-eyed country folk and pale Midwestern collegians returning to farms for Christmas. Even as he slept, he radiated confidence and the healthy flush of outdoor life. All night the bus had stopped at darkened central Iowa towns, rousing him with cold blasts as the door opened. People around him would talk quietly before the sound melted into the whine of the diesel engine; interior lights would dim and the bus roll into darkness, snow-flakes drifting through the headlights.

Someone shook him awake. "What is it? Am I there?"

"Are you where?" wondered an old man in coveralls and worn Hudson Bay coat. Smallish, with the creased face and knotted hands of a laborer, he had bristly white hairs poking from his ears and nos-trils as well as from under a stocking cap.

"Is this Dickeyville?"

"This ain't there. I know Dickeyville, Wisconsin, son. We're still in Iowa and your stomach's growling."

"You woke me for that?"

"Yup."

The young man shook his head. "I haven't eaten since yesterday. In the Bahamas."

"I felt like talking to someone," said the old man, displaying in dimmed lights scraggly rows of yellowed teeth.

"You woke me so you could talk?"

"Yup. Your stomach's growling."

"Nothing's been open. It's night."

"Yup. I know all about it."

"About what?"

"That everything closes at night. Goin' to Dickeyville for the hunt?"

"Hunt?"

"Killer pig. The Horror."

"Don't know what you mean. I'm meeting my fiancée's family."

"Or the Grotto. Eighth wonder of the world if you ask me. Course you didn't ask. You cold?"

The young man yawned. "I'm starved and ache to my bones."

"Ought to eat then."

"I told you, there's nothing."

The old man plunged his blunt-fingered hands into opposite armpits and, settling back, let his craggy, whisker-stubbled face sink onto his chest. Immediately he broke into a snore like the crushing of aluminum cans.

After an hour of peering from ice-frosted windows into the darkened facades of one-stop towns, the young man finally fell back to sleep. His eyes re-opened in some pre-dawn hour to a crinkle of waxed paper – the old man was unwrapping a thick sandwich. Slabs of homemade bread; lettuce, pickles, brown mustard, mayonnaise, black olives, relish, cheddar cheese… The jaw-locking sandwich had more a perfume than an odor.

"Would of woke you when the bus stopped, but you seemed to need the rest," he said, eyes squinted in ecstasy as yellow teeth plunged in like a pitchfork driving into a hay bale. "Nobody can cook like them Amish people. They make their own cheese and bread. Sell the sandwich for two bucks. Best damn – pardon my French – sandwich in the tri-state. Old world cheese, if you catch my drift."

The young man mumbled a vague assent about "drift", whatever it was. Everyone else on the bus was eating sandwiches, including the broad-shouldered driver now steering over icy roads with one hand. A delicious aroma flowed along the icy jets leaking into the bus.

The old man balled up his empty wrapper and dropped it under the seat. He prodded the young man with his elbow. "You're not from around here."

"What was your first clue?" the young man asked.

"Your tan. And your clothes."

"I hadn't noticed. You mean to say everybody on this bus isn't wearing linen and doesn't have a tan?"

The old man was impervious to sarcasm. "Yup. Nope. People in the Midwest don't have tans like yours or wear flimsy clothes."

"What a surprise." The airport temperature had been eighty-six when he'd boarded the plane in the Bahamas. Because of the blizzard he had landed in Des Moines instead of Chicago, where he'd planned to pick up cold-weather clothing.

"Yup. Pathetic clothes."

"Not that it's your business."

"Nope. Pretty nippy in Iowa," the old man warned.

"You think?" The young man pretended to go back to sleep.

"Know why?" the old man persisted.

The young man sighed, slowly opening his eyes. "No, why?"

"We're pretty far north. It's cold and windy here because the sun's farther away than in summer. It snows around here, son."

"No kidding."

"It's not your fault you don't know. They should have taught you in school. These days schools ain't worth a damn." The old man settled back and closed his eyes. He slid a few inches down the seat.

The young man lay his head into the hard corner over the metal armrest and window. Exhausted, he let his eyes close.

"D'you read?" – The old man leaned close, cheese-breath warming the other one's face, making his eyes pop back open. The oldster's forehead was furrowed with concern.

The young man turned away and coughed. He didn't like old or fat people breathing on him. A true Californian, he regarded infirmity or ugliness as disease. He didn't like to inhale the air of the afflicted. "Of course I can read. The schools aren't that bad."

"Ha! That's pretty good, son. I mean *really* read."

"Isn't reading just reading?"

"Shows how much you know. I mean like the Midwestern writers. I only say that because you ain't from around here."

The young one shrugged. "I've read some. Wasn't... uh, *whatshisname*, from the Midwest?"

The old man snorted. "Sure. Most famous of all."

"Look. I need to get a little – "

"Because if you're going to travel in the Midwest, you better read the literature. Only a damn fool wouldn't. Want some gum?" – He fished out of his pocket a rubbed stick of Wrigley's that might have been there for years.

Hungry as he was, the young man regarded it and shook his head. "I'm only visiting, not moving here."

The old man continued: "There's a smell in the springtime. Can't say anybody's ever described it right, though. Comes around March when the ice starts to break and the wind starts to warm up and the earth thaws. Smells a little like something dead. Well, the thawed hog pens smell that way. Only it's like all dead things: at first it smells strange, but eventually it gets sweet and takes on that wild smell." The old man nodded to emphasize some point the other didn't get. "You know, when the earth thaws?"

The young man considered. He hadn't thought about frozen earth.

"You look like a man who's always been young, and always will be," the old man said.

Go away, the young man thought.

The old man squinted, focusing eyes like red buttons pressed into mud. "You seem like a man who'd like Roethke. A Minnesotan. Knew a lot about love. Course, all poets do; that's why they're poets – because they can't spend *all* their time fornicatin'. Makin' poetry and makin' love have a lot in common."

Suddenly alert, the young man glanced at those sitting nearby, but nobody seemed to be paying attention. He looked back at the old man to see what he had in mind.

The old man stretched his hand toward the window, past the young man's face. The young man pulled back as the old man pressed a dirt-caked finger onto the fogged glass and wrote five names: Wright, Roethke, Duffy, Bly, Sandburg. He said, "For prose, Hemingway's Nick Adams stories, maybe..." The young man appeared interested, so the old man continued, unaware that the other was noticing that his skin had the color and odor of prunes: "If you're going to live in the Midwest you've got to read it. It's an old land and after a while you'll want to understand it."

"Said I'm just visiting. I'm going to meet – "

"Because it's like the winter insomnia, when it comes. Like a bare bulb swaying while a blizzard pounds your hundred-year-old farm-house. Same place your Pappy and Ma was married and died in, buried in the family graveyard next to your grandmother and father. Same storm rages in your soul, son. Nor-wester of hunger and fear..." The young man watched some inner light switch on behind the old one's eyes, a light revealing more about darkness than day. The man began to gesture, shaping air and words between callused hands. "On those winter nights you could lose the pieces of your soul like a hunk of feed corn worried by rats, until there's nothing left but an old dried cob..." The young man glanced to see if any other seats were available. "Hell, I oughtta be a poet myself, eh?" Then, as suddenly as it had switched on, the light of the old man's madness dimmed and he shrugged, "Or you could make the winter storm your companion. Find solace in the long hours. Go to church and read and learn the earth through poets and takin' up a handful of the soil and smellin' it and workin' it. In spring you could walk out on your two hundred acres. At twilight go by the fishing pond and scuffle your boots into the earth. Maybe turn over an arrowhead been there three hundred years."

The young man pulled himself a little further into the corner of his seat. He glanced out the window, recoiling as huge snowflakes brushed against the glass and swirled away.

"You warm weather types don't think enough about dyin' because you don't live winter after winter when things die. Don't think enough about death, so you don't know about living."

"I think we do all right."

"No. Don't suffer enough. On the other hand, look at the way you're dressed."

"I said I was in the Bahamas."

"Just goes to show," the other concluded. "Things happen too fast in warm places, 'ceptin' geological time. That's the same everywhere."

"At least we don't obsess."

"So you say. See, Hemingway wrote how in Spain's financial hey-day some folks had swimming pools who didn't used to take baths. Seems to me you California dreamer-types are like that."

"Maybe I'm from Florida."

"Don't think so... Man like you is always hungry. What's it you hunger for?"

"You don't even know me. You can't just – "

"Think. What is it?"

"All right, *breakfast*. I'm starving on this goddam bus."

"Nope. That ain't it."

"I think I'd know."

"Huh-uh. Something else."

"*You're* something else. What's 'California dreamer' supposed to mean? Something you heard in a song." – Hick, he thought. He glanced at the other passengers: ugly, pasty-skinned provincials. He felt a sudden hated for them all.

"Stegner himself – that's Wallace Stegner – was born here in Iowa. Right in Lake Mills. Didn't know that, did you?"

The young man peered out the window again. "Looks like the storm's getting bad."

"I seen storms, son; this ain't nothin'. I was gonna say Stegner's maybe a little subtle for you to start on. He's considered a western writer 'cause he moved there. Hemingway was from Illinois. We'll start you on the Nick Adams stories. More narrative drive."

"Start me? What are you talking about? You a teacher or – "

"Sure am. Teach everywhere I go. Didn't I just learn you something? Anyway, what kind of man isn't a teacher?" – He pushed one of his dirty, stubbed fingertips into his whiskery cheek. "How many kids you got, son?"

"None. I'm not married."

"No kids at your age? What are you, homosexual?"

"What?" he snorted. "Because I don't have kids? Told you I'm meeting my fiancée."

"Sure, son. Well, nice talking to you but I got to get some shut-eye now. Before long we'll be in Wisconsin." – The old man turned his head and closed his eyes.

The young man waited a few moments until the other began to snore softly, then prodded a finger into his shoulder. "Hey. You ever been to Disneyland?"

"Huh?" the old man snorted. "What's that?"

"I said, have you ever been to California. Disneyland."

"Sure. I was there with my family in the summer of... let's see, uh, 1962, it was."

"Did you read any comic books first?"

"Did I what?"

"Read any comic books. Only a damn fool wouldn't. If you really want to understand Disneyland you gotta read lots of Duck. Donald Duck. But as a beginner, maybe we'll start you on Mouse. He's more subtle than Duck but you being experienced and all, you'll probably pick it up. We'll bring you up slowly to Gyro Gearloose. He's pretty much considered the epitome of the California Disney sensibility."

A half-smile crossed the old man's eyes, but lasted no more than a second. "I hope you stick around long enough to find what you're looking for, son. And to learn what you should – that hunger and desire are the same thing."

"I told you, I'm not hungry for anything except – "

But the old man tipped back his head and began to snore.

Chilled and exhausted, he watched the snowy morning come through bare trees passing outside. Just after dawn the bus came upon an accident. Several passengers stood in the aisles looking at cars stopped ahead, but the young man focused on a farmer working in a barn beside the two-lane road. Faded paint across one end of the barn read "Twiny's Twist Greek Chew"; the young man mouthed the words as if they were clues to something.

The barn's doors were wide open to the freezing air where the farmer had gaffed a white hog from the door header. Oblivious to the icy dawn and stalled traffic just twenty feet away, he wiped a thin-bladed boning knife across a pink-smeared apron. The young man rubbed his frosted pane to see better and made out a blue-pink pile of knotted entrails at the farmer's feet. Steam rose from the innards and carcass.

The bus accelerated to what seemed an unsafe speed on the narrow snowy road. A featureless countryside marked by hillocks and slight depressions rolled by like a black and white movie. It came as a relief when the young man heard the driver announce that the next stop was Dickeyville, Wisconsin, the town named after the settler ancestors of Daphne, his fiancée. Feeling a sudden intimacy for the place where she had been born, he peered hard out the window and, like the unveiling of a miracle, the blizzard briefly opened. The bus passed snow-covered fields stretching to a hazy, indistinct horizon. White farmhouses, charming, strangely familiar... the young man felt as if he were discovering something he already knew. In a few minutes he would see his fiancée, the woman who would someday have his children and share his life. He would see the environment that had shaped her life, the town half-owned by her parents. He would meet the people she knew. He had never before married, and he looked forward to the fact that at age twenty-nine his history was about to join another's.

The snowstorm again enveloped the bus as it climbed a gradual rise and passed a sign announcing Dickeyville, population 999. Picket fences and white houses, just as he'd imagined... However, when they came to a halt halfway between a sign identifying the Dickeyville Diner and Rifle Club and a small, plain-faced wooden structure with a sign indicating Dickeyville Industrial Park and Shooter's Mall, no one was waiting for him. He glanced at his watch, saw that it was 7:15 a.m., exactly when the bus was meant to arrive. The snow turned to sleet as he watched. Wind gusts battered the bus.

He grabbed his carry-on, a sleek leather duffel containing Coco-Tan Lotion, a ragged ancient beach towel dedicated to the virtues of Bushmill's Irish Whiskey, a pair of flip-flops, sunglasses, Hawaiian shirt and white slacks, his favorite diving mask and a pair of swimming trunks still damp with salt water. He remembered with a pang that he'd cut short his working trip by two days. As he walked down the bus aisle, every head turned to watch. Perhaps the faces expressed gratitude that the god-ling had blessed them with his presence?

Nobody else got off in Dickeyville. The driver sprang from his seat to pull suitcases from the slush-caked belly of the bus, but the young man shook his head no as the door folded open, a rush of cold air sweeping in. He jumped off the last step and moved quickly to the lee of the diner, which was closed. Alone, glancing up at pale faces peering at him from the bus, he experienced an alarming premonition that he ought to get on board again and ride until he could catch a plane home. The vehicle pulled out in a cloud of diesel fumes, sending up rooster-tails of icy mud. Nobody had arrived to meet him. He pushed aside premonition to concentrate on his face numbing from cold.

He had skied in Tahoe and Colorado and, if asked, would have said that he knew cold.

He didn't know cold.

Within a minute his toes began freezing inside his canvas shoes. He stamped his feet and glanced around. There were trees in Dickeyville but those near enough to see in the white swirl were spidery skeletons dripping with sleet. The sky was not so much dark as absent of color, although a bruise-toned sheen tinted the sky in the east where a sun had risen somewhere behind a thick ceiling of snow cloud.

He dropped his duffel and thrust numbing fingers beneath his armpits. He glanced up and down the two-lane highway that he supposed bisected the town. He could imagine when it was a dirt road, the place's sole link to an outside world. Across the street from the diner houses began, and he supposed in horse and buggy days people living along the road had been the lucky ones. But years had passed, bringing the sputter of horseless carriages.

The wind slowly rose, driving the sleet almost horizontal. In a moment of futile fury he swept at his hair, which had blown nearly straight up. Pulling back under the building's awning, he felt heavy slush caking down his waist and legs. His nose had gone numb.

He didn't want to miss Daphne and her parents, but it wouldn't do to freeze to death waiting. Squinting into the blast of wind, he searched, then tried the door of the diner and swore at the sign:

Doors Open Every Day at 6 a.m.
No shirt, no shoes, no service.

No shirt or shoes – as if! His teeth began to chatter. He glanced at his watch: 7:17. He'd been waiting two minutes. He pulled his bag in front of his ankles. Very resourceful, he thought, looking at the icy accumulation on it. They'll think that when they find my body.

A pickup with clanking tire chains materialized out of the storm veil, driver bending over slightly to peer at the blond stranger. He dared to hope, but the truck continued past. The wind howled through wet, bare trees. Sleet stuck like demented glue to the side of the diner and the young man's dufflebag and jacket.

2

The blond Californian started to worry that something might have happened to his fiancée and her family. Daphne had told him that the only things between Wisconsinites and death in winter were fireplaces and furnaces. But no, that was silly. An accident on the dangerous roads? Too horrible to think. He imagined people thrown from cars to bleed on the slushy pavement. They'd last five minutes. He wrapped his linen coat around him tightly, grabbed his bag and leaned forward into the sleet. He could see a Skelly service station down the road but couldn't tell if it too opened its doors at 6 a.m. Every Day.

It did. A bell chimed as he went in. Hunch-shouldered from the cold, he looked around and found a short, wiry man his own age standing reading a book beside a space heater. "Excuse me," he said. "But do you have a phone? My cell phone," he explained, "is sitting under twenty fathoms of Caribbean."

The attendant put down his book and took in the stranger, top to bottom. "The boss don't like me to sit down. Says it looks bad for the customers. Now don't that beat all? I been here over an hour and no one's been in." His eyes were close together, his chin small and cleft. He sported a wispy pencil-thin mustache that reminded the stranger of strands of thread.

Thin, straight black hair, parted into a ruler-straight exposure of white scalp, hung in bangs over his forehead; he would do perfectly cast as a dim medieval peasant. Smeared streaks of what appeared to be dirt or motor oil covered a pale cheek. Stretching his shoulders, our Californian thought: a knight's half-wit squire in *Monty Python*.

"I said, 'don't that beat all?'"

"Hmmm, I guess it does," he said, shrugging himself out of his frozen muddle. Over the attendant's shoulder was a long window looking out on a poorly-lit garage space. Without really thinking about it, he supposed the guy had been working on the big four-wheel drive sitting there with its hood up.

The attendant was meanwhile waiting for him to say something else but, when he didn't, reached under the counter and pulled out an oil-smudged phone book. "Here go. Phone's outside. We gotta keep the book here on account of people – mostly from outa town – stealing the pages. Can you beat that?" His little eyes bored hard, as if the tall stranger had done time for page-napping.

"A heinous crime," he muttered, scanning the book for "Dickey". Finding none, he momentarily panicked, thinking he'd heard the bus driver wrong and exited at the wrong town. Then he realized he was looking in the section for Gordondale and, flipping pages to what was obviously a smaller burg, Dickeyville, found dozens of "Dickeys". Locating the one he was after, he borrowed a pencil and copied the number. "Wouldn't dream of felonious ripping," he added.

The attendant evidently wasn't amused.

The handsome stranger thought of something else. "You have any food here?"

The guy perked up. "Got peanuts. Moky's Smoked and also Brittle Brand Candy-coats. Get you some?"

"In a minute. Got to phone." He pushed open the door and went out on the sleet side of the building and put two quarters in a slot. No dial tone. No change back. His frozen wet suit sagging on his body, he hurried inside. Compared to earlier, the sleet seemed slightly abated.

"Tom fool phone." – The attendant put down his book again. "Thing gets wet and don't work every winter. Where you trying to call? Long distance? Get you a few packs of nuts now?"

The tall man bent, strands of thick blond hair draping dramatically over his forehead, and rubbed his hands in front of the heater. "Local. I'm trying to call somebody who lives here." He looked at the attendant's book. *Reading Digest: World's Greatest Leaders.*

The attendant stopped midway in shoveling a handful of foil-wrapped packages toward him. "Hell's bells, you should of said something. Go ahead, use my phone."

The stranger thanked him and, thinking he knew the expression but had never heard anyone so young use it, lifted the receiver of the wall phone. No dial tone on this one, either. The attendant sharply tapped the phone button a few times with an oily forefinger but no better luck. He chewed at what would have been a fingernail tip if he'd had any. "Nope," he said, "I s'pose we're incommunicado today." Turning his attention from the two bills the stranger dropped on the counter for the peanuts, he nodded towards his book. "You ever read about Alexander the Great? Hear about the Gordian knot?"

"Huh-uh. Never did."

"How 'bout Theseus and the Minotaur's maze? Should read that."

"Umm..."

"This here Alexander the Great book was written by a genius. An' I mean a genius. Do you read? I mean, really read?"

"Don't start that shit again."

"Beg pardon?"

"Nothing. I read Bly. And – um, Stegner."

"Good stuff. But Theseus and the Minotaur's maze?" The attendant wiped his nose with his sleeve. "That's what you oughtta read."

The tall man looked out the window past "Nightcrawlers" and "Rifle Repair" signs as he picked up a package of peanuts and bit at a corner. Teeth clenched, he managed to grunt: "Never heard of 'em. Any chance you could direct me to the Dickey house? Charley and Winona Dickey?"

The attendant looked up. "The Dickey's place? Why didn't you say so? Sure, I know them." Something passed behind his eyes. "Better gimme back them peanuts, mister."

"What? Why should I? I haven't eaten for so long I could eat – " He looked around the room " –a can of Porter's Oil Additive."

"Heard your stomach, all right. But you wouldn't want these." The attendant snatched the package out of his hand and swept the counter into the garbage. "Changed my mind. These ain't for sale."

"Now listen here – "

"I thought maybe you was some guy here for the winter hunt, is all. Didn't know you was here for locals."

"Hunt? You're the second to mention it."

"Dickeyville Horror Days. Anyone with a brain knows about 'em. You don't?"

"I'm here for the Dickeys."

"I know the Dickeys. Know 'em real well. They own half this town. In fact, I went out with a Dickey girl for years."

Mat smiled tolerantly. "Probably not this one. I'm speaking of Daphne Dickey."

"That's the one. You kin of theirs?"

He looked at the attendant. He took in the man's hatchet-thin and slack-eyed face, his low, grease-smudged forehead and moustache looking like glued-on pubic hair. Glancing down at the man's book, now sitting print-side up, he saw that it had extra-large type. "Sort of kin," he answered. "Is there more than one Daphne Dickey?"

The attendant examined his face. "Where you from, Mister...?"

"Roper. Mat Roper from California." – He held out his hand.

The attendant wiped his own quickly on his coveralls and stuck it out. "Ed Hieman, at your service. Though if you're around long enough, folks in these parts call me Buster."

"Pleased to meet you, Buster – "

"But I hate to be called that, Mister Roper. It bothers me something fierce." – With a cramped, laborious style, as if he were not used to drawing or writing, he began to inscribe a map on a blue paper towel. "Come in on the bus, did you? Why didn't you eat at that Amish place down the road? Best in the state, I hear."

Mat grunted.

"Peanuts are stale, is all," Buster went on. "Just for the damned tourists, get my drift? I get a dime on every package I sell. Came to nearly ninety bucks last summer." He thought of something. "Say, you want to share some of my knockwurst sandwich? Big dill slices on it."

Mat was starved, but not that starved. "I'm a vegetarian."

"Oh? Doctor animals?"

"No, *vege*-tarian. As in vegetables."

Buster straightened up. "You mean to say you crazy Californians got doctors for your gardens?"

"What I mean... Just sell me the peanuts. I've got to eat something."

"You California boys must think we're a little unsophisticated out here. No way I'm gonna sell you stale peanuts." Buster scrawled on the map, pausing to ask if Mat Roper happened to be an actor.

Mat began modestly, "As a matter of fact I have – "

"There she is, good as a gold grape," Buster interrupted, pushing forward the map drawn on a windshield towel. "By the way, you ever heard of organic food?"

"Of course. That's the best way to – "

"'Cause ain't all food organic? Ain't pretty much everything?"

"No, it's food grown without – "

"Well, better get going now. I got a carburetor to clean."

Mat took the map. He saw that the streets ran crooked, almost in a maze. He inquired if he might call a cab, but the attendant snorted and said he might as well call a buffalo for the good it'd do him. Mat took up his duffel and thanked Buster Hieman.

"You see Daphne," the latter said as he went out the door, "tell her refusing her marriage proposal was the dumbest thing I ever did, hear? Tell her that." Standing, he cackled as he took up his book. "Tell her to come ask me again."

The door swung shut.

Sudden gloom came over Mat as he set out to cross the small town. Overhead, a snow-caked banner drooped forlornly across the main street; plastered with snow, the lettering was indecipherable. The message might have been comforting, but it gave no pleasant greeting to him. He considered what he'd seen so far: a busload of homely people, one crazy coot and a mildly retarded pump jockey. Small wonder everyone moved west.

According to the map, he had only a half-mile to walk. The sleet stopped; muddy-gray sky lightened by degrees. Perhaps the cold had abated a trifle. His feet were numb and no longer pained him, but a heaviness not related to his dufflebag settled down. He blinked at clean snowfall on the yards and filtered sunlight reflecting from the white houses trimmed uniformly with contrasting shutters. Passing two white churches, both small, perhaps one great room each, both with absurdly high steeples topped with crosses barely discernible in low clouds, he thought of Salvador Dali's elongated art. Pausing before the Epiphany Church of Salvation, which had twin stained glass windows representing the Garden of Eden and the Last Supper, he wondered at the fine craftsmanship and how such a small town could support it. A figure moved behind the glass, gesturing, perhaps beckoning. Mat hurried on.

As he went up and down the rollercoaster street, snow packed inside his pathetic loafers. From the bus window southern Wisconsin had seemed flat and bare, but he discovered it now to be gently heaving and, despite bare branches, rather arboreal. Close to his destination, according to the map, he came upon a quaint graveyard. Old weather-worn headstones protruded above snow, a crucifixion monument with several figures too distant to see clearly. Glancing across it, he saw a brick structure – the Holy Ghost church according to a sign – and what he took for a typical small-town park. As he came closer, rising from snowy earth, the park disclosed creations so bizarre that he almost failed to register what they were. It was a garden of monuments, the statuary at once hideous, despicable and marvelous, like the riotous colors festooning a gaboon viper. So weird was the place that Mat's initial sensation was that it served as a warning. A sign read: DICKEYVILLE GROTTO.

He'd never seen anything like it. Nothing could have been like it, at once so chintzy and ridiculous that it was magnificent, a work of excess so beguiling it had to be the labor of brilliant lunacy. Despite discomfort from the cold and uncertainty as to whether he should run, Mat felt compelled to press closer. Like a mouse walking toward piled loops of a coiled snake, he had to see, and what he saw were snow-capped mounds framed in concrete, decorated with thousands of seashell bits, glass shards, rocks, buttons or mosaic tiles and stones. A couple of these monoliths were gated and large enough to enter. All had themes: Christopher Columbus; Christ the King and Mary; the Holy Ghost; a petrified tree column with limbs and leaves detailed in glass; patriotism and government; the Sacred Heart. Never had a monument been rendered so artless, never such effort been put into constructing edifices to bad taste. Mat felt breathless, like a child dazzled by the riotous gayety of Chinatown. If you gilded the Statue of Liberty with bottle caps, adorned the Mona Lisa with glitter sunglasses... There were other dedications, so numerous and gaudy, reminiscent of artifices like piñatas or disco mirror-balls, each one made up of what seemed like millions of embedded decorative shards.

The grotto was so alien it might have fallen to earth. Simply observing it, Mat could not have been more horrified or embarrassed than if it had been dedicated to him. If sights were sound, he would have heard the cacophony of a pachinko parlor, a circus calliope, Disneyland's *Pirates of the Caribbean* melody in duet with the Macarena and Hell's fire alarms amplified through a madman's sewer pipe.

"Unbelievable. Freaking, fucking un-believable... If a parking lot carnival cooked meth, went schizophrenic and shot steroids, this is what it would look like."

As he stood riveted, he heard a sound not quite of the wind. Glancing around, he caught a motion as a side door at the Holy Ghost church shut. Turning, he hastened down the street, seeing Christmas trees in the windows of white houses with pathways beaten through snow to sheds and sidewalks; plywood nativity scenes behind picket fences. A cocker spaniel trotted across a yard to wag its stumpy tail at him through a fence. All these things would have, for this past six months since he'd fallen in love with Daphne, filled him like a cup. Now, emptiness. He hurried under the skeletal trees along sidewalks on crooked streets, remembering that back in California, winter was the season when the world became green.

Here he was in Daphne's town. Where she'd grown up.

3

Daphne had bellowed her way into Mat's life. She'd come to California as a substitute delegate to the American Livestock Convention in Sacramento, where the Wisconsin pavilion emphasized the virtues of "Wisconsin dairy", primarily cheese, a hundred sample wheels of which the Wisconsin consortium had brought along for tasting, as if cheeses were novel for Californians. The convention was, Daphne later told Mat, the first time she'd traveled outside Wisconsin not related to Green Bay Packers' football. When Mat laughed, she didn't.

Mat's presence had also been as a substitute delegate. He'd come to the convention to assist a buddy who provided a seaweed supplement for organically-raised cattle. The guy's beach-bum partner had bailed out at the last moment, at a critical point for seaweed sales, so out of desperation the guy had promised Mat a hundred bucks a day plus expenses to help run his booth. Being one more beach bum-actor short on money, Mat had jumped at the chance. As a vegetarian, he thought beef repulsive.

Daphne told Mat as they leaned on the fence rails of the Iowa hog exhibit that she felt "right at home". He sized up her shape within tight blue jeans and red blouse unbuttoned to cleavage, lively blond hair falling below a cowboy hat. She had a face made for modeling, perfectly stunning, unusual too, though he couldn't say why.

Daphne had arrived at a time when Mat's nights were frequented by leather ladies, mostly blondes, who seemed to exist at the beaches and to age only in an epidermal sense, women who otherwise seemed perpetually somewhere between twenty and the precipice age of thirty-nine, hungry for sun and man-flesh and cocaine and alcohol before their looks were gone. It didn't enter Mat's mind that his and his peers' skins weathered too, from countless hours sitting on surfboards under blazing sun. Nor did he notice the appetites of the wealthy leather men, who trolled the beach bars for young beach bums. He never considered that his peak would last only as long as his looks. Mat was mostly indifferent, self-satisfied and immune.

Immunity was armor. The zen of indifference.

In the beach bars everyone knew everybody. Society of Beach Bums (SOBB t-shirts, available in tourist shops) members moved easily and carelessly between them, greeting every rich skipper who took his yacht out on lazy swells with a cabin-load of hard-bodied women and hard-liquored buddies, skippers with perfect white hair and wearing weathered white captain's caps who came into harbor under motor too fast, mainsails flapping, harbor police fussing only when some other rich guy's rub rails beat against his pier. In the bars older ladies bought drinks for the beach bums with defined pectorals who landed bit parts as extras in movies from one week to the next. Parading bare-chested across the beach or posing with drinks in front of a bar TV, these 'actors' all dreamed of steady parts in *Sea Watch*. Each was on the verge of "something" – a professional term tainted with malignant ennui.

A timeless drift, a timeless place, where people remained young until they miraculously aged in a night of sudden revelation…

When Daphne had seen Mat walk by her booth, she'd bellowed a hog call that rolled like a tsunami over the hubbub of ten thousand people in the California State Convention Center. The sound, crossed between a foghorn and a castration, had shivered Mat's scalp under his blond hair and retracted his testicles to somewhere up around his spleen. He had stopped (or rather his feet had failed him) and listened as she sold herself to him. When he'd steadied himself to leave for his booth, she'd threatened another hog call.

Please, no.

She asked, "What's your name, mister? I'm Daphne Dickey. And how do you get a tan like that on your feet?"

Mat's eyes tracked to his sandals.

"And this black t-shirt and the white slacks. God, you're a real piece of work, mister. You are something rare."

"Not really."

"Who are you?"

"Mat Roper. And 'how do I tan'?"

"Just getting to know you, Mat Roper. A girl's got to know the best and worst right away."

He laughed. "I'm a free-spirit kind of guy, Miss Daphne Dickey."

"You do look that way, if it's a euphemism for broke. But aren't you the good-looker." Daphne had turned and waved toward a booth under a banner: WISCONSIN CHEESE: DO IT WITH COWS.

A raven-haired beauty waved and hog-hooted back, at which Daphne immediately linked her arm through Mat's and asked him to "promenade the fairgrounds".

The crowd parted like the Red Sea as she led him away, nearby faces seeming to smile from within a mist. She was the odd one.

"Don't play the sophisticate with me, Mat Roper. I hate phonies like fox hate crow, OK?"

"If you say. So are you what they call a 'hick'?"

She laughed. "I'd answer to 'hick', yeah."

For the next half hour she led him around stockyard pens. When they came to the pig pavilion, she stopped beside a big boar lounging in a bed of hay. Pink-skinned and bald, the indolent creature looked obscene to Mat; its testicles bulged like tennis balls in red spandex.

Daphne glanced at the boar with disinterest. "You ever hear of the Dickeyville Horror?"

"The what?"

"Nothing, really." She hung over a fence. "What is it you want, Mat Roper? What gallops your mule?"

Gallops my mule indeed, he thought, tossing a pebble into the pen and seeing Gary Cooper in his mind's eye. "I dunno. Maybe the same things most guys want. A woman who loves him, some kids and – "

She laughed. "Puh-leeze."

He tried again, eyeballing her chest. "Tell you what I'd like now – "

"Stop it. In farm towns we learn young that's not a big deal." She reconsidered. "A big deal until it's done and then not until it's a big deal again. Tell me. What is it you want? Right now?"

"Who knows until you get it? Short term, a drink. Long term, enough drinks, enough babes, free rent, and my own show..."

"I'm enough woman for anybody. And I know shows don't grow on trees. And the price for anything free is always too high."

Intrigued by such presumptuousness, Mat looked hard at her. "I'll tell you something, Daphne Dickey. Everything in life but money came easily to me. At one time, even money came easily."

"That's a start," Daphne said. "I hate bullshit. And I'll tell you this: until recently, with everything but money, it all came hard for me."

When the convention ended, Daphne drove Mat to L.A. in her rental car, moving that first day into her own apartment, laughing when he'd reluctantly invited her to stay with him. Her apartment was expensive, big and situated with an ocean view, though not right on the harbor as was Mat's – he shared with anywhere from three to five other surf bums, depending on couch space. Hers was one of those places loved by junior law partners and single doctors and young financiers, most of whom drove Porsches or Escalades or who had no car at all and wore it like a crown, commuting on rollerblades, their daddies' money or four thousand dollar bicycles. These guys Mat knew from the Harbor Club where, instinctually, he and they understood that, while he had them all now, later, when his looks were gone and liver spots came out, the bouncers would stop him at the door.

Before two weeks had passed, Mat learned Daphne came from money. Big farmland, bigger than he could imagine... She said big money. Mat liked big money. "Big money" had a nice ring to it that kick-started his surrender to the charming Wisconsin girl, whose parents, according to her, also owned half the town named after them and called every night to check on her. This was bad, because for all the women that he'd rolled over during the past ten years Mat was a babe in the woods in the love game.

When he went to Daphne's place, he'd find her at the pool surrounded by junior yuppies who always seemed to have conversation that didn't involve surfer-dudes. He remembered miserably why he'd avoided love in the first place and immediately felt stifled by the relationship. She grew on him, but even that admission felt like a sizing for a straightjacket. If he didn't call her at night to "check in", she would call him. She was so cheerful he wanted to scream, "Get away from me. Can't you leave me alone?" Yet he recognized with a horror that, if he didn't see her, he felt he was going a bit nuts.

Early in the acquaintance, to evade the love trap, Mat conjured an excuse to leave her at home and headed for the clubs. He went to the Del Mar and knocked down a couple Irish whiskeys neat. It was early, nine-thirty. Two women found him within a half hour. Secretaries at Seaside Marine – he'd seen them before; they knew of him.

A miserly exchange, verbal economy... The two led Mat from the bar, Eva plain-faced and dirty-blond, fine body, and Roxy, bubbly dark-framed glasses and a reed-thin body and face of a goddess. Between them he'd choose the best parts.

They took him to an estuary condo. "It's like that, huh?" he asked when they led him straight to the bedroom and he stood staring at a king-size bed. The condo smelled of lavender beeswax candles.

"It's like that," Eva said and, pouring three doses of Stoly into water glasses, pulled off her blouse and stretched languidly on the bed in her bra and skirt. For her part, Roxy, still completely clothed, gulped the vodka, started coughing and rose to turn down the light. She put her arms around Mat and kissed him, her breath tasting of salami and vodka, and pulled his black t-shirt over his head. Eva pulled them onto the mattress and the two women promptly snuggled into one another.

Mat lay on his side watching. He had never had two women at once and had never planned what would happen. Momentum gathered at the women's paces; they decided the game.

He stayed somewhat passive. Perhaps women with exotic tastes weren't attracted to him? Maybe exotic women regarded him as conventional? It was an accusation he could confess to. He availed himself lackadaisically, leaning against bars, laughing with acquaintances, looking good. A woman usually chose him before final call: her agenda. Mat wasn't dull, he simply had never needed to try hard.

He watched the two women kiss.

Roxy pushed away, saying she'd never done anything like this before; she wanted to leave but oh God she was so drunk...

Mat snorted.

Eva's face, red now, buried itself into Roxy's blouse, teeth clamping onto tiny pearl buttons, the material tearing open.

"Hey, that tidbit you just destroyed cost eighty bucks at Hagman's!"

"Mmmph," Eva replied, going for Roxy's throat.

The women began pulling at each other's clothing. Mat stripped off his own and reached to touch them, but Roxy pushed his hand off and told him not yet. He settled back, sipped vodka, coughed into the glass as the ceiling fan turned lightly and women breathed heavily. He leaned towards the bed table and switched on a radio. Harpsichord, Mozart, which he changed to soft rock. The night had barely begun; it was before ten-thirty. The women sighed.

A niggling. Puzzled, he set the hook and expected to reel in a sardine of a thought, but on the deck, examined, everything sloshed out like a gutted yellowfin. It was so alien he was almost dizzy... Guilt. There it was: Daphne, alone at home waiting for him... Daphne two thousand miles from Wisconsin... dependent on him.

"Damn!" he swore.

The two women froze momentarily. "Be patient," Roxy purred.

"It's not that." He didn't owe Daphne anything, hadn't promised a thing, not even that he'd date her. She'd just come along from Sacramento. He hadn't said no – how could he? It's a free country. They were barely lovers – just ten or so times, whatever, like a dozen other girls he knew casually. "It's not that," he repeated.

"Shhh," Eva hushed him. "If I'd known you were such a talker, I'd've given you a Mexican Quaalude."

"Not that we've ever done something like this – " Roxy explained, her words muffled in Eva's crotch.

"Oh, can that crap, will you?" Eva grumbled, sitting up to reach for her vodka. "He doesn't give a damn how many times we've fucked."

"I mean, who the hell does she think she is, coming in here and ruining my gig?" – Mat eyed Eva's breasts.

"Who?" Roxy said. "Eva ruining it? Or me ruining you and Eva?"

"*Daphne*, of course."

"What's she look like?" Roxy asked.

"You trying to break us up, Roper?" Eva asked. She pierced Mat like a kabob with a steely stare.

"Not that there's anything to break up," Roxy said.

"Not you guys." – He jumped from the bed.

"*Guys?* Is this some Freudian sexist shit, Roper?" Eva wondered.

"You two," Roxy said, "I'm getting bored here..."

"I mean, she's been here a few stinking days and she's already trying to pull this commitment crap." – He pulled on his slacks. "Be damned if I put up with it."

"Man, you really can pick 'em..." Eva started on Roxy.

"Me? Who wanted a guy in the first place?"

Mat had left his old Karmann Ghia at the Vista Del Mar and ridden with Roxy and Eva. He called a taxi to get back and mumbled the whole way. The driver, a Russian with a black moustache thick enough for filter feeding, watched him in the rearview. "Troubles you are having? You have money to pay for ride?"

"It's my girlfriend – " He found himself impaled by the word. *Girlfriend!* Never in his life, a girlfriend. That's it, he thought. He'd fix that Daphne. He'd tell her that he'd left two women in bed to come to her. He'd tell her and go back to Roxy and Eva's condo. Daphne would be crushed, but it had to be done. Best to break off quickly. Poof! Then the healing process could begin; eventually Daphne might love again. To trust again after the hurt of losing Mat...

It stung to imagine the pain in Daphne's eyes. But he would mine the diamonds of his righteous anger. It was over.

He had the driver take him to her complex. By the time the cab got there he'd imagined her alone after he read her the riot act, after she understood this was the end. He softened a little at the thought of her grief and loneliness. But be firm, he thought; so she doesn't hold out false hope. He buzzed her apartment from the security gate.

Nobody answered. God, he hoped she hadn't gone out looking for him. He thought of the girl, hurrying from bar to bar, desperate, perhaps crying, dark eyes liquid with grief. But that's why this had to end, tonight. He'd see to that. He forced back thoughts of mercy. The severance had to be sudden, complete.

As he stood at the security gate, Mat heard laughter out by the pool – splashing, a party, from the sound of it a small but a loud one. A woman hurried out the gate and Mat pretended to fumble for keys. She stopped to eye him as he dashed through. Mat went around toward the blue glow of the pool and lit tennis court and there found Daphne in the hot tub with four guys. On the table he could see a half-pitcher of margaritas and two empties.

"Oh, hi Mat," she called out when she saw him. "Where've you been? Come on in. We're celebrating my new apartment."

"I was just coming to see you."

"Look away," one of the guys said, and Mat saw he was deep in his cups. "Have a good long look. Then go 'way."

"Shush, Terry," said Daphne. "That's not nice."

"Terry's rarely nice," said a pink-skinned guy with red hair. "I'm nice though. Nice guys always finish last, Daphne. Just for a change let's say the nice guy finishes first. Jes' for a change, you know." His margarita glass slipped from his fingers and blubbed to the tub bottom. The guy rolled in like a red-baked porpoise in pursuit of the glass. He was wearing underpants.

"You looked. Now go 'way," Terry repeated, trying to be dangerous.

Mat snorted, but laughter seemed suddenly to go out of the party. The guys climbed from the tub, one in underpants, three naked, and mumbled goodbyes. He'd seen these guys before – amateur predators, young but wealthy. He took Daphne's keys and went upstairs to her apartment. She followed soaking wet a few minutes later. He was sitting on the couch with the TV on. It annoyed him when she scooted her wet rear end next to his and leaned into him. He ignored her.

"Oh Mat, pretty girl alert." She reached behind her back and fumbled momentarily. Her bikini top fell off and she pressed against his side. He grimaced and said nothing. She pulled his hand to her bikini bottom. "Rowwrrrrr," she growled.

He took away his hand.

"You're acting weird." She fell back on the cushions. She smelled of margaritas and chlorine. "What's wrong?"

"Nothing," he said. "Just that scene, is all."

"What scene?" She leaned forward to nibble one of his ears, but he pulled away.

"Those guys."

"Guys in the complex? We were just having a few drinks – great bunch of guys. Invited me to share a pitcher."

"Three pitchers."

"Dropped in to help me finish up. Just goofing around in the tub."

"You were. But they weren't thinking just drinks out there."

"Who, those boys? They're barely out of college. A guy like you couldn't be jealous."

Savagely he stabbed the TV remote. "If you got drunk, they wouldn't have been so harmless." – He hated this; it wasn't him.

"Them and me? Mat, you need a reality check. One, you don't own me. And two, I can handle myself. Three, you and I've only just met, OK? Isn't it a little early to concentrate exclusively on each other?" – Daphne retied her bikini top.

Mat rose from the couch and stood in front of the window. He felt knotted up inside. He could see beyond the streetlights and restaurants along the shore and dark mass of the ocean beyond, broken in the distance by running lights from two boats coming in. He saw the lights of a few visiting boats without dock space that had tied to anchor buoys just outside of the marina. The inky mass of the sea met a moonless horizon bright with infinity stars.

"I thought we had something special here. You don't see me hanging out with anyone, do you? I thought this was going to be different."

Daphne appeared surprised. She scooted closer and smoothed his hair. "I didn't mean it like that. I don't want anyone but you. But we hardly know each other. Maybe you'll want to go with some other women. And it's OK if you do; I'll work things out if that happens. I just want you to be straight with me, remember? To tell me true. If you don't want just me alone, then I can live with that. I know a guy like you isn't used to just one girl."

He turned from the window and sat beside her, cradling her face in his hands, amazed at how beautiful she was – yet was not. Was, or... "Right now I'm not thinking about other women," he said, and meant it. Very strange. A web he'd blundered into.

"That didn't take long," she said, smiling. "The bigger they are, the harder they fall."

"Huh?"

"Hard guys always drop like flies when they think they're losing."

"What do you mean?" – He had a physical sensation of being pulled underwater.

"Nothing."

The second he had her again, he doubted he wanted her. Again.

This emotion, this thing happening, wasn't passing around leather ladies with Society of Beach Bums clansmen. In that company, the usual gang, Mat found himself on the uncommon ground of introducing his "friend" to hustlers and rich skippers and surfer boys, all of whom were smitten by, first, Daphne's beauty, second, her money.

She was the kind who liked men, a man's woman who went easily among them and drew them like minnows around a bright coin. She was not like the luckless women who fell for bad boys. Mat became vulnerable, drowning or falling in love – same thing to him.

Every moment with her seemed full, like his first trip to Disneyland, like seeing a former nun dress for her first date. He had to ask, did he want it to stop? Spending time with her, sometimes skipping the bars, going to movies – corny stuff... Borrowing a boat and fishing, anchored, falling asleep in the cabin while the boat rocked in the swell beyond the surf's draw, wine glasses rolling around deck... Drinking beer at the beach... Sharing a towel...

He hadn't done so much laughing since he was a kid.

At Mat's ratty apartment over the Oyster Club one morning, his roommates off somewhere, Mat, pulling on shorts for a lifeguard gig, said, "Must be good not working. You get by."

"I told you. Money comes easy. Never been short of the stuff."

Mat plugged in his electric razor. "That's what my mother used to say, just before there wasn't any. What was it you said came hard? everything else?"

Ignoring him, she slipped into a shirt to make coffee. Slate-gray sea, completely flat; no swell or shore break; cormorants and grebes diving just off the Oyster Club's pier... "When am I going to meet her?"

"Who?"

"Your mother, of course. She sounds like a lively one."

Mat laughed ruefully. "Not the word I'd choose."

"So... when?"

"Sometime." He paused, switching off his razor. "Have you told your folks about me?" – The talk's implications were ominous.

"Good point," she admitted. "Not yet."

Yet? Even more ominous.

They bought a lottery ticket together and their luck held: they won five dollars and bought chintzy flamingo salt-n-pepper shakers at a rummage sale. Daphne took the pepper, insisted he take the salt, that the two shakers would one day be reunited. Omigod, he thought.

She seemed flawless from twenty feet; but if he stood next to her she seemed imperfect, though he couldn't tell why. She'd pursued and hog-tied his heart and leashed him like a puppy. He didn't want to do anything without her; it was pathetic and he knew it, just like all lovers know it, and he didn't give a damn. It went on for six months and he couldn't remember being so happy and miserable at the same time, always afraid she'd see him for what he was: not so good as her, not so sure of anything, not such good material as the yuppie pups at her apartment who adored her or rich older guys at the marina who professed their love, all patiently awaiting the time when Mat would make a fatal mistake, because guys like Mat always turned wine into water. Mat, knowing this, watched himself around the hottest beach girls like a drugged man fighting off sleep.

Away from Daphne he was as confident and self-assured as ever. If he thought about it, which he didn't, he'd know that outwardly at least he seemed seamless, impermeable and cool. His doubts seemed like lava in a lamp, rising from somewhere in his subconscious to trouble him briefly, then recede. He dismissed trouble; impunity had been his main virtue.

At times he wanted her to go away, disappear and take the feeling of dread, first nagging that she was too good, second that he was abandoning freedom and would finally hate her for it.

Ambiguities…

His opinion of other men in love: it made them fools at first, after which they were no longer fools because they fell out of it. If married, they became prisoners, either fat and complacent or lean and hungry. He had belonged to a non-exclusive club of which the best and the worst you could say was that, even as they aged chronologically, SOBBs remained younger than married men. Not necessarily a grand attribute, but they lived the libidinous fantasies of the married – what most men longed for: perpetual immaturity, the pursuit of short-term gratification, non-reflective existence, just waiting for waves, Jimmy Buffet as spiritual guru to the tune of "Margaritaville". Ecstasy and fear. What if he looked back on this thing with Daphne as wasted time and regret? What if he broke it off and regretted that?

Ambiguities of love…

Meanwhile, sirens sang as always to plague and tease him. The wealthy yacht club wives and daughters were drawn to him by the pheromones of love and innocence, drawn to his vulnerability. The yacht club daughters… girls who came easy when he was their age. Mat saw the boys those girls wanted; he'd seen one in his mirror. For the first time in his twenty-nine years he was charting the seas ahead. Over Daphne's shoulder he watched older members of the SOBB clan and what he saw unnerved him. The beach bums were broke and hungry for something. What had seemed right, casual and inevitable, the same faces in same places doing the same things, the melodrama of sitting beside the pool with a tall, ice-sweated Havana harbor on the table and falling asleep to wake five or ten years later with everything the same except the leather skin, seemed no longer noble tragedy but something grimmer. These days he occasionally wore the blue blazer Daphne had bought him, though he usually wore it over a black t-shirt.

It was like going home after the fatal three year limit. What he'd known had become strange. He couldn't see things the same and felt simultaneously cheated and relieved, although he couldn't tell which more. He missed the action and found himself fantasizing, thinking like a married guy. Before, he had mocked their fantasies, thinking, just *do* it; don't sit around whining. Now he felt guilty, thinking: I feel bad for thought crimes. What in hell's wrong with me?

Leave her, stay with her. Who knew? But when he thought of her gone from his life, ice water seeped into a hole in his chest.

The ambiguities of love…

After a storm, before sunrise and footprints trod the beach, they looked for things washed in. "You know that rock and roll heaven song?" she asked, "And their hellacious band?"

He yawned. "Yeah, so?"

"Except for John Lennon, those guys couldn't carry Mozart or Beethoven's jockstraps."

"What?"

She knitted him a sweater. He hadn't worn one for fifteen years, didn't even own one. This sweater was red. "I don't care if you wear it," she said cheerfully. "But where I come from every girl knits her guy a University of Wisconsin sweater."

"It's, um, very red," he said, holding it over his chest. He looked like a stop sign.

"It is, isn't it?" she answered happily.

How could he not love her?

She poured a glass of lukewarm water from the tea kettle.

"There's cold water in the refrigerator," he said.

"You know how some things are neutral? I like neutral water. Boiling does that."

"What?"

She bought him new tires for his Karmann Ghia. "I'll be damned if I'm going to get killed for the price of new tires on your death-trap." A tailored white dress shirt and gold cuff links: "No way I'm dining French with a guy who thinks black t-shirts are the pinnacle of fashion." Several silk ties, a male makeover (waxed body, plucked eyebrows, styled and moussed hair). A blazer, Tito Raboni loafers. Other things he could neither afford nor would buy if he could.

At first he welcomed the gifts, later not.

"But I've got money," she argued. "What's the big trip? It's a gas to drive those other beach bums wild." He knew she didn't mean it in a bad way. But it was bad. Older women had bought him drinks, women who appreciated the attention. This was different.

"That's ridiculous, Mat. If not me, then who could be more right? Would it be any different if you had money and I didn't?"

End of argument for her.

"It's not the same. And even if I didn't know the word, it doesn't make you look good to be with a guy who mooches off his girlfriend."

"Piffle," she said.

"*Piffle?*"

"Exactly. I care more about you than what others think."

She left him standing there. "What in hell is 'piffle?'"

They rarely argued, only one big one. That started over nothing. She goaded him about using the wrong fork. A trifling thing. They'd split a bottle of zin at her place before walking to a nice restaurant, her treat. She commented when he started his salad with a dinner fork. Not rudely, but still…

"Who cares?" he asked. "That's a hick thing to mention."

She looked as if he'd slapped her. "Did you just call me a 'hick'? Did I hear that right?"

Mat smiled, she didn't. "No, I was just saying."

"Do you even know what a hick is? Tell me what a hick is."

He should have known better. He chuckled. "Someone who has sex with animals?"

"So I'm someone who has sex with animals? You think my mother has sex with animals?"

"Course not," he stammered. She called herself "hick" all the time.

Daphne dropped her napkin into her plate. "So exactly who are these people you think have sex with animals?" Her tone was equal parts venom, contempt and hurt.

"Um, everyone in the red states?" Another joke.

"Why, you arrogant pig. Are you saying everyone in the Midwest has intercourse with animals? That's what you're saying?"

"No, of course not. I'm kidding. Forget it."

She'd caught this one by the tail. "You're the worst kind. You Californians think you're the stuff, don't you? You're cocksure the rest of the world just hangs on your every – everything you do. From Disneyland to who's sleeping with who in Hollywood. From surf-boards to redwoods to goddam Death Valley. From San Francisco to Los Angeles to – to *Tahoe*. From tie-dye hippies to silk-tie yuppies and dot-commers."

"Listen, Daphne – "

"No, you listen. You Californians think manure is manna. And I'm so tired of it."

Mat's eyebrows raised. "Well, some things start in California, sort of. I didn't mean – "

"I'll tell you who lives in California. Cocky bastards full of themselves and their easy lifestyles. Fully committed to the notion they're better than everyone else."

"Come on. Nobody thinks that. We just live easy."

"That's the worst part. You aren't even aware of it. You've got looks and confidence and your tan body and your vegetarian diet..."

"Whoa? How I eat? What's that – "

"You don't know what it's like for everyone else in this world!" Tears streaked her cheeks. "You don't know." She grabbed her napkin over her eyes and fled from the restaurant.

Mat glanced around. He loathed seeing these kinds of scenes, much less participating in one. "Good God," he muttered. Several people watched discreetly but not discreetly enough. "Good God," he repeated, dropping a couple of bills and rising from the table. He hurried past their waiter. "I think we're eating at home tonight."

He ate crow; side dishes of apologies. He learned that committed men choose their fights carefully. Daphne stayed mad for two days, longer than Mat had ever carried a grudge.

Time slipped past. He began to know her in ways he hadn't known other women, mostly because he'd spent time with women only in bars or bed. He grew comfortable with her paying for clothes, dinners and drinks. It did drive the surf bums crazy to learn her family had that money. But by now Mat convinced himself he would have felt the same about her without her "big money".

They drank Havana harbors at the Mackerel Club and one of his buddies kidded Mat about making Daphne an "honest woman". Daphne turned as furious as Mat had seen her, calling the guy a "sexist asshole incapable of recognizing 'honesty' in any of its manifestations and if [she] were a man [she]'d kick his ass". Mat rolled his eyes to tell the guy to get lost. Daphne ranted that when she married, it would be for love, not honesty, and did she have to marry Mat to make him honest? Before slipping out through the kitchen they paused at the bar to have Clyde refresh their Havana harbors with dashes of bitters. On the Mackerel's dock, a little drunk, he thought: sure, maybe I could marry her one of these days – someday in the future, maybe when she's closer to her inheritance. He chuckled to himself; the concept

seemed appealing. Someday after they'd known each other longer...
It seemed comforting. He glowed in the acknowledgment of their love.
Meanwhile, under the dock lights a school of baitfish rose and skipped
across the dark water. Something bigger flashed underneath them.

Daphne seemed forthright to Mat. He knew her well. That's why
he felt comfortable speaking of marriage, marriage in some indistinct
future five or so years away. He ordinarily avoided the word like sane
people avoided eating puked-up fur balls or flushing their eyeballs
with Drano or touching flame to ether.

Daphne turned and caught him in her arms. "Oh, Mat! Mat!" Tears
sprang from her eyes.

Oh God. For the second time Mat felt sucked into cold water.

4

Here in Dickeyville the streets curved, crossed one another; they
curled like knots, slowly rising, because the town covered a knoll above
spreading farm country. Mat had never imagined such entwined little
streets lined with quaint little houses. But at last he arrived at a shoveled sidewalk before a house with the correct address. It was an old
house, craftsman style, one of the nicest he'd seen, off-white, trimmed
a tasteful pine-forest green. Smoke rose cheerfully from a brick chimney and curled between two spreading bare trees at each side of the
yard. Such massive trees must be at least a couple hundred years old,
he guessed, and something that solid, that stable and permanent,
comforted him. A newer Chevrolet pickup sat in a driveway that ran
alongside the house and seemed to curve behind it. He swung open
the gate and walked up a flagstone pathway beaten through the snow
to an enclosed front porch. He climbed the steps and knocked on a
varnished door with a leaded-glass window in its center.

Footsteps clunked inside. He listened, making out a voice.

"Someone's here."

"You get it?" came another voice.

"Who, me?"

"Who you. Who else? Get the ding-danged door."

"All right. I got it." The phone began to ring. "You get it."

"The phone?"

The door opened, and out came a rush of warm air smelling of slow time and cinnamon and odors that seemed familiar but not instantly recognizable because Mat's nose was running from the cold. Before him stood a white-haired woman, short and aproned. She glanced at his dufflebag. "We don't need any," she said, starting to shut the door.

Although her ears distracted him – leathery flaps with long lobes poking through fuzzy hair so that he could not avoid staring – he recognized something in her features. "Mrs. Dickey? It's me. Mat Roper."

The woman looked at him as if he were delivering a dose of measles. "Father?" she said over her shoulder as she edged from the door.

An old man appeared, slippers clapping the floor, bare-chested except for suspenders strapped over white hairs covering a narrow torso. Over a thin but rich mustache sat the oddest nose; it was bulbous and turned up at the tip so that you looked straight up the old man's nostrils. Mat had the uneasy notion that with enough light he might see the man's brain.

Nose, hair and clothing reminded him of something and Mat couldn't help himself: "You must represent the lollipop guild."

"What?" The man's eyes narrowed. "That was Agnes on the phone, Mother. Says there's a man on our porch."

"Sure there is, you durn fool. Here he is."

"It's me," the young man explained. "Mat Roper. You know, Daphne's fiancé? She was going to meet me at the bus stop. I just talked to her on the phone the day before yesterday."

The old people blinked at Mat. At last the woman spoke. "Better get your gun, Pa. This salesman's got a pitch like I never heard."

"Fiancé?" the old man asked. "You like the Packers of Green Bay, Wisconsin?"

"Daphne? Where is she?" Bright spots darted before Mat's eyes. His head felt light. "We're supposed to be married," he blurted.

5

One day after his quasi-proposal to Daphne, his mind in a fog, Mat had driven Daphne downtown to a swank jewelry store called Nine-Window Goldman's to choose a ring. The entryway to Nine-Window Goldman's consisted of a riveted bulwark of copper sheeting and dense black glass. At eye level, a few feet above a weathered antique copper doorknob, a pair of stainless steel cupids drew their bows, arrows notched, perhaps intent on piercing passersby. The cupids were familiar to Mat but he could not recall why.

The store's facade offered conflicting impressions of commerce and art. Although no connoisseur of art and inappreciative of commercialism or calculated marketing, Mat was not such a neophyte that he didn't recognize expensive trendiness. The pricey portals of Nine-Window Goldman's hinted that whatever lay inside would be costly and of quality and that the management would not so much keep their prices in line with other stores as guarantee theirs were higher. Certainly the same diamond could be purchased for less in a mall, that is if one wished or, God forbid, needed to pay less.

Another thing did not escape Mat's attention: Daphne had led him straight to the most expensive jeweler in the beachfront community.

Inside they were greeted by a wooden cigar store Indian whose stony continence had been artfully but not undetectably altered to include a cherry-red smile and upon whose wrist hung several strands of what Mat supposed were paste diamonds. His and Daphne's shoes sunk into a plush wine-colored carpet that echoed the store's tasteful burgundy and copper exterior. Before the door had closed silently and solidly behind them, they were approached by a familiar-looking young man, well-appointed in a tailored black suit. Mat remembered how, off the Yucatan, he had once watched a barracuda cut through a milling swarm of baitfish and then swing back to chop up the cripples.

"My name is Rolphe, and I will be your jewelry consultant today," this one said, directing Mat and Daphne to a counter. Raking moussed hair with his fingers, smoothing back stiff blond clumps as if preparing for Wimbledon, center-court, the 'consultant' presented tray after tray of diamond rings. "How much do you wish to spend, sir? Or is money the object here?" He snorted an airy guffaw and smacked his humorless lips to imply his contempt for discussing money.

His own lips suddenly dry, Mat spoke a number. Rolphe's eyebrows barely rose.

Meticulously he set a few half-carat sparklers beside rings in the price range Mat had mentioned, revealing how scrawny Mat's choice would be, how skimpy the stones. Amazing how poorly the teeny rings fit Daphne, either too small or too large for her finger. Such tiny stones on the rings, only just discernible… Easily discernible though were the jeweler's and Daphne's disdain and Mat's first inkling of panic.

Indecision went regarding the marketing-versus-art battle.

Daphne said she'd chip in for a bigger stone; she "could afford it".

Mat's jaw tightened.

His brain said this cannot be happening. I am not really here; I am stuck in someone else's bad dream. Only an idiot could be badgered into buying a ring he can't afford by some smiling dickhead jewelry store clerk. Mat's trance-induced mouth betrayed his skimpy bank account by asking, "How much is that ring there? Yes, that big one. You like that, honey?"

Mouth, stop this right now. You're where I'm gonna stick the gun barrel after I'm out on the street rummaging for aluminum cans.

"It's okay."

A carat-weight of carbon costing a half-year's salary for me, he thought. "Well, you know," he smiled airily as he indentured himself to a rock smaller than a lentil.

The ring fit perfectly and she spun it once around her finger, then extended her arm. Everyone in the store, customers and other "jewelry consultants", clapped in appreciation.

Then the actors bowed out and the curtain closed on this act.

There it was, and there it would sit, until death did them part.

Sign here.

As he stood at the counter, armpits damp, shirt sticking to the center of his back, Mat was suddenly mindful that he had a rehearsal soon for a minor non-speaking role, though he could not say precisely the origin of the recollection.

His was a sweat common to other men in similar situations, situations where someone else's absurd dream has snatched him up and carried him away like an owl clutching a rodent. Mat Roper, the incredible human meadow vole, he thought. What had Beat poet Gregory Corso said about marriage being the "commonest of situations"?

Was this pretense necessary? He looked carefully at the clerk, better appointed than many attorneys, who bore himself like nobility, some Czechoslovakian baron whose title had been confiscated by a Communist regime.

The jewelry consultant wouldn't say shit if he had a mouthful.

The dopey ceremony, the smarmy words repeated by stuffed buffoons. How to say in public what you felt privately? Where was the dignity? Vows before an assemblage, he supposed, his beach bum buddies there to scrounge free booze. He could see them sidling up to the grub and snatching canapés stuffed with salty goop during the ceremony while caterers shot disapproving glances. Mat and Daphne could make their vows in a foreign language so nobody understood. They could speak coded English, dropping the consonants. They could exchange wedding vowels. One of his drunken acquaintances, another wave chaser, grabbing the microphone during the drunken congratulatory speeches: "First time I met Mat..."

Shit.

Anyway the ring would be genuine, best his money could buy. But a stable family to marry into, Daphne would do well to forget that.

Mat's mother, a woman Mat's friends perceived as wealthy because she lived in a Hollywood mansion… At that thought – his mother at his wedding – something went Boing! in the back of his head like a runaway pinball. He could see her huge Hedda Hopper hat, moth-eaten fox stole and a feathered gown out of the Ziegfeld Follies, sash-aying about like royalty and calling everyone "darling". It was not so much embarrassment. Other than the ring-purchasing ceremony, which was like a naked erection at a sixth grade dance, he usually wore indifference like armor; he possessed the impunity that allowed a dozen British soldiers to lord it over eighty thousand heathens. But he desired to protect his mother from herself. He didn't stop to think his acquaintances – and certainly Daphne – would like his mother, the way people like eccentrics if they're sincere and harmless. Half his acquaintances' parents, most from Hollywood and all from southern California, were weird anyway.

His mother wore knee-high white boots, for God's sake. And a Dolly Parton-sized wig.

The next day he ate lunch at Nate's Bistro, people-watching and sipping a Perrier. A pair of transvestites passed his table – leopard-skin tights, ostrich boas and stretch pants, cigarette holders and sequined, oversized Elton John sunglasses. The pair daintily flipped metaphorical rose petals to their audience, gyrating to the cheers and clapping of luncheon tables. At that moment, visions of Daphne's Midwestern aunties dancing through his brain, Mat resolved to do something. He dialed. "Mom? How are you?"

"Mat, darling. I am fabulous. Why haven't you called lately? I've been worried sick over you."

"Sick? Only lost fortunes sicken you, mom. You could have called. They call that box attached to my phone an answering machine.'"

She tsk-tsked. "Don't be smart. I've been busy getting ready for a huge party next month. You've simply got to be here, maybe with a few of your friends in the industry. A few of the successful ones, Mat. Not the bums."

"Industry" meant the flicks, the movie world's support system. Directors, producers, editors, gofers, grips, costumers, casters, chauffeurs, set designers and locators, extras and the hundreds of others behind the final print. By bums, she meant everyone like him. Guys on the edge who lived for the beaches. Los Angeles was full of the beautiful and damned: the best and most gorgeous of Booneyville, Kansas, who, armed with piano and dance lessons and two whole summers at the Midland Arts Festival, where they played a key role in *The Music Man*, busted out of their hick towns to head for New York or Los Angeles, where he or she promptly found fifty thousand others as attractive with a bit more talent – which was when the Wolfe axiom kicked in, and Crawdad Falls, Minnesota, suddenly receded in the psyche but not the heart and time passed and the breaks and acting jobs didn't come, except for opportunities in skin flicks or on the street or bit parts on casting couches. Home was the place you couldn't go back to. All lost. Clichés had legs for a reason.

Mat was born into the Hollywood social scene. Sex at fourteen standing in a pool with an English actor's wife who took off her bikini bottom but wouldn't take off her top. She puffed a joint and he puffed at her. Sipped martinis and learned to like them by fifteen. Snorted the first line at sixteen. Had he known, he would have traded every second of it for what the others had left when they rolled toward L.A.. He could only guess what had passed in the blur, suspected it was better not to have money when one was young than to have had and lost it.

Mat's mother's "gala" affairs depressed him. An assortment of aging B-actors who showed for free drinks, she flitting about – "Darling, darling" – brittle bouquets and arrangements cut from a garden that hadn't been tended for years and everyone pretending not to notice the state of the paint and drained pool, bottom cracked from the quake of '84... Parties of sad suits, wrinkles and double chins, of dropping names of people who had starred in black-and-whites and bleach-haired ladies with cigarette holders and eyebrows lifted nearly to their widows' peaks, flamboyant gay boys in love with Mat's mother's feathery forty-year wardrobe – no outfit too outrageous...

"Be there if possible, Mom. I've been pretty busy myself. Listen, I called to ask you about that trust from father."

"Oh?"

"Yeah, I need the money now. I know I didn't want it before, but something's come up. Can you get it from the bank, or do I need to?"

"Now, Mat, what do you need it for? I thought you didn't want to dirty your lily-white hands with money from your father's death."

"That's the only money I ever turned down." He didn't like being reminded of the source. Tainted money. "Can I get it today?"

A pause. "It'll take time. I can't just take out the money like that. It's tied up."

"In bondage? Sorry to hear."

She ignored that. "Takes time to get the money."

"How long?"

"Aren't you full of questions. Soon as I can. Meanwhile, come to my party. And dress sharp."

"Can I get it in a week? It's important I get it before seven days."

"Sure. Absolutely. One week. You're not the type to blow money on some chippy, so what's with the change of heart?"

"Nothing. I just need it. What I don't need is a third-degree." He had a thought. "Mom, pretend – just suppose – that I were to get involved seriously with someone. And one thing led to another and I got married. Would you come to the wedding? I mean alone?"

"What? My baby boy getting married? Mat, if only it were true."

He squirmed. "Would you come alone?"

"You foolish boy. We'll have the event of the year. A poolside party attended by the glitterati of Hollywood. Catered by Puccini Rosso, flower arrangements by Dornans, Wynton Marsalis performing. Billy Graham presiding as a personal favor to me. Think about the paparazzi howling to get a glimpse of the guests. Too bad Michael's no longer with us, but if we could get Liz, wouldn't it be something."

Mat snorted. "Uh-huh. Event of the year. Mother, Liz Taylor is dead and you haven't even asked about the girl."

She tsk-tsked. "One's pretty much the same as – is she an actress?"

"I've got to go, Mom."

"Well, is she?"

"Listen, I was just thinking aloud. I'm not dating anyone right now."

"You're not getting any younger, bub. Looks are fleeting. Think of the elder Barrymore or – "

"Got to go, Mom."

"If you must. You're not in trouble, are you? It wouldn't hurt your film career to schmooze a little with some of my guests."

His film career. Grip jobs, underwater shoots, bits in films like *Hooter Hounds of Malibu* and *Surf-Bored Bunnies*; films with no more than ten speaking actors because guild rules obligated pay for spoken lines; films with actresses who barely concealed their talents in string bikinis… "Frankly, I don't have a career. If I did, those guys couldn't help me pull scum off a pudding. Thirty years ago – not now."

"You just turn your back on some of the biggest star-makers of all time, people who really knew how to make movies, not like these Steelburck movies."

"Spiel-*berg*. And you haven't even seen any of them. Mother, look, I've got to go. Get my money. Please. No later than a week. It's important." He was sweating again. He had a sudden premonition, not a good one, though Daphne had said he wasn't one to believe in anything he couldn't see.

6

Vinnie the Tide didn't get his nickname from tiding over the needy with short-term loans. Actually he had nicknamed himself. He was proud of his inspiration and thought it clever on several levels. He was like a baker except the ingredients for his bread were fear, confusion and desperation. The suckers who needed him referred to Vinnie-the-Vulture, though not to his face. Tide-you-over until you pay me back, Jack, at 20% the first week; 30% after that; 40% by the end of one month. After that you pay with meat. Held court at the Wet Stork. Same table for thirty years.

Mat sat with Vinnie, same as Mat's father had many years before.

Vinnie had hassled Mat's father just before he'd died. Rather, killed himself. "Don't wanna take it out on your family," Vinnie had said. For the 500 Gs Mat's father borrowed to add to his kitty of several million. "Go for this one," Mat's father had said. "This is the one sure thing I've seen in forty years of producing flicks." Vinnie and Mat's father both were about business.

Mat's father said if you think something's a sure thing, ask a friend to bust your chops. The old man, worth four or five million, swam in a school of bigger fish. Some of them also went in heavily on the sure thing. They lost some; he lost it all. In the Industry, movies, once someone had the scent of failure, the scariest odor, there was a lot of dead time between phone calls. Money was oxygen in Hollywood. Life went flat faster than a ten dollar retread once you left the fast lane; even the B producers and stars stopped calling – until they were running out of air, too.

That's the way the fortune cookie crumbled.

Mat's father's motto: "Never trust a fat man. Fat woman, okay. But never trust a fat man." So here was Mat.

Bloated like a beached marine mammal, Vinnie glowed a greasy pink-bronze from weekly hours in his brother-in-law's tanning salon. Body shrunken from its former 230 pounds in his fighter years, Vinnie looked like a glazed potato on toothpick legs. The two guys seated with him, Bob and Buck, were born of silent Ozark granite.

"You know how it works. You're a good boy. I see you sashay around like a king. I like that. It's never personal with me. That's my motto. Isn't it, boys?"

You ought to hear my father's motto, Mat thought.

The "boys" said nothing, their attention seemingly attuned to some long-past evolutionary branch separating carbon from silicon. It wasn't clear which path their ancestors had taken.

"Not personal. Not with your father, not with you. So here's my advice: don't do it. Don't borrow shark money. It's in your blood to fuck-up." Vinnie leaned forward, his fat cheeks puffing, to spit three olive seeds into the ashtray.

Mat knuckled the table. "Difference is I'll have the money."

Everyone in Hollywood, playing parts. Mat the prototype handsome beach-bum with the good heart who wins the girl; Vinnie the shark who bites the chumps; Daphne the rich innocent Midwest girl come to California... They didn't make movies so much as live them.

Vinnie an escapee from central casting: greasy, fat, one lazy bug-eye... He twisted linguine around his fork. "Sure. They all see a shark because they got the dough."

"Have it in a few days."

"Just like your father. One stupid sonuvabitch…" Vinnie liked to fuck with them. Make 'em crawl for the dough. That was pleasure, more than interest on the loan. Vinnie's thick fingers sliced through thin hair. "They're all going to have the money, you fucking putz." He sighed and sat back to watch the show of human foibles, not so much a spool of film as a loop. Fat Vinnie didn't need money anymore; his heavyweight fight with Sonny Liston had set him good with a half-block waterfront slum in San Diego. When developers came calling, he'd held out for a share. A fighter who'd wearied other fighters by offering his head, Vinnie's meteoric career, up and down, saved him from a too-mushy brain, but mushy enough to be dangerous. Biggest pleasure came when some dumb fuck bailed on the payback.

"Mat, you're a fuckin' snake getting ready to cross a freeway. You don't even see what's coming." Vinnie smiled. He liked that, snake crossing a freeway. It was a good line. I'll have to remember that, he thought. It was gone as soon as he put it away.

As Mat looked at the fat man seated before him, into his fleshy face, he knew Vinnie wouldn't loan him the money. "I won't screw up."

Vinnie slurped *rustica*. Looking at this young man he thought of the money he'd put on the kid's father. Money he'd collected from the guy's estate. That was a long time ago. The pasta was good here. What the hell.

Vinnie took a mouthful of sherry. He imagined shooting Mat when he didn't come up with the bucks. Random killings were for punks, the new breed of sharks. Didn't go for that shit. Drive by and shoot up a house full of babies. Pathetic.

Laughed at himself. Fat, old, soft.

"What's so funny?" Mat asked.

Vinnie waved him off. "Wonderin' how you'd look in a bullet hole."

He knew things about people. No respect for skippers. His guys pinned skippers to the floor. Vinnie straddled them. Liked to hear them beg. Pussies. They always begged. "I'll get the money, Vinnie. I'll get it. If I have to rob a fuckin' bank. I swear. Please, please. I got kids. Don't do this. You know me, man. You know my family."

Let them go on a while. Good to hear them cry. Think they're winning you over. Then sit on their chests, push your balls right up to their noses and show them the pistol. Piss-ant short-barrel revolver. Let 'em see it. "No, Vinnie, god no!" Press the .22 caliber loaded with shorts into the guy's chest over the heart and pull the trigger once. Shorts better than longs or hollowpoints. Takes longer. Prolongs Vinnie's pleasure. Gotta enjoy something, right? Didn't like to fuck anymore. Too much work. Chance of a heart attack like that fucking New York governor. Look pretty fucking sad lying there fat and sweaty and dead and naked on top of some bitch after shitting himself when his heart blew up. He thought about it. Big old turd sneaking out his fat cheeks after he convulsed and died... Actually the stuck turd had some appeal. Maybe he should try fucking again.

When the skipper stopped flopping and the hole stopped leaking, place the barrel in his eye and put one through the jelly into the brain. Make other clients think. The eyeball bullet and empty socket always clamped their assholes. What's the problem?

Vinnie shrugged. "Your funeral." He farted, shifting slightly so the old couple at the next table would hear. Shifted his bulk again to get the stink around. Laughed. His bodyguards didn't laugh. Vinnie didn't give a fuck. He was used to them.

Mat was amazed at how much of what he'd been doing lately involved perspiration.

7

Mat didn't flaunt fortune, not his looks or dates, but this was different and he liked the sudden respectability. Do things all the way. Marriage implied the country-club notion of respectability.

He parked his Ghia in front of Nine-Window Goldman's. So what if these feelings were based on expectations of a hundred movies and novels imprinted in the collective psyche? Mat knew it and gave himself up to it. In his pocket were eighty one-hundred dollar bills, still crisp and scented slightly of Vinnie's *pasta rustica*.

Marriage, possibly even children, little Mats or Daphnes running on the beach with dripping-wet long blond hair, coming back to the towel to gulp warm soda pop and snatch sandy fistfuls of potato chips... He passed through the entrance, once more intrigued by the stainless steel cupids. Where'd he seen them before?

His tranquility evaporated when he faced the same obsequious jewelry clerk who'd helped him previously, same little dick who'd stacked the knuckle-sized sparklers beside his original tiny one. Mat impatiently drummed his fingernails on the countertop.

The clerk smiled brightly, eyes eager. Mat realized he would probably collect a sizable commission for trading a tiny rock attached to a thin band of gold for a fistful of hundred dollar bills.

"Beautiful stone," he explained. "Cut in the style of the Orlov diamond, supposedly one of the eyes of a Buddhist statue." He leaned slightly toward the stone, as if to bow.

"That's nice," Mat said, lifting a palm-sized box and peering at the ring within. It was rather nice, he conceded, the diamond collecting the light of the room and casting it into his retina. "I guess I'll take it."

"The Orlov belonged to the Persian Nadir Shah who was assassinated for it by one of his Afghan mercenaries," the man expostulated, taking the box from Mat's hand and pausing to snap open the lid to look inside, as if ghosts had spirited the ring away.

"Mercenaries? Does that bode ill, or would you know?" Mat joked.

The clerk's eyes found his. "Sir, levity regarding omens is bad taste. Are you aware I once saw a bat fly out of a pipe organ during a wedding in a Frank Lloyd Wright-designed church?"

Mat was startled. "No, I didn't know. How could I?"

"It didn't last three months."

"The church?"

"No."

"Oh. The bat."

"The marriage, sir."

"Oh," Mat said thoughtfully. "Where was it?"

"Flying in the air."

"Not the bat. The wedding."

"In Wisconsin. Madison."

That's a coincidence. Wisconsin. "Anyway, I want the ring."

The consultant's eyes narrowed. "Or was that the Pitt diamond?" One index finger worked persistently at his temple.

Mat was impressed by such determination to ferret out facts. "I don't know."

"You should find out."

"Does it matter?"

"Everything matters, Mat Roper."

Mat's eyebrows lifted. "Do I know you from somewhere, Rolphe?"

"Are you serious? You don't recognize me? I thought this was just an act. I bartend at the Wet Stork. See you three/four times a week. In fact, I gave you a free drink last Wednesday."

Mat had to admit he couldn't remember the face, but a free drink was hard to forget. "You're Wormie from the Wet Stork?" The same Wormie whose dry, blond hair normally bristled over his head like straw poking from a horse's mouth? Wormie, who was also bassist for The Hump, a professional opening band?

"Guess you won't be bonking any more babes for a while, eh?"

"But you said 'Rolphe'."

"Rolphe is just for the sucker money. My uncle owns this joint. The markup on wedding rocks is bad enough, but in this place it's obscene. I guess your rich chick will help, though. I wouldn't mind scoring a few of your castoffs. Is your address book available?"

Thus Mat was robbed of even the dignity of the transaction. Ill omen if ever there were one. As he passed through the door of Nine Window Goldman's, he realized where he'd seen the chrome cupids: on mud flaps of Peterbilts.

In her apartment, Daphne cried and couldn't finish her clam linguini when Mat gave her the ring. They had a couple of mai tais at the Bambuko, then went out to the Harbor Yacht Club and everyone dined them and bought them Havana harbors and got them drunk and the band played *The Wedding March*, and later, before closing time, Daphne spilled a drink down the front of her dress and they walked back along the piers to his place, staggering arm in arm and she collapsed on the couch and he couldn't wake her and didn't care.

He was very happy and drunk when he fell asleep, and knew finally and forever that everything was well.

Until he woke up. Then blossomed the common harvest of commitment: anxiety and futility.

Even though he wasn't cheating on her, he felt like it every time he looked at a pretty woman, followed by sensations of anger for feeling guilty. For God's sake, he thought. I'm not Warren Beatty.

Outwardly he seemed happy, but doubts itched at him. Partly it was the momentum and power of tradition.

Like polliwogs inside their eggs, initially invisible, Mat's apprehension hatched after a few days when women he barely knew congratulated him and planned bachelorette parties for Daphne. Married people started offering invitations to the betrothed couple, and Mat couldn't help but notice these folks seemed more interested in cultivating Daphne's friendship than his. When he no longer hid his anxiety Daphne pooh-poohed it, calling it fear of change, saying their initiation into the club of married life would gift him the happiness he'd always craved. "So much," she gushed, "comes of this kind of stability. Mat, you can't imagine what it will mean to your career?"

Oh, yes, he thought, there's always my career as professional beach bum to think of. Equally odious: most married people were boring.

All of it was like pulling the crucial rock out of an earthen dam.

In the first place, looks aside, Mat wondered why would anyone want to marry him. He was charming, to be sure. And he had an air of dignified certainty – confidence and solidity – that was contagious. That was who he was. But it was like his bravery in water: he did nothing to earn it. He sat over a gin and tonic at the Club Mako, the bartender there being a surfing acquaintance. Mat asked,

"Curt, why would she even want to marry me? What in hell do I have that she'll want in five years? Can you imagine?"

Curt wiped a towel in a glass. "You're right. I can't imagine."

"I mean, what have I done these last five years? Slept with about a hundred women – safe sex, of course. Been an extra in twenty or thirty movies, did some gripping and diving on shoots, a little life saving and sailing. Not much. Lot of surfing."

"Nothing," Curt suggested.

"And what'll I be five years from now? No career..."

"About thirty-five," Curt added.

Mat nodded unhappily. "*Thirty-four* and no career. Still looking at beach babes out the corners of my eyes. God."

"All your looks gone," Curt said. "But still arrogant as hell."

"You think so?" He glanced at his reflection in the smoky mirror behind Curt. "My looks?"

"And still arrogant as hell. You've never had to work for a thing, have you? Women, money, looks. It's always been there."

Mat paused. "What's that supposed to mean?"

"The worst kind. You don't even know you're arrogant."

Mat cocked his head. "I ask again: what's that supposed to mean?" – Daphne had said the same thing. Arrogant?

Curt shrugged. "Dunno. Guess she'll eventually leave you," he said, smiling ruefully and holding the glass up to look through it at the porthole lights adjoining the bar. He began to furiously rub at the same spot. "Best you should let her marry me, Mat. It's apparent the poor girl's about to throw herself away on a bum without enough sense to go out with the trash."

"Come on. You know what I mean."

"It doesn't figure, does it? Fortune doesn't always roost in the coop of the worthy."

So: Curt was one more guy in love with her. Mat left without paying. If so many men didn't want her, he'd be able to know if he really loved her. Love was like an old brick made valuable by virtue of everyone wanting it. It was Daphne's rarity. She was like a Babe Ruth autograph. Everyone wanted it whether or not they wanted it because everyone else wanted it. Maybe he wanted Daphne because they did. Tug of war with a rope descending into the underworld. He could either pull up the devil or be dragged to hell.

He'd believed he'd achieved a Zen indifference because he hadn't really cared – about anything. That was his mantra: Immunity... Immunity. Immunity. Drum talking in his psyche. When others let something dig at them, some niggling annoyance, he'd despised it. Made him feel good in a way to hear acquaintances complain. Fucking shine it, he'd advised. That's what he'd do.

Well, now...

The inevitability of marriage weighed on him, and it was better not to think about it, except that his sudden silences made Daphne angry that he wouldn't "communicate". She decided to plan the nuptial event by herself. The logistics were numbing, even if no dates had been set. When would she meet Mat's mother? Mat hadn't even told his mother yet. Marry in Wisconsin or California? Mat didn't care, which infuriated her. Endless exploratory shopping trips with "best buddies" Daphne hadn't known two months before; expeditions to boutiques where wedding invitations cost twenty dollars apiece, caterers charged one hundred-fifty a plate, flowers for the hour-long ceremony cost five grand and up and a five-tiered "champagne" cake covered with sweetened lard would run three grand... Gowns began at four thousand for, as Daphne said, "crappy little rags I wouldn't be caught dead in."

Rags, she said.

Mat began to see how superfluous a groom was to the whole process. Initially an integral part, once he had committed he was out of the loop. "Honey, couldn't we just have a small justice of the peace wedding? Just you and me?"

He might as well have kissed her with a dead fish in his mouth. "What? God, Mat. A girl waits her whole life for this." She added: "Anyway, traditionally, the bride's parents pay for it."

He squirmed – another thing besides sweating he was doing a lot of lately. "Waits her whole life for this?"

"Well, practically," Daphne replied… this, from an avid feminist.

"Sort of like a Barbie and Ken double-bed set."

"Screw you." – She meant it.

Transformation of the abstract into the concrete, the process was like an ice pick to the temple. But once he was put on ice by Daphne, the preparations went along nicely without him.

"So where are we getting married? Here in California? Back there in Wisconsin?" By now he favored there; his mom and the SOBB wouldn't make it.

"Out here, Honey. My relatives will come. They all want an excuse to visit Disneyland."

He'd meet them on his own turf. All right, he didn't care. What did it matter? All he wanted was certainty. No doubts.

One evening he walked on the jetty to watch the sunset. Daphne had said she and someone next door were going to do some girl things. The northwesterly breeze, sweeping a cloudless indigo sky, came up strong. As he watched yellow and orange light of a dying sun shimmer with the swell gently rolling up against the breakwater, the last rays of disappearing light warming his cheeks, Mat saw the black silhouette of a big dorsal fin rise to the surface not twenty yards off the end of the jetty. In maybe twenty feet of water. Incredible. A big fellow, over twelve feet, no way to tell what kind. Mat stood and looked down the public beach in the direction the fish was headed and saw in the faded light that not a hundred yards away a woman sat on a beach towel while her two children frolicked in the dimpled surf. The shark's fin sunk below the darkening water.

Mat had dived with sharks in the Yucatan and off Cuba and in a cage off the Farallones and had a thrill with a big Tiger once. He had swum with sea snakes off Australia's Barrier Reef and on Christmas

Island during filming of a bonefishing segment for *American Sportsman.* He'd swum alone at nighttime on the sea more times than he could remember, and once in the cold water north of Santa Cruz he'd helped carry someone out of the surf who'd been shark-slashed on the calf. He'd never felt greatly afraid of things he couldn't see. This was something he could.

He yelled for the woman to get the kids out of the water, but his voice drifted away in the breeze. The woman didn't hear, didn't look. Mat hunched his shoulders with anticipation and saw the fin come up again not a hundred feet from the kids, closing steadily, slipping along just outside the surf. He yelled again, desperation powering his voice, but the woman didn't respond and the children splashing in the waves appeared not to notice the huge dorsal, a fin looking for all the world as ominous as the phony one in *Jaws.*

It sliced on through the water twenty feet behind them.

When it had gone Mat slumped onto a concrete chunk. He'd never seen anything like it. The thrill of a lifetime, he thought. If she'd seen what he had, the young mother wouldn't let her kids in the bathtub.

It was all about fear.

When the chance came the next day, Mat leaped at the opportunity to replace a diver, Beetleman, for a week-long shoot about drug smuggling in the Bahamas.

"I'm sick, Mat. I've got some damned body rash I picked up on that Baja shoot last month. I think I'm dying," Beetleman said. "You should see my dick."

"I'll pass."

"My body looks like a bloated blood sausage. I'm bleeding out of every hole."

"Dude."

"Well, practically. I think I've got dengue fever. You know the stuff everybody's getting in the tropics? I heard Spielberg and Coppola both had it. Arnold may be dying of it even as we speak. It's *the* disease right now. And it's usually fatal, if I may say."

"Is it that bad, Beetleman? I mean, if there's anything I can do..."

"What could you do, hold my thing for me? Just go on this shoot. I really wanted this one, but... It's good money for a diver, and I'd just as soon you got it. Listen, buddy, I might not be here when you get back. If I don't make it, I want you to have my diving stuff and my surfboard. The whole tuna, man."

"I don't know what to say," Mat said.

"Just go. It's enough to know a stud buddy is getting the bucks."

"I'll owe you one, man... Listen, if you feel better, you can have any work that comes up while I'm away. All right? Just check my message machine. Pin number five-oh-five."

"If I'm not dead, I'll check. But I'm likely a goner."

Blessing the god of serendipity, Mat hung up to call his agent and pack his gear. The trip and the money were just what he needed.

He rang Daphne. She decided to go home for a few weeks, to tell her family about Mat. He could meet her in Wisconsin.

8

Nothing had happened to Daphne. Within a half hour of his arrival at the Dickey house she called from Des Moines and explained that her plane had been re-routed because of mechanical problems. Her cell phone wasn't working, she said. She was disappointed when Mat told her he'd broken the news to her folks about their engagement. She'd meant it to be a surprise.

He stood in the kitchen speaking into a rotary-dial telephone, the first he'd seen in years, while the sleet that had frozen into his slacks melted and dripped on a linoleum floor. Mother and Father Dickey hovered around him, apparently unaware how to react to the sudden appearance of a future son-in-law.

"Well, it *was* a surprise. And what in hell was I supposed to do when I showed up at the door and they'd never heard of me," he growled into the phone. "Stay at the Dickeyville Marriot? There isn't even a goddam taxi here."

Daphne began crying and he said he was sorry. She sniffed and promised to be there after dinner. He felt the beginning of a head-ache. His dufflebag still sat beside the front door. Looking at Mother and Father Dickey, attempting not to stare at her strange ears and his proboscis for the tenth time, Mat wondered: how could he introduce these embarrassingly homely people to his mother and Hollywood friends and say this was his new family? The thought of the wedding reception, his mother, her friends... he tried to put that away.

The house was warm, a fire crackling in the fireplace. Mat's nose had cleared and he recognized some of the surrounding smells: old people, Persian carpets, brewed coffee, clothes worn comfortably long, old linens, boiled cabbage, ginger cookies and other baked foods; those, and the passage of long years. An old brass and marble clock depicting time's winged chariot ticked loudly on the mantel above the fireplace. There was a fine old Steinway piano. Pictures – tintypes, caricatures of Daphne and the old man and woman but some with even stranger noses or ears – hung in wooden frames in the living room; but there were no photos of Daphne. Doilies hung over the arms and backs of a deep-brown leather couch and old wing chairs. Along one wall rose a floor-to-ceiling bookshelf filled with volumes, some old and leather-bound. After the old woman bid the "men-folk relax and get to know one another", she headed into what she said was the kitchen, and the living-room filled with deep silence, except for crackling of the fire and deep, even ticking and occasional chime of the clock.

Mat stood in front of the fire drying his lightweight suit. The old man, now wearing a shirt at the old woman's insistence, rocked quietly and smoked his pipe. *A meerschaum pipe* – amazing! Looking at the guy, Mat could think of nothing to say.

Ten minutes, twenty, passed away as he slowly rocked. "Some weather we're getting. You're getting, I mean," Mat ventured.

The clock ticked.

Five minutes later the old man answered. "Seen worse."

Silence became so prolonged that Mat imagined he could hear the snow that glowed briefly as it drifted past lighted windows. He wondered if the old man was deaf.

Steam rose off his pants legs before the radiant heat of the fire. His stomach ached from hunger and tension. "May I call you Father Dickey?" he asked. Something seemed to empty the room, like a submarine with a pressure leak. Mat rubbed his already warm hands over the flames. "Heh-heh," he chuckled uneasily. "Heh-heh." He picked at some lint on his suit, his eyes searching the room for something to bring into conversation. "Ahem," he cleared his throat.

The old man finally plucked his pipe from between his yellow teeth and fixed Mat in a level stare. "Asked you earlier, you like the Packers of Green Bay, Wisconsin?"

"Umm..." This was an important question. Mat's mind cast about. "I follow the '49ers. But the Packers are all right. Got, umm... Bart

Starr, eh?"

"49ers? Never heard of them. This is Packer country and I follow the Packers." The old man rubbed vigorously at his odd nose.

"Waiting for Lombardi to rise and lead the cheese-heads to the promised land?" Mat smiled, but the other stopped rocking and stared at him over his glasses. Deciding something, he resumed rocking.

Mat was readying himself to bolt from the house when the old woman bustled into the room carrying a cake covered with pink frosting and strawberries, a tall cylindrical cake on a silver platter that she set grandly upon a deep-varnished mahogany end table. "All this man-talk," she chided. "You're too late for lunch – we just finished."

Mat glanced at the clock. Ten thirty. An hour and a half 'til noon.

"Up since three," the old man huffed. "Breakfast five hours ago."

"Now, how about strawberry layer cake? It's my specialty," the old woman explained to Mat. "I unfroze the best berries for you."

"I'm honored," he said politely, eyeing the cake eagerly. His stomach rumbled, but neither of these old folks seemed to notice.

She set TV trays beside chairs around the fireplace and asked Mat to sit. She brought a pot of tea and three cups. A ceremony.

"So what do you think of the Dickeyville Grotto, dear?" she asked.

Mat glanced at his hosts. "Well, it's certainly something to... to think about, isn't it?"

"Of course, our family doesn't go to that church."

Mat brightened. "I can see why. If a small-time carnival cooked meth, went schizophrenic and shot steroids, that's the grotto. That place made my stomach – "

"We feel the same way, son," the old man said. "We love it too."

"Yes, well, it certainly warmed the, um, my stomach..."

"Gets darn near thirty thousand visitors a year," Pa said.

"Father Minus will give you a personal tour," Ma said.

"Sure. Thanks for your hospitality." Mat held up his saucer as she forked over a large cake slice. "I guess I was kind of a surprise, wasn't I?" He felt ravenous, remembering he hadn't eaten since breakfast the previous day.

The woman laughed. "Why of course not, dear. There's been others come for Daphne. You're quite welcome here."

He paused, his fork in mid-air over the cake. "Others? You mean that fellow at the station? Butch? I mean Buster?"

She tut-tutted. "There's been some low class ones, too. Low-lifers. See, Daphne's never been lucky in love. Until you, that is."

Mat thought about Daphne. An extremely beautiful woman. Intelligent and witty, strong-willed. He felt an emptiness in his stomach again, emptiness that wasn't hunger. "Are you sure we're talking about the same woman? You have only one daughter?"

The woman laughed. "Eat your cake, young man. And I'll get out her baby pictures after."

"I don't see her on your wall."

"No, and you won't. Daphne prefers it that way."

Mat stabbed his fork into the cake, a gooey strand of pink frosting stretching as he lifted a bite. "Mm-hmm," he said, until the alien taste filled his mouth.

The woman watched him. "I hope that frosting's okay for you. Father's stomach gets upset from strawberries, but he likes them fine. So I whip Pepto Bismol into the frosting."

The old man nodded. "Mighty good, Mother."

After Mat explained his stomach was wobbly from the bus ride and he wasn't hungry after all and could eat only that one bite of his treat, Father Dickey insisted on eating the rest. Mat watched him, noticing that for such a wizened old man he had the appetite of a wolverine. For her part, Mother Dickey ate no cake, giggling and insisting that the "calories didn't do a girl's figure good at all".

Snack finished, the old man returned to his rocking, this time with a newspaper. He ignored Mat, who glanced about for the TV and saw none. For a long time, until Mother Dickey finished the kitchen chores, Mat watched flames flickering on oak logs. He listened to the cracking of embers, now burning down.

The old guy rustled his papers into a tidy heap and tossed them into a box full of short wood chunks beside the fireplace. "That's that," he said. "Isn't it?"

"Umm...I guess it is," Mat answered.

"And why do you think that is?"

"Why what is?" Mat wondered.

"Why *it* is, of course."

"You mean what 'that' that was that, is?"

"Exactly," the old man said. "We see eye to eye on that, anyway. Come with me." He stood, bones somewhere in his wiry body cracking loudly, and led Mat into the rear of the house, through what appeared to be addition after addition. Although the structure had seemed somewhat large from outside, Mat realized that two thousand square feet – maybe more – had been built on to the rear. They threaded through halls passing darkened, musty-smelling bedrooms with pulled curtains; chilly rooms closed off to the warmer rooms up front. Rays of wonderfully bright light sneaked in from seams along the edges of sills. Mat had a premonition he was being led toward a room containing dismembered bodies of former "gentleman callers".

"Almost there," Pa said.

"Where?"

"To it. Could be in the Guinness book if I were a vain man… It's back here." He led Mat down a final dark long corridor to a door Mat thought might be the rear of the house but which revealed, upon opening, another door set at the end of a six-foot long hall that opened to the right. They passed through this door and were immediately confronted by two more. This is it, all right, Mat thought: they'll never find me here. "Add-ons," the old man meanwhile explained. "It's a big house dating back some one hundred-fifty years. Like one of them mazes, you might say."

"I hear you own several hundred acres around these parts," Mat replied, to make conversation.

"Hah! A damn sight more'n that," the old man said. "I guess you're not one of those gigolo types, eh? Even if you look like you might be."

"I don't think so, Mister Dickey."

"Father Dickey. Or Pa Dickey."

"Sure. Father Dickey."

Mat was hopelessly lost. How could a house stretch so far back?

"This is real exciting," the old man said, pausing before a door. "Close your eyes."

"Close my eyes?" May as well, Mat thought. Better I don't see the ax and the retarded cousin wearing the skin of one of the prior suitors.

"Close 'em. That's right." He guided Mat into the room and clicked on a light. "OK. Open 'em up."

Before Mat a great multi-hued mass squatted, bell-shaped, filling the entire room. The thing had a diameter of maybe twelve feet and nearly reached the ceiling. "Incredible," he said. "It's – just incredible."

The old man cackled. "It is, isn't it?" He pulled open a shade so

Mat could see better.

"What do you call it?"

"It has no name. I just call it my string collection."

"It's… certainly tall."

The old man sat in a chair beside the window. Through it Mat saw a child building a snow fort next door. Father Dickey also glanced out, his potato nose profiling into a misshapen ramp. "There's just one problem. I'm not so young as I used to be, and I can't find the end to add onto. I don't suppose you could help, could you?"

Mat looked at the behemoth. He could see that it was made of thousands – millions – of different strings all knotted together and wound horizontally. Standing next it, he searched for the end. Touching the mound, his fingers slipped into its soft mass. He jerked back his hand. "Damn!" A shudder of disgust went through him. It was like the time he was part of an Indian shoot and they'd been filming in the sacred Ganges: he'd touched something meaty in the water.

"Maybe you ought to just pick a thread and cut into it."

The old man snorted. "You ever heard of a henway, Mat?"

He thought. "What's a henway?"

"'Bout three pounds. Maybe four." The old guy chuckled. "Point is, a man ought to know what he's cutting into. This, for instance. I've been trying for two years and I've got to find the end." He paused. "You know what you're cutting into, young Mat Roper?"

Voices came down the hall. "Yoo-hoo. Come here, Mr. Roper. We've got visitors," the old woman's voice floated through the maze of passageways. "It's the reporter from the *Gordondale Gazette*!"

9

Each woman took one of Mat's arms and guided him like a cripple onto a burgundy velvet couch dating probably back to the turn of the 19th century. He chuckled uneasily as he sniffed the reporter's perfume. It was vaguely reminiscent of machine oil and violets.

Mrs Link was a thin middle-aged woman with cupid lips under a long nose. She explained that she had come to do a feature on Daphne's engagement. "Nobody around here thought she'd ever land a man. And such a handsome one!" She squinted seductively at Mat while pulling a small note pad and an impossibly small chrome camera from her purse – the kind of camera used by spies in old movies.

Mat chuckled again and nodded toward the camera. "You want a picture of one of my freckles? Maybe one mole?"

"That's not funny, dear. I'll just snap a picture of you. And if we can have a recent photo of Daphne we'll print it in tomorrow's issue. I'm sure all Daphne's old friends would like to see..."

Mother Dickey rose from the couch and left, ears bouncing at every step, then brought back a leather-bound album. She lifted out a photo and handed it to Mrs Link. "It's not new, of course, but it's how I like to remember her." She sighed. "She was such a dear child."

Mrs Link accepted the picture, then handed it to Mat. He stared. "But this..." The photo, black and white, framed the face of a high school graduate. She wore the standard white blouse, black vest; had straight blondish hair, nice mouth, beautiful dark eyes – and the same honker as Father Dickey and ears of Mother Dickey. Yet he recognized the face, too. "This is Daphne?"

"Before she got the nose-job. And the ear-job," Mother Dickey said. "Did I mention this is how I like to remember her? She was such a cute little duckling."

"We all know what kind of duckling," Mrs Link snorted. "Surely she mentioned her surgeries, Mr. Roper?"

"Um, sure. I just haven't seen this before."

"You'll get used to it," Mother Dickey chided. "Your children are sure to have the Dickey nose." She sat in father Dickey's rocker. "Dickey noses blow others out of the water."

Mat dropped heavily back in the couch. "Children?"

"I must be off," Mrs. Link said, standing and snapping a shot of Mat slumped into the cushions. "The presses must roll. Tootles." She crinkled her face as if she were sniffing a fresh-baked cinnamon bun. "So nice to meet you, Mr. Roper."

Mat sat up quickly. "I say, Mrs Link. Couldn't you hold off on that story a bit? You know, that way Daphne and I can surprise anybody she wants to surprise?"

Mrs Link pooh-poohed the idea. "Don't you worry. Everybody will be surprised about Daphne. Take my word for it."

She left, and Mat melted back into thought while Mother Dickey rose from the rocker and sat next to him on the couch. Smelling yeasty sweet, she opened the album and showed him great aunts and uncles, grandfathers, mothers – Dickeyville's founders, nieces and nephews, most with the appalling gall growing on the ends of their upturned noses. "Typically Midwest," Mother Dickey said. "It's my belief that was why the founding fathers left Europe in the first place. The whole of the Midwest is populated by immigrants with unique noses."

Mat nodded. "Hmm."

"These others, Winders – my side of the family – all have big ears and marry Dickeys. In our blood sure as Dickeys have big schnozzles."

"Ahh. Ahh." – Mat glanced to the wall without Daphne's photos.

Later he was led upstairs to what Mother Dickey called the "gentleman caller" room. He said he felt tired, though really he needed to think. But when he had showered and changed into fresh slacks and stretched bare-chested on a quilted coverlet, he had nothing to think about except the advice he'd always given engaged acquaintances: a man should see a woman's mother before he married. To his credit, he paused to reflect that a woman ought to look at her guy's father.

Mat decided he'd like to board a jet and arrive back home in California in four hours, but he was trapped. No transportation to Des Moines until tomorrow.

Over a deep-varnished pine dresser a framed tintype of a pioneer Dickey glared, sternly confidant that the genes would march on, his nose like a two-holed kiwi above a bushy mustache. Pale egrets strained heavenward on jaundice-colored wallpaper. Sitting up, Mat groaned and pulled on his shoes. He tried to find something to read but could locate not even the *Reading Digest* Mother Dickey had said was next to the bed. He had a ghastly vision of his mother, who had never adjusted to the family's economic reversals, fainting when she met Daphne's parents. He pulled off his shoes to stare restlessly at his socks until he lay down again and drifted into a midday nap.

10

He awoke ravenous, momentarily disoriented in the unfamiliar room. He sat up, rubbed his eyes, saw in twilight a snowstorm raging outside the window. Voices and laughter sifted in beneath the door, then a ghastly hog call. He recognized that. Somewhat refreshed, he switched on the light and stood up. Pulling on a short-sleeved shirt and tucking it into his slacks, he slipped into his canvas shoes. His mind was clear about one thing.

He followed the noise downstairs and stepped into a living room full of Dickey noses and Winder ears. He saw it all in an instant: men of many ages, some bearded, some nearly as tall as he, square-shouldered, heavy-set, hair dark, short-clipped and razored white over the ears in what used to be called "fenders with white sidewalls" when he was a kid; men in white t-shirts gabbing with drinks in their hands and deep, sonorous voices, nodding as others spoke; short dark-haired women with small waists and high, cushioned breasts and round, compact rear-ends and trim ankles; laughing farm women in plaid blouses with clinking highball glasses, bustling about full of cheer, as if they were surprised to be meeting long-lost loved ones; children slipping noisily through the crowd chasing one another, stopping to snatch at colorful ribbon candies or rum balls in bowls or Christmas cookies on platters; white-haired grandmas in white aprons and grandpas in suspenders and red flannel shirts. As Mat entered the room, dozens of huge noses and long flappy ears turned his way; the party silenced and all faces looked as if they could not have been more stunned than if the dead had risen from the earth and fish fell from the sky. First one muscular young man's mouth opened into a grotesque "O", then another's; soon the whole clan was hooting hog calls. Mat's legs wobbled as he scanned the space for Daphne. He smiled woodenly while Mother Dickey shouldered through the guests to him.

"Where's Daphne? I need to talk to her right away."

"She called while you were asleep. Said she can't get out of Des Moines because of the weather. Can I get you a drink?"

Mat groaned. "What about the bus? Can I get to her?"

"Full-blown blizzard. No buses run in this, Mister California boy. You just better hold your nose and pick your horses. Bourbon do? Mulled wine or beer?"

"Any food? I'm starved."

"Course there is. Got German potato salad, shrimp balls, Polish sausage, Swedish meatballs, crackers and cheese, chips and dip, veggies cuts. Try some." She paused. "Beg pardon, did you just growl?"

"Sorry, no." His stomach tightened.

"Work your way to the tables. Introduce yourself to everyone."

Mat hadn't pressed five feet into the throng before meeting cousins and uncles, aunts and nephews and nieces, all called together for an impromptu engagement party. He bore their intimate derision and heard from across heads twice more the hog call that had roped him. He stared straight up the bushy nostrils of Uncle Tylee, who discussed the prospects of the Packers and the "new" league – the what? forty year-old American Conference. He glanced over and saw Dickey sons and cousins whose thick corn-fed muscles swelled Packer and Wisconsin Badger t-shirts as, squint-eyed, they sucked down something called Leinenkügel beer from bottles that whetted the tips of their Dickey noses. He saw giggling honker-nosed Dickey daughters and knitting matrons impassively bearing their fleshy burdens; heard the fsst! of beer cans and clink! of wine glasses and smelled the bread smell of old women and pipe smell of old men filling the roomful of Dickey and Winder portraits; and he knew – knew it even in his teeth – that he could never stand to hear that hog call again or the story behind it. What had seemed dear and precious now hurt in his molars. He tossed back a shot of Canadian whiskey that someone placed in his hand, and then tossed back a refill.

As the evening passed he never reached the food table twenty feet across the crowded living room, heated, sweltering nearly to ninety. Muscled Dickey sons who asked: Dude, tell us about your hot beach babes? hooted out into the snow, yelling and throwing beer cans, while one daughter disgorged in the downstairs bathroom with the gusto of someone strangling. Matrons placed wet kisses and pinches on his handsome "surfer" cheeks while ruffling his "beautiful blond locks", referring at least a dozen times to him as "Goldilocks". His arm pumped and hand was crushed within iron fists of Dickey and Winder men, his own good nature peaking in ecstatic leaps of acceptance and plummeting down sloped nose-jumps of depression, until in drunkenness he no longer saw ears or beaks as twin Dickey daughters with honking-big noses and rabbit-lobed ears sandwiched him in a corner between lusty farmer's daughters' breasts and nuzzled his "eensy-teensy, itsy-bitsy" ears and promised him heaven in a haystack, until he drank beyond abandon from half-filled glasses off the mantel or piano and then drank more, accepting numberless invitations from faces suddenly familiar and remarkably endearing, crying with Father Dickey, nose-to-nose draped in each other's arms, wretched sobs over the missing end of a string ball and the profound beauty of family ties and undying pain of losing a daughter but gaining a son the old man had never had. Mat remembered lastly giggling as his flimsy shoes squeaked in dry snow while he peed beside the porch, then kicked a full beer can across the street to the cheers of the young Dickey and Winders in t-shirts, who stamped their feet in the yard despite the thermometer hovering around 20 degrees. Then came sudden reeling collapse in the snow, dick still in chilled fingers, and strong but gentle hands lifting him into the house and onto the couch.

11

Morning, he awoke fully-dressed on the couch, his brain thudding inside a dehydrated skull. A strange sound was scraping and scrapping outside. He staggered to the window and pulled the shade, exposing raw eyeballs to a blast of intense light. Glorious day in Dickeyville. Squinting against fierce sunlight reflected from dazzling snow, he watched Father Dickey shoveling. The old man, mittened, scarfed and booted, looked up and waved cheerily before scratching the shovel under a next scoop of drift.

Heart hammering his ribs, red blobs pulsing in his skull, Mat collapsed back onto the couch. Taking stock, squinting again, he saw that the living room had already been cleaned. He felt a slither of bile surge up his throat, but fought it back. Mother Dickey bustled in.

"You up, dear? I thought I heard you stirring, so I put on your breakfast." She set a tray on the coffee table. "You're quite a sleeper. We've been up for hours."

"How nice for you."

"By the way, what you asked last night – about being married."

"I asked?"

"What I meant to say is that it's safe. After thirty years I feel safe."

Like I care to know, he thought. Mat pressed his temples between his hands. "I feel hurt."

"When you're young it doesn't sound romantic, but you watch life die all around you. Even if safety is an illusion it's a thing you can grow to. It takes a lot of time and trust to grow to that."

Sounds great, he thought. Like an airbag or bank account.

"I know folks from California rarely marry. Your parents married?"

"Who told you that? People get married in California."

"Oh." – She seemed disappointed.

"My parents were married."

"Well, you better eat," she said.

On the tray lay a half-dozen sausages oozing light yellow oil, heavily peppered scrambled eggs, coffee, hash browns with a dollop of catsup and sour cream, toast, orange juice, hot cereal and a small bowl with what looked like homemade strawberry jam. Mat felt the grip of starvation, but his stomach sent up one queasy bile-burp in protest and he knew he could eat nothing for hours. "I don't eat meat."

"Of course you do, dear. Everyone does."

Too hungover to argue, he opted instead for a shower. More than ever his mind was set. He staggered to the bathroom and threw his clothes into a heap. As streaming hot water relaxed away some of the ache in his shoulders and head, he again felt a momentary warmth for these rather unique people and their homespun manners. He lathered, or rather rubbed the hard cake of soap over his body without the bar noticeably shrinking or foaming. It was heady and solid and did not waste away with water – soap as solid as the Midwest, honest, durable and lasting through plenty of scrubbing. He had a sudden inspiration: He could take this stuff – this regional product – back to the coast and maybe market it. He sniffed the bar, finding it a tad minty, a trifle too strong. Maybe have to talk to the manufacturer about that. The idea of becoming a soap baron appealed to him. A regular job. His mother would like it if he were a CEO. And performed in his own ads.

After he'd finished showering he found that his clothes had been removed from the bathroom floor, and, somewhat curious that someone had been in the room with him, he had to call for his dufflebag.

Mother Dickey laughed from the next room. "We're country folk, Mr. Roper. Naked men mean less than a plucked chicken." She didn't bring his bag but tossed a handful of clothing into the bathroom – jeans, shorts and a t-shirt. Then a pair of big boots and an article of clothing he didn't at first recognize. "Put those on, too."

Mat leaned over the pile. "Boots? What's this other thing? Is this decent? Didn't I see these in a leather shop catalog?"

"Long-johns. Your union suit. The bun-flap is standard. Those and the boots are Cousin Ken's, but he's off to the University of Wisconsin. His mother sent them over. They'll be a little wide, but not tight like Father Dickey's would be."

Mat picked up the long-johns and stared at them with disgust. He'd never worn a pair in his life and wasn't about to start now. He stuffed them into his duffle, then dressed. Remembering his frozen feet from the day before, he slipped into an extra pair of socks and pulled on the big wool-lined boots and tied the laces. Like the soap, the boots were solid and honest.

"Better hurry up," came Mother Dickey's voice. "The boys are waiting in the kitchen for you."

"What boys?"

"I have to wonder about you, Mister Mat Roper. Your memory's as short as the day is long. You promised the boys you'd go along on the shoot today. The hog shoot."

"I'm sick. Why would I do that?"

"Mat, in Wisconsin a promise is a promise."

"In California a promise is an egg," he mumbled, "Sometimes you have to break it."

He couldn't remember saying anything about filming hogs. Maybe he'd told someone about the job he'd been on last year: gripping in Maui on a Nature Channel shoot about feral pig damage to the pristine ecology. Thought he deserved a production credit because the director had used his suggestion that they add the People for the Ethical Treatment of Animals objection to Nature Conservancy policy of shooting non-native wild pigs to protect habitat.

Nothing better than two non-profits in a cat fight.

The effort of chuckling caused him great pain, tacks stabbing under his eyelids. He gulped three aspirin from the medicine cabinet and washed them down with a swig of Listermint.

He shaved and headed for the kitchen. There he found three hulking, big-nose young Dickeys and a flap-eared hulking Winder sitting over cups of steaming coffee. The dour-faced boys glared at him as if he were a poisonous snake. Mat was instantly alert.

In the depths of hazy recall he recognized a couple of these guys, whose muscles swelled the red-checkered shirts under thick camouflage coats. Three of them wore stupid wool stocking hats. In short, they looked ridiculous. Mat issued a half-hearted good morning to the three Dickey noses and pair of Winder ears.

"Maybe it is, maybe it isn't," said one. "An' maybe it's in between."

The others chuckled like this was a good joke. Mat smiled warily.

One of the Dickeys, the biggest and obviously oldest, the only one not wearing a stocking cap, took from his head a different ridiculous bit of haberdashery: the first raccoon skin cap Mat had ever seen. He hadn't known that they existed outside of Disneyland.

The four looked like an audition for *Deliverance*.

The big man caught his stare. "Well, Mister Roper – "

"Last night he said call him 'Mat,'" interrupted another Dickey, younger version of the one in coonskin, so young that he still had facial skin cratered by pimples.

"Um... Mat," the older one continued, "while you been sleeping late we've been here an hour. Auntie made us breakfast. Everyone else has left already."

Mat recognized this for an accusation and rubbed his hair. "Who left? For where? I'm sorry, but I can't remember anyone's name. Can we go over them again?"

"People around here, Roper – " the big man began.

"Mat," the young one interrupted.

"People around here don't like it if you forget their names. That means you don't care enough to hear."

Mat looked to see if he was kidding. Unusually for him, he took an instant dislike to the guy. "I was pretty tired," he shrugged.

"I'm Verne," said the other, pulling on his tattered coonskin and sticking out a hand. He appeared to be around thirty-five, though Mat would later learn that he was in his forties. "My brother Brodie. Cousin Nels and second cousin – a Winder – Bascom."

Each took Mat's hand in firm, callused grips. "Pleased to meet you all," he said, confused, still waiting for the aspirin to kick in. "Now what's this I hear about – "

Mother Dickey interrupted. "All right, all right. Out of my kitchen. You young men skedaddle and go on your shoot before that tom-fool old husband of mine changes his mind and goes too. I need to wax the floors and do some cooking before Daphne gets home." She handed a picnic basket to Bascom. "Fried chicken, Wisconsin smoked cheddar sandwiches, cider, deviled eggs, hot coffee with a dash of the Irish, and warm double-chocolate chip cookies. Little snack to hold you."

"But I – " Mat started.

"Get along with you. Grab Father Dickey's coat and muffler off the hook as you go out."

There seemed no appeasing Mother Dickey, and anyway the young men were moving impatiently toward the side door off the kitchen. Verne snagged Father Dickey's coat – a camouflage wool carbon copy of the boys' – and handed it to Mat, along with a scarf, gloves and a green woolen cap with earflaps, a hat even more ridiculous than the others. Mat stuck it in his pocket. The clothing smelled of diesel fuel and Old Spice. The sunlight through the window hurt his eyes. "But it's sunny out there. I don't really need this coat, do I?" He sniffed the thing. "Gads." It reeked of every combustible he could imagine.

"Please don't go taking the Lord's name in vain, Mister... uh, Mat?" Nels asked. There was bliss in his face, but Mat would learn Nels was most blissful when he was pointing out someone else's sin.

"'Gads' is taking the Lord's name in...?"

"Nels has gone over to the Gordondale Baptists," Brodie explained as Mat tried to wrestle his way into the coat. "We know you Californians aren't used to non-secular ways, but we try to indulge him." Unlike the others Brodie was pudgy and seemed friendly.

"Amen," Nels said.

"Well," Mat said, "I don't need a coat today, anyway."

"You're a tough one then," Verne said, "since the temperature's about five above zero. You from California's polar region?"

The others laughed.

"It's sunny out," Mat explained.

Bascom nodded. "Some parts of Alaska they put things in refrigerators to keep 'em cold without freezing harder 'n bulls' balls." Bascom's voice, like his ears, was big with drawn-out vowels.

"Jeeze – " Mat said.

"Mat..." Nels warned.

Outside, the icy air, driven by a steady breeze, struck Mat's exposed skin like a bag full of nails. He pulled up the coat collar, wrapped the scarf round his neck and pulled on the gloves and cap. Instantly he regretted not wearing the long johns, but said nothing about going back; the boys were too antsy. He was being kidnapped.

He needed to talk to Daphne.

The sky was as blue and deep as he'd ever seen. Crystalline air. He squinted into a slow, freezing breeze. Looking past the rear of the Dickey home he surveyed the land, saw it slope away from the flat rise upon which Dickeyville had blossomed over a hundred years before. You could see the far horizon beyond islands of trees, matrixes of farmlands spotted here and there with barns and houses dotting snowy fields on the forever expanse. It was like looking through time to a hundred years before, like seeing a land where your great-grand-parents came from. For the second time Mat had the strange sensation of remembering something he hadn't realized he'd forgotten. It all appeared as wholesome as *It's a Wonderful Life's* Bedford Falls. He realized also that he could never call this place home. How did people live in places like it, he wondered.

"Clear sky now, but look over there." Brodie pointed to the southwest, where a gray expanse nudged over the flat earth.

Father Dickey, wearing only tennis shoes, blue jeans and a faded green Packers sweatshirt, leaned on his shovel and nodded at "the boys". "Wish to hell – beg your pardon, Nels – I was going with you. But mother's on one of her tizzies about the upcoming marriage." The old man glanced at Mat. Some fifty yards of driveway had been cleared alongside the house. Sweat dripped from his thin red face, but he wasn't breathing hard.

Taking stock of his hangover, Mat doubted he could even lift the shovel this morning, but he took the wicker lunch basket out of Bascom's hands. In a little while he was going to have to eat, acid stomach or not. "Maybe I better stay and help..." he suggested.

"Come on," Verne growled. "We haven't got all day."

"Yep," Pa lamented, "get up in the morning with nothing to do and by sundown you're half-finished."

The truck was an old Dodge pickup painted somewhere between pea and baby shit green, a color indicating the vehicle had once belonged to a government agency. Terminal body cancer, rust was devouring the lower body and brown holes riddled the fenders. On the hood was a bowling trophy ornament and inside a gun rack bristling with rifles. An "NRA" sticker blocked a hole in one side window.

Bascom climbed through the truck's passenger door and waved in Brodie. Verne took the wheel, then in climbed Nels and lastly Mat to settle on Bascom and Brodie's laps. "Hell, Roper," Verne said, "you in here is like trying to squeeze a nightcrawler into a straw."

The others laughed uproariously.

Mat was certain now: he did not like this guy.

"Gol-dern heater doesn't work, but we ought to be cozy with five in here," chuckled Verne.

Brodie laughed. "Ain't that why we're bringing along Mister Ro–ow!" he yelped.

"Owww! You quit squirming and watch your bony butt, Nels," Bascom boomed close to Mat's ear.

"Is 'butt' in the Bible?" Nels wondered.

"Sorry, Bascom. I got my knife in my back pocket," Nels answered.

Verne started the pickup and tried to shift around legs into first gear. Mat ducked his head to keep from banging the roof. Racked rifles pressed at the back of it; if he tilted and ducked, he could almost see through the windshield. He imagined the truck overturning as Verne drove fast down the slushy, twisting street. There were no seatbelts.

"You smell something funny?" Brodie wondered.

"Sure do. Smells darn fine, like Mat's been using some of Uncle Dickey's – Look out!" Verne yanked the wheel and the truck swung sideways, wheels drifting neatly around a black Labrador standing nonchalantly in the road. Mat's stomach flipped.

Verne rolled his window down: "Fritz, get your sorry ass home!"

"Cousin Otto's dog," Bascom explained.

They rubbed frost from inside the windshield. "So, guys," Mat said, swallowing the bile that threatened to rise completely, "What're we shooting today? Video? Something a little primitive," he chuckled indulgently, "like Super 8? Bergman shot a few reels of 16 in, I think, *Persona*, and it turned out great on the big screen."

"Don't talk," Verne instructed. "First, I don't know what in hell you're talking about. Second, Old Scratchy's got no defroster, and you're icing my glass." He rubbed the window with his sleeve; the brothers helped. "Breathe easier, men. Better yet don't breathe at all."

The truck ground in first gear, swerving through Dickeyville's twisted, snow-crusted streets. Verne wrestled to pull the stick back into second around jutting knees. Mat was disinclined to let him up-shift. It was his intestines that were shifting.

Not filming. *Hunting*. In Mat's mind, a cretin's sport. These weren't his kind of people. Were these guys anybody's kind of people? Were these people *people*? He wondered, did they do meth? Looked like it.

Staring through the frozen windshield, leaning to see past the hood, Mat determined that, yes, the ornament on the old Dodge was the figure from a bowling trophy, perfectly poised, legs bent deep as the tiny gold bowling ball hung on its fingertips, ready for release.

"What does everyone do in a town like this," he wondered aloud. "What do they do for a living?" Thinking meth again.

"Can't speak for all, though I pretty much know what they do," Brodie said. "Me and my big brother Verne are polliwog ranchers."

"Right. That's a gut-buster."

"Did you say 'Buster'?" cousin Nels asked. "Talk about one of your all-time great guys."

"Sure. Unique human being," Mat said. "You raise polliwogs?"

"Polliwog ranchers. You can't find polliwogs in winter in the Midwest – too cold. So Verne and I raise them. We've got a pond in our basement and several in a dairy barn we lease from our uncle Heywood. You met him last night."

"Grow polliwogs? As if."

They didn't bother to explain. "You gotta meet Heywood."

"I met so many I don't seem to remember." Mat glanced sidelong at Brodie to see if he was kidding and decided he was.

"I guess you'll remember when you see him today," Brodie went on. "How so?"

"You promised to visit. Everyone calls him 'Hollywood' Heywood on account of his time in California."

Mat thought about that. "What did he do in Hollywood?"

Bascom interrupted. "That 'Hollywood'. He's really something."

"Yeah, ol' 'Hollywood'," Nels echoed.

"Personally, I make my living in the Jehovah's Witnesses biz," Bascom said.

"That so," Mat said.

"I bought into the franchise years ago. Got in on the ground floor and got a protected territory that includes a quarter of Wisconsin."

"You're not a Jehovah's Witness."

"No, but I do have the south state franchise. Anybody who does door-to-door conversion in the area pays me royalties. Cleared around fifty thousand last year. I almost won a Cadillac and a trip to Hawaii."

Mat smiled. "Good deal."

"Of course you couldn't get in so cheap anymore. Franchises have gone up. Everybody wants in. It's not like the old days."

"Just my luck to miss out."

"Hope to recruit a few managers this year. You interested, Mat? As a future cousin I'm prepared to offer a tidy package for, say, twenty-five grand. You'll have to bring over a few converts first."

"Sure, count me in."

The unplowed streets were ribboned with tire tracks and footprints of pedestrians. The truck continued down the same route as Mat had trekked the previous day; he was struck now not so much by the quaintness of the houses, as by the serenity and tidiness. The town looked like a Rockwell painting or a Jimmy Stewart movie set, and he was touched not by cynicism, as he would have suspected, but by a longing he could not understand. He thought hard as it unreeled past to discover why he felt a touch of nostalgia. No reason came.

"Verne, your transmission's howling. Sounds awful," Bascom said.

Mat sat forward. "Give me that lunch basket. I've got to eat."

"Under my feet," Brodie said. "But I couldn't lift a pea pod through this tangle of legs."

It wasn't until they were nearly at Buster's Skelly station that Mat read the big banner stretched over the two-lane highway: WELCOME HUNTERS TO DICKEYVILLE HORROR DAYS!

"Dickeyville Horror?" – Envisioning yokels with ski masks and chain saws. "I heard about that somewhere."

"Everything you need to know is on that banner," Verne said.

"Must be the secret of Tiny Town, 'cause it doesn't tell me much."

"You gotta learn to *really* read to survive here," Verne warned.

"So I hear. What's the Dickeyville Horror?"

"Don't you California guys know nothing?"

"A monster," Bascom said, sticking a finger into his huge rubbery ear and picking at it. "We talked about it last night. You heard us talk a half-dozen times this morning. Got a comprehension problem, Mat?"

Bascom's ear probe looked like a breadstick attacking an abalone.

"He isn't kidding, Mat. The Horror's a monster all right. At least a kind of one."

"Come on," Mat insisted.

"A boar," Brodie volunteered. "European wild boar. A killer who runs to five hundred pounds, judging from the hoof prints."

"Hoof prints."

"I've personally not seen the beast, but he's been seen by plenty others. We've all seen his hoof prints, though. They go about this big." Brodie touched one middle finger to another and one thumb to another, creating a circle as big as a cantaloupe. "Verne's seen him, all right.

When he was about twelve."

Verne nodded, a dreamy look in his eyes. "In the Mazy, driven by dogs. Not fifty yards away."

Mat looked at the circled fingers. "A pig that size?"

"Wild boar," Brodie repeated. "No domestic pig. A boar this big stands four feet at the shoulder, six feet long. Smarter than a dog, faster than a quarter horse for a hundred yards, meaner than hell's fire."

"A-men," Nels said.

"You guys want to shoot it? What for?"

"Not just us. Everyone," Bascom explained. "Everyone everywhere. Guys from other states."

"A *killer* boar."

"Blood-thirsty murderin' killer."

"Most dangerous animal in North America."

"So why not call in the National Guard? Or poison the thing if it's that dangerous? Or shoot it from a helicopter or set steel traps?"

"You gotta be kiddin'."

"Couldn't do that."

"That's wrong."

"Wouldn't be sporting."

"What are you, some kind of animal hater?"

"Hater? I don't even eat animals," Mat said, scrunching his head lower to see through the windshield.

"That's a good one. Everyone eats animals."

"I wear them on my feet," Mat admitted. "Have a leather wallet."

"That would be abuse. Are you an animal abuser?"

"I don't shoot or abuse animals," he said flatly. "I'm opposed to it."

"Oh no, Mat. Abusing animals is a way of life out here. It's as American as John Deere tractors," Nels said.

"They're made in China these days," Mat suggested.

Verne thumbed the end of his big Dickey nose. "Illinois," he said. "You can't joke about something sacred as John Deere, Roper. But we were talking about the Horror, and when I say mean and smart, I'm not joking. One year Ole Johannsen put a handful of buckshot into the pig's guts when the old guy found him in his pigsty breedin' sows after busting through a new fence. Ole thought that was the last of it. Except two nights later that damn boar – beg pardon, Nels – came back and plowed down nearly a hundred acres of top-flight hybrid."

"Hybrid?"

"Corn," Bascom explained.

Verne nodded. "It had to be nothing but vengeance because the boar didn't eat but a bushel of the stuff. Just ran up and down the rows, right over five-foot-tall cornstalks. Leveled every row in the field."

"Maybe some kids with a car," Mat suggested.

"Naw. Whole town came out to see the tracks," Brodie said. "It was the Horror."

"My God," Mat said almost under his breath.

Even Nels forgot to chastise Mat. "He's been on the loose in these parts for, what, Verne? thirty-five years now? Since we were babies and our fathers went after him?"

"Or weren't even born," Brodie said, absently picking at a pimple.

Verne nodded. "And beyond. That's how long there's been hunts for him. Some say the hog is immortal, some say he's the Devil. That's stupid, though a few put lead in him and he bled out plenty without dying. Once, when I hunted with Lloyd Thatcher and his boys, young Bailey got a quick shot at it before it shivved his leg from knee to thigh clear to the bone. Said he heard the beast crashing through the brush maybe a hundred yards away as some guys pushed him out of a thicket, and as young Bailey lifted his .30-30 the boar was into a small opening in the brush before he could aim. Said the boar was fast, faster than anything he's ever seen, and maybe his shot went into the big hump on its shoulders before the beast came under him. Flipped young Bailey nearly fifteen feet in the air and was gone, swallowed up by the Mazy wood.

"We got Bailey to the road and called on Uncle Bill's CB for an ambulance and they said Bailey's femoral artery was missed by a quarter inch. Anyway, me and his brother Tate and his dad followed maybe a gallon of boar blood spread a half mile through the Mazy." He paused and rubbed at the windshield. "Dammit, I knew that window would fog up."

"But he didn't die?" Mat asked.

"The Dickeyville Horror, or Bailey?"

"Either."

"Neither. At the time I thought maybe the Horror would die, and I wanted to find him. But Bailey's dad Lloyd wanted that boar more."

"Lloyd Thatcher had a heart attack right around Easter last year,"

Brodie said.

Verne shook his head, coon tail bobbing over his mangled ears. "The monster'll take more killing than that. By the next spring there'd been two sighting on the edge of cornfields and the beast had broken through the side of a barn to get at a sow. Tore through siding on a silo, too. I saw that out at the Hayes' place. Hair stood up on my neck to see those giant hoof prints and that torn-up metal siding ripped clean through the rivets like a walking can-opener got it."

"A can-opener?"

"His tusks," Bascom said. "Biologists say a European boar this big will have nine-inch tusks as sharp as skinning knives. Pretty near everybody in south state has seen sections of tree trunks where the critter sharpened and rubbed his tusks. Looks like an ax fight."

"And you saw the boar when it got that Bailey guy?" Mat asked.

"He didn't see it then," Nels said. "Saw it when – "

Verne interrupted. "There's not so many tusk-rubs anymore."

"Maybe he's dead," Mat ventured.

Brodie snorted. "Last year he got caught up by a six-pack of those Tennessee blueticks. Tough sonsabitches – beg pardon, Nels. Boar shivved two and ran the rest clear onto the Millawney ice after a freeze. Damn dogs broke through and the owner fell in and got wet getting them out. I haven't laughed so hard since we set Ruby Winder's shirt-tail afire that New Year's."

"He's out there, all right," Verne said. "I can damn near smell the beast. Like death and fear and all evil things. Waiting."

"Sure. Milt Thackeray put a shotgun load into his head before I was born. Wasn't even hunting the Horror but chanced onto him." Brodie laughed. "The devil of a beast turned for him, but Milt's a spry old coot and went up a tree. Dropped his shotgun. Said the beast's face streamed blood but he circled the tree for the next three hours snorting and pawing and tusking the trunk."

Bascom roared. "Milt hasn't gone to his outhouse since. Shits in a pot 'cause he thinks the Horror's laying for him!"

Mat shook his head. "So why hunt him in the snow? Why not when it's warm?"

Brodie fielded this one. "'Cause of the 'maze'. Eight square miles of dense virgin forest along the Millawney River clear to the Mississippi. And miles and miles more second-growth swampland as dense as it was two hundred years ago. In winter, with no leaves, you can almost see your way as you push through the brush. In summer you can't see three feet. Would you hunt a five hundred pound killer boar if you couldn't see him coming?"

"I wouldn't hunt him now," Mat said. "Call the National Guard."

"Told you. There are sporting rules – "

Verne interrupted. "Ole Johannsen. Not a week after his corn field was razed, old Ole disappeared. He was one of those Scandinavian bachelor-types, but he had a cooking lady, if you get my drift. She said he heard something by the barn one night. Took his shotgun and headed out with a lantern. Last anybody ever saw of him."

"It was the pig? The boar, I mean?"

"The irony of it was, there was a killing frost that night. It would've killed the crop anyway, since it killed everyone else's too. But the frozen ground – no tracks. Cold trail for the dogs. So we hunt the beast."

"Doesn't the landowner care? What if you shot one of his cows?" – Mat could see himself shooting a cow. It would be the only thing he ever shot. That is, if he knew how to shoot.

Bascom chuckled. "Owner? Mat, it's the wilderness. A wilderness so vast you could disappear an army in it."

"No exaggeration," Verne added.

"Like wilderness out of time," Nels said, eyes dreamy and distant. "Like God's land hundreds of years before even Indians lived upon this Wisconsin earth. Land that's never been cultivated other than a few apple trees, never stamped by the mark of humankind, never cleared except for a few acres around the original cabin. The Mazy family was nearly original pioneer stock and owned the land for over a hundred years. They died out with a girl named Dead-Alice."

"That name probably kept away riff-raff at her coming-out party," Mat suggested.

Brodie continued: "Mazy woods. When we were kids and she was alive, we used to say: 'Dead-Alice Mazy, crazy old coot, leather-face like a beat-up boot.' But when she died she left eight square miles of land along Millawney Creek. It's what'd be called the commons in Europe. A trust owns it and pays the taxes. But anyone can hunt it. Across the river are close to six thousand acres of state park. Next to that are thousands of acres of what we call 'flood swamp'. Black water swamp where hardly anybody goes because the mosquitoes would carry you away. Then there's the Mississippi River. So if you shoot a cow out there, it isn't a cow, it's a bear. And as for anybody caring, they wouldn't even hear your shot, it's so remote."

"So that's where this boar lives."

"Sure," Verne said, downshifting, the tranny gears grinding as legs got in the way. "The man who kills the Dickeyville Horror will become a legend."

Mat snorted. "My lifelong ambition. To be a living legend in Dickeyville, Wisconsin."

No one responded.

Verne turned the truck into the Skelly and Buster dashed out, stopping long enough to lock the station door. He wore a green-checkered woolen cap with earflaps, a hat that looked vaguely familiar. Mat guessed Buster had an IQ of about sixty, slightly more than a cabbage. His head was so small that he looked like an earwig. Then Mat felt his own head and realized where he'd seen another of those hats.

Buster stuck his into Bascom's open window, surveying the truck's interior. "Hey, men. Oh, and you too, Mister Roper." He looked slightly disappointed. "Gads, what smells? That you, Mister Roper?"

Mat cleared his throat. "Call me 'Mat'."

"Boy oh boy, it sure smells good," Buster said.

Verne smiled broadly. "Guess you'll be piling in the rear, Buster. Seeing as how piling in rears is your lot in life." The others laughed.

"Why not let Buster take my place? I mean, how I feel abou..." Mat's voice trailed off.

"Business of mankind, to subjugate the beasts," Nels explained.

Buster shook his head vigorously. "No, Mister Roper. But thanks for asking. I guess a movie star from California ought to ride in front. I'll just climb into the back and sit alone. I kind of like the cold and solitude. I'll just sit out here. No need to worry about me. Never let it be said that Buster Hieman ever displaced any rich celebrities."

"Don't worry, Buster. We won't worry," Brodie said, laughing.

Buster started to climb into the bed, then paused, tweedling his ridiculous pencil mustache. "Bascom, I forgot my gun. Can I use your twelve gauge?"

"Buster, why do you pull this kind of shit? I don't suppose you have any shells, do you?"

"Buster, you got matches in the station?" Nels wondered. "I need to fire up my pocket warmer and these idiots don't have any."

"Last match I had was when Superman died," Buster said, then started laughing. He laughed so hard he could barely climb aboard; he snorted so hard snot came out his nose. "Buster, you are a funny man," he congratulated himself, wiping his nose with his sleeve.

What planet am I on? Mat wondered.

Mat saw "Dickeyville Horror" signs in windows at Humphrey's Hunt & Hardware; Stumpjumper's Sporting Goods, Ammunition and Auto Parts; the Dickeyville Diner and Rifle Club; below the NO VACANCY sign on the Dickeyville Motor Motel and Ammo Store; Graybow's Groceries and Hunt Shoppe; and the Freedonia Feed and Ammunition Building. In the streets some dozen men and a couple of women stumped through slush in heavy insulated boots, carrying rifles, all walking the same direction. Verne slowed and offered rides to maybe two-thirds of them, and they climbed into the back with Buster. Several huddled their heads together and glanced toward Mat.

The truck swerved to the curb beside a bent, quick-stepping old guy whose headgear caught Mat's attention. The man waved as the truck slowed and swept off a top hat with earflaps to reveal long, scraggly white hair. He pressed an arm into the cab and introduced himself as Dickeyville Mayor and owner of the Freedonia Feed and Ammunition Building, "a place Mat would want to call his gun and ammunition headquarters" if he and Daphne settled in Dickeyville. "And just what do you do for a living, Mister Roper? And what's that smell?"

"Mat Roper is one of the biggest names in Hollywood," Buster volunteered, peering Kilroy-fashion around the corner of the pickup bed.

"Buster..." Nels said.

"Are you saying, Buster Hieman, that our Mister Roper has actually been in glamorous company in the City of Angels?"

"That's what he told me."

"Damn it, I never said that," Mat argued, eyeballing the Mayor's bizarre camouflage hat. "All I said – "

"Such language!"

"Shush!" Verne suggested, finger over his lip. "You're beginning to frost up my windshield again."

"It's ridiculous. I'm not even a bit player." Mat had a queasy feeling in his stomach, not all of it hangover. News obviously traveled quickly in a small town.

"It's true you were that guy Indiana Jones?" someone asked from the back. "That you?"

"Harrison Ford? How could I be someone else?"

"Make-up. Everyone knows that," another suggested.

"Special effects," came a voice.

"Lot of people want to meet you, Roper. Everyone."

"*Mat,*" Brodie suggested.

"Right. All thousand Dickeyvillians want to meet me." Mat turned to the Mayor.

"Less. Nine hundred and ninety-nine. Course that's counting Daphne and not you, and who in hell knows where you two will settle. Once we reach one thousand we'll incorporate and be qualified for an extra thirty thousand in state rural development funds," the Mayor explained. "Right now most of us are dependent on the Dickeyville Horror to some extent." He chuckled, brushing imaginary specks from his hat with crabbed, arthritic fingers before pulling it on, then said: "Good luck to you today, Mister Roper."

"How so, dependent?"

Nobody bothered to answer.

The bent old man climbed briskly aboard and Verne let out the clutch. The bed of the truck bristled with rifles, shotguns, red coats and stocking caps. A few faces were those of boys, one looking about thirteen. "Perhaps you'll do a documentary on our burgeoning metropolis once we incorporate, Mister Roper," the Mayor yelled over the roar of the over-revved engine.

"I don't do – " but Mat's words were blown away as the truck picked up speed.

Verne drove across the highway, right past the "Entering Greater Dickeyville, pop. 999" sign, and turned onto another road, unpaved and rutted with dozens of tire prints. The truck turned past a small wooden sign that Mat hadn't time to read, but a banner stretched over said: WELCOME TO DICKEYVILLE HORROR DAYS HUNT! PARKING $10.00 ALL DAY, 8 MILES. GOOD LUCK!

"Guys," Mat said, "Guys, wait a minute. I'm not sure about this."

"He's right," Brodie said. "He doesn't even know what he's going to use. Personally, I got him figured for a pistol man. Want my .357?" Brodie pulled a heavy chromed handgun from a holster under his coat and dropped it into Mat's lap. Brodie might just as well have produced a rattlesnake: Mat froze, the weighty thing sitting cold and solid against his legs, a fact Brodie seemed to accept as compliance. "Thought so," he said.

"But... what'll you use?" Mat hated guns. He'd never fired one.

"Just my hands," Brodie said. "Maybe some small twigs to fend off the monster. But don't any of you worry about me. Just see my mom gets what's left after the hog's done with me."

"He'll probably leave your dick 'cause he won't be able to find it," Bascom said. Then he assured Mat, "There's an extra thirty-ought-six." Just then the truck bottomed out in a rut.

"Too much weight in the bed," Nels said.

"About six hundred pounds too much. You better slow down, Verne," Brodie suggested.

Verne slowed, but the axle dragged slushy ground on the next hump. "Dammit. Beg pardon, Nels. But I replaced the axles after haying season when I took that big load down Lukenville way."

"Why don't you just have some of the people get out?" Mat wondered. "Would they mind?"

"Can't do that," Bascom said.

"You'd rather ruin the truck? They'd be pretty selfish to mind."

"Tell me, Mat," Verne said, "if this were your truck in, say, Los Angeles, would you ask these guys to get out?"

"Sure. To keep from ruining the truck. They'd understand."

"Well, these folks'd understand too. They'd understand that your truck was more important than them."

"Not really. It would just be a precaution."

Verne was silent a moment, thinking, as the truck pitched and rolled over a short stretch of moguls and ice patches. "I don't mean to sound like a preacher, but I guess that's how it'll come out. And I'm not calling you a numb-nuts, okay?"

"I'm sure you'll tell me anyway."

"Here's the most important lesson about living in a small town. You can apply this rule to nearly every interaction. In a small town the good will of your neighbors is beyond money. Once you learn that – really learn it – you'll be a local, at least welcome when you visit. They'll accept you as one of their own."

Like that's something I care about, Mat thought. A colony of hicks.

The Mayor poked his head in the window. "Riding together we

save on parking fees."

The road rolled deeper into a densely treed forest, dense even if some of the trees were deciduous and bare, limbs naked except for caked snow, appearing dead to Mat's eyes. Ancient maple, hemlock, white and black oak, hickory trees, bare limbs crowding over thick brush… Soon the truck entered stands of dark and majestic conifers rising tall as hardwoods. Under the trees were dry, brown thistle, sumac and wild currant, shoulder-high. Tall leafless brush and twisted bare vines snaked upward into the trees' lower branches; bare sticks, head-high and impenetrable. Spears of dead ferns, tall wild roses, wild currants and huckleberries rose from dirty brown snow splashing off the dirt road onto the shoulders. The loamy forest floor was deep, dark and dank beneath scraggly canopies of branches. The ancient and twisted forest stretched for miles, for all practical purposes unending to the men packed into the bed and cab of the pickup.

Mat's knees had pains shooting through them where they pushed against the AM radio.

The truck passed a small ticket booth stuck in the middle of the road. It was manned by a smiling child, blond with white skin, perhaps thirteen years old. His eyes were flat and as tranquil and expressionless as a mannequin's under a blue stocking cap. He took a ten-spot from Verne and handed back a parking receipt and pamphlet. "G' luck, Verne. You too Nels and Brodie and Bascom. And mister?" he nodded toward Mat.

"Yes?" Mat asked.

"You be careful, mister," the boy said. "You look like the kind of guy who in the movies gets killed."

"Oh? And what kind of looker gets killed in movies?"

"Your kind of looker. I seen it lots of times. A guy who doesn't know shit from shinola."

"You're a cute little wiseass," Mat replied.

Everyone laughed.

"Shit from shinola? Shit from *shinola*? Young man," Brodie said, trying to catch his breath, "if I tell your mama you're talking like that, there'll be some 'shinola' somewhere all right."

"That does it," Mat said, reaching for the door handle and trying to move his body. "I'm getting out of here."

Of course there was no way out of the truck and it was miles back and, as the men pointed out, "so cold he'd freeze to death and they'd catch hell from Daphne, and hell had no fury compared to hers, as he probably knew".

He didn't know, no.

"Listen, Dexter, you better be polite…" came a voice from the bed.

"Pay the boy no mind," Bascom said to Mat. "He's Buster's little brother, and…"

"And what?" Mat asked.

"Probably has to do with Daphne."

"What about her? And how's the little creep know who I am?"

Bascom shrugged, jiggling his earlobes. "Small town."

The truck reached the road's dead-end, a snow-plowed parking lot cut from the forest. Mat had expected maybe one other car; there were at least fifty. "Looks like there's a few," Nels said.

"This is incredible," Mat said. "What did you say this was?" The guys were climbing out of the cab and the bed, leaving him to sit alone.

"Read the brochure," Verne said, lifting a rifle from the gun rack and shouldering it.

"But I'm just starting to get warm." He was numb, not warm. "I'm not sure what to do."

"Just take the .357 magnum," Bascom said. "Then go hide in the woods. When the horror comes," he started laughing, "kill it!"

The others laughed as they shouldered rifles and shotguns. Verne turned to Mat. "Stay here awhile, OK? I'll be back for you as soon as I get these guys going. The pistol's just in case."

"G' luck, Mat," Buster shouted back. "Shoot that sonuvabitch if you get the chance, before he kills you."

Mat waved weakly.

The men split up and slipped under snow-laden boughs, disappearing into the woods like quicksilver into floor cracks. The last thing Mat heard was Bascom's big voice exhorting Buster to "Get that goddam gun oughtta my face." If there was a reply the words swept away in a rising cold wind.

Sitting in the truck with both doors open, Mat had a sudden feeling of vulnerability. Steam clouds billowed from his nose as he breathed; the temperature in the cab, which he'd been thinking of as cold, now dropped from thirty to around ten degrees. Mat realized he could die – freeze to death – just sitting there. He pulled down the earflaps of the ridiculous hat, glanced in the mirror – Christ.

He turned his attention toward the great silence that had settled over the clearing full of cars, a silence broken by some distant crow's *caw!* Alone, he lifted the weighty pistol from his lap. Without it pointing into his eyes, he angled the barrel so that he could see the bore. The dimensions of the hole – its size and the imagining of a bullet coming out and hitting a body – repulsed him. He had no idea what kind of damage a bullet hitting bone and muscle would do. He'd seen the kind of carnage re-created by actors' makeup, but those displays might be excessive. Given Hollywood's tendency, he suspected so. But he'd also seen pictures on the news of people lying dead, shot, stretched out inside chalk lines. Unimaginable quantities of blood. It was like the bleeding Santa Cruz surfer: the guy kept bleeding and bleeding from the rip the shark slashed in his thigh, bleeding long after everyone thought he should have run out of blood.

Mat set the pistol, barrel away, on the truck seat.

12

The minutes passed. Another pickup arrived, this one with Michigan license plates, parked beside Verne's truck, and a passenger and driver got out. They wore camouflage jackets with red bibs, and Mat noticed that both had wires running from backpacks into their boots, wires strapped with duct tape around their waists, thighs and calves. Suicide bombers! Mat thought.

He reconsidered and guessed that the wires were for boot warmers. The men slung rifles over their shoulders, turned expressionless glances toward Mat and then, without speaking, melted away into the dark underbrush.

Seconds later one of the hunters re-emerged from the woods as quietly as the two had disappeared. The man's face was angular with a stubble of beard and hard, intense eyes. He stood unsmiling, rifle slung, staring at Mat for almost a minute. Then, in a very deliberate way, he reached into his coat pocket and pulled something out. He dropped it onto the ground and turned away into the brush.

Freak, Mat thought. The guy probably thought Mat was waiting to steal stuff from the vehicles.

He waited. He tried closing the doors against the cold, but it made no difference at all, and in the end he opened them again. Pine siskins peeped in the trees with chickadees. A junco pecked on bare earth under the tires of a Jeep. Crows cawed from conifer tops. The forest was foreboding, as if it had eaten the men who'd stalked into it for the Dickeyville Horror.

Mat looked at the cars, mostly four-wheel drive rigs. This was like a phantom auto mall for low-mileage trucks, he thought. The lot for Flying Dutchman Dickhead Used Gas-guzzlers. There wasn't a foreign-make in the bunch.

While he sat shivering, now that he had time to think about it, Mat doubted that the creature even existed. How could a pig, even a wild boar, live that long in this cold? Or get so big? It couldn't. Most likely the Dickeyville businessmen had concocted and fueled the idea, same as commerce-minded Scottish businessmen fueled the myth of Loch Ness. Mat chuckled aloud, but the sound was swallowed up by the surrounding forest, sucked into the black hollows below the trees.

Thirty-six hours ago he'd boarded a flight from the Bahamas, and now he was stuck with a bunch of retarded lunatic hicks with giant ears and noses, hunting for a nonexistent pig in some primeval wood. While Daphne – lovely Daphne who used to have a nose as big as a plum and ears like bagel halves – was drinking a martini in an airport hours away. He looked at the clear sky. Jets fly in this kind of weather and runways could be plowed. But a new storm was coming.

Then he had a memory of something – an aromatic field outside Santa Barbara one summer night when he was eight, and a television actor, a visitor to their beach house, sent Mat out beneath a starry sky with a flashlight and a burlap bag to hunt for birds. Snipes.

This was a snipe hunt.

He looked at all the trucks and thought of the steely-eyed Michigan hunter. No, it was no joke. It was something else. This was hard, more primitive than a snipe hunt. This was a thing without humor.

Mat felt lonely, isolated. Not that he hadn't always been a loner. But this was different; this was a world not his. He wrapped his arms around himself. It was damn cold. He remembered the lunch sitting on the truck floor. He was as hungry as he was cold and alone.

A bough on a tree bounced, sending a cascade of snow globs to earth, and Verne stepped into the parking field. "You and I are headed over by a branch of the Millawney where we might have luck. My guess is these guys aren't going to do much but push around that pig."

Startled by the sudden appearance, Mat sat back. "I'm a little famished. Mind if I eat?"

"I don't really mind, but the boys would be royal pissed. It's sort of a tradition to wait until we're all together to eat."

"Maybe just a little piece of chicken...?" Mat asked hopefully.

Verne stuck his rifle in the gun rack. He dug his keys from his pocket. "Guys'll be pissed."

Mat eyed the basket before he set it on the floor. "The hell with it. But wait a minute." Climbing out of the truck, he clomped on the frozen dirt to where the Michigan hunter had disappeared. Stooping, he picked up brass. He turned it in his fingers. Winchester, .30-06, it said.

"What'd you find?" Verne called.

"Nothing. A bullet."

"Used, we call 'em shells. Get in."

"I don't suppose you'd drive me back to the Dickeys if I asked."

"Don't ask."

"Not even if I said I don't want to hunt anything."

"I said don't."

Verne started the truck and U-turned. He hunkered over the steering wheel, his breath coming in big clouds and the gray fur of his coonskin ruffled by air gaps in the cab. "I got those boys set up by No Luck Spring, but there were tracks around – human tracks, I mean – so I don't think anything 'll come of it. But I don't like the boys to be moving around too much; you never know when one of those fools from out-of-town might be trigger-happy and start blasting away."

That was a comfort to Mat.

A half-mile down the road Verne suddenly pulled the wheel to the left and drove into a wall of pine boughs. Limbs slapped the windshield but the truck slid smoothly through onto a narrow tire-tracked road that ran straight into high weeds and scraggly brush that threatened to grow across the opening. The truck rolled and pitched on the rutted trail, but Verne seemed not to notice. Mat hoped they wouldn't break down; he had no desire to freeze to death with Verne in some impenetrable forest two thousand miles from home.

"Where'd you say we're going?"

"Around-side to the Millawney. There's a way to get behind Big Buck Flats under the bluffs. By the old lead mines and shot-towers.

Not many go there anymore. When we drove in, I saw there weren't fresh tire tracks, so I thought you and I'd take a shot at it."

"Great."

"Another reason we're here is that you can't get lost this way. All you have to do is hit the road to see the truck. More people get killed in this kind of country by getting lost and freezing to death than by driving drunk or shooting one another or getting gored by the Horror. Know how to read a compass? You can have mine. Just in case." He shifted his body to pull a circular object from his hip pocket.

Mat took the compass. Its worn brass casing rested in his gloved hand. "I wouldn't know which direction to head for."

"Just watch. That's what you should do in strange country."

Like Wisconsin. "Yeah. It is that, isn't it? All of it."

The tail on Verne's coonskin cap bounced with the ruts. For twenty minutes the truck plowed virgin snow, then stopped. The road went on, but Verne switched off the ignition in a place indistinguishable from any other. He turned to Mat.

"You know how to use that thing?" He nodded toward the pistol. "Not much more complicated than a compass."

Mat shook his head. "No idea. Don't know if I want to."

Verne said, "That's up to you. But I better show you because if you need it you may change your mind. You probably don't have a hunting license, do you?"

"Hardly."

"Doesn't matter. You won't see the boar anyway, not smelling the way you do and as loud as your stomach is."

"Smell? You mean the soap."

Verne laughed. "Uncle Dickey sure as hell beats all, don't he?"

"What do you mean?" Mat sniffed at the back of his hand. The soap was strong and had left a delightful lingering odor.

"Come on," Verne said, picking up the pistol, "Lesson time." He half-cocked the hammer and spun the cylinder. "I can't show you how to hit anything with it. But I can show you how to cock it and how to see if it's loaded. Also, you'll need to bring the picnic basket."

"What for?"

"Maybe we'll need provisions, never know. Now about that Colt..."

Shortly they were out into the icy air. Verne slipped the pickup keys under the front left tire "just in case" Mat needed them and pointed up without speaking. Mat saw that the distant cloud bank had come closer, blocking more of the sky. The clouds were a curdled gray, mottled lower on the horizon. Mat didn't know much about local weather, but he was mariner enough to know storm signs. Cloud covered the whole of the northwestern horizon above the ancient trees.

Verne pointed to his watch. "Three hours, no more or less. We better be out of here by then or, even if directly as the crow flies we're not eight miles from town, it might as well be a million. Forecast calls for a big one... Come on." Verne turned into the woods. "Check your compass. This way is southeast."

Mat held the pistol like he was shaking hands with it, barrel pointed down. He took a big breath, thinking how much he hated this day, then followed Verne into the woods.

Verne stopped once, as if listening for something, then turned. "Daphne told her Pa you have balls. That you've dived with Great White and Tiger sharks. That true?"

"Whites off the Farallones. Cold water dive in a shark cage, no big deal. Big Tiger came for my legs one night off Australia, during a Barrier Reef filming. Could have been bad, but again no big deal."

"Huh. We'll see about that."

"What?"

"Just thinking."

Verne set a steady pace and they walked for twenty minutes through underbrush. The ground beneath the trees was mostly bare of snow but damp; springy mats of twigs and leaves and needles were soggy and black. Heavy air muffled the sounds of their passing, and Mat heard no chattering of snowbirds or cawing of crows: the coming storm seemed to have quieted the forest. Other than stepping around several frozen ponds, they headed straight, Mat noted by the compass. He was relieved to see that he couldn't possibly become lost.

He was sweaty by the time they stepped into a small clearing alongside a flat-bottomed depression he recognized to be an iced-over creek. From the cut of the bank he guessed the water underneath to be slow and deep. Twisted limbs rose from the ice like the arms of tortured bodies. Animal tracks covered the snow over river ice. Mat had no idea what kinds of tracks they were.

"What I'd do is sit over there under those boughs and watch the meadow across this channel. Main body of the Millawney's about two hundred yards that way," Verne explained. "I'm going past the old Mazy cabin to check the Spider Cage."

"Spider Cage?"

"Just a blown-over silo by the old orchard. Not much more than an opening in the woods these days, and I don't figure that boar will be in the open. So you ought to be fine here. I want to look for tracks before the storm blows in. I don't think anybody'll get into these woods for a few days, and I want to see something. Just stay here, okay?"

"Where the hell else would I go?"

Verne started to leave, then turned. The breeze, stiffening, ruffled the long hairs of his coonskin. "Another thing. If you weren't going to marry my cousin, I wouldn't bring you here. There's not three dozen people in this county who know where the old Mazy place is."

"I guess I should say thanks."

Verne shrugged his big shoulders.

"It's all a little strange for me. This isn't what I know."

"Figure you've got more to learn than you realize."

Mat looked around. "Where is it? I don't see anything."

Verne pointed across the channel to the far edge of a clearing seventy yards beyond the frozen creek. "That's the remaining wall. Just past it, in those trees, you can find the old family gravesite. Wooden markers are still there, though they're hard to find unless you know where to look. Past that there's the remains of a plane wreck."

Mat lifted the green-checked hunting cap from his head and let the breeze play through sweat-matted hair and over his ears. The chill was sobering, refreshing. He felt the hangover's echo recede.

"This is an old land out here," Verne went on, "and the people who touched it – the red ones and the white ones – left something here you can feel. I mean some can, many can't. When you die a little every winter and get reborn a little every spring, life leaves a thumbprint on you. You tend to touch the earth deep, even if you don't leave any marks, if you get my drift. This is the sort of place where time comes to die." – He turned to leave. "But not me. Don't shoot me when I come back, okay, numb-nuts?"

"Fuck you."

Verne dropped over the bank and crossed the ice on the creek, his shoulders bunched against cold and the weight of his slung rifle. He crossed the forest opening and was gone.

Mat sat back in the hollow under the boughs of a tall pine alone among the hickories and maples surrounding the small clearing. He could imagine the opening in the forest shrinking over time, the trees closing in on the cabin until their winter-blackened limbs covered its garden, then covered it too. He imagined leaves falling year after year onto slowly sagging rafters, imagined the creeping entropy of sweltering summers and spring rains and freezing winters. He imagined the dampness of the place, creeping mildew and wood rot.

He couldn't decide whether this land was the most beautiful or most forsaken he'd ever seen. He wanted the sea, wanted its moods and the melancholy abandon of being on it, because he knew that place. He thought about Daphne, about what she was bringing him to, trying to make him a part of – this land, these people, even though he and she would never live here. No, she wouldn't want this – not any part of it, she had said, but even in California she would bring part of him here. He sensed it and felt something waiting for him to give in.

He felt something changing inside, something alien and formidable. And even out of the wind he was chilled. He compared it to winter swimming, when the ocean's cold sunk slowly into you, reaching toward the body's core. He wished to hell he'd worn that ugly-ass long underwear. His backside felt frozen to the damp ground, yet he knew he wasn't as miserable-cold as he soon would be. He set the huge magnum pistol in his lap with the barrel pointed away and plunged his hands into his pockets. He could not see into the past. The feeling that there was something he couldn't remember, a thing familiar but beyond reach, something he should understand, again teased at him. He couldn't figure what it was he had forgotten. He thought about the crazy old man on the bus and what it was he was supposed to learn. Then, just when he admitted to himself that he didn't know and couldn't see, and that he probably would never see, whatever it was he missed, he suddenly discerned what was left of the cabin wall through dark shadows of great hardwood trunks. He imagined cans rusting away forty years under fallen wood, the crumbling remains of a syrup can in the shape of a log cabin. In the loamy earth he saw bottles and even a small sack of marbles lost by a boy; old pennies dropped in the snow one winter evening, pennies lost into the earth during spring thaw… In this land of frozen time ghosts breathed and walked again, although it would be some time before Mat understood them.

13

Dead Alice Mazy wasn't old when that lugubrious moniker was hung on her. Her story was well known to the townsfolk of Dickeyville: it was her Lazarus-like resurrection, first at her nativity, second in her thirteenth year, that brought the name about.

Stillborn to a dying parent in January 1921, her tiny blue body had been carried out to the porch by her father and set in a wheelbarrow while inside her mother was attended to by Doc Lander. Her father intended to wheel her into the woodshed and let her rest there until spring thaw had softened the earth so that he might spade her a grave in the family site deep in the Mazy woods. A pitiful wail stopped him before he had stepped back in the cabin door.

During her thirteenth year, several months after her father's fatal brief struggle against diphtheria and shortly before the good women of Dickeyville attempted to save a virgin by removing her from the wilderness and placing her in the Lutheran Children's Home in Fond Du Lac, Alice was hip-chucked into a white oak by a startled draft horse as she attempted to plow the acreage around the family home. One of her suitors happened to visit and found her lying face down in the newly turned earth. Doc Lander, summoned, declared the girl dead a second time, an announcement precipitating great excitement. At last the great Mazy woods, Alice's inheritance could be logged and cleared. Last of her line, she had no relatives to claim thousands of acres of swamp and forest – worthless except for timber, hundreds of thousands of board feet.

Dickeyville's harvest would be bountiful. Alice's right to the land was as tangible as blood. Her great-grandfather Frederick Mazy had served in the Twenty-sixth regiment, Wisconsin Infantry Volunteers, the so-called "German Regiment" returning at the Civil War's close to West Bend under its organizational name, the Washington County Rifles. On the train home, feeling lucky to have survived many battles, he drank and cut a deck with a young Englishman who smoked a bowl of twist and sipped brandy like a proper fellow. Alice's great-grandfather lost the cut, but the Englishman, a sportsman headed west to shoot buffalo, laughed and traded Mazy's princely four hundred dollars for title to a swamp forest, a vast stand of no worth, as he believed, which the Englishman, who put his faith in and gambled under a banner more efficient than luck, had stolen from some other hapless veteran.

At that time the large oak woods of the north were under assault. So, after first visiting his swampland and failing to find another willing to purchase it, a dejected Mazy pulled on a pair of stagged trousers and caulked driving shoes to work the Chippewa and Flambeau Rivers as a "river hog". There he and others like him rode and wrestled white pine logs with peaveys downstream to the sawmills. The job paid two dollars and fifty cents daily wages and all the red horse (corned beef), murphies (potatoes) and firecrackers (beans) a man could eat. Mazy watched the timberlands of northern Wisconsin disappear.

The pillage of God's wilderness served as genesis for a religious man's mandate to *preserve*, much like John Muir, another Wisconsinite, would discover years later in California's Yosemite Valley. Eventually Mazy married a young woman of pioneer heritage from Illinois who did not rebel against his curious preservationist ways. A child of the forest herself, theirs was a happy union, as was their son's.

Their grandson's was not. He married a woman influenced by good folk in the township who, like most people of the era, preferred subjugation to stewardship of wild land. Her constant task of convincing her husband unnerved him but did nothing to move him. What she considered potential industry and financial boon, he saw as heritage, a notion that was almost heresy in farming country. The unhappy harpy died in childbirth; the fruit resultant of their loveless coupling – Alice – survived to be seduced during her childhood by her father's faith: preservation of the wild land.

A two hundred acre clearing had sufficed these families until all in their time lay in a plot next to the homestead, surrounded by thousands of acres of virgin forest. By the year of Alice's birth the then-named Mazy was highly coveted. The great stands of the north state were long gone and envious eyes surveyed the forest adjoining Dickeyville township. The forest meant jobs for the townsmen, but only if it were subdued.

At thirteen Alice Mazy was pretty and slender-waisted, five-foot-four, with dark hair and thoughtful brown eyes. She was already a girl with strange ways – loved the land, sometimes hated it, could not leave it. She had grown up in the woods with no friends other than her lonely father who believed, partly rightly, that his obstinacy had killed his wife. In spring the girl, in a white dress, would gather wildflowers in her forest, dark hair falling over her face as she bent to pick sprigs of Queen Ann's lace. Her own forest. Young men's faces would turn as she'd enter the hushed dark interior of church on Sundays, their shy glances assessing her wealth and blossoming beauty. Their mothers' disapproved, for Alice had something of the forest about her, something dark, untouchable, untamed: mystery, the smell of new earth after the spring thaw, a taint of the wild, the unclaimed.

It was not the girl's land others wanted, not the deep-mulched black earth; it was the trees. And they wanted her, too. By now the Mazy woods stretched three miles along the meandering Millawney River and beyond, just beyond the city limits of the town; in fact, Mazy woods defined the southern borders of what the locals called Dickeyville Town. The Midwestern hardwood and pine forests had receded like the great Wisconsin Glacier past the northern parts of Iowa and Wisconsin and other states. The forests had become farmland – beautiful farmland, land green and rolling, with loamy black soil that sat moist and fragrant in a farmer's callused hands, dirt so rich it seemed perpetually damp.

One week after Alice's father died, strangling when his burning-raw throat closed off his breath, Musgrave Winder, age twenty-two, showed up, hat in hand, on her porch to ask her to marry him. Not because of his Winder ears, Alice said no; she knew how Musgrave saw the land. In her loneliness she invited him into her cabin and poured two cups of mint tea from a kettle hung over the fireplace – her fireplace. To his mother's shock Winder stayed two days before Alice kissed his cheek on the path from the cabin in Mazy woods, her woods, and sent him away.

He never spoke about it. His mother did, to the Dickey Township Quilting Guild, after one of Minnie Rutherford's tongue-loosening elderberry tonics. Said that for three days after he left the cabin Musgrave refused to eat. Ate only after his mother, Mrs. Henry June Winder, had threatened to tear out her own heart for fear of his health.

Other young men went to see Alice; smelled the wild apple blossoms in her hair; smelled the musky odor of forest that clung to her slender body and reflected darkly behind her eyes. None could ignore the tract, the wealth of land. None could subdue her.

After Doc Lander's second pronouncement of her death Alice had been carted into Dickeyville to Doc's other office, where he hung his mortician's sign. Stretched indecently naked under a sheet, she had given a choked gasp and sat upright. Looking around, she screamed, swung her feet to the floor, grabbed her dress and run naked right out the door. To the townsfolk ever after she was *Dead* Alice Mazy.

Despite town women's misgivings, she continued to live in the woods. Nothing touched her desire to protect and possess virgin land; not wealth, not her neighbors' goodwill. Her resolve didn't waver during the Depression years, nor later when she was approached by east coast speculators. She reasoned that she would not find more happiness elsewhere than the forests and small clearing where her parents, grandfather and wife, and her great-grandfather and wife were buried. She had enough money to survive, to pay taxes. The Mazy went on.

So did Alice, each year the same. Sundays she went to church, unmindful of bachelors' – and married men's – sidelong glances at her and peeks over hymn books. On Wednesdays she would visit the library in Platteville, returning the week's books and collecting the next's. Suitors would appear, and some suited as long as she wished, but none would claim more. She incurred the enmity of some for her strangeness, her alien and aloof demeanor, but when she opened her Mazy land to hunters during World War II, animosity toward her strange ways mostly went underground. There had always been enthusiasm in Wisconsin for deer hunting, but occasionally someone, sometimes married, by invitation left his tent to sleep in the rough cabin in the Mazy clearing, site of the annual hunt camp.

Dead Alice grew wilder. Her eyes, though clear, took on the haunted, timorous expression of hermit women, witches, tribal healers. In hermitage she dressed and smelled of smoke, forest, sweat, clothes worn too long; she took on an odor of old time, pioneers, the long-past Fox people who had lived in this country. Her hair streaked early with grey, though her ankles and waist, not thickened by bearing babies, remained firm and thin, and her face escaped the lines of wives who labored rearing children, cooking up soap monthly, sweltering over wood stoves in summer, canning and sewing and helping with the harvest, nursing sick animals and humans and the boredom of endless hours of each day stitching together the fabric that made the tapestry of life possible or the men with skin weathered working fields in driving snow and blazing sunshine, whose bodies slowly bent with rheumatism and ill-set broken bones or limbs lost in threshing machines and harvesters or broken by stock or by axes and tools and combines and tractors capable of a thousand ways to harm.

Decades passed. The settler Dickeys and Winders and other pioneers were supplemented by Gradys and Joneses and Butlers and countless other farm and small town families. During the '60s, teenagers of Dickeyville melted away to the cities, Madison or Milwaukee or other bigger, more exciting places, both west and east coasts, and time seemed to stagnate in the town. Population slowed, then stopped growing. Alice went on as before, growing stranger each year, more remote, welcoming only during deer season the townsmen into her forest. In line with her nickname, she seemed obscure, and sinister ideas grew up about her. Children heard stories of the woman of the woods, gathering mushrooms and toadstools, eating bugs in summer and chewing unidentifiable dried meat in winter. They came to fear her, and when they slept outside on warm summer nights Dead Alice stories lit their imaginations. Dead Alice, her hair long and scraggly, streaked with grey, showing a habitual furtiveness when she came to town... She didn't wear underwear, they said. Centipedes and spiders lived in her hair. She slept with snakes; ate them; climbed into windows to suck the breath of sleeping children. She could fly. Her glowing eyes could see in the dark. Stay out of her forest!

As the town modernized, she no longer plowed but bought market groceries. Her field went fallow; the woods pressed in on the acreage surrounding her cabin, and the hunt camp pressed into the meadow closer to it. Alice inherited money from a distant aunt, a relative she'd never met, her last living. Her new wealth, ample, was greatly exaggerated, and resented by those still intent on Mazy's timber. Taxes were now not even a remote encumbrance. She had long stopped worrying what people thought; maybe she never had.

During her sixtieth summer she bequeathed her great but unappreciated gift to the people of Dickeyville: she imported a wild beast from Germany's Black Forest. Farmers' heads in John Deere caps nodded in agreement: the creature would breed escaped domestics; its feral offspring would ravage their crops. She had imported something for the hunters – a European wild boar.

When it arrived crated by train in Platteville, *sus scrofa* weighed only one hundred fifty pounds. He had tusks not quite an inch long. Sparse black hair covered his body, a scraggly tail and small black eyes. "Drug dealer eyes, or a child molester's," said Nate Dickey, at the station peering between the bars into the creature's face.

"Ya, it ain't so much," a Swede said.

"Bullshit," Alice exclaimed, to no one's surprise, because by now her eccentricities were common knowledge. "It isn't either one of those. You'll see."

"Exactly," Ben Winder said, plucking at his overall suspenders, "what I'm afraid of."

Alice hired a wagon to haul the crate to the Mazy. She wiped snow-white hair from her damp forehead and pried a crowbar into the reinforced slats atop the crate.

Freed, a strange scent, a not-quite-right odor, came strong to the boar as he crossed the meadow – the lure of natural decay and standing water, of river and fallen trees, of crushed wild brush, of moist fen; of the black mud under the swamp, the myriad insects and box turtles and big snappers, the alligator gar, the sunfish, the muskies and shovel-nosed catfish and channel cats, badgers, beaver and squirrel, bears and deer, the wood ducks and mergansers and great pileated woodpeckers and hawks and northern or barred owls and song birds, the nitrogen-rich decaying and damp leaves fallen and accumulated for thousands of years until they created blackened, humus-rich topsoil feeding patches of musty morel mushrooms beside rain-leeched acorns... The boar left the meadow opening and ran for miles until he scooted across the edge of the Dickeyville cemetery with its weather-worn headstones and old oaks and pushed into a thicket of locus brush across from the border of Mazy woods. Sniffing at the town to size the boundaries of his new home, he turned back into the Mazy. Except for sudden yet brief silencing of hordes of disturbed crickets and cicadas, the woods swallowed his passage.

Men hunted the boar, and his notoriety grew beyond Dickey County. His cunning and his body grew. He feasted on forest bounty and sometimes raided crops. Two decades on, he weighed over five hundred pounds and stood over four feet at the shoulder. Faster than a horse, dangerous as a cornered grizzly and twice as intelligent, he could be killed by no one. When he was still young, several men had shots at him and several put lead into his sides. Buckshot destroyed one of his eyes. Two decades passed. Men brought dogs to run him, dogs bred in southern states to hunt Arkansas razorbacks; and the dog packs howled and plunged deep into the Mazy, usually to find nothing. More resolute packs rushed silently through the unending forest and swamp and sumac-meadows and dense pines, occasionally pushing the beast, twice in four years bringing him to bay. When the men who tracked dogs by telemetry collars arrived, they were winded, faces torn by branches and brambles; the dogs with heart and courage were dead or dying, and cowardly ones dragged their tails and whimpered for fear of what they'd found, instantly becoming hand-licker hounds never again worth a pound of poop for pig hunting, so pig-broken that they'd slink their tails as soon as someone dropped bacon into a skillet. *Outdoor Life*, *Field and Stream* and *Sports Afield* carried articles on the Horror. *Outsdoorman* television did a spot. First a congressman, a year later a senator showed for the hunt. An AP article described the hunts and Horror's hoof print size.

Dead Alice took up flying one fall before the snows, and she was a sight in her blue biplane, yellow scarf whipping behind, crawling so slowly against a thin wind, rising up on the thermals to look down on it all, the great Mazy forest she had built at the cost of love and happiness, but never having seen it all for what it was, her triumph. Perhaps she glimpsed the long, narrow black back of a ghost, the boar as it trotted down one of the twisting trails cut into inscrutable features of the wood, trails like lines etched into an ancient man's face.

Rising one day into the spring sky, with the mud far below starting to thaw and crocus buds peeking from beneath the black earth, crisp air ripe with expectation and a first channel appearing like a black jagged ribbon in the frozen Millawney's surface, Dead Alice climbed against a pale sun. She laughed a vintage laughter she'd saved nearly a lifetime to uncork, a special brew reserved for one whose vision had been clear and who'd suffered for it. Distant fields greening with the season, Dickey and Winder fields stretching to the rolling horizon... Below lay the tapestry of her history, Dead Alice's wilderness legacy, the Mazy and great boar – Alice's wild hog, already older than any pig wild or domestic had the right to be, bigger, stronger and faster, the beast an abomination defying reason and nature. More wiry hair sprouted along his back, like on the shoulders of grizzled men who had aged hunting him. His tusks grew, his remaining eye no better than if he'd had two... Her unholy creature.

Like him, Alice served as mother's milk for myth. Successive generations of Dickeyville children had dreamed of the hermetic witch wandering Mazy forests named after her, haunting labyrinthine trails in search of mysterious herbs, talking to animals, brewing secret potions in unknown glades while her wild hair dangled damp with sweat, untidy with twigs and leaves and insects. Her piercing eyes in troubled dreams wove into visions of the great red eyes of the boar. In backyard tents, children told late-night tales of the beast and witch-woman, until they dashed through kitchen doors screaming. At forest fringes, Friday night teens tipped beers beside their cars but watched warily the black forest's wall. Young children drank the milk of fear: the Dickeyville Horror. The Horror is out there.

For generations it was more threatening than tyrannosaurs, child-snatchers, rattlesnakes, ravenous bears, closet monsters. Nights when a child walked home from her friend's house, it haunted and stilled her breath as she listened to imaginary clattering hooves of the foam-mouthed beast, tusks clacking as it burst through a neighborhood hedge in pursuit of blood. Moonless nights boys hauled out garbage and heard its breath in darkened lilac bushes, from which blood-red pig eyes were focusing on its next victim, skewered upon bloodied tusks, shish-kebabed body screaming into the forbidden forest, the Mazy, where it would devour the victim alive, and a grieving mother would bury her face in a pillow every night for twenty years in lamentation for sending her child out – it was certain the boar got him, though for all the Horrors that lived in the imaginations of tousle-haired children, all the wild fears of protective parents, all the hours peered away into darkened corners of bedrooms or strange backyards during the late terrible hours before dawn, not a single child died from either the beast or fear of it.

But Dead Alice died, to be reborn in myth. Stories multiplied the number of those who'd loved her in her cabin. Her stubbornness had shaped the land of the Mazy, and shaped the lives of those at the forest's perimeters, while the real Alice grew stranger and greater than her myth. Land grew more valuable, and Dickeys and Winders and other farmers thrived. The excesses of the 1970s and '80s were so far in the past that farmers couldn't remember money borrowed for giant combines and farm investments led to failure of family farms dating from the Civil War. Producers from Disney considered a movie based on Dead Alice and the Horror; lumber investors inquired into the land tract. But discouraged by an iron-clad will and trust, hoards of mosquitoes and an icy reception, exploiters fled the provincial outpost.

Three decades after Mickey Mantle had passed his prime on Verne's baseball cards, the boar entered his in the dense wood. He grew still more massive, yearly gobbling thousands of pounds of acorns and grubs and fallen apples, occasionally pillaging and crushing cornfields, grubbing washed-up carp or shovel-nosed catfish or snakes or fresh shoots and mushrooms. Each spring he broke through pen fences to breed sows. Farmers marveled at the funny weaners like striped squirrels, the Horror's spawn. Farmers didn't set loose the unholy offspring, they butchered them.

A few witnessed her descent. In spring of 1990, Dead Alice and her biplane spiraled down four thousand feet into the Mazy, landing not a quarter mile from the place she had been born. The inspector who came from the Aviation Board in Chicago said that it was lack of fuel and he couldn't figure anyone failing to notice the fuel gauge. "Hell, it's right there in front of your nose!" Old-timers claimed it was nothing but one of Dead Alice's catatonic spells and one night she would rise again, this time from the earth of the Mazy where they buried her next to her ancestors. But Dickeyville children in their dreams knew: there had been no burial.

14

The snow swirled heavier around Mat, settling in a feathery powder on his shoulders. He had been sitting – mostly sitting, then standing, slapping his arms, sitting again, pulling cold handfuls of pine needles over his legs to keep warm, huddling deep inside his coat – for nearly a half hour. The flakes were getting bigger, visibility shrinking. Verne's tracks in the snow across the creek were no longer visible. Dry drifts fell from treetops in airy, muted cascades.

Silent woods. No birds sang. Mat heard nothing of the trucks he and Verne had left behind. When he turned to the picnic basket, Mat saw how much snow had accumulated – three inches or more. And still it fell from the gray sky, inexorably, in flakes larger than he imagined possible. The storm had arrived without wind, quiet enough that he could hear the flakes slide down his jacket and pile in his lap. Cold air, silent penetrating cold. When his legs started falling asleep, Mat's anxiety increased. He knew about hypothermia in sea water and guessed it was the same, coming with cramps. Shivering, he felt for his nose to make sure it was there.

Terrible, pervasive silence. He was a solitary man, but this was different. Here the solitude came close, oppressive, indistinct like the white earth, hazy sky, white-dusted brush, trees. The earth seemed scourged, dead white, sterile. Visibility, thirty feet. Relentless snowfall.

White silence.

Mat jumped to his feet hearing a gunshot; it was muffled by snow and trees, but close – very close. Then he heard a scream of terror. Another gunshot, then a demonic squealing that stood up his hair. A voice screamed his name.

Mat answered, voice hoarse with cold. "Verne? That you?"

Silent woods.

"Verne? You okay?"

Mat stood hunched, shivering, the grotesque flakes settling on his body. He couldn't see the clearing across the creek.

"Verne!" he yelled. "Verne!"

Great emptiness. Impenetrable whiteness.

Go for help? If he went toward the flat and got lost, it wouldn't do anyone any good. He pulled out the compass. It would be easy to hit the road, although he no longer had tracks to follow. He started to turn, then an image flooded in: Verne, torn and ripped, bleeding to death, guts pierced by the demon boar. Mat remembered blood flowing from the surfer at Point Año Nuevo near Santa Cruz, the man's fingers clutching into tanned arms of the surfers carrying him.

"Dammit!" He swore. He couldn't feel his feet.

Numb fingers thumbed back the hammer of the .357 magnum as he staggered toward a bank. "Shit." Gored and eaten by a wild pig wasn't the death he'd envisaged. He imagined someone finding his and Verne's half-gnawed bodies frozen and red like raspberry popsicles after the storm.

Stepping onto the ice covering the creek, his feet went out from under him. He landed hard, flat on his back. "Woof!" Winded, he gasped, the pistol pointing skyward between his hands. "Bang!" Mat said, looking into the haze. "Take that."

The relentless snowflakes landed on his face.

Carefully he rolled over and crawled across the ice on his knees. A sudden squeal, louder, brought him up. Then silence. The sound had come from dense brush by the side of the old cabin. Mat gripped the pistol in two hands to steady it. He checked again: cocked.

Again the horrible squeal, and he knew it was the enraged boar, the killer. Then came tortured human moaning, a sound that brought Mat to his feet. He dashed across the clearing; plunged blindly into brushy forest. The blurred meadow compressed into a thick canopy not penetrated by snowflakes, damp earth padded with pine needles.

Immediately he smelled smoke. It hung dense in dark limbs and brush around his face. He couldn't see ten feet within the bush of black pine draped with dried creepers and bare hardwood limbs sprouting in wild profusion. Vegetative chaos. Mat crashed in deeper, pressing his body into dry brush. "Verne! Verne, can you hear me?"

Again hysterical squealing, nearer this time. Mat slowed. He was sweating, body clammy, shaking with adrenaline. Blue smoke drifted through entangled limbs under the pine canopy, twisting thickly out of trunks of huge trees. Was it smoke from Verne's signal fire?

Close now, he could hear moaning just ahead – twenty feet maybe. He parted the brush with the pistol and pushed into it, expecting any second to be ripped to shreds. He whispered loudly: "Verne? Are you okay?" But his words were sucked into the heavy air, sucked away over the carpet of decayed needles and smoke hanging like blue moss against stillness. Just ahead, scant yards, he could hear something, a sort of muffled clucking, and the thought came that it was a sound of suckling boars, that the beast was protecting its young, but that was wrong. Pigs don't nest, he reasoned; and the beast is a male.

Then it came. Brush split apart and the monster was on him, head like a blackened turkey, a dark, alien shape, mouth red, scimitar tusks, tiny mean eyes. The pistol bucked in Mat's hand, roaring once, two shots as fast as he pulled the hammer and squeezed the trigger, as if he'd done it a hundred times, muzzle flashes and smoke and blind panic, a primitive snarl in his throat. He leapt sideways to avoid the upturned tusks. Eyes wide, he screamed. The boar's head stopped above Mat's. It hunted him.

He lay still, terrified, listening, senses hyper-attuned, heart thudding in his chest, gulping air like a beached fish. Then the boar's head sucked back into the brush.

Mat raised himself halfway. He heard a sound clearly now. It was… laughter. Of many people. The head pushed out again: a hideous rubber boar head attached to a pole.

"What the – ?"

Mat rose unsteadily. He pushed past the head into the brush and came into a small clearing crowded with men dressed in hunting garb and stupid hats. Some he recognized from the night before. Shadows danced beyond a fire blazing. Verne stood with a fistful of five dollar bills in one hand and bottle of whiskey in the other. Mat was bewildered. Nels and Brodie, laughing, stepped forward to shake his hand.

Mat blinked. "What in hell?"

Hearty spirit filled the atmosphere as men pushed toward him. Later he would remember seeing the Mayor, hand extended, wiry white hair poking from beneath his top hat, haloed by the big fire.

It would have been better if Mat were the kind of man to laugh easily; not cry or love or hate easily, a man immune to easy emotions, good and bad. A man who didn't play jokes didn't take them well. The whole thing sunk in slowly.

"But… how'd you get here?"

"Humped it clear across the woods," the Mayor said, and they started laughing again. "Sweaty work but it was worth it to see your face."

"You sons of – " Mat dropped the pistol at his feet and turned from their hilarity to push back into the brush, past the rubber boar head, under the pine canopy. Brodie and Bascom followed him to say *wait, we can explain*, but he ignored them. Out of the clearing and over the frozen creek… He would walk from the woods.

The two caught up to him part way through the meadow.

"Mat, it's a great story."

"Get away from me. I don't have any idea what you crazy fuckers are talking about and I don't want to know."

"Don't take it hard."

"It's just a joke."

When he reached the picnic basket, adrenaline suddenly switched into Zen hunger, a sparkly pitch somewhere between mere ravenousness and outright starvation, a light-headed transcendental state that exceeded fear and mere appetite to achieve a gastronomical fever bordering on delirium, as if his fury were directed not at the perpetrators of the boar charade but at the circumstances of life itself, as if food alone could console. He wanted to stuff his mouth, wanted to roll gobs of food with his tongue and crush it between his molars.

But something had gone wrong. The basket lay trampled into a tangle of wicker. "The hell. You guys did this, too." An imperturbable man not by design but by innate temperament, Mat burned with anger at the thought that he'd avoided eating so as not to "piss off the boys".

Bascom and Brodie pulled up short, their eyes wide. "Mother of God," one said quietly.

Mat noted the scattered wrappers, mangled plastic containers, torn napkins. "All the food gone," he whispered, too struck to say it aloud.

"Not the food. Look there."

Then he saw tracks punched into the earth through powdery snow.

Later, when the five of them piled back into Verne's truck, four were near laughter's fatal stage. Mat wasn't close. Crowded in as they were, the windshield progressively foggier from hilarity, nobody noticed the cloven prints crossing the road. Verne, tears coursing down his cheeks, drove over them unseeing. The truck lurched over bumps, its heater puffing a thin stream of iciness over Mat's frozen legs. Now sure that he didn't like Verne, didn't like him at all, Mat decided the man was a jerk and felt an almost overwhelming desire to blindside him in his laughter-teared eyes. It was no pleasant ride. Mat sat on the outside, nearest the door, window open despite polar temperature. He sulked. He would have walked. They tried to explain, but kept breaking into puerile laughter. Verne tried to share the bet money with Mat, saying that the odds for him coming in to save Verne had been two-to-one against, and that information drove the idiots into further fits of hysteria. It appeared that the "secret place" was somewhere called Mazy Meadow Road that everybody in town knew. Half the men had waited to see what Mat would do.

"Did it ever occur to you idiots I could have killed somebody blasting away like that?" were Mat's first words, and would have been all if he hadn't remembered something.

Mentioning the pistol bent the idiots in laughter again. Verne had to pull over and wipe his eyes. "We may be idiots but we're not going to let you kill us – not with a pistol loaded with blanks." Brodie snorted, Nels howled, Bascom whimpered in misery.

Mat was a long way from Southern California. But at the mention of killing, he had a sobering realization: his first installment to Vinnie was due soon. He calculated and his eyes widened. Today, the first money due..."Get me home. There's something I have to do."

It wouldn't matter to Vinnie whether Mat had put the payment with a bookie or that he'd been stuck in some hick town two thousand miles from L.A.; when payment was due, it was due. It would be easier to squeeze water from a baseball than stiff a loan shark.

"Don't you want a drink first? Everybody'll be buying at Pepper Joe's Bar and Scope Shop," Brodie said. "Be a sport. There'll be sandwiches and everything."

The sandwich part almost got him, but they'd laughed too long and too hard. "A *sport*. Look, I don't have to justify myself, but this isn't anything to do with that boar bullshit." – Mat had a way to get money to Vinnie but he needed to phone from the Dickey house.

As they pulled onto the town's winding roads, the subject changed to the tracks by the picnic basket. "Never heard of the Horror eating domestic food unless it was still growing in a field," Verne said peering through wiper blades dusting back dry drifts of snow. He toyed with the radio knobs. "Also never heard of him getting so close to someone. Mighty strange."

"Probably knew Mat was shooting blanks," Brodie suggested, and the hicks broke up again.

At the driveway as the truck slowed, Mat bailed out, slamming his door behind. Father Dickey, red-faced and sweaty despite the cold, was still laboring at his shovel, a Herculean effort against the falling snow. He caught Mat before Mat could reach the sidewalk buried a foot deep. "Hey, Pa. I'm in sort of a hurry...." The truck idled halfway onto the drive behind him, then the engine shut off and doors opened. Mat ignored the men getting out.

"Won't this make a hell of a story," the old man said, brushing aside slush. "You're lucky."

Mat snorted.

"Gosh o'mighty!" the old man yipped, stooping to pick up something. "I finally found it."

"Found what?"

Father Dickey held up a ten-inch strand of muddy string. "This must be my lucky day. Ma said she saw this string last night before the snow buried it."

"Glad it's someone's lucky day." Mat shook his head. "You shoveled fifty yards of sidewalk for a foot of string? With a hangover?"

"I don't have a hangover. Why should I? Anyway, if you're not a fanatic, nothing gets done."

"I gotta get out of here," Mat mumbled.

"Been a couple calls for you," Pa said.

"Daphne." – He trudged up the driveway already filling with snow.

"A gravel-voiced guy."

"Huh-oh. Did he leave a name? Was it Vinnie by any chance?"

Pa shrugged. "Beats me."

That put fuel on Mat's fire. I really gotta get home, he thought.

He heard Pa call as he reached the house, "Did you face the hog? Did you do the right thing?"

As the old man laughed, he tromped into the utility room, pausing to glance in the mirror at the hat he was wearing, that orange-lined monstrosity, green-pleated, with earflaps. Stupidest-looking thing in the world. Made him seem as if he had an IQ of sixty. People in California would never wear anything like it: Californians wore only baseball hats – wore them backwards, even to weddings. Anybody wearing a hat as stupid as Mat's should be reincarnated as a Moscow bum swilling hair tonic filtered through hard bread. Mat scraped off the hat and dropped it to the floor. Glancing into the mirror once more, he saw that his hair lay crushed and sweaty.

Pushing past Ma in the kitchen, he even pushed past a tray stacked high with golden toasted cheese sandwiches. "Later," he mumbled both to her and his rumbling gut as he went into the living room. "I need to make some calls. I'll pay you back, okay?"

She answered: "Did you go in to save Verne, or what? I had fifty cents on you."

Mat cursed under his breath and dialed his mother's number. The phone rang a dozen times. "Come on, come on," he muttered. Finally a man answered: "G' day, mate, I'm not sure whose 'ouse this is."

Mat heard a party in the background. "Is Missus Roper in? Could you get her? This is important."

"Sure, mate. What's she look like?"

"It's her house. Your hostess, the older woman. Probably wearing white knee-boots and lots of makeup." His luck to get Crocodile Dundee on the line.

"Oh, that cute old broad. 'Ang on." The receiver rattled onto a table. As it dangled, Mat heard music and noise and from it guessed that the party must be big.

"Hello?" came a voice.

"Mother? This is Mat – "

"Mother? Why, honey, I've barely reached puberty by Hollywood standards. Who is this? Are you in the Bizness?"

"This is her son, Mat. Please put on Missus Roper, if you please – "

"I got it, honey," said a muffled voice into another receiver. A fumbling, then: "Mat, darling, where are you? Are you on your way over?"

"What's going on, Mother?"

"Darling are you on your cell? Aren't you here?"

"If I was at the party, why would I call? My cell fell overboard."

"Mat, dear, you're such a funny boy."

"Listen, there's something you have to do for me."

"You silly thing. I've already done it. All your friends are here. There's so many people here I didn't even know you weren't. I don't think you've even been missed."

"Missed? Why should I be?"

"Because it's your engagement party, silly. Aren't you coming?" Her voice moved from the receiver. "Byron? Byron Schuster? So good to see you. Love you, too, dear. Give me a call sometime?"

"Hello? Mother? God, is Schuster still alive? He must be a hundred and fifty. Did you say an engagement party, for me?"

"Oh, and dear, there's some real thug types – from casting, I think – looking for you. I do wish you'd hang out with a better crowd."

"Looking... Listen, mother, that money I wanted you to get? I need it now. I need you to send it Western Union or something. Today. I mean, no, I need you to give it to someone there."

She laughed. "You are the comedian, aren't you? I couldn't do that."

"Why not?"

"Because I spent it on your party. Now you better get right over here. This might be the event of the year – hey, isn't that Lon Chaney? Funny, I thought he was – "

Mat broke into a sweat. He dropped the receiver into its cradle. This was the grandfather of bad days. Lon Chaney won't have anything on me as far as death's concerned, he thought. He didn't want to imagine Vinnie's thugs coming for him.

Then he brightened, remembering something obvious. He could make the first payment anyway. What a moron to be so concerned, he thought, dialing his agent's number. Another good thing: his stomach had stopped growling. Most likely it starved to death.

The call went right through. "This is Mister Russ."

"Ike? It's me. Mat. Calling from Wisconsin."

"*Wisconsin?* What in hell 're you doing there? Did you know there's a couple of thugs looking for you? Ball-breakers if I ever saw some. I told them you were on a shoot in the Bahamas."

"They know different. They called here."

"You in with a shark, Mat? Listen, I didn't take you for a sucker. You crazy or what?"

"Yeah, crazy. Did the bucks come through from the Bahamas shoot yet? Maybe I can stall this guy."

Silence. "Mat, babe. You didn't hear?"

"Hear what?"

"It's in the can, the shit-can. The shoot was a front for a coke deal. The whole troop fell even before their shoulders were dry under that big Caribbean sun. In all the trade papers. DEA guys were here to talk with you. Seems you skipped out just before stuff hit the fan."

"DEA? Are you shitting me, Ike?"

"I wouldn't shit you, you're my favorite – "

"Yeah, yeah."

"Heh-heh-heh. Remember *The Last Detail?*"

"Be serious. I'm in trouble here."

"All right, all right. It's true. Huge coke deal. Hell, this phone's probably bugged."

"I don't know anything about any coke, dammit, Ike." He sat on the bed. "I don't feel very good."

"Yeah well, you know how the studios are these days. Scared shit-less over any drug scandals. Public image and all that. The studio police and L.A. narcotics called me; they think you're dirty. I told 'em no way my man has dirty fingers, but they're sniffing around. Two hundred kilos is a lot of blow, man; they're looking to hang it on a few heads. Are you sure you're clean? I got a reputation, you know."

"Right, Ike. Your reputation." Then: "Of course I'm clean, What am I, stupid? The '70s are over. Long time ago."

"Then I won't tell you the rest of the news."

"Good or bad?"

"You mean, 'How bad?'"

"What else?"

"You asking? Okay, you're gonna get it. You know that guy Beetleman, sick guy whose place you took on the Bahama shoot?"

"Sure. Good man."

"Yeah well, the word is that he was taking your calls after he got better and got a gig on a feature. Tit-and-ass job. Seems one of the regular divers on the *Sea Watch* team stepped on a sea urchin; damaged some nerves and needed surgery. Beetleman checked in on your call and wound up with a regular gig."

"I thought he was dying."

"From stepping on a sea urchin? You kidding?"

"No, I mean Beetleman. Never mind. Regular gig you say?"

"Yup."

Mat's heart sunk. "On *Sea Watch?*"

"To the tune of one hundred K a year for a few dives a week. Contract, no less. Gets a studio union card." Ike paused to catch his breath. "I hadn't thought about it, but this might make a great screenplay. Docu-drama. No, comedy. Perfect. Get Owen Wilson and DeVito together. This could be big. Mat, you hear me? Listen, if the goons get to you, call me right away, before you call any medical people. I'll fly out on the first flight and blow this bigger than OJ. You there, Mat?"

He'd hung up. I'm not anywhere, he thought. Sure as hell not here.

Digging a card from his wallet, he found a number. Sweat dripped from his forehead onto the paper, but when he tried to dial there was no tone. Mat heard the brothers come into the kitchen. He tried the phone again, then went into the living room.

Verne, Nels, Bascom and Brodie were by the sink. One bottle clinked against another – a toast. They were having a good time.

Mother Dickey sat in the couch having tea and reading *Redbook*. She smiled as Mat took a seat. "Better, dear?"

In addition to laughter coming from the kitchen, Mat could hear the rasp of father Dickey's shovel still scraping the sidewalk. Sure bet for a coronary, he thought for the second time. Doesn't that old man ever tire? "I feel all right. Missus Dickey. Do you have the number where Daphne's staying? I need to call her."

"Something wrong, Mat? You're not getting cold feet, are you?" She giggled and tossed her magazine to the floor. "That's a Midwest joke. Anyway, the phones haven't worked since this morning."

"I just used one."

"Oh, good; glad to hear it. But she can't be reached right now."

"I need to talk to her – private things. If you could get the number?"

The woman sighed, pulled at a floppy ear. "Fact is, that friend of hers, Mr. Hieman from the Skelly station, heard she was in distress. Little while ago his mother stopped by to say he left in a Power Wagon for Des Moines to pick her up. So I'm sure she'll be home tonight."

"Hieman? Buster Hieman?"

"That boy surely does get around."

"But – that's rather indecent, isn't it? I mean, she's my fiancée."

The woman tsk-tsked. "Things certainly *were* different when I was a girl. But you being from California and all… I mean, I don't like the neighbors to know, but we view *Sea Watch* in this house."

"Don't remind me about *Sea Watch*."

"Too spicy for you?"

"You think the buses might be running today? It's my mother, you know. She's not been too well since – "

"Buses? I'll tell you, Mister California beach boy, no buses or anything else on that interstate. Some heavy duty four-wheelers."

"Like Buster's got?"

"He doesn't even have a bicycle. Borrowed the Power Wagon."

Mat shaved; sat on his bed; tried the phone, but it was down now. He thought about Hieman picking up Daphne, but the thought was too ludicrous – the guy was a major idiot. But Mat wished he'd known Buster was going; he could have hitched a ride to the airport and flown home. Hieman would still have had Daphne all to himself for a few hours – not that it'd do him any good, though the thought of Daphne in a truck with Buster amused him. Also troubled him; but not so much as a mandatory twenty years in a federal penitentiary for a two hundred kilo cocaine deal he hadn't even known about.

Even that wasn't so troubling as thinking about Vinnie's loan; not so troubling as imagining a .22 caliber pistol pressed into the chest while two androids held a struggling man's arms. Pop! Then life bleeding out a hole small as a dried pea.

There was nothing to be done. He'd always been an imperturbable type; it was too late to change. He took up the *Gordondale Gazette* Mother Dickey had set on his pillow and turned to page four, the last page, and saw his blurry image beside Daphne's high school photo. He looked like her grandfather. "Local Girl To Wed," the caption announced. By the quality of the photo, he thought it should have another headline: SURFER PAEDOPHILE ARRESTED FOR ASSAULT OF TEENAGER.

He wadded the paper and tossed it into a corner. He shut his eyes, hoping for a catnap.

15

As he lay on his bed, Mat could still hear "the boys'" muffled laughter. Still wearing baggy clothes and wet boots, he lifted his feet and dropped them on what he guessed was a hand-stitched bedspread. Again he looked up at the yellowed wallpaper printed with elegant egrets stretching necks skyward. "No egrets," he said. But lots of regrets. Outside, the snowstorm raged silently, huge flakes swirling, brushing the panes and dropping into a growing mound on the outer sill. The neighbor's house forty yards away was completely obscured. A small guest alarm clock which hadn't been there the previous night ticked steadily on the dresser. Mat's stomach rumbled incessantly as it had earlier and, looking down the sunken abdominal washboard of muscles, he cursed it.

All of it. Looking to the Dickey and Winder patriarchs and matriarchs, he cursed them, too, for good measure. Hicks, he thought.

Warmth began to push out the cold in his bones, and with heat came intoxicating stupor. His eyes began to close, his breathing deepened. He dreamed.

He was in the funny pages, black and white, humping with Blondie, frozen solid in *flagrante delicto* with Dagwood's busty wife, right there on Dagwood's favorite couch. The thing was, he was aware of someone opening the paper and looking at him with his pants around his knees. His two-dimensional eyes strained to catch a glimpse of who it was... "Ma! Come in here and look at this, will you? Mat's in the paper and he's – he's committing a sin with Blondie."

Mat strained harder to see, and he just made out Ma bustling into the kitchen and leaning over the table to look.

If he could blush, if it were the Sunday color paper, Mat's face would redden. "Hah!" Ma cried. "That's not even a good drawing."

Someone knocked softly at his door, and Mat snapped awake.

A voice asked, "Are you awake?"

He sat upright. "Daphne! I'm awake! Come in." He sprang from the bed to the door.

Ma Dickey stood behind the door, wiping her hands on a flour-dusted apron tail, a slightly embarrassed expression on her face. "Sorry, Mat Roper. I guess Daphne and I must sound alike."

"Didn't mean to startle you," he said, on some level disturbed by the revelation that mother and daughter sounded so similar.

Ma shrugged. "The boys're leaving. Seems like you have a visitor."

Something touched his heart. Then he realized the visitor couldn't be Vinnie. "They left because someone's here? Then he's welcome with me. Uncle – Haywire, is it?"

Ma coughed discreetly into her hand, a puff of flour poofing into the air. "You mean Uncle Hey-*wood*? No, but you're supposed to visit him today. It's someone else. Reverend Weems, to see you."

" Do I know a Reverend Weems? Why's he want to see me?"

"Why, to join his congregation, I suppose. It's his job to recruit and gather the holy lambs to his breast."

Mat snorted. "If it's sacrificial lambs he's after, he has the right boy."

"It was just a prank, Mat. They don't mean any harm."

"A *prank*? A short-sheet is a prank. Shaving cream on a toilet seat is a prank. A handshake buzzer, or maybe even an exploding cigar." Mat felt something pound in his temples – his hangover – as his blood pressure rose. "It's not a prank when you think someone's getting eaten alive by a giant pig with – with six inch fangs."

"*Tusks,* Matthew Roper. And more like nine inches."

"Tusks, then. But where I come from, that's no joke."

Ma sighed. "No, I suppose it's a cruel joke. If it makes you feel better, that same joke – or some variation – has been played on pretty near everyone in town."

"I mean, they're probably going down to the Dickeyville Diner and Rifle Club to have a big laugh at my expense."

She shrugged, smiling. "No, they're probably going to Pepper Joe's

Bar and Scope Shop to have a big laugh at your expense."

"What a day."

Her expression settled. "Listen dear, knowing how you feel I don't mean to put a too-rosy glow on this boar thing, but a guy could use the experience to buff up his life story."

"Life story. Like I don't have one?"

She shrugged. "Who hasn't got stories?"

He thought of something else. "What happened with Verne's ears? They look like he went through a lawn mower."

"Best ask him, dear."

He shrugged. "This hasn't been a very good day for me." He slumped onto the bed. "It couldn't get any worse."

"Don't count on that. The Reverend ought to make it a little tougher, if I know him."

"I don't want to see this Reverend Weems. And I need a phone. A cell phone. You have one?"

"You don't?"

"Lost it."

She shook her head, earlobes jiggling cheerfully. "In a town like ours, someone with a cellular phone would look conspicuously extravagant. No one I know has one."

"Daphne does."

"Daphne," she sniffed, "is another thing. Everyone expects her to be a little testy."

"Testy? You must be kidding."

"I can't help with the phone. Is it life and death?"

Mat laughed ruefully. "Worse. Can't you send this guy away?"

"Mat Roper, you have to understand how it is in a small town. When you marry into a family you marry the town too. I can't send away Reverend Weems because it wouldn't be decent. If I did, it'd be all over town in an hour that you wouldn't see a man of the cloth. In two hours everyone would be thinking that you were an atheist or some such abomination. By nightfall everyone would be thinking you were kin to the antichrist. You aren't an atheist, are you?"

Mat chewed this over, chewing his lower lip as well. "I just don't believe in things I can't see or – "

"Because if you were an atheist, Mister Roper," she interrupted, "it would go very hard on you in a small town. Most of the 'free thinkers' in a small town just quietly find excuses to do other things on Sundays, like watch Packer football game."

He thought how, when his surfboard dropped into a trough and he couldn't see over the swell, everyone else seemed to be erased from existence. "I'm not really looking to find God."

"Everybody wants to find God. Every golf ball wants to find the fairway."

"Huh?"

"Every kernel wants to find its cob, Matthew."

Groan. "This place is too conservative for me," Mat said.

"That so. Well, Democrat liberals are the worst thing," Ma said.

Mat smiled indulgently. "So you're a Republican."

"Why, they're as bad as Democrats. Didn't you know that? Honestly, Mat. I thought Californians were free thinkers."

"Some are."

"That's true enough. As long as you're courteous about it. Does anyone pray for you?"

Mat considered. "I had a great-aunt, but she's been gone for years."

"Whether a person believes or not, it's a sad world when nobody's praying for you."

He changed the subject. "Marry the town when you marry the girl. It's funny, but I had a similar thought. I was thinking a guy should see the mother before he – ah..." He glanced at Ma Dickey's ears hanging out of her gray hair. "Guess I shouldn't keep the Reverend waiting."

"You said you were famished, and the boys ate the cheese sandwiches, so I put out a platter of home fries, Wisconsin cheese, oatmeal cookies and Macintosh apple slices sprinkled with cinnamon. Does that sound good?"

Mat's stomach writhed. "I'll be right down. I want to get out of these clothes."

In five minutes he was descending the stairs. He went into the living room to meet Reverend Weems just as Mother Dickey rose to leave.

Weems sat on the couch – a thick-bodied man with gallons of excess skin and fat. He wore a dark blue suit that seemed like a serge tent that might hide a couple of kegs of beer. His hair was steel gray so deep and thick that it looked like he wore a helmet. A dark-skinned man, his eyes were heavy-lidded but bulgy, the eyes of a sensualist. His arms ballooned within his white shirt and his throat seemed suspended exactly between a wattle and a jowl.

He rose, standing not quite so tall as Mat, and extended a thick arm. "Ah, Mister Roped. Such a pleasure to meet you at last. May I introduce you to Missus Dickey?" He extended his arm toward the retreating Ma, then chuckled uneasily. "No of course not. She's your future mother-in-law and you already know her." He measured Mat's height. "We stand mighty near to heaven, you and I, Mister Roped."

"Rop-*er*."

"Mister Rop-*er*. But as I was saying… tall and close to heaven."

He sat. The clock ticked on the mantle. Outside Pa's shovel scraped at the driveway close to the house. Almost done. A few dying embers crackled. Plates rattled in the kitchen.

"Yes, I have met her," Mat said at last. The Reverend's skin was oily, lustrous in tone. It was healthy skin, almost blue, vibrantly supple. Something about the face struck Mat.

"Met who?" the Reverend wondered.

"Ma Dickey."

"Yes, well… You certainly should meet her."

"Yes," Mat said.

An almost-empty platter rested upon the coffee table. There remained a single apple slice. The Reverend followed Mat's eyes. "Do you mind?" he asked, bending foreword to snatch the slice into his mouth. "I haven't eaten since breakfast, and the Lord's work always makes for a hearty appetite."

Mat sat in a corner chair. He noticed a bowl of hard Christmas candy within reach.

"So. You're going to marry our Daphne, eh, Mister Roper? You mind if I call you Mat?"

"Not at all. Your first name is…?"

The Reverend cleared his throat, a sound that began down deep in his belly. "Reverend."

"You're the Reverend *Reverend* Weems?"

"No, I mean you should call me Reverend. It hardly seems appropriate to call a man of the cloth by his first name, does it? I wouldn't think you'd think so."

"Oh."

"God's flock. The beauty of Heaven has never been surpassed."

"No, I suppose not." It was the Reverend's eyes. That was it – how blue they were. Beneath the hair they reminded Mat of a blue crab's wriggling eyes peeking from beneath its shell.

"There's a great full banquet in the sky, Mat. Every day is Sunday and the lambs feast in His name. Amen."

"Hmmm-hmm. I could use a feast."

"Could you now. That's good news. I'd hoped you'd feel that way."

"What way?" Mat lifted the glass lid to the candy bowl. Red, green and yellow ribbon candy. Green-banded pineapple candy with flower designs. Red-lacy cherry and lemon wedges. He hadn't seen this stuff since he was a child.

"A garden of Eden, full of beauty and the bounty of God. Not unlike the Viking version of Valhalla, although" – the Reverend chortled – "we of course don't cling to the version of nubile beauties." He winked, waiting for some response, and coughed uneasily.

"I suppose not," Mat said, wondering. The ribbon candies reminded him of his parent's house when he was five. A pang struck him in some deep place.

Reverend Weems was pointing a thick finger toward the ceiling. "Up there, Mat."

Mat looked at the ceiling just as Ma Dickey came in. "My, you boys certainly were hungry." She swooped up the tray and departed.

"And we enjoyed it mightily, too, I must say," the Reverend called after her. "Where was I? Oh, up there... Up there in His great bounty is a feast, Mat, a feast of the soul. Where men never hunger for the tainted flesh, for beauty is His banquet, and love, and a table as elegant as the Last Supper was plain. Do you get my drift, sir? Do you understand what I am saying?"

Mat nodded as he picked a lemon wedge and pinched it between his thumb and forefinger. The candy refused to budge; it was welded to the other candy. He wrestled harder, with a kind of desperation.

"What have we got?" the Reverend asked, leaning in. "Mind if I try?" He plunged his fat hand into the bowl, mining for a candy, and grunted. Beads of sweat rose from his meaty forehead; blue veins bulged along his thick neck. Even his hair seemed to bulge. "Like grappling for hungry souls," he grimaced through clenched teeth. Suddenly, with a sticky crackle, the whole clot of hard candies came free of the bowl. The Reverend examined it briefly, minutely; sniffed it. "Would you like one, Mat?"

"Umm, no thanks, I guess not."

Weems shrugged, put the cluster back and lifted on the lid. "And that is heaven, for you, sir. The banquet of the Lord. Will you partake of it?" His eyes rolled to the ceiling. "WILL YOU?" he thundered.

Previously mesmerized by the candy bowl, Mat jumped in his chair. "Oh! Sure. Whatever."

"My son, my son. I saw you that first week. Watching with hunger."

"Yesterday, you mean? When I was walking by?"

"Perhaps." The minister shrugged. "Do you believe in the bounteous feast of the Lord?"

Mat was noncommittal. He didn't know that he believed in *any* kind of feast.

"Do you wish to partake of His banquet of Plenty in Paradise?"

"Mmm."

"I take that for a 'yes?'"

"Oh, um, most yesly. Yes indeed. Very yesly. Sort of."

"Good. Then it's settled."

"Settled?"

Surprisingly nimble, the Reverend's blue bulk sprang from the couch and extended a hand toward Mat, who rose and crossed the room just as Mother Dickey entered.

"Leaving so soon?" she asked.

"All has been decided," the Reverend told her.

"It has? Already?"

The Reverend turned to Mat. "We didn't excommunicate Darwin in our church, not that he belonged of course. There's room for all appetites at the Lord's table in the New Reform. Room for flowers of all colors. Any utensils imaginable. A dish from every nation, as it were. All flavors, all seasonings, all are welcome. You'll appreciate that, being from California and all. Heh-heh."

"Ah," Mat said. "Heh-heh."

"I must be off. The Widow Spencer has invited me to sup with her today." The Reverend donned a blue hat with a jaunty, tastefully-small feather in the band, Tyrolean. "See you then, Mat. Be prompt in making arrangements. No, I know the way out. You two relax." He swept out of the room. The front door opened and closed.

Mother Dickey cleared her throat. "I'd have thought you'd first want to speak to Daphne about those arrangements. But a man does what a man must, even if his actions are rash."

"Say what?"

"Tut-tut. You know what."

"That guy's pretty strange, you know."

But Mother Dickey had already turned toward the kitchen. Mat started to follow her, but she waved him off.

"It's a rule of this house, Mat Roper. No one in the kitchen after four while I'm making dinner. If you want something else to eat beside that huge snack you just had, check the refrigerator on the back porch. Help yourself."

All he found was Leinenkügel beer. He took two and went out to stand on the porch. The thermometer on the side of the house showed minus ten. Pa Dickey was nowhere to be seen.

Mat went back in. The day seemed unending. He popped the cap off one of the "Leineys". His stomach gurgled. The beer tasted wonderful. He tried the phone one more time. Dead. He turned on the TV. Daytime TV. He went back to his room and sat. He drank the other beer. He lay back. Just before he fell asleep he realized what it was about Reverend Weems: he reminded Mat of a younger version of Vinnie-the-Tide.

16

"Are you going to sleep away the whole day? It's time to rise."

Mat sat up with a start. "Whazzat?"

Mother Dickey clapped her hands. "Come on, now. Chop-chop!"

His eyes blinked and focused. "Mother Dickey? Again? What's going on? How long I been asleep?"

"Ten or fifteen minutes."

Mat groaned, easing back. "I need to sleep."

"Can't. It's time to go see Uncle Heywood. Honestly, Mat, you can't keep making these appointments and not keep them."

Mat rubbed the sleep from his eyes. "But I didn't – "

"Oh, you did. You most certainly did, because I heard you."

"Right. Last night?"

"Right."

Mat had his feet on the old bed quilt, something Ma certainly would have noticed. "Oopsy," he said, sitting up. "How will I get to his house? There's no taxi and I wouldn't dream of putting you out for a ride. Maybe I could just call?"

"Nobody I've ever known expired from walking, Mister Mat Roper. Anyway, it's only eight blocks to Heywood's house. You must have passed it on the way from the bus stop, so I think you can survive the trek. And don't forget what the Sherpas say."

"Sherpas?"

"Tibetan guides in the Himalayas. Don't you ever watch the Discovery channel?"

"Just what do they say?"

"They say, 'Cold feet, put on a hat'. For when you go walking."

"Right, one of those hats that make your IQ drop. You suppose I can find a snack around here?"

"This close to dinner? Not in my kitchen, young man. Merciful heavens, haven't you had enough to eat for one day? Two snacks already? You must have a hollow leg." She started to leave the room. "Incidentally, I hate to bring it up, but being as I'm Daphne's mother I need to ask. Is there something I should know about any bad habits you have? I mean, I know people tend to be a little wild in California, but I'm a little concerned."

"Concerned about what?"

"Some man who said he was from the DEA called for you. And I read enough to know that stands for the Drug Enforcement Agency."

Mat covered his ears with his palms. "Believe me, I didn't do a thing. Well, not for years. It's a mistake. I've got to get back home."

"Mat, about your visit today..."

"You mean the visit you say I have to make?"

"It's just that... I like you, Mat. I don't want anything to make you feel..."

"What?"

"Nothing. Feel like you did about the Horror. Just have a good time. And be careful."

Mat brushed his teeth, washed his face with the amazing soap and promised himself to check into marketing the stuff. He tried the phones: still no luck. Through the window he was startled to see snow falling thicker than it had earlier. In the living room he found Pa sitting in his rocker with a book and a pipe; he was wearing a rumpled and thin bathrobe over his pants but bare-chested. Slumped as he was, the grizzled and sunken chest sucked into the chair, Mat figured the old man would go maybe one hundred and thirty pounds. A stubble of beard and moustache poked out from the small half-face under his bulbous Dickey nose.

"Say, Mister Dickey, you think I might scrounge anything to eat around here?"

Pa looked up from his book. "Not likely. Ma's pretty strict that way. She doesn't like anyone in her kitchen close to dinner." He went back to reading.

"You tie on your string?" Mat asked.

"I told you; can't find the end to tie on to. I've got a mile of string I can't even tie on."

"Sorry. Say, do you know where – "

"Because," Pa interrupted, "it just isn't right to tie where there isn't an end. The kind who'd do that would be the kind of man who'd... cheat on a deal. I can tell you're not the kind of man who'd ever cheat on a deal. Because there's no telling what would happen to a guy who'd cheat on a deal, Mat."

I already know, Mat thought. Just ask Vinnie. "Any chance you know anyone has a cell phone?"

"Ma said you sounded excited about something. Said you needed a phone pretty bad."

"I do and it's important. You know where I can find one?"

"Most likely anybody with one wouldn't advertise it. Folks around here rather frown on conspicuous display."

Mat laughed. "*Conspicuous?* A cell phone? A red Ferrari is conspicuous. With a donkey dildo hanging from the mirror. Not a cell phone."

Pa cleared his throat. "Anyway, Daphne has one."

"A donkey dildo? Or a Ferrari?"

Pa cocked his head sharply, but failed to respond.

"Just joking," Mat said hastily. "I know she has a cell phone."

"Well, you know how Daphne is. But I wouldn't make that donkey joke with Ma."

Mat shrugged. "It's just a guy thing."

"Not necessarily a *father* thing."

"Sorry. Since you're the second to say, just how *is* Daphne?"

Pa cleared his throat again. "Settle down, son. And since you brought it up, speaking of laughs, Ma said you were also pretty upset about the boar hunt."

"That's one description."

"Verne and the boys said you didn't take it well."

"Am I supposed to?"

"Can't speak for all. You weren't the first and won't be the last."

"O, do I feel good to know that."

"Boys didn't mean any harm. Anyway, you tried to save Verne. Some of them who were laughing high-tailed it for town when the joke was played on them."

"Bunch of yokels," Mat muttered.

Pa closed his book. "I suppose."

Mat half regretted his words. They were all, all of them, inescapably part of the whole lump sum: Dickeyville hicks. "Not that it's so bad to be a 'yokel'," he added but thought, unless you're engaged to one. Need to think about that.

"No, you're right. We're pretty much hicks in these parts, though I think the polite society word would be 'provincials'."

"I just don't think it's very funny to pretend someone's getting killed," Mat explained.

"To hear Verne tell it, it was," Pa chuckled and within seconds had worked up a belly laugh. "Wish to hell I'd been there."

Hicks, Mat thought, stuffing himself into the stupid hat and heavy coat and storming out into snowflakes as large as quarters and finding that he couldn't see across the street piled knee-deep in powder. He had Heywood's address on a piece of paper. Maybe this "Hollywood" guy was different from the others in this one-horse town with nothing better to do than mess around.

The funny thing about walking in snow, plowing his legs through the stuff, was that Mat quickly grew tired and overheated. He pulled off his stupid hat but was almost immediately cold. If he unbuttoned his coat to let off the heat, he grew chilly. It seemed to be either hot or cold. He chose hot because he was better adapted to it. "Dumb-ass Sherpas," he thought. "I'd kill for a 7-11. A Quick Mart. Even the Osgood's Twenty-Flavor Popcorn Emporium like the one in Santa Monica that for some reason – he figured delirium was near – leapt into his mind. The popcorn idea seemed especially appealing as he plowed, half-starved, down the snowy sidewalk.

"Oh, Mister Roper. You don't mind if I call you Mat, do you? Hope you're enjoying your stay."

Mat looked up to see a middle-aged woman, hugely fat and barefoot, sweeping snow off her porch. She wore a floor-length overcoat that hung like a pink tent around her and, by the absence of particular nose or ears, appeared unrelated to Winders or Dickeys. Her door was ajar and the most wonderful scents drifted out. Mat smelled buttered toast and hot chocolate. Maybe popcorn; he'd just been thinking of popcorn. He was amazed how acute was his sense of smell. "Oh... hello. Hello!" He had no idea who she was. He stopped.

"My neighbor told me about you. She was right: You are the cutest thing I've ever seen."

"Thanks," he replied absently. The smell was maddening.

"They say you're a big star out there in Hollywood."

"Now listen – "

"So are you connected?" she interrupted.

"Come again?"

She looked perplexed. "I know how it is. After all, my husband's practically a star too."

"Oh. Sure."

"So are you connected?"

Not even to the internet, he thought. "Hmmm."

She clapped her chubby hands together. "I knew it, I just did. So you wouldn't mind looking at a property, would you? I was thinking maybe Opie would want to see it."

Huh-oh. "You mean Ron Howard? He's kind of busy."

"But this is hot. I mean it."

"These guys are hard to get to, Missus...?"

She laughed. "I'm such a hooty-hoot. How about Mister Spielberg. I hear he's always on the lookout for something."

"Right. He rarely comes across anything. Just sits in his big hilltop mansion hoping something will pop up."

"Okay then, it's settled." She swayed her big hips in a pirouette. "Well, ta-ta! My coach awaits." She drew into her lungs a swell of icy air, and her great bosoms ballooned huge, seeming ready to burst through the tent flap; then she turned and slipped inside and shut the door before Mat could say another word.

Numbed, he stood for several seconds before trudging on. The interaction troubled him: it demonstrated how confused he was now –

he should have manipulated something to eat.

In a matter of minutes he arrived at the New Reform Church. Hurrying past, he still wondered at the massive spire on the little building: it disappeared into the snowy heavens.

A few minutes later he approached the Epiphany Church of Salvation, which had an equally massive spire. Here, however, he was not mindful enough to pass quickly, and it came as a surprise when he heard his name called from the front door.

"Mister Roper! This is indeed a fortuitous meeting, a spark of light in the darkest day. A veritable glimmer. Won't you please come in?"

Had it not been for Mother Winder's admonition regarding the state of affairs, so to speak, of small town theology, Mat might have followed his inclination to feign oblivion and hurry on. But there could be no polite escaping this speaker, he realized, so he turned to where the voice had originated.

On the porch of the church stood a short, slender man with bright red hair and a black frock from shoulders to feet. As Mat trudged up the walkway, his eyes were drawn to massive stained glass windows he'd noticed the previous day – images of the Last Supper and the Garden of Eden – that dominated the church front.

"Welcome, Mister Roper. Welcome to the Epiphany Church of Salvation. Tallest church in Dickeyville. Come in, come in." Completely confident that his request would be obeyed, the man turned to lead Mat into the church. Mat felt compelled to follow.

The main aisles were covered with red carpeting that ran between more pews than he would have guessed possible. The tidy building seemed larger inside than out and was quite chilly. On the wall behind the pulpit a huge red tapestry hung from ceiling to floor, perhaps 300 square yards of material. Mat had no idea if the material had theological significance. As he tilted back his head to look up into the lofty reaches above the great room, high into the dark rafters of the spire, he saw his steamy breath rise before him. Opaque light spread under the great stained-glass windows and diffused across the hardwood floors between uncarpeted pews.

The reverend led Mat to a place near the front and gestured for him so sit. Simultaneously a phone began to ring behind the pulpit. Excusing himself, the man hurried behind the choir benches. As he said "Hello", Mat had a realization.

"Hey, can I use that phone when you're done?"

The minister's head nodded as he spoke into the receiver. "I know. He's already arrived and is here right now, as real as the Savior, blessed be His name. Thanks for the warning. Good-bye." He ducked back behind a curtain, and Mat heard the phone slip into its cradle.

Someone had been watching him and had informed the minister of his progress down the street. It seemed curious that the guy didn't attempt to hide this fact; he seemed to take it that Mat wouldn't care.

When he reappeared and moved back to the bench, up close, he was even shorter than Mat had first thought. Skin, ruddy red, quite mottled, had the appearance of having been burned. Thin, greasy hair, fiery-red and slicked back from his forehead, looked like wet feathers on a bantam cock. Even his eyes were red, the fiercest eyes Mat had ever seen, eyes that lived up to the cliché of "burning like lumps of coal", the eyes of a madman on his way to the gallows.

"You may use the phone after I'm done speaking to you, Mister Roper. No sooner, no later." He sat at the end of the pew across from Mat's, red eyes studying. He appeared not to like what he saw, for his mouth's corners sloped down. For several minutes he merely studied.

"Is something wrong?"

"On earth there is much wrong, Mister Roper, though that is not what I now contemplate. That's sucking the monkey's nose, if you know what I mean, and I think you do."

"Monkey's nose?" Mat asked, but there came no response.

He averted his eyes from the man's stare and looked instead at the tall stained glass windows casting light across the benches. Beautiful work, masterful perhaps. He couldn't help noticing the uncanny detail in the Garden of Eden. "Amazing," he murmured. "Simply amazing." He stuck out his hand. "I haven't had the pleasure...?"

"You'll have to excuse me. I have a condition with my hands and cannot shake with anyone on my doctor's orders. Danger of staph, don't you see. I am the Right Reverend Rantin."

"Pleased to meet you Right Reverend. Is that what I call you?"

"Right."

"Okay. Pleased to meet you, Right."

"Reverend."

"Reverend Right?"

"Wrong. Just don't call me late for salvation, okay?" The Reverend snorted a few times, then lapsed into silent contemplation of his visitor. "You may have noticed that I am a short man, Mister Roper. A short man, a red one and a humble one. A short man is nearest to hell, where all fallen men are made equal. I'm here to tell you, I had a boy come in here today because he could no longer stand the touch of his own sinning right hand that had stolen – stolen right here in Dickeyville – two Cherry O'Harry candy bars from Higgan's Grocery and Gun Shop. We are reminded that children are shorter and just that much closer to hell, Mister Roper. Remember that. It's not kissing the monkey's nose we're talking about, but sucking it. You get my drift?"

"Oh, sure," Mat said. He was examining the minutia in the Last Supper window. Along with the disciples and Christ, who was pointing at Judas, behind and off to one side he could make out what looked like a waiter at another table administering the Heimlich maneuver to someone. The disciple at Christ's side appeared to be tossing something over his shoulder. A salt shaker lay on its side before him.

"Hell is an ugly place, Mister Roper – you may simply call me 'Reverend' – an evil place reserved for the sons of Adam. Men will gorge themselves at the carnal trough and drown in their own vomit, Mat – may I call you that? Thanks. Or starve or freeze – "

"Starve and freeze? Yes, I can relate to those."

"But they will suffer. They will suck the monkey's nose, Mister Roper. All of them. There is no recourse, other than starvation."

Mat saw that the Right Reverend Rantin wore a gold wedding band, and he couldn't shake a sudden grotesque image of Rantin and his wife humping. As horrible as that seemed, another notion came to him – that one would say of their humping, everything was red.

"Are you with me so far? Because if you need it spelled out, if you need it snapped over your head like some cloying plastic bag to cause your blackening flesh to swell and putrefy, then I will give you my attention. I'll help you see the terrors of hell. I'll help you understand. I mean, if hair were worms, where would they defecate? Into your brain, that's where."

"Gads," Mat replied, surprised.

"Because if you want to see it, if you want to surrender to it, then tonight at midnight ask of Satan that he attend you. Invoke his name 'Beelzebub' or 'Baal the Fly King' that he might claim and drag your living, screaming entrails under the earth; that the vultures of hell might tear out your living eyeballs and consume them upon the bare, quivering, throbbing breasts of the woman you love. Are you with me so far?" The little man's eyes flared with passionate fire. They seemed to shine into a part of Mat's humanity that he didn't want illuminated.

"Whoa, it really is time to be going, isn't it?"

"You are right about that. Because we are all 'going' to be going. Do you read me loud and clear? Do you 'grock' it? Comprendo, señor? Do you get my drift? Are you with me? ARE YOU?"

Mat stared at the Garden of Eden window. If he squinted his eyes, he could see tiny ants toiling over the fallen fruit which lay at Adam and Eve's feet. Adam appeared to be stepping on as many as he could. Deeper in the woods, just behind Eve's leaf-obscured breasts, a homeless man could be discerned collecting cans. Another man, partially obscured, appeared to be masturbating while checking out the naked couple. "I hear," he whispered.

"And I am red. Why am I red? I am red that all may know that man is born a sinner. Red that man might know the hellish horrors that await sinners. That we are closer – closer, I tell you – to hell beneath our feet than heaven above our heads. Will you join me, Wilbur?"

"Um, my name is Mat. I really have to go now."

"Mat, then. Will you join me? Join in rising up from hell?"

"Sure. I guess so. Sometime. I have an appointment with – "

"Jump."

"What?"

"Jump. Jump up. Now." The wiry Reverend Rantin rose from the pew. His knees bent slightly, then he sprang a few inches into the air. "Come on. Join me." He began jumping in the aisle.

"Oh, thanks, but I – ah, never jump, um, on an empty stomach. I really think I ought – "

"JUMP! Rise above the burning grip of Satan, as high as you can."

"Well, I – "

"Jump as if the deck screws of hell were being driven under your toenails! Jump as if Satan's box cutters were slicing into the festering flesh of the bottoms of your feet! *Jump!*"

Mat reluctantly stood. He jumped twice, barely raising his heels. "Whew! That was great. Now I've got – "

"Jump! Jump from the eternal fires!" The little man sprang higher above the carpet-padded aisle. "Higher! Jump like the dark one's flaming fingers were reaching to crush your testicles!" It seemed that the little red man might lift off. He bounced like a flea on a hot plate. "JUMP!" he screeched.

Mat began leaping into the air. His stomach growled ominously.

"Hear them? Hear them? The rumbling of hell! Jump! Jump! Jump!" the little man encouraged, his robe billowing and collapsing. "Leap above hell!" Heating up now, his breath billowed from his nose into the cold air.

Mat jumped. They both jumped. They sprang like maniacs, over and over springing upward.

At last both men dropped into the pews. "Oh, yes," the Reverend gasped, head lolling over the bench back. "Yes, yes, yes, yes. Oh, God, if only I hadn't stopped the sin of smoking I'd light up now." His red hair standing damp, he looked all the more like a bantam cock. "Thus will you rise above hell, Mat. Will you join us in rising above the dark forces?" The Reverend lifted a finger toward the rafters above.

"I dunno. I guess," Mat panted. "But look at the time. I've got to run." There actually were no clocks in sight, so Mat glanced where the reverend pointed, impossibly high above in the darkened beams.

"I'll let Mother Dickey know," the Reverend said.

"Know? What?"

"Your ascension. You've made me very happy, Mat. Happy in this red, red world. Was it good for you, too?"

"Whoa, the churches in this town are sure tall," Mat said. He rose from the pew and, stomach growling madly, hurried toward the entrance, glancing and noticing that Christ's stained glass image had excessively large ears. Winder ears.

"...red, red world..." The words flapped behind.

He burst out the doors into the day, a day colder than even the little man inside the frozen church. Mat mumbled under his breath as he dug the slip of paper from his pocket to re-read Heywood's address. Glancing at the streets, they seemed like a dream as he strained to see as far as he could in the swirling snow, straining to see his way home, a home far away from the strange people and customs of Dickeyville, a place as strange as in some bizarre Fellini movie. If a passing hearse full of the living dead offered, and it was heading west, he would have accepted a lift. It couldn't be much stranger than Dickeyville.

With a start, he realized he'd forgotten to use the church phone.

Hell with that, he thought as the dry snow squeaked under his boots. He walked, passing a new Ford pickup parked alongside on whose bumper a sticker read: "THERE THEY GO AND I MUST HURRY AFTER, FOR I AM THEIR LEADER."

Mat smiled. He'd seen the same bumper sticker in California. But ten years earlier.

17

In a few minutes he'd reached the correct address. He hadn't been looking forward to meeting somebody – anybody else – in this town, but he hoped at least that "Hollywood" Heywood might be "his kind of people", whatever that might mean.

It was a large house, taller than Ma and Pa Dickey's, painted pale-blue with white trim. Smoke billowed from a chimney beside the front porch. The curtains were drawn, all mortuary black. Mat rubbed his hands and slapped his arms. He hoped greatly for food. He struggled up the unshoveled walkway and stamped his feet on the mat before ringing the bell.

No one immediately answered, to his partial relief – he was ready to go back to Mother Dickey's to demand something to eat. He figured what he'd say: I'm starving here, Mother Dickey. Starving. Isn't it the Christian thing to do to feed me? What will Daphne think when she comes home to find her fiancé dead?

As he turned to leave, the door suddenly cracked and an eye peered through. "Mat Roper?" came a voice. In the background he made out a funereal dirge, Mozart's *Requiem* playing through a tinny speaker.

Mat tried to see inside. "Yes, it's me."

"So you say."

He stood on the freezing porch. "Didn't we meet last night? Can I come in?"

"Met someone who looked like you. Can't be too careful with – what I've got. How about this: What's the sign say above Hollywood?"

"Am I at the right place?"

"You're at the home of Happy Hollywood Heywood. So what does the sign say?"

"You mean the Hollywood sign?"

"Uh-huh. What's it say?"

"It says 'Hollywood'."

"Okay. You're you. Come on in quickly so nobody sees."

"Sees me?"

"Sees them. Come on."

"Who?"

The door opened and an elongated hand snaked out to pull Mat inside. Any hope of normality disappeared as he entered a house like none other. Except for one over the La Brea tar pits, it's unlikely such a building existed. The ground floor was nonexistent, the space inside the outer shell open like a barn, cavernous; only half of the second story had any floor. The interior resembled a stage more than a home. Bare dirt-smeared walls were covered with black curtains and an occasional picture. A massive excavation of earth had been dug perhaps fifteen feet below street level, a pit surrounded on four sides by halogen floodlights on ten foot stanchions. A refrigerator, partially dirt-covered and obviously unused, poked through the upheaval along one side; just beyond it was a lit fireplace. A great mound of earth covered the wall to Mat's right; beside it a ladder rose to the second floor, or rather half of a floor, where apparently hid hastily-conceived living quarters. In what had probably been a bedroom, toasters and microwaves lay littered and a small cook-stove sat precariously near the edge of the precipice. Mat saw steam rising cheerfully from a pot. The solemn music evidently came from a small clock radio, volume turned above speaker capacity, atop a toaster oven.

A little voice inside, his mantra, repeated: 'I've got to get out of this town, got to get out.'

"It's pretty much what I said, isn't it? The jolliest place in town."

He turned to take in "Hollywood" Heywood. He was as tall as Mat but so thin that the skin hung on his bones. He seemed to hang everywhere. His Dickey nose hung so far down an extended jaw that Mat's first impression was his face was melting. His hair was thick and long over his ears; coffee-and-milk-brown, it seemed younger than the rest of him. His extended hand had long, big-jointed fingers. Mat guessed that Heywood might be in his forties.

A fine wide smile, with gapped teeth. "Glad you could make it, Roper." With his saggy skin, he suggested a human bloodhound.

Mat put his hand into a firm grip of simian fingers. "Good to see you again, Heywood. Even if last night is a bit... fuzzy. Do you suppose I might use your phone? The phones were out a while ago and I need to make an important call."

Heywood was dressed in dirty dungarees and a plaid work shirt; a happy face patch had been sewn over one of his elbows. "I hear it ring once in a while, but it's buried somewhere. I think I used it a few months ago to call a museum, but otherwise I'm happy as hell to lose it. If you can find it, use it. Can I get you a cuppa?"

Mat glanced at the mounds of earth covering every square foot of ground and shrugged. "Thanks."

It felt warmer inside than out, so he unbuttoned his coat and took off his stupid hat. At least he couldn't see his breath. He glanced around – no chairs – so tossed the coat on a mound of orange-colored earth. "What do we have here? An accident?"

Heywood turned to walk around the pit which seemed to extend almost the entire breadth of the floor. "What we talked about last night, Roper; luckiest thing to ever happen to a man. Like I said, nobody else's been in here in over six years." He scrambled up the big dirt pile to the ladder and climbed to the second floor while Mat looked for anything to sit on. As there was nothing, he settled at the edge of the pit and looked in. His breath caught. He stood quickly, eyes widened in amazement. His mouth failed. He could only stare.

"Nobody been inside for six years, and they can't understand why. Heck, I've practically been a fugitive in my own town."

"This is impossible," Mat reasoned. "It can't be real."

"Oh, they're real, all right. I couldn't believe it myself when we first found them. I didn't even believe in this stuff. Too good to be true. It's is the real thing, all right. What would you say they are, dinosaurs?"

Mat shielded his eyes from the floodlights surrounding the pit and leaned forward. "This is... absurd. A joke." He shook his head. "I got to get out of this town. It's like a spider web."

"Of course it's a joke. I know it is. You don't think I believe it, do you? Only a fool would believe this." Heywood extended his arm and wiggled his long fingers in distaste. "But here it is. In fact, when we first discovered it my wife Helen didn't want me to dig further. Wherever she is, I'm sure she doesn't even talk about it now."

Mast looked around. "Why, where is she?"

Heywood shook his long head. "Gone. Because of all this. And I don't even care."

"It is kind of... drastic." Mat tried to imagine what the house had been like before the destruction, imagine it with a woman's touch. Then he looked into the pit again, disbelieving. "This is ridiculous. I don't even believe in this kind of stuff."

"You said that already."

"No, you said it."

"For six years I've been working here. Six years of hard labor. Day and night. Best years of my life. Do you understand why?"

Mat laughed, but no happy laugh. Something about it made him feel nauseous. "How did you find... um, this?"

A sound escaped Heywood, a stifled sob. It embarrassed Mat in the way of a stranger's barstool confession, the long drink of self-pity.

"I was clearing an extension on our root cellar about eight years ago, just digging out four or five cubic yards to put in some more canning shelves for Helen. I hadn't been digging two hours into the virgin earth when I uncovered what you see, the tip of that one's wing bones. I called Helen and our daughter Ruthy and we all dug some more. Guess you could see why we were excited. Pretty quickly I was into bedrock and had to use a chisel.

"Was I giddy. Couldn't be happier. Of course, I broke my thumb once when I hit it with my two-pound sledge. Also got a chip of rock in my eye and had to see a specialist in Chicago to get it out – just before the big dirt collapse that sucked down part of my neighbors' foundation. But none of it brought me down for a moment."

"What happened to the neighbors when the foundation went?"

"House collapsed. Cost me a fortune."

"I see."

"Took six months' work to get the fossil head excavated. Day and night, sometimes sixteen hours. I lost my job at Osgood's Video and Gunsmithy, but man was I feeling good. Everybody said I looked like hell, tired and done in, losing weight something fierce. When Helen saw the whole head uncovered, she turned right upstairs and said she was leaving and taking Ruthy and did I want to come along. She said to bury and cover it with cement and we'd move that night and never tell a living soul. She wouldn't spend another minute with that – thing. But I was too happy. Still am happy, too." He sniffed.

"So I said, 'Are you crazy, Helen? This is the chance of a lifetime, ten thousand lifetimes. We'll be rich. We'll be more famous than anyone who ever lived.' But then she was gone. It took me six years to get this much dug from the living stone, and so far nobody's found out. Until you, that is, but I can't keep it secret anymore. They think I'm eccentric, but I don't care. Maybe I'm feeling too good about this, but," he said with conviction, "it's enough to make any man gleeful. They don't call me 'Good-time' Hollywood Heywood for nothing!"

Mat shook his head, swimming with the implications of what he saw. He shook it again and tried to make the enormity of it recede, to scoff at the image below, but the extent of Heywood's joy – the ruined house, ruined lives and bones held fast in dark rock... It couldn't be; but those things wrestling in stone were so frighteningly real. The whole character of it had the unmistakable visage of a truth so compelling that words – denial – would break against it like a storm tide rushing into a jetty. There could be nothing other than ruin to unearth such a thing, and Mat felt awe at the hugeness of it all.

A long silence ensued.

"This is... I mean, it's like Biblical proportions, man."

"Cecil B. DeMille," Heywood said.

"D. W. Griffith," Mat replied.

"Erich von Stroheim."

Mat thought a second. "David O. Selznick."

"Hmmm. Victor Fleming?"

"You're saying *Gone With the Wind*?"

"It's all I could think of," Heywood explained, shrugging.

They stood staring into the pit. At last Heywood sighed. "I feel that you... feel like, well, you know, being from California and all..."

"How's that?"

"You know. Like Eddie Arnold puffing up with joy in *The Toast of New York* before the gold scheme collapse."

"Uh-huh. When were you in Hollywood, Heywood?"

"Got there in the spring of '42."

"How many years were you there?"

"Years?"

"Yeah. How long in California?" His eyes never left the pit.

"About six weeks. I was stationed at Pendleton before shipping out for the South Pacific."

"The big war? How old are you, anyway?"

"God, I don't know. Not anymore. Eighty, ninety – I've lost track."

Mat examined his face. "You look pretty preserved for eighty. More like forty, I'd say."

"Yup. Best years of my life, these last six."

Mat stared into the pit and listened to the astounding but somber *Requiem*. It seemed like Heywood's good luck matched his own. The man had been in California for six weeks, at a marine boot camp. Mat thought about his own hopeless condition: no money, fiancée far away, surrounded by the weirdest hicks in the world, hunted by a goon who'd break his legs before he shot him when – no excuses – payment didn't come; also wanted for questioning regarding a cocaine deal he hadn't known about. He remembered what he'd seen years ago in northern California, by Trinidad, painted on the face of a beach rock: No disco. No fat chicks. No future.

God, he was glad not to be Heywood.

No one could be as happy as Heywood.

Mat watched as a jewel-like tear made a lengthy and precipitous journey down the man's drooping nose. "I'm crying with happiness," he sniffed. "Just crying with happiness."

Mat disliked the weight of depression, and his natural inclination toward calm rebelled against this particular brand of joy. Something, an idea, began to take shape.

"You know, maybe we're taking this all wrong. Maybe you were on the right track before, and your wife was wrong. You said 'opportunity'; you're right, Heywood – right!" Like a thin summer haze hanging over a flat southern sea, gloom was dispelled by a vision. Mat stood suddenly. "What am I thinking? This is incredible, the biggest thing in history." He reached down and dragged Heywood to his feet. "Bigger than, say, even Marilyn. You were right, you're going to be famous. Famous and rich. There hasn't been anything like it in all history. You and me, Heywood. We're going to make this work!"

"The greatest show on earth." Heywood smiled wanly. "That's why they call me 'Smilin' Hollywood Heywood'."

"No, really."

It was funny. Mat felt different. All his life he'd seen people act like this, but it had always been beyond him... well, maybe when he fell in love with Daphne, at first anyway. He felt strange, but good, and excited: *enthused*. He, usually so level, was ruffled, and he liked the feeling. It reminded him of something, though he couldn't quite remember what. It took him back to something and, if he couldn't recall what it was, he knew it was good.

Heywood nodded. "It's what I said. We'll be really, really happy."

"No, listen." Mat caught Heywood by the collar. "It could be great."

"I know. We'll be really, really, really happy."

"Let me in on it. To make it work for you."

"I don't know if I should let you be so blessed. It may not be healthy to feel so good. Being this happy hasn't necessarily made me less sad. You know what this is, don't you?"

"I'm not too good at this stuff, but I think so. It scares me, but I think so." Mat grabbed his coat and pulled it on. "I've got somebody to call, if I can ever get through again. I'll talk to you later."

"Man, I feel great!" Heywood buried his face in his hands. His shoulders shook.

Mat headed out the front door and noticed that the walls, unsupported without adjunct walls or rafters, shook and reverberated when he slammed it. On the porch he stopped and buttoned his coat, took stock, then turned and walked back in. Heywood was sitting beside the pit with his melting face hanging through his fingers.

"You don't happen to have anything to eat, do you? No? I didn't think my luck would be that good." Mat shuffled through the dirt to the side of the pit and looked down again. He was reminded of the most famous and valuable fossil of all time, archaeopteryx, the feathered dinosaur, preserved for millions of years in stone. Here, half-emerged from a gray, bedrock slab he could clearly discern the two fifteen foot-high skeletons, one with a human-like skull, two bony masses and a web of spindly skeletal framing extended from both shoulder blades in a sweeping arc reaching almost to its feet, clearly a wing, the other with claws and taloned toes and two horny bumps rising from a reptilian skull. Frozen in time, colossal, hands to each other's throat, they appeared to be locked in mortal combat.

No way, he thought. Yet so unlike dinosaurs... Slowly he exhaled. It felt like he hadn't breathed for his whole life. He felt as good as Heywood did. And when he felt so good he usually called his agent, because that brought him right back to earth.

"And, Heywood? Change that radio station, okay?"

18

The snowstorm eased somewhat as Mat walked back to the Dickey house. It was still cold though, and his pensive mood broke occasionally as he covered his nose with gloves and blew to warm himself. His lips felt like frozen liver. He pulled down his stupid hat and crossed the street to avoid the New Reform and Epiphany Church of Salvation. He wasn't sure why, but he also avoided the house where the strange large woman lived. There was no traffic, not even children playing in the snow, and Mat figured this was because snow held little novelty for local kids. They were probably tired of snow in all its manifestations: pea-snow, wet snow, powder, icy snow, frozen flakes, breaking glass snow... the myriad fabled varieties, thirty or so, identified and named by who was it? Eskimos? Mat tried to recall, having read it in some script, but failed. What the hell did it matter? He had something going now. Something incredible.

He couldn't believe it, especially away from it. And yet he had seen it. His thoughts swirled around it like snow as he walked. There were some Christmas displays but not as many as you would expect. The town looked abandoned, like a set after a day's shoot. Sets were lonely once everyone had gone, places where time and life seemed suspended, empty as the remains of a good party. Few cars were parked on the street now. Earlier there'd been cars at the curbs, where there were curbs, curbs where lawns ended and streets began, cars with snow plowed up against wheels; now there were tracks from escaped cars, as if everyone had left to avoid an air raid. Snow in the middle of the street was rutted from tires. The town was like a movie where humanity has ended for all but one person. Post-apocalypse... Mat, of course, had pretty much felt like that his whole life: blessed, but alone. The only sound was his shoes crunching snow. It reminded him of bare feet crunching pea-gravel below the surf line during a minus tide.

He wasn't aware of a pickup coming in the sound-deadening snow until it was almost upon him. "Hey, Mat! Jump in; we'll drive you to it," Verne yelled.

Nels leaned behind Verne and waved. "Hey-ya, Mat!"

He continued along the street while Verne's smiling head rested on his forearm in the window of the idling truck. "I certainly would like that, Verne. Maybe along the way we could stage the abduction of a few children for the town's amusement."

Verne shook his head. "Suit yourself. If you want to play the ass-hole, fine with me." He gunned the engine and tires slipped, tossing behind a snow rooster trail.

"See you at the house..." Nels' voice receded into the snowfall as the truck caught traction and vanished.

Mat felt a spike in his blood pressure. No doubt about it: Verne got to him. If he stayed another day in Dickeyville, they were going to fight. His blood was hot for it.

Nels had said they'd see him. At Ma and Pa Dickeys'? He hoped not, because he had some heavy phoning to do. Serious phoning. He didn't care if he saw Verne and those others ever again; he just wanted to phone, eat and sleep – and get the hell out of Hicktown, USA.

As Mat got close to the house, he noticed that trucks and cars were parked as densely as at the Dickeyville Horror lot in Mazy Woods. Some in the street were double-parked; bumper-to-bumper, pickups, Ranch Wagons and SUVs were stacked along the curb. Mat could hear yelling and recalled the previous night, Winder and Dickey college kids swilling their beer. What were they drinking? What had he drunk? Lime and bugles? *Leinenkügel*s. The word leaped into his head – "Leineys". His hangover, almost completely dead, pulled itself together long enough to kick him right behind his eyeballs, a sharp goodbye throb. He wouldn't do anything as stupid as last night – that was a promise.

At the house, there were dozens of people outside in the yard, young people. Four-wheel drives were pulled up on the lawn and side-walks around the neighbors' houses. Kids were dressed the same as the previous evening, despite cold wearing t-shirts, jeans and sneakers – dressed just like California kids, kids everywhere. That was it. They seemed to be wrestling in the snow until Mat saw a football rise from a pile of bodies, then disappear under writhing young legs and arms. Steam rose off the bodies. They held up when they saw him, grunts ceasing and a howl lifting into the snowy skies like some wild Norse supplication, a howl that immediately modified into that familiar and particularly grating wail, a hog call. Mat clenched his teeth. The sound hurt him to his bones, right through his jaws and into his skull.

"Merry Christmas, Mat," they yelled.

There were maybe thirty co-eds in the yard, many wearing the red t-shirts of the Wisconsin Badgers, while an overflow crowd of similarly aged and older townspeople milled around front and side porches. A racket of polka music and voices came from inside; there seemed little concern that teens drank beer openly. As Mat walked up the path, the kids cheered and a beefy one stepped out to grab his arm.

"Roper, hey. That was pretty good today, huh?"

Mat was surprised. He removed the hand and looked the kid over. Nineteen, maybe twenty, he had a definite Winder air about him – long, elastic ears, solid body. His t-shirt displayed "Badger Guzzle Squad", but his wide-shoulders and muscle-corded arms suggested he might be a wrestler. Vaguely Mat remembered this kid from the night before, but he had the discovery at Heywood's house on his mind and anyway nothing to say. "Pretty good for everyone else" – Mat started to push past but saw that the kid was drunk – "not for me."

"No, wait. I had about a half-semester's worth of beer money on you, Mister Roper. This Leiney's for you." He held out a beer, and the other kids toasted Mat.

"I hear you don't eat meat," one said. "That true?"

If his body was a temple for the Church of Mat, there wasn't room in it for antibiotics, hormones and cholesterol-swollen fat. He didn't say that, though. They'd figure 'organic' for themselves.

"Man, that's too weird. How'd you get so buff?"

Mat glanced at the boys' builds. The girls were muscular, too. "What about you guys? Taking 'roids? Personal trainers?"

"Liftin' Leineys and hay bales," someone said.

"Is it true that because of the feminists, it's against the law to build a snowman in Los Angeles?" asked a young woman with a dark pony-tail and eyes that glittered with mischief. She won Mat in an instant.

"No. In Los Angeles it's warm and there isn't any – "

She groaned. "It's a *joke*, Mister Roper."

"Oh." He smiled. "Yeah. Call me Mat."

"What's that smell?" a kid asked. "It's kinda weird, but familiar."

Mat started to explain, instead nodded toward the beer. "I don't get it. Everyone thinks it's funny that a bunch of drunks tricked me by faking someone got killed. I don't pretend to know much about small towns, but hasn't anyone got anything better to talk about?"

The young man shrugged, set the beer back into a nearly empty case. "I dunno, Mister Roper. But those weren't bums out there. That was the Mayor and some county supervisors and the big farmers. Pretty much the respected people in town."

"And I suppose they're all here for another laugh?"

The kid looked surprised. "No, sir. You really don't get it. We're not here to laugh, we're here to celebrate. I bet sixty bucks on you. Most of the other kids bet on you, too. If I'd lost I'd have bailed hay free for a day. Hardest work I know. It was mostly old ones bet against you."

"I should be flattered?"

"After last night, I knew you'd come through for Uncle Verne."

"And what if I ran? I'd be laughed at by everyone."

A short kid snorted, his stomach bulging through a tattered t-shirt printed with the words *No Fear–Whitewater Grand Canyon*. "Half the guys bail out when they hear that pig snortin' in there. I did. Nobody thinks nothing of it."

The others agreed.

"So how many of you bailed?"

A couple kids raised their hands. "You fuckin' bet I did," one said. "I been shittin' my pants about the Horror since I was old enough sit up." The boy was built like a fullback.

Right, Mat thought. "Those of us gullible enough to fall for it, eh?"

"Everybody – every guy, that is – falls for it. They do it to everyone, if they like you. It's hazing, like in college, only here it's better."

"If they do it to everybody, doesn't everybody know the trick?"

"Nobody tells the kids," someone said. "It's like an institution."

"And nobody's been shot?"

A woman with a Dickey nose and short jet hair passed another beer through the steaming bodies. "You big-city boys sure have some funny ideas. You're just a little tense. Want to roll in the snowbowl?"

"No, thanks. I've got to make a call. Several calls," he corrected.

"Well, cheer up and Merry Christmas. Wanna smoke a reefer?"

The football rose above the kids, bounced off outstretched arms and disappeared toward the ground. A flurry started, pile of bodies. Unopened beer in hand, Mat tried the stairs into the house. A wall of jammed, steaming bodies, backs to him, blocked the way. He had to get to a phone. Walking round to the side door, the kitchen door, he found just as many bodies and each one just as oblivious to his attempts to pass. Those on the outside of the porch, none of whom he recognized, grabbed his hand and pumped it, congratulating him. But they wouldn't let him through.

Mat walked around the house's extensive addition until he spotted a door without a porch and steps three feet above the snowy earth. He banged on it, but all that happened was a hump of snow dropped at his feet. Stretching, he was able to try the knob. The door opened, and he stepped high and shut it behind him.

He switched on a bare bulb hanging just inside. Hallways ran in three directions from where he stood. As near as he could tell, all three of them seemed to run into dead-end walls. It was nearly as cold in this section of the house as outside. Mat pulled off his gloves and blew into his hands before heading toward the house's front.

At the end of the hall he opened a door to the side, glanced quickly in and was starting to close it when something caught his attention. The small room, smelling strongly of dust and abandonment, was lit only through a window by blue twilight and early streetlamps; but that was enough. Tables had been arranged around the walls; on them were ranges of rolling hills and valleys. A meandering river filled with water ran along the back, curving through a tiny forest stretching the length of the room. Going in, Mat saw that a drawbridge, now lifted, had been built to accommodate the doorway. When the bridge was down, the countryside wrapped round the room. Then he noticed the purpose of the layout. Tiny railroad tracks circumscribed the expanses. Coming closer, he saw a miniature town with crooked streets and tiny houses behind a bustling station. Passenger trains and freight trains waited off the loading dock. There were tenders and Pullman cars and cabooses, all realistic. The work of a serious hobbyist, all had been painted appropriately and scaled to size. Weeds glued to twigs made convincing trees; roads were painted on table surfaces. Mat bent closer to look at carefully-detailed people less than a half inch tall standing beside automobiles and trucks, all replicas of early '50s models. There was a fire department, a feed store, another feed store, a park with swings and a slide, a grocery store with clerks carrying out bags for old ladies, kids playing baseball on a diamond, the police department... Winding streets should have been a tip-off, but not until he noticed the two churches with incredibly tall steeples did Mat understand. Sure enough, there was the Dickeyville grotto, which, because it had such a quirky aspect, was the least-convincing item on the board.

Looking closely at the water behind the town, Mat saw that it was clear acrylic. Along the riverbanks tiny people fished or swam. A rowboat was beached in a cove where a tiny couple lounged on a checkered spread and ate a picnic. Bending close, he saw that they had sandwiches and glasses of juice or wine, a bowl full of potato salad, apples and something on a plate – ham maybe. He noticed something further and bent even closer, eyeballs scant inches away from the little people. They had big ears and noses.

He looked back at the town's perimeter along the river. A smile crossed his face. A black pig ran down the railroad tracks.

Mat tried another door. Opening it, he saw that he'd been there before. It was Pa's string room. Again, despite his hurry to reach a phone, he felt compelled to go in. The other room had smelled dusty, but this one smelled more so. It smelled of decades passing.

Though the room wasn't well-lit, you could see how the multitude of strings had been tied together neat, end to end, to create this voluminous object now collapsed of its own mass. It was as if the ball had melted, pooling at its bottom. Mat acknowledged the effort involved.

The strings represented tens of thousands of varieties, from thread to cord. Each end had been meticulously knotted and clipped, so that the affect was of a continuous multihued string. How long must the strand be? How many countless hours had gone into it? Mat had never seen anything like it. He wondered what might possess a man to succumb to such an obsession. Of course, he realized, it never would be completed. It would go on and on, for a lifetime.

A horrible thought came, an analogy for the ball of string. Marriage... Ma and Pa Dickey's marriage. They'd been married, according to Daphne, for over forty years. Never anybody else.

Mat had had at least one or two new lovers every month since he'd been seventeen. And here was this old married couple with only each other. The thought depressed him. Had he seen any sign of affection between them? Was indifference the outcome of long love? Was it even love and, if so, did anyone really want it? Did older people pretend it was what they wanted because they were afraid to try anything else? Why did married people seem so happy when others married? Was it that misery loves company, the expedience of a live-in squeeze, or was there something more, something Mat didn't understand?

Misery or happiness? Rhetorical question, since he'd never know unless he married... The rub was, if he tried and didn't like it, he'd still be married, at least for a while. But to try something on the chance that he might like it seemed so... insincere.

Following a plotline already explored, he tried to imagine himself and Daphne in twenty years, but the only images that came were of two photos, tintype portraits like those on the wall of the guest room, which revealed nothing of ancestors' hearts and minds. He couldn't see himself with Daphne for that long, living on her money, living on his beauty and hers.

Old couples grew complacent, too tired to look elsewhere, collapsed like Pa Dickey's ball of string into something bottom-heavy. Or they grew quaint, comfortable with each other, collecting a long succession of memories. Like an old garden grown into natural harmony.

A buzz of fear droned inside Mat's brain, like he was some web-trapped summer fly. He shut off the sound just as he had fifty times since he and Daphne had gotten engaged. But eventually, he knew, he was going to have to face it, one way or the other.

Leaving the room, he tried other doors into other ice-cold rooms. Most were filled with storage boxes and old stuff: baby carriages – the woven wicker kind – cribs and playpens, huge doll houses, old baseball gloves and worn footballs and braced tennis racquets from another era, two ancient rocking horses, countless boxes labeled clothes, boxes labeled "misc. household", an easel with a terrible half-completed oil painting of a square-rigger on a stormy sea, boxes labeled "old schoolwork–Daphne", boxes labeled "Toys–Daphne", dozens of old chairs and tables and end tables and sideboards and chandeliers and hutches and coffee tables, butter churns and lunch pails with pictures of Deputy Dawg or The Beatles or The Dukes of Hazzard. Rooms stacked full to the ceilings with musty stuff that should have been in a massive rummage sale... Finally he swung open a door into a throng of people seated around a big screen television.

This room was heated, and welcome air rushed out at Mat. Since the Dickeys hadn't turned on a set since he had arrived, he didn't know if they spent time watching. In fact, Ma and Pa were not present; these were the folks older than them, maybe a dozen, seated in overstuffed chairs and on a pair of ottomans. They all looked up in surprise when Mat entered.

An aroma struck him. His eyes followed his nose to three oversized, uneaten bowls of buttery popcorn on a table in the corner. The folks were absorbed in watching a western. "Who the hell are you?" asked one old man, mottled Dickey nose like a pickle rolled in sand.

Mat stuck out his hand. "Mat Roper. Pleased to meet you all."

"Jee-sus Christ. You gonna talk us all to death, Roper? Why don't you just shoot us and get it over with."

"Look at that hair. You a faggot, Roper?" This one looked Mat up and down. Same Dickey nose as the other. Could be twins. Tiny glittery eyes; Mat imagined a demon's eyes.

"Hush boys," said an arthritis-bent woman. "Let it be."

"He's the groom," said another old lady.

"What? Daphne's marrying a fag? Nobody told me."

"Makes her a lesbian, don't it?"

"A dam clam lapper."

Laughter.

"Hush up. I can't hear the show."

"Idiot. Just because Roper's a queer doesn't make my great grand-niece a lesbian."

"Well, excuse me for living. You got your homosexuals, you got your bisexuals, you got your trisexuals and transsexuals and god knows what else. How the hell can I keep 'em straight."

"Oughtta mount *women* like the Bible says, Roper. What in hell's the matter with you."

"Jee-sus Christ, ever tell you I liked to mount 'em from behind?"

"About ten thousand times."

"Who the hell didn't like that?"

"I still like it."

"I like rodeo style myself."

"What in hell is that?"

"Well, you mount your wife from behind and reach around and squeeze one of her tits. Then you tell her it feels like her sister's tits and try to hang on for eight seconds."

One of the old ladies lifted a purse and slugged the man's arm.

"Why, it's Mat," a rheumy-eyed old woman said, waking suddenly, her face crinkling into a wide, gummy smile. "Good to see you today, young man. That was quite a wing-ding last night, wasn't it?" A few others greeted him, women nodding old gray heads and men finally extending weathered hands.

Mat guessed that most of them were in their seventies or eighties or more. Leathery Winder ears and Dickey noses all round.

"Merry Christmas, son."

"Hello, hello," he said, reaching to shake many mitts as he edged his way toward the greasy popcorn. "Whatcha watching?" Carefully high-stepping across bony legs, thin ones and fat ones, legs wrapped in baggy stockings or white socks, even a pair of wicked-witch red-and-white striped socks, stepping over varicose legs in clunky orthopedic shoes, legs and maybe shoes almost a century old, Mat had almost reached the bowls when somebody answered, "Video movie from Milt's Flicks 'N Fishin' Supplies. Now enough goddam chatter."

"Uncle Josh, Mat's the guest here today."

"Well, he's not my guest. He isn't even from Wisconsin."

"He isn't? Where 'n hell's he from?"

"Shush, now."

"Jee-sus Christ, they won't even get me a drink," one old man complained to him. "Not before five, anyway. Would you get me one?"

"You seen the Dickeyville Grotto, Roper? Nothing like it on earth."

"He ain't a Korean, is he? What kind of name is 'Roper'?"

"Hesh, you damned fool. Course he ain't from Korea. I hear he's from New Guinea."

Mat glanced at the beer in his hand but paid little heed to the folks as he made his way to the popcorn. "Haven't seen so many old legs since *Antique Road Show,*" he said. "Heh-heh."

"Very funny, Roper. You want to hear jokes about dumbass California boar hunters?"

Mat shrugged. "Old poop," he mumbled under his breath. Almost there. He was truly starving now; if he didn't eat soon, his body would start digesting itself.

"Hope you like that, young man," a tiny woman said from where she curled in a chair, bright eyes shining beneath the fold in a blanket. "Most of the young 'uns won't eat popcorn sprinkled with Metamucil."

"Ooh," he said, but didn't care enough to pass it by. By now he'd eat the goddam popcorn if it had passed through a chicken. He grabbed a handful but didn't raise the puffy kernels to his mouth. His attention was suddenly arrested by the television. "That movie. It's not... not..." He had only seen it once, but he'd never forget it. This movie had played a pivotal part in his life.

"Yup, *Heaven's Door.* Pretty damn underrated, if you ask me," one old guy said, rubbing the white stubble sprouting from his scalp. "It's got a little bit of everything."

"It ought to. It cost forty-four million dollars," Uncle Josh grumbled. "Now can you shut up so we can listen? Say, does anybody smell something funny?"

"I didn't do anything," the first old fellow said. "Forty-four million? That ain't nothin'. It probably brought in millions."

"Yes," Mat gasped, "about one and a half of them. Forty-four was a fortune back then."

"Smart aleck. They got damn good western costumes."

"Costumes..." Mat muttered, his appetite fleeing, his mind numbing when he heard *that* movie mentioned. Popcorn kernels dropped through his curled fingers. "*Heaven's....*" He couldn't finish it; these words that were genesis for all things painful in his youth.

"Yep. Used to be, people liked westerns."

"We watch it once a month. That's the good thing about bein' old and forgetful."

In his current mental state pain hit him like a hundred-year wave. Turning, he carefully retraced his steps over the old legs, stopping to set his Leiney on the table, then leaving through the door opposite the one he'd come in.

He was in a bathroom. Quickly he locked doors on opposite sides and sat on the edge of the tub. The room was morose, '50s style, with brick-patterned linoleum and pastel-blue checkered wallpaper. A big bar of Ivory soap rested in a chintzy plastic holder. A fuzzy blue cover hid the toilet seat. Standing quickly, Mat jerked up the lid and bent over, but his stomach was empty as a junkie's purse. He rested his elbows on the seat, breathing heavily, eyes closed.

19

Aegus, his father, had been a movie producer. He and his wife Marina had been what polite people termed "comfortable". They would sit beside the pool behind their Hollywood Hills mansion with tall drinks and fall asleep. Roused every few months, they would see that their lives were good, so good that it was a happy accident when Mat arrived in 1981, thirteen lucky years after the Summer of Love. The family had money and looks and a bankful of "hip". They were prototypes of the rich Hollywood Californians who passed easily through phases of the psychedelic '60s, the cocaine '70s and the dotcom '80s. Their summer home in Santa Barbara was a "beach house" only by virtue of what equally wealthy owners called their adjacent houses.

Raised under a Hollywood sun of easy large money and connected to "the industry", Marina and Aegus weren't bad parents so much as absent ones. It was nice to have an attractive child, but they had their lives and he had his. Mat's parents loved him, spent minimal time with him and weren't willing to let his tiny life limit their evenings. An *au pair* took care of his needs; a cook prepared meals; he attended a private elementary school for wealthy children of "the industry".

What Marina and Aegus no longer had was youth. The people they liked best were getting older. Some were getting dead. Attendance at pool parties dropped off because their actor friends could no longer be seen in swimsuits. Liposuction was still a few decades away.

Hollywood was flush in mediocre productions; money to be made, but not like in the past. Fear was that the videotape industry would ring a death knell. With remakes of classics, Hollywood was becoming a parody of itself.

It was during this time of disquieting emptiness that Aegus saw a film that rocked him like none had for years. It was a movie that caught the viewer and shook him until his jaw dropped; caught him in its talons and squeezed him until the juice was gone.

It was a great movie.

Immediately after Aegus saw it, he walked out to the ticket counter to watch it again. He watched for flaws. Then he called up his wife's father to see if he'd seen the film. He too was a producer.

"Loobie? Aegus here. Have you seen – "

"Saw it last night. Best in maybe six, seven years."

"Kidding? Best since *Strangelove*."

"Maybe since *Kane*. Or *Coming Home*."

"Don't go off the deep end, Loobie. But I admit this is bona fide."

"Pretty much. Whaddaya think of that guy?"

"Director?"

"Acting, too, but yeah, him."

"You know what it is, Loobie."

"What is it?"

"Perfection. That's what. I'm trying to go all the way on his next one. Deep-sea."

"Might go in too. Just might." Loobie chuckled. He'd always thought Aegus was too careful; not a guy to go for the ring.

"I mean it. I've never seen a sure thing before. This is what it looks like." Aegus decided at that moment. "Word has it, Loobie, you're inside his next one."

"Been there, done that. Already."

A fateful moment. Aegus hadn't known, and would have denied it, but he'd always been a believer just waiting to happen. It was like catching the mumps: the later in life, the worse.

After he'd hung up, Aegus called his banker. Then he called his broker. He wanted to be in early, because he knew there would be a long line. He had money in another film, but had to get more for this one. First sure thing, and he leaped for it like an ad man hearing Jesus' voice on his answering machine.

The new project was on the table and the money men were already queuing. Big money muscling up to the bar, Hollywood sharks smelling blood – a medium-rare talent-steak, a one-of-a-kind genius director, a can't miss. Aegus never blinked, even though the project was a western. The golden boy director had made the decade's best flick; so many wanted in, there was barely room for Aegus' fortune, supplemented by all he could borrow and all he could mortgage. After a twenty-year sobriety, he was intoxicated with recklessness.

Mat was eleven, a time when most kids begin distancing themselves from their parents, but he and Aegus had grown closer. As the boy assumed a careless sophistication, Marina too came closer to him. Mat was slender and blond, with patched hippy jeans and long, uncombed mane that he flipped over his shoulder. The old man caught while Mat tried his pitching arm; he hauled the youth dutifully to Dodgers' games during his flirtation with baseball. Mat played 1st base on the Hollywood brat-pack little league team, which performed badly but fielded the attractive long-haired sons of the rich and famous. Though it wasn't winning, girls followed the team, partied, poured packs of peanuts into bottles of orange Nehi and chewed sunflower seeds. Mat hit in the .400s and had the attention of higher leagues.

Aegus took Mat deep-sea fishing for yellow-fin off Cabo once a year. He gave him swimming and tap-dancing and guitar lessons. The family summered in Santa Barbara, where Aegus and Marina re-discovered one another; they became a real family. Mat did a few spots in commercials, never staying long enough to catch a sitcom, which suited Aegus – he preferred his son to be out of the industry. "Too many guys with a shake in one hand and a knife in the other. But if it's what you want, I'll show you around. Help you get your feet wet." Mat did want, but only if he failed to play ball for the Dodgers. He modeled a few times but grew bored.

"It's not like I pray for a movie career for him, even if he's got the looks. He's not very hungry," Aegus explained to Marina as she mixed evening martinis.

"He's just a boy, Aegus. Do what you're doing."

With expectation of financial bliss, Aegus' paternal instinct blossomed. It justified his madness: building a legacy for his son – the sure thing, all in, savings, investments, annuities... He took out a mortgage on both houses. He put the bite on all of his friends and relations. Marina fretted. "Are you sure about this? You've got a family, you know." Aegus waved her away.

Every dime he could lay hands on. When he could scrape no more, he visited a loan shark who hung around the industry: Vinnie-the-Tide. Aegus hit Vinnie, who he'd known since post-war years, for every cent the fat man would loan. Got a break on payback time.

Marina lost her housekeeper and cook, but Aegus didn't care: the money would be there in stacks to the ceiling when the film came in – the sure thing. Not death, not taxes, nothing was as sure as this. Aegus would bet his life on it. And he did. All in.

Production started and Aegus relaxed. All he had to do was watch.

And watch. The family retreated to Santa Barbara, where day after day Aegus and Mat made sandwiches and lemonade and went to the beach. Mat surfed; Aegus read trade magazines and gossip rags from under a ragged straw hat. Mat turned a happy twelve with his father. That went on for months. Then everything changed.

Production costs started to climb. And climb. The phone started to ring with reports that threw Aegus into rages. Loobie called sometimes two, three times a day.

"The director wants what? Are you serious? Wants what? Cowboy underwear? Who in hell is going to see it? With whose money?" Aegus would slam the receiver into its cradle and plow his fingers through his hair. "It's going to drive me goddam crazy, honey," he'd tell Marina.

Directorial perfection turned into obsession.

Mat went to the beach alone. Marina and especially Aegus were too tense to accompany him and couldn't offer a pretense of companionship. It was the beginning of lonely years, but Mat didn't yet know it.

News worsened. Aegus was on the phone constantly. Production slowed as costs rose. Hollywood tabloids began hinting at the director's lunacy. Multiple shots for everything; authenticity to no purpose... Perfection.

When industry tabloids hinted, people ducked. Constant ducking made people sweat. There was a lot of sweating. Loobie drove up to Santa Barbara twice a week. He had nearly as much as Aegus in this and took it as badly. Aegus carried a Maalox bottle in his coat pocket and started martinis in the morning before the phone rang.

Production costs soaring... Aegus ran his copy of *The Bear Shooter* on his Beta VCR. Good as ever. "I ask you, is this the same director?" he'd wonder. He'd pour another martini and sit up all night waiting for the sun to come up over the coastal mountains to lighten the ocean fifty yards below. "Has to be good."

Nothing had to be anything. "Nothing" came wrapped in an expensive package. Forty-four million dollars later, in 1980 the successor to the great film *The Bear Shooter*, sure thing *Heaven's Door,* opened to laughable reviews and empty theaters

The film grossed one and a half million dollars.

Now, in Dickeyville, Mat sat in the dark bathroom, bent over a porcelain bowl, tears glistening as he recalled. He could hear merriment outside, old people laughing through one door, riotous start of a party through the other. His stomach knotted as he fought down hurt.

Aegus hocked everything not bolted down to pay off Vinnie-the-Tide; there was no bankruptcy for shark loans. Marina couldn't help herself; she ridiculed Aegus, berated his foolhardiness. Her father, Loobie, couldn't help; he'd lost nearly as much. "Hell," Aegus said, "everyone I know is bleeding because of this." Aegus tried to borrow from old friends in the industry. He looked everywhere; nobody answered his calls. The bank padlocked his yacht. Vinnie called twice a day as loan payments came close; he'd loaned Aegus big bucks.

Mat's parents tried to shield him, but failed. In youthful confusion he transferred his fear into something he could control; in an obsessive way he came to view his baseball performance as a buffer to protect his family, especially his dad. His exhausted parents failed to see his preoccupation, and the boy's love for the game turned into desperation. Mat smacked balls in batting cages until his shoulders ached.

Aegus died by degrees, then all at once. He drank to oblivion. He hawked a nugget he'd worn around his neck since childhood, including on twenty-nine missions over Europe. Financially destroyed, he seemed intent on punishing himself by killing what was left. He was verbally abusive; pushed Marina to the living room floor when she mocked his drinking. Shamed, he started crying: Mat saw through the kitchen window. The boy watched, not understanding, his ears and cheeks burning at his father's humiliation.

Aegus, plowing his hair with his fingers, plowing as if he could plant a solution in the furrows within his thick locks... Marina stopped badgering him and started tiptoeing around the house when he drank. Finally she made no effort to conceal her bitterness from either her son or her husband. Loobie had never looked so old, so helpless.

Vinnie was leaning on Aegus to sell his houses, but the banks already had the notes. The family stayed as long as possible in Santa Barbara, and Aegus and Marina looked for breaks where there were none. Everything was on hold: their lives, their finances, their love. Aegus' pleas to relations resulted in twenty grand, enough to keep Vinnie at bay for a few days. The fights with Marina got worse.

"Don't worry, dad," Mat counseled, stuffing his jersey, cleats and glove into his dufflebag. "Four for four today, okay?"

"Sure, kid." Aegus put down his drink but didn't turn from the window. He'd been thinking of flak over Dresden and a city in flames.

"If I'm four-for-four, I'll wear my jersey wrong-side-out as I come up the drive. You'll know I got four hits and everything will be great."

"Sure, kid. Everything will be great."

"It will, dad. You'll see."

"Go get 'em."

Mat walked up the drive after the ball game to the sound of a scream. Fifteen minutes later an ambulance and two police cars were outside. Everyone said accident, too bad Aegus had been drinking, too bad about that cliff behind the yard, what a curse it was he was so despondent and got careless. Privately they suggested he was clever enough not to let it look like what it was. The family would get the insurance, a bunch of it. Unlike George Bailey, Aegus was worth more dead. Aegus had no Clarence. What risky flights over Europe had failed to do, a movie bomb accomplished.

Marina attempted to protect Mat, but Mat knew his father had jumped. And he knew he had done it because Mat had forgotten to wrong-side-out his jersey when he'd come up the drive.

Sick with shame, he told no one. He quit baseball, spent hours locked in his room. Ten thousand times during the quiet hours of night, he agonized about forgetting the jersey. He knew there was more to it than that, but in confusion and agony he played the endless loop in his mind, an endless saga of *what if?* Maybe inside-outing his jersey would have changed everything.

Vinnie took only what had been loaned, which was a bundle. That was a concession, but the fish was dead, right? Vinnie saved face. He'd ridden Aegus hard. He had to. But what the hell, he didn't have anything against the guy. This was just business. Vinnie was happy to get the money back. That was the last time he'd lend that kind of dough to someone in the flicks.

Marina and her son kept the Hollywood mansion and scraped by on small change. Blustery-brave with the boy, Marina hinted that secret finances would arrive like welcome wagons as soon as "that movie received its due". At some point in teenage, Mat emerged from his stupor. He understood that delusions, no matter how powerful, couldn't hold calamity at bay. Only indifference could do that.

He spread out his Bushmill's Irish Whiskey towel and waited for girls to come to him. A loner by nature, indifferent, with striking looks, he had an aura of immunity, a quality that drew their attention. He seemed to know things about life he was hardly aware of and most boys would never learn. Nurtured by the sea, surfing or swimming out, he liked the feel of deep water. Not overly imaginative, he was the only kid of his crowd who would swim at night, sometimes a couple hundred yards offshore. He was a strong swimmer and the L.A. sea was warm, the swell gentle. It was good to tread water in a dark sea and turn to watch the beach fires. He'd seen big sharks around Point Conception when his father had taken him fishing, but didn't regard swimming to be a matter of courage; he was simply unafraid.

Girls with coltish legs pulled into faded jeans, thin tanned arms swinging casually from sleeveless blouses, salty blond hair pulled back into pony tails, thought a good deal of his indifference, which mirrored their own. To them, behind quick cold eyes that seemed to miss nothing, he seemed an embodiment of tragedy, of cold beauty destined to be pulled beneath emotional black waters by something primitive and inexorable. They watched him from across the fires and whispered secrets among themselves, laughter sometimes skipping over their voices like sparks flaring in air; then they would sink into private, inaccessible quiet. Standing in front of the flames dripping wet, with a towel hung over his thin but strong shoulders and nubbled with goose bumps, he would be chosen by one, and he would lead her into the lee of some cold dune, shadows shifting and stretching far into darkness from the breeze-churned fire behind. He would spread his lucky towel on the sand and kiss her salty soft lips and press against her goose-bumpy flesh, hot but also cool. In the dark of shadowed driftwood their young bodies would play to indifferent rhythms of surf and everything would be suspended for them as they discovered unfathomable freedom that could not be recaptured; the breathless mystery and giddy fear of summer nights when they realized that they were beyond the reach of parental control... It killed few, though for him it fed an indifference that was like a malaise.

So passed an early phase of his life. After quitting baseball he could stop grieving for his father; only his mother's fear of poverty would affect him. There wasn't much money left from the insurance, but it was enough for a small trust which, by an inflexible ethic, Mat rebuffed for years as "blood money". They rescued the Hollywood house but not Marina's spirit. No fool, she existed on interest from the insurance settlement and inheritance after Loobie's passing two months following Aegus'. Maintaining a carefree demeanor, she watched and lamented every dollar that disappeared. Other than capricious and alarming extravagances such as for Mat's engagement party, she nurtured a meanness about money that made Mat afraid of it while breeding unconscious envy of others.

A junior high psychologist and private shrink tried to figure why he hadn't cried over his dad's death, citing delayed burial syndrome, sublimation, substitution, whatever the fad-of-the-day. They figured it would come out sometime; it did from time to time... like now.

He leaned back on the bathtub edge. A moment of vulnerability when the past laid siege to the present...

His mother had tried to get him into the industry, saying "it all has to work out, all the disaster and bitterness" and the best way was to follow his stars. This brought him to the present, a time when he owed money for a wedding ring he wished he'd never bought.

Well, maybe not that. He needed to think; to get home. Wiping his eyes and sniffing, feeling slightly ridiculous for his emotional outburst, even though it had been private, he stood up, realizing again that he had to get to that phone. Opening the second bathroom door, he stepped into a party bigger than the previous night's.

20

The room was so crowded he had no space to move. Faces turned toward him, and several people started to cheer, then started hog-calling. Mat nodded miserably, tried a sickly smile. "Hey-ya, Mat!" He heard Nels' voice. Hands reached toward him, and he shook them. One hand held out a small glass of something dark, and he took it down in one pull. It burned. Good whiskey. "Nice work, today," somebody said. "Way to stick with 'er."

"I'm so hungry," he said in a voice no one seemed to hear. The alcohol spread like poison in his stomach but felt good. Just the one drink, he thought. Last night had been too much; just the one. He saw Verne and Bascom huddling and laughing across the room with other men. It was one reason to get drunk. Maybe this was Mat and Verne's night – he was spoiling for it. Just one more drink, to calm his nerves.

He plunged into the noisy, milling crowd of Dickeys and Winders and friends who must have numbered one hundred or more, counting those outside and packed on the porches. He took a beer handed to him and tried to make his way toward the phone in the adjacent room but couldn't pass anyone without his free hand getting pumped or a cheek getting pecked or being told how handsome he was by some matron or hugged or introduced to someone he had no intention of remembering or being asked how he could survive without eating meat (he wondered how he could survive without eating anything) or being asked to tell "all about Hollywood" as if you could do so in one hundred words or less or as if he knew everything about Hollywood anyway. Some mustachioed uncle laughed in his face with boozy breath while telling about how he'd had to "go in" to face the Horror back in '62, as if Mat cared. Before he had crossed halfway to the dining room Mat had already reached for another beer and taken another shot, this time peppermint Schnapps offered by a shy-smiling lady not more than seventeen, who had a siren's cupid-lips and wore a gingham dress with high-button collar which looked like it came straight from costume, *Little House on the Prairie*; a girl with the sweetest, most cryptically-sad smile that Mat had ever seen, and he knew if he were drunk enough he would want to cry with her, hug her innocence to touch what he missed, the sweet bitterness of a dead father and lost mother. He passed further into the crowd until he came face to face with Ma Dickey carrying a tray with eight or nine plastic cups of draft beer on it. He drained his bottle and took one of them.

"Mat, I've been looking for you. I've got to say, I'm not too pleased."

"I saw the model layout in one of the back rooms."

"Oh that. Pa built it in his spare time after we married."

"I saw the pig in the train station."

"It's a boar, Mat. You're comparing pussycats to lions."

"You said I'm in trouble?"

"Your telling both Reverend Weems and Reverend Rantin that you'd be getting married in their churches. I'd have thought you'd ask Daphne before committing to something so big."

"I didn't say anything like that." He felt the drinks working on him, working in a bad way, and fought back.

Mother Dickey seemed exasperated. "I personally heard you say so to Reverend Weems today; he's here, ask him. Then I just bumped into Reverend Rantin and he says you stopped at the church and pledged to join. Really, Mat, you just can't go on promising things to people and not following up. That's not how it's done around here."

"Well, this place can... can just..."

"There you go again. It's off the subject but I've been meaning to say. It was that damn – pardon my French – Sinclair Lewis."

"What was?"

"*Main Street*. Before that, everyone pretty much knew small towns had about the same ratio of bad and good people as cities. After *Main Street* everyone thought Midwest small towns were enclaves of the small-minded, bigoted and malicious."

"Has it ever occurred to you nobody gives a – "

"You travel much? Europe? Asia? Africa?"

"Been to Australia. Cuba. India. Christmas Island. Mexico of course. Recently the Bahamas. I've never been much the traveler. Never wanted to. Can I get a beer around here?"

"In your hand. As I was saying, we're all pretty much shaped by where we travel or live. I was in New York for 15 years."

"You?"

"Sure. Wanted to dance and sing. Wound up as a secretary. One day Pa came and fetched me. Said he'd waited long enough, since we were high school sweethearts."

Mat thought of Ma's ears on stage – a sobering thought – just as a matron passed behind him and pinched his ass.

"What I'm saying is, to absorb a culture you have to be receptive."

"Culture. This is a pretty white-bread place to live. Any other cultures around here?"

"Pretty much country culture." She swung her arm to present the crowd. "Mostly German Catholics. But not all."

"People a little prejudiced?"

"You mean race? I see. Would you say a Mexican village without black people is prejudiced? a town in Turkey without Japanese? Or does it count only in an American town? You Californians are supposed to be the sophisticates and skeptics. Someone says 'diversity is good' and your little noggins bob in unison."

"See, that's what – "

"Fact is, Mat, diversity is neither good nor bad; it is just a thing. Anyway, my cousin's married to a Hispanic man. There are a few folks here tonight who weren't born in the US."

Mat glanced around. "Yeah, but everyone's alike."

"I don't think so."

He shrugged.

"So are you prejudiced? Against people in the Midwest?"

"I was just thinking – "

"There's a few bachelors here live with other bachelors. A few gals live with their 'best friends'. So what? What's there to say? It's just people, and people here aren't meaner or kinder than anyone anywhere else. You've got to absorb the culture. Whatever it is."

"Everyone around here is pretty good at advice on life. I wish they'd quit messing with mine." He drank his full cup.

"People get set in their ways the whole world over."

"More country wisdom. I wish Daphne were here."

Ma smiled wanly. "Never wish for something that increases your chances for a heart attack."

"*What?*"

"Country wisdom. One more thing. You got three or four calls today when you were out."

"Daphne?" – He was relieved to hear that she'd called: he wanted to talk to her, wanted to hear her say she loved him, something familiar. *Maybe* he wanted to hear; he didn't know.

"No, some gruff-sounding guy. What was his name? Vincent De Hyde? That ring a bell?"

"Vinnie-the-Tide called? That's no good. So it was Vinnie that talked with Pa. How'd he get the number? What'd you tell him? Not your address, I hope. Not where I'm at." He felt stone-cold sober, but that feeling passed quickly enough. He drained his beer.

"Why wouldn't I tell your friends how to find you? Honestly, you're the funniest man... Here's Daphne's number." She handed him a crumpled slip of paper.

"I know her cell."

"It's not working there. This is the hotel. Don't jump at everything you see or hear, all right? I worry about you. How you feel about yourself." She patted his cheek.

"I'm sorry. I can't talk now. I gotta do something."

Desperation assisted Mat's plunge through the crowd toward the phone. He managed to avoid outstretched arms and overt expressions of new-found familial affection and dialed Vinnie's number. An answering machine clicked on to say that Vinnie had had to go away on business in the Midwest; if the caller cared to leave a message, he would get back to him as soon as he'd taken care of a few things.

Yeah, my knees, Mat thought. He remembered that Daphne had left her parents' phone number on Mat's answering machine "just in case" they got separated. So Vinnie had a number and an address. Said he'd hunt a runner to the ends of the earth as a matter of honor... which meant Dickeyville, pretty much past the world's end.

Mat had to get out.

But he wasn't so shaken that he couldn't secure his fortune, even if he had to spend it in a wheelchair. This thing with cousin Heywood... it would make millions; a sure thing. Mat tried to call his agent, but Ike was out of the office. Getting another answering machine, Mat covered the receiver and spoke quietly: "Ike, baby, I'm onto something with a guy name of Hollywood Heywood, something like you've never seen in your life... bigger than Sinatra. Imagine something so big there's no venue for it, get me? I'm talking bigger than the Beatles, bigger than the apocalypse and just as well-attended. Listen, I'm crapping my britches here because we could sign this thing today.

"Ike, something else came up. You loan me a few bones to cover a debt? You know I'm good for it. Call me, about both things. Thanks." He repeated the Dickey's phone number.

Then he tried the number to Daphne's Des Moines hotel room. The office said she'd checked out. What to do, Mat thought. I want to go home but can't, because of Vinnie; he may be on his way. Mat set down the receiver. It occurred to him he had nowhere to go.

He heard uproar and absently looked around. He spotted people surging toward the front porch and had a sudden hope that Daphne had arrived. He pushed forward to reach the commotion, but couldn't move aside bodies.

The couple of drinks had been just right for his nerves. He would have felt almost human, if not for his hunger and new fear. The thought of the fat man and his little pistol... It was nothing personal to Vinnie: Mat's would be an objective execution.

He shook out his arms the way you might shake sea water out of your hair. The drinks helped, but it would do no good to get stinking drunk like last night. Getting blitzed was out: his mood was wrong; he knew he'd go right after Verne.

Vinnie said it was genetic, in Mat's blood to lose. Vinnie was right.

In front of Mat's face was the back of a head. He tapped a shoulder, and a young man turned. "What's up, mister?" he asked.

"I just wanted to see what's going on. I think my fiancée got home."

The young guy, maybe twenty with a boyish face, the type that gets carded at bars until he's thirty-five, shook his head. "Naw, it's my professor. He's telling about the guy we filmed today."

"A professor? What's he doing in a place like Dickeyville?"

The kid shrugged. "It's his hometown and he's got a project. He usually drags a few students wherever he goes. He likes an audience."

"Someone like you."

"Six of us. Grad students. We've been working on a set since last semester. Man, it'd curl your blood to see this thing." He did a double-take. "You from around here? Don't look like it."

" L.A."

"In pictures?" The kid boxed Mat's face between forefingers and thumbs. "Great face. Damn!" He held out his hand. "My name's Willander and I'm a cameraman. Well, I shoot for the University film department; it's a start. Are you connected?"

Mat smiled and nodded, starting to leave; then he paused. A familiar voice came from the next room. "Who's the professor?"

"'Hecklin' Heywood Dickey. Probably the funniest professor at the University. Everybody loves him. The guy 'd do anything for a laugh. He's the cocky sonuvabitchin' prankster to end all. If he gets his teeth into someone – and he does every semester – he never lets go. I've seen him bring students to their knees."

"Tenacious?"

"Like a pit bull hanging from your nuts." The kid started to turn.

"Whoa. What's that set, Willander?"

"A project started by students before my time. Cement and plaster mixed with granite powder; skeletons bonded right into stone. They're fighting, and it's too grisly for words. You gotta see it. And you should see what we caught today with hidden cameras."

The guy's nose started twitching, and Mat understood that he was being sniffed at again. "Today?"

"Yeah. Suckered some poor hick. I was having lunch so I've only seen footage on the editor. Say, you *are* in flicks. I've seen your face before, and I know it was in a movie because I never forget a thing I see on film. That's how my mind works. A steel trap."

"You say a set?"

"No, a steel trap."

"No. I mean you work on a set."

"On a grant. Professor 'Hearty' Heywood Dickey, they call him – well, he calls himself – modeled it after an old Wyandotte Indian skeleton he's got. Which he shouldn't have, but does, and he's got the skeleton hung in his office as a hat rack. He's named it 'Cigar'. Get it? Smithsonian guys'll be after him for that eventually. Anyway, someone in the art department at the University welded the wing bones from patio-umbrella spines."

"A fifteen-foot tall angel-dinosaur?"

"You know about it?" The guy laughed. "It's not completely clever," he conceded. "We gutted a condemned house without the shell falling down and killing us."

"Gutted the whole house?"

"For a set. On a grant. Didn't you say you were in film?"

"Yeah."

"Which ones?"

"Went straight to DVD."

"This project's worthwhile. It's a great Halloween joke around town. Started for a class project and got out of hand. Good set for a grad film. Should be able to scrounge a couple grants."

"Grants. Great."

"Kinda incredible."

"Anything for a laugh," Mat said, smiling weakly.

"That Heywood,"

"Heh. What kind of idiot would believe something so foolish?"

"Everybody knows. Only a Dickeyville hick would be gullible enough to fall for it. This guy's the first and I'd hate to be him. Fundamentalist hayseed with an IQ of fifty."

"Heh-heh."

"Just some local yokel."

"Heh-heh. Heh-heh."

"You gotta get out there and hear Professor Heywood Dickey tell this story. Doing it right now. You'll die, man. He's the funniest sonuvabitch in the whole department. Nobody makes bigger fools of people than he does. Crusty pro at telling stretchers to the rubes."

"Heh-heh. Heh-heh. Heh-heh."

As Willander chuckled, Mat pushed through the crowd to get to his room. Ignoring slaps on the back and hearty handshakes, he paused once to take an offered beer which he drained in two pulls. Releasing his grip on himself, he was buzzed instantly.

Everyone seemed to know him whether they knew him or not – an awkward notoriety based on gullibility. He was not particularly a man to be embarrassed; mostly he was indifferent to derisiveness, because he'd experienced little of it; he felt secure. But he burned at the idea of falling twice in the same day for not just stupid jokes, but really, really stupid ones; flummoxed by hayseeds he looked down on. The idea of the professor playing the heart-broken rube for him and then telling everyone... The hicks would laugh him out of town and he'd be glad to go. Daphne should never marry a fool.

Starved, hung over, confused, far from home… understandable having been so stupid. They'd all know about it before the night ended. Nature of a small town…

He thought about Heywood as he shouldered through partiers. "Hollywood", right. In California for basic training and these guys think he's the toast of L.A. Mat passed a young guy bent over, nauseated, leaning against the wall outside the bathroom.

"I don't feel so good," the kid offered. He had on a Hawaiian shirt.

"Welcome to the club."

A hand caught Mat's arm – the fat, smiling woman he'd seen earlier. Tonight she wore a navy pantsuit that fairly clung to her body. It resembled an automobile seat cover. "Mat, so glad to catch you. I just heard they nailed you pretty good with the boar joke."

He started to pull away.

"But a guy like you didn't really bite on that angel bones gag. Hell, nobody falls for that, not even me." She chuckled self-deprecatingly.

"Listen, I've got to go. What did you say your name is?"

"Lana. Lana Winder."

"Pleased to meet you again, Lana. Now if you'll excuse me – "

"Wait. You said you'd read my manuscript. I have it here." She unhitched a shoulder bag, lifted out a thin folder and handed it to him. "You don't have to read it now because it's pretty long – twenty-one pages. Some stuff is missing and happens between the pages so you got to imagine. I was thinking of putting it in but I figure Hollywood guys have big imaginations to think what goes on between pages."

"Big imaginations," Mat nodded. "They're notorious for that."

"I hear they just throw around money to anyone with a good idea. I've got a great idea about these people who fall in love, then something comes between them. I'm not sure what. But then they get together again towards the end. Read the opening – the part where they fall in love – and tell me what you think."

Escape blocked, Mat sighed and peeled back the binder cover to read: BIG BROADS IN LOVE, by Lana Winder.

"Interesting title."

"Think so? It's just my working title. Read the first page. I'm really proud of how it gets your attention. As my friend Martha says, it feathers your fancy when you read it. I should warn you," she added, her face reddening, "it's a bit spicy."

Mat smiled weakly and read: "Like a covey of destroyers, she thrust her proud beauties toward his panting hand palms. He took them under appraisal feeling the nipples harden like arteries. Their faces met in the middle. His tongue charged out like a rare black rhino painted pink, to chatter squirrel-like upon her hot burning fiery lava lips. She responded to the giblets of his caresses, tongue writhing like a spongy sexy snake into his suddenly full mouth with the words unspoken, I love you, I love you. She was big, really big, and he felt the beginnings of love. 'I want your *****,' she said. 'I want it now.'"

"Hmm," Mat said. "Very interesting. Quite... um, powerful."

Her cheeks were flushed. "That's it exactly – powerful. I'm not really sure yet whether to go for the best-seller crowd or stay with the 'arty' types. I hope the publishers don't want gratuitous cheapening of it just to cater to the public, if you know what I mean."

He didn't know what to answer. She was enthusiastic and had a nice smile, in a sad sort of way. He hadn't had many friends, even fewer women friends, but one he'd liked was a fat chick who was always on the make for stud muffins. "It's hard to find a hard-body who likes 'em fat," she'd say. "And when you do, there're lots of other fat chicks who want to take him away."

"I don't think these days it's necessary to use asterisks instead of anatomical words," Mat spoke up. "What word did you mean? Or maybe you better not say."

She cocked her head. "What are asterisks?"

"Don't worry."

"I used to be married. I'm sure I would've worried in those days."

"Sorry."

"He left me 'cause I'm fat. Broke my heart."

"Umm, that's too bad. Wish I could help."

"It's not your fault."

"No, I had nothing to do with it. I was in L.A. and didn't know."

"You probably have no fault in this."

"I never saw you before yesterday."

"Then you're likely okay."

"Probably."

Someone tapped Mat on the shoulder and he turned to see Father Dickey wearing his sleeveless t-shirt and carrying two beers. "Thought you might need these, Mat," he said.

Mat took both cans. Two Leineys. "Thanks. I just might."

"I thought you would. That damn Heywood's telling everyone you fell for his angel-demon fossil spoof. That lyin' sonuvabitch."

"Heh-heh."

"What I wanted to ask is, were you in my string room earlier? Someone was in there."

"I was. Didn't know I shouldn't. Sorry."

"It's all right if it was you, but it would really grab my gonads if it was someone else."

Mat shrugged, feeling more oblivious than before to what was going on around him. Oblivion felt good; he'd have to try some more of it. "I was looking for the end," he lied. "Couldn't find a thing." He liked lying right now; it seemed truer than the truth. "How'd you know I was in there?"

"Molecules rearranged."

"Thought so." He leaned close to Father Dickey and whispered. "Pretty much everyone's commented on the way I smell after using your soap. Does it smell bad?"

The old man sniffed. "Smells damn good to me at the price of fifty cents a cake."

"You mean 'bar'?"

"No, a cake is what they call 'em. Hey, there's Elmo Winder. I gotta talk to him about my bacon shares."

The old man disappeared into the crush of bodies, and Mat returned to the woman. He suddenly felt talkative. "What were you saying? What's your name again?"

"Lana. Look, I'm kind of drunk."

"Who isn't?" He offered her one of the beers.

She shook her head. "I drink the low-calorie kind. Anyway it's silly, my talking to you."

"Why?" He tipped up a Leiney and drank until he finished it. He felt memories of his father sink away, like a black-mood submarine.

"You're so handsome and everyone's just dying to talk to you. All of the women."

"So why aren't they? Seems like you're the one talking to me."

"They're shy because you're pretty. I got divorced not long ago."

"I'm supposed to get married soon – " her eyes seemed tiny, like a pair of olive slices dropped on a pizza; homely, but the smile was nice " – to someone who used to look like a Winder and Dickey."

"I know. To firecracker Daphne."

"That's not the Daphne I know."

Lana shrugged. "She used to look different."

Over the din, speaking a little loudly, Mat expounded on Mother Dickey's nose theory. "... So that's why all the funny ears and noses in Dickeyville." Instantly the din died. The convivial chatter ceased. Silence. Mat looked around. People were looking at him.

A voice spoke loudly from across the room: "What funny noses?"

Mat quickly went to get another beer. Jeeze, he thought as he glanced at the crowd: they're pretty thick-skinned when it comes to joking other people.

By the time he'd gotten back from the kitchen with a few more brewskies, he was well along. He sat down next to Lana again.

"I have a fall-back plan," she said. "I wrote a cookbook. French."

"You were in France?"

"Do I look like a damn frog?"

"Well, you look qualified to write a French cookbook – no, that didn't come out right."

She giggled. " I shouldn't change the subject, but do you know you smell kind of divine?

"Everyone says that."

She cocked her head and batted her eyelashes. "So will you do it?"

"Damn right," he said. "What?"

"Sponsor my screenplay."

"Oh, that? Sure. Can't miss Academy Award winner." He straightened an imaginary bow tie. "And in the category of Best Screenplay, for *Big Broads in Love*, we have Lana! We also have some other screenplays, but – the hell with them. Everyone knows the winning screenwriter is Lana. Come up and get your Academy Award, Miz Lana."

Lana turned her head coyly and bowed from the waist. "Academy members, television viewers and all you important people who idolize me, first I want to thank my good friend Mister Mat Roper who got me started. Mat, come up here and take a bow."

Mat laughed. "You have to remember how many of these things get pitched to directors and producers every year."

"I'll bet there are hundreds," Lana postulated.

"Every day."

"I'll only get my hopes up a little," she said.

"We'll get each other's backs."

"Say something sweet."

"For a fat girl you don't sweat much."

"Shucks."

21

"I gotta eat now," Mat mumbled, grabbing his beer and sitting up. "I'm a little hungry."

As he pushed through the throng, a familiar voice stopped him. "Feeling better?"

Mat looked into Verne's mocking face. "I'm King for a day. I feel better and better every time I'm crowned royal buffoon."

"Just curious. Don't bite my head off."

"I feel like this town squeezed me in a lovelock."

Verne's mouth jerked slightly. "You're such a prodigy. You been here what, two days? And you've already got it figured."

"I feel like I've been here a month, and how in hell long does it take to know? I feel like I stepped in a pile of Dickeyville."

"These people might be a little intimidated by you. Ma and Pa Dickey, here comes the unknown fiancé of their only child. The others – just a bunch of small town yokels happy to welcome a new in-law. You're taller and look better than most of us. Don't have the big ears or noses you seem to think are so funny. It isn't like we haven't tried to make you welcome."

"Boar hunt and angel dinosaur bones… I feel like I've come home."

"Heywood goes over the line by poking fun after he tricks people. Most of us don't like making people eat it after they've stepped in it, but that's his business. I'd have headed off the angel bones with Uncle Heywood if I'd thought there was a remote chance you'd fall for it. None of us yokels did. Nobody else for that matter, not even his artsy-fartsy film students."

Mat set down his drink. He stared into Verne's smirk. Voices around the two faded. "You might have canceled the boar hunt, too."

Verne's smirking didn't abate. "There is that, isn't there? I misjudged you, Roper. You're not half the man I took you for."

It was coming up now in Mat's blood. "Go ahead. Just go ahead."

"Not many outsiders even go on the Horror hunt. Some people felt it would suit a diver and movie-maker fine. Let's just say, Roper," Verne paused and looked around the room at others, "that they thought you'd have the balls and the spirit to hang 'em on."

"I haven't got much spirit for playing the fool. You wanna play some other game?"

A further thought momentarily erased the expression on Verne's face. "It's only ourselves that make us play the fool, man. You know that. Same way we play the loner. You and I know better 'n most."

"This game's crooked as snake shit on a rollercoaster."

"You're the only one playing it now."

"The play I got in mind will make *you* wiser."

Verne shook his head, "I don't think so."

"Come on."

It hinged on the moment. Mat was a large man, strong, a swimmer, built lean. Men didn't challenge him. He wasn't intimidated by Verne, who was heavier. Mat ached to hit him, hard. But somewhere on some level beyond drunkenness he knew that what was getting to him was more than just Verne. It was all of it: confusion about Daphne, marriage, career, his father, Vinnie, the DEA, being a public fool, jealousy that the fucking hicks had something he didn't...

"I've had a bellyful of your arrogant California shit," said Verne. "You been one prima donna, lording it over us. Tomorrow morning: be dressed at six. I'll be here."

"*Now.*"

Verne shook his head. "You think I'd fight my cousin's drunk fiancé in my uncle's house? You want to fight, tomorrow we'll head for someplace where it isn't spectator sport. You and me. There's young people here. We don't act like that in front of kids."

"No, you act worse. I'll be ready."

Verne started to turn, then hesitated. "Nobody here holds anything against outsiders," he added. "Just stay away from me tonight."

Mat was tensed, the muscles in his back bunched; then the mean drunk in him slipped out like a snake leaving its skin. Anger went as quickly as it had come on. He also felt some other, more subtle shift, as if on some level he'd moved on, though he couldn't say to what.

The party went back to being a party. Nobody seemed upset. A

Winder kid, maybe in late-teens, brought Mat another shot of pep-permint Schnapps. "Uncle Verne sent this, Mister Roper. He's a pretty good guy, once you get to know him."

Mat snorted but took the drink.

"I doubt anyone ever had the balls to stand up to him like you."

"That's not necessarily a virtue, you know."

The kid scuffed one foot. "Listen, about the angel bones – "

"Thanks for the drink."

"Yeah, but did Heywood – "

Lana, the fat woman, hooty-hooted him from a couch and waved him to join her, but Mat, waving back, pushed through the crowd and paused by the dining room table to lift a Leiney from the case set there. He tried the phone. Dead.

In his room he pulled off his shoes and lay back on the bed. He was half-drunk; more than half. The Dickey ancestors, quiet as ever, watched from the wall. Regal noses and ears. Or just plain hanging honkers and flaps. Either way, they seemed disapproving of his con-duct. Seemed to disapprove that Mat Roper might marry their proge-ny. He sat up and looked closely at them, old pictures, tintype portraits and, from a later time, studio photographs. He was more aware than ever that, as well as a mate, you married a family. And he wanted no part of this one.

What was left for him? He couldn't go home, not now. But go where? The shark's arms were as long as the law's. And that was another matter, the law. Someone had fixed him with a smuggling rap. He couldn't afford a lawyer. He could just see it: court-appointed pub-lic defender telling him to plead guilty to a lesser charge, like drug-dealing instead of smuggling. The lawyer, on his first case, too young to shave, twenty-four, just graduated from a place called California Internet Institute of Law, website two years old, courses taught by "professionals" who couldn't pass the bar, visiting Mat in jail because Mat hadn't been able to post bail, a baby-faced gremmie flopping open papers he'd never seen before that minute, perusing them for maybe sixty seconds, then announcing: "For a plea-bargain you'll only get five years, Roper, ten max. We go to trial, you'll probably do twen-ty. They got four drug dealers ready to cut a deal with the DA for reduced time. They say you masterminded the whole thing." Then the guy would set down his pen in a manner meant to be meaningful and

add: "I personally don't like drug kingpins. But I gotta do my best to –
what do they call it? Oh yeah, *defend* you."

What do they call a guy who graduates number 124 in a law class
of 124? Your attorney.

During Mat's trial the guy would have a nervous breakdown and
confess that he'd gone into the legal profession only to please his mom
on her deathbed; he'd really wanted to take up ballet.

"But I'm innocent!" Mat yelled, sitting up in bed.

It wasn't like he had anywhere to go; so he could go anywhere.
There'd be no trail; he had no roots except in L.A. Pull off a disap-
pearing act? There were always women who'd help, always had been.
He thought of the Virgin Islands or maybe back to the Bahamas.
Maybe Maui, Kauai; Bali. Sitting on a white-sands beach with a rich
leather lady, sipping margaritas, water so clear that at forty feet you
could make out tropical fish and coral clusters; later, white cotton deck
clothing for lobster and champagne cocktails aboard her sailboat…
The image got hazy; he saw himself paraded around like one of those
Brit or Australian trophies adored by rich divorcées – "Matthew, darling, bring me a mai tai, would you? And put a little umbrella in it. You
know how I like little umbrellas in my mai tais, Matthew. There's a
good boy. Do remember the little umbrella, won't you?"

She would languish on deck in her string bikini while the sun
destroyed her skin; lie in a deck chaise with the *Wall Street Journal*. And
the sun would dry her out, dry up the juice and laughter and novelty,
and she would resent him.

He glanced at the window to see if snow still fell. A little, lighter.

He'd turned down the gilded prison before. Good when it was
good, when he was twenty-two, though the heiresses were younger
then too. Not leather ladies, but healthy young women with white
skin under bikinis that drove college boys mad. The indifferent and
immune, the young and rich and beautiful lying bronzed and oblivious and well-oiled on beach towels brought from St Tropez or Monaco
or a secret spot on the *Golfe du Lion* where the rich played, topless,
sometimes bottomless, under midday sun, cooled by sweat and salty
air… Mat could do that again – slather on someone's suntan lotion.
It was, he thought ruefully, what he knew best. Do it until he no longer could – a leather man. The beachfront restaurants and bars were
populated by slightly balding guys whose looks had been legendary

in their time. The leather ladies got old and died and never left anything to the beach bums they loved; if they didn't have children, they
left all to their nieces or nephews – revenge for having bought love.
The blond guys with white pants and British accents and good tans
and black t-shirts or Hawaiian shirts bumming drinks and hustling
disinterested young rich girls in Miami Beach and Maui and Malibu
and Santa Cruz and a hundred other places, envying younger guys
who took their places in the seaside nightclubs with roofs bright with
seagull shit... California sea lions barked on floating docks. The aging
playboys waited for that one and only, wealthy sweet-hearted girl who
would rescue them from themselves, the girl who'd love them for who
they were, whoever that was. She would look just like the girl from
tomorrow night, or the night after that. It was hard to tell... There was
the sea. The ocean's many faces, summer-translucent-blue to winter
gray, from gentle swells to foam-topped whitecaps; diving and snorkel-
ing or walking the shore... Deep-V motor cruisers plunging through
northwestern swells, anchored parties aboard yachts, sailboats, wind
surfing... Winter rainsqualls and summer fog; sunsets off Catalina;
deep-sea fishing, albacore out in the shipping lanes, abalone diving
by the Monterey Peninsula and north to Fort Bragg; cold-water surfing and sail-boarding, driving the Oregon coast in winter, camping
deserted miles of the Olympic Peninsula, sailing the San Juans, nights
with the SOBBs... It came back to that.

And no snow.

But: there was no appeal to looking over his shoulder for Vinnie;
waiting for that little bullet in the heart on some desolate Baja beach...
Mat had spent twenty-nine years perfecting an attitude of no concerns.
Too late to start a new career.

Daphne could be the solution: rich, good-looking after plastic surgery, hog calls... Escaping Dickeyville, little town with twisty streets
and twisted jokes, she'd go wherever he wanted. She didn't care, as
long as he was there.

But her family – Ma and Pa Dickey. The uncles and aunts and
cousins. And Verne and Nels and Brodie and Bascom and all the others, who were even worse. Crazy beer-swilling hicks with muscles by
Jake. Being an outsider for the rest of his life...

Daphne could loan him money to hold off Vinnie.

Couldn't do that, take money from her. He could work and send checks from somewhere.

That was it. Yes. But... the hat didn't fit either. None did. No suit tailored for Mat Roper.

He climbed from the bed and went to the bathroom. He looked in the mirror for signs of aging around his eyes. Staring, mind alcohol-hazy, perhaps swaying slightly, he saw pallor, vagueness not so much a sign of physical malady but of spiritual malaise. It wasn't that his life had been disjointed, though it had been; it was the indecision. Answers came by patience. But... no time for that. If he married Daphne, he'd regret it. If he didn't, he'd regret it.

Mat picked up the cake of soap and looked at it: better in the bright glare of the bathroom's light to think about something other than being decisive. The soap was round, slightly opaque. It felt waxy to the touch and foamed poorly but left his hand moist and clean. He sniffed the cake; the scent took him back to some indistinct hour and day he could not recall but had pleasant connotations. He sniffed more deeply – a sweet-minty odor, entirely pleasant. He wondered why people had commented on the fine aroma.

He dried his hands and combed his blond hair, carefully and drunk-enly lifting curls over his forehead and letting them dangle there, sexy, above one eyebrow. Like most preening drunken men, he winked into the mirror – his best buddy.

The party had grown in a half hour, the crush was worse. Outside younger Winders and Dickeys and others were whooping, squealing, laughing. That nobody seemed upset at the youths' boisterous drunk-enness didn't strike Mat as peculiar: in Hollywood of his young years worse than alcohol and marijuana had been tolerated.

Snowballs thudded off the roof and outside walls, followed by a bel-low from Pa Dickey somewhere in the house. Mat pushed through the guests, taking what was offered to drink and hunting for snacks, ignor-ing the few who asked about Heywood's dinosaur bones.

Big smile on her face, Ma informed Mat that the Reverend Weems had telephoned to inquire after him and remind him the feast of heav-en awaits those who partake of the banquet and thank him for com-mitting himself to his church. Hearing no trace of irony in her voice, Mat snorted. She said also the "horse doobers" were long gone and smiled foolishly, pleased. Mat didn't care about food.

"Can I fetch you coffee?" she added.

"No thanks." He looked around, recognizing some faces. "Tea?"

"Not a tea drinker. I'm fine."

"So what keeps you going when you wake up?"

"Not sure. Indifference? What about you?

She didn't even have to think. "Fear."

People kept arriving with cases of beer or bottles of liquor. One of the girls, neither Winder or Dickey, brought Mat a peppermint Schnapps snow-cone and, after he finished it, he went outside for another, joining for a few minutes the teenagers crowding the yard.

New snow had fallen over old and everything was capped in white mounds. Under the streetlights very light snow fell delicately; "pixie dust" as a blond child in blue snowsuit called it. He talked to Mat from atop a wooden crate while building a "snow-troll", a six-foot monster dubbed Thor. He mashed in a couple of tennis balls to serve as buggy eyes and stuck on beer caps he'd scrounged. A running commentary, voice muffled by a woolen wrap… Mat listened, charmed, until his butt chilled. The boy remained as oblivious to teenagers in the yard as they were to him and still spun his story after Mat had gone.

The sky seemed like black cloth, close, soft and yielding. Cars and pickups kept arriving, sliding on slicked pavements. Folks came into the Dickeys', bags in hand, yelling Merry Christmas though the holiday was still a couple weeks off. Wearing stupid-flap hats that made Mat laugh, they, seeming to know him, mocked his "beach attire."

Mat's legs felt sometimes rubbery, at other times wooden. He lurched back into the house where everything seemed to float past him – sure sign he was in his cups, he thought lucidly; but then that was gone. Beside the coat hooks just inside a poorly-lit porch, he was snatched and pinned to the wall by two young women, a homely pair, who laughed as he struggled to escape, and he blinked hard to see if his eyes were tricking him but, no, they were twins, and he vaguely remembered them – Dickey-Winder hybrids with Winder ears and Dickey noses but lovely long blond hair, like palomino horse tails, he thought, giggling. They nuzzled his face with icy cheeks and giggled back most appealingly, teasing his hair with busy fingers and laughing until he laughed, few words passing except nonsense and Ooh, you're so cute or I could just gobble up those ears, as they ruffled his curls and tweaked his nostrils and bit his chin and pulled his earlobes, until he felt suffocated like a puppy or kid mauled by some favorite aunt. When he at last pushed free and stumbled through the pantry door, he was woozy as a child leaving a roller coaster.

Immediately he was met by Bascom, who gave him a hug as he came into the kitchen, and Mat was hugging back, but then pulled away as he remembered suddenly why he was supposed to be angry, and pushed on until Pa Dickey found him and asked him again if just perhaps, just maybe, he had found the end to the string when he was in the string room, and Mat told the old man that, sure, he'd find it someday if it was the last thing he ever did, and then they were outside together clinking a couple of Leineys and draped arm in arm, Pa wondering how come that damn boar had gotten so close to Mat and worrying about that damn weasel Buster Hieman up there sniffin' around beautiful Daphne, lovely Daphne, the best damn daughter and best damn fiancée a father or guy ever had, then worrying for Mat about that damn, no-good lying Heywood telling everyone that he had fallen for the angel bones trick. Then Mat told about Vinnie and the whole Mafia wanting to kill him and the DEA after him for smuggling four hundred kilos of cocaine into Los Angeles in his suitcase. Pa asked, and Mat replied, well they were small kilos – but only so he could buy Daphne everything she ever wanted. How he loves that girl, how he loves her! Pa Dickey crying with Mat again, Mat confessing he didn't really smuggle anything but it sounded good and then staggering back in to look for consolation, which he found on top of the refrigerator in the form of a pint bottle of Canadian whiskey and, even though he was an Irish drinker, what the hell, except that there was a cigarette butt in it and he came up gagging and cursing.

"Hold your tongue, son. Lest you be the subject of a sermon at your new church," someone said, and Mat turned to see diminutive red Reverend Rantin, face etched in disapproval.

"I choked... someone left a butt..." He held up the bottle but lowered it when he registered Rantin's expression.

"It's a small bottle, but mighty Satan dwells within, Matthew. I hope when you begin services at the Epiphany Church of Salvation you'll learn to avoid temptation by unholy spirits."

Mat sobered briefly, formulating words, "You know, about joining your church – "

The Reverend interrupted. "I hear that the beast approached you today, Mat. I hear he came close and snorted at you – growled, some-one said. Is it true?"

"Not quite that, but if the guys weren't playing – "

"I hear that part was no trick. Oh, this is a bleak day, a red day. Can there be any doubt that reckoning is near, when the minions of Satan walk the land? Bleak day indeed."

"Right, well, the wedding plans of Daphne and – "

"We all suck the monkey nose at some point, Matthew Roper, even me, while the Devil's red fingers reach for our feet from the fiery bow-els of hell." Rantin leaned in conspiratorially. "Heywood's blasphemy has not gone unnoticed, mind you."

Mat thought he detected a sneer on the Reverend's face, but said nothing. "I mean about me and Daphne's wedding – "

Rantin brushed fingers through his stubbled red hair. "No need to thank me, boy. This is my marriage, after all, marriage to my flock, and my bane is to watch them fall, succumb to the sins of the flesh."

"Yes, but you see, about the wedding – "

"Verily wedded to their despair and ecstasy, their triumph and fail-ure, flesh and spirit, blood and bone... You are right, you are right. My bane, though weighty, is nothing compared to the red flames of hell."

"Daphne and I haven't made up our minds yet."

"To what kind of ceremony? Don't worry; I'll choose. And so I toil on. Seen any sinners in need of redemption, Matthew? Look around! The room is full of them, so I must jump to confront evil when I see it. Are you prepared to jump into the fray against sin with me?"

Mat shuddered. "Maybe some other time."

With that, the small red man slipped between two burly backs that miraculously parted like the Red Sea, then closed around him.

"Wait," Mat protested. "I need to talk to you."

He was gone.

Mat felt fingers close on his elbow. He turned to find a mousey woman whose hang-dog eyes bored intently into his.

"Oh, hey," he said. "Hey."

"Hay is for horses, Mister Roper. I have something else in mind."

"I don't think we've met. Have we?" Alcohol glazed eyes took her in: average hair, face, build; human wallpaper, real life "extra" made for the crowd, but... glittery eyes. Mouse-basset eyes: determined.

She took him in tow and led him to a couch where he asked what she had in mind. He was staggering now and only his eyes remained sober, not his mind or voice or even ears. But by God he could still see straight, so show him what she had in mind.

"A property," she whispered. "It's big. Bigger than anything ever!"

Mat groaned. "Don't you people have any idea – "

"Because when you hear it you're going to go nuts. It's that good. That good. Promise you won't steal it. Promise."

"I can safely promise. You have a beer by any chance? Schnapps? Irish whiskey?"

"You've had quite enough. Now listen."

"Who nominated you to be my… whoever gets nominated to whatever it is."

"Sh. There's this young soldier, special ops."

"Ooh. Military lingo. That shows promise."

"I know. Anyway, he returns from Afghanistan to his wife and daughter. He becomes a cop in a small town in the south run by a cor-rupt politician – drug dealer. The vet-cop arrests the dealer who gets out of jail right away and swears revenge. The cop's wife and daughter get mowed down and for the rest of the movie the cop kills the drug dealer's gang one-by-one until there's only the drug lord."

"Wow. Original. You figured that out all by yourself?'

"Pretty much. You can see why I want to keep it secret."

"I gotta pee."

"The cop has a best friend from his old neighborhood whose sister is beautiful. The cop and her don't hit it off at first but then they sud-denly kiss. The drug lord tortures and kills the best friend, kidnaps the girl and threatens to kill her unless the cop fights him to the death. See, the drug lord and cop both happen to be weapons and karate experts."

"No kidding. What a surprise twist."

"Yes. They battle to the death and the cop wins and gets the girl."

"You go to many movies?"

"All the time. Why?"

"Just wondering. I gotta pee."

"You know, you smell terrible," she said.

"Are you kidding? Some people love this smell. Sniff it again."

He raised his arm to offer a whiff, but she leaned away. "I'll bet they do. Verne, Brodie, Bascom?"

"How'd you know? Hey, you got anything to drink?"

The Mouse pulled within herself, face going blank. "I don't think your response is appropriate, Mister Roper. I'm offering you the chance of a lifetime, to get in on something bigger than you ever imagined." This was the defining point in her existence, he realized, as if each day had led irrevocably to it; as if her parents and ancestors had lived and trekked and worked and scrimped and married and died that she might be at the right place and time to fulfill her destiny.

22

"I have your word? To keep our secret until we're on paper with the bigwigs?"

But Mat was slumped, barely conscious. He lunged forward, sitting suddenly, and gave the Mouse a kiss on the cheek. "I see your point," he slurred. "We never should have bought Alaska. Where am I?"

"On the verge, Mister Roper, of my ticket out of Smallville."

"We gotta go. They're all around us."

"Indeed they are."

"I need a drink." He rose and lurched from the couch.

The party showed no signs of abating and when he passed a clock he saw that it was nearing midnight. Even the children were running around, wild, out of control.

"Here he is," someone yelled beside Mat.

He turned and looked behind. "Here who is?"

"You," said an elderly man with bushy eyebrows like hippie caterpillars. "The guest of honor. The man responsible for the party."

"Wha 'd I do?" The room started spinning.

"I'm surprised at you, young man. I'd have thought someone as experienced at life would be more polite and perceptive."

"Well, you can politely – "

"Politics, did you say, Mister Roper?"

Mat peered at a vaguely familiar top hat with earflaps. Then he looked into the face beneath it, a face haloed by a crop of white scraggly hair. It belonged to the hunched Mayor.

"Whose politics?"

"And why not? As Mayor and owner of the Freedonia Feed and Ammunition Building, I'm interested in a man with the savvy to take over my job once I retire when I get old."

"*When* you get old?"

The Mayor nodded. "Since you've expressed your interest."

"I did no such thing," Mat protested. He abhorred politics because they were anathema to indifference, and indifference was his specialty.

"Young man, when you've been around as long as I have, you'll learn not to pay attention to people who contradict you. And I say it's as plain as the nose on your face, you aren't cut out for anything but politics. The pundits say my numerous bids for the assembly were thwarted because I'm so damn ugly, but with your looks and my credo we could get Dickeyville in the Capitol building in Madison."

Mat's eyes widened in mock horror. "I'd rather be eaten one inch at a time by a great white – "

"Speech! Speech!" Mat was interrupted.

"Let the man speechify!" someone yelled, and immediately came shouts from others. A chorus rose and could be heard outside. It seemed impossible, but more people from outside began crowding into the house. "Let the orator speak!"

"I want to hear the actor make a speech!"

"Come on, speak!"

"I don't wanna make a speech," Mat protested. "Why should I go speeching around?"

"For facing the Horror today," the man with bushy eyebrows explained. "For meeting fear and facing it down."

"But it was just an old boar head. Wasn't even real."

"But did you know that? No, you did not. Unfortunately, if you hadn't gone in after Verne you might have shot the real boar."

"I could have shot it? What'd I wanna shoot some poor pig for?"

"*Boar.* It could've gored and eaten you," the Mayor said, adding, "Of course, better you get killed than it. Think of the publicity."

"What?" Mat asked.

"And the tragedy. Of losing those tourist dollars."

"What tourist dollars?"

"The ones the Horror brings to Dickeyville," the old man said. "Without it, we'd have nothing to bring in outside folks, 'cept the Dickeyville Grotto, rightful eighth wonder of the world. Tourists 'd all go to a big place like Gordondale. Where would our kids wind up?"

"Whoa," Mat said. "Lured by the bright lights of Gordondale?"

"Exactly, young man. I knew you were the astute player. Why, they've got a shopping center with a movie theater inside. There's even a bowling alley."

"Gads. What am I doing here when I could be there?"

"But no Dickeyville Horror. Oh, they've tried. Had Rattlesnake Roundup Days, Gordondale River Leech Week, even tried Tick Terror Days. Big flops."

Someone grabbed Mat by the arm and dragged him off. "I gotta go," he explained to the Mayor as people clapped and slapped his back. He was led to a piano bench sitting between the dining and living rooms and boosted up on it. "Speech!" they yelled.

"Come on. I dunno what to say."

"Speech!"

"We talking honorarium here? How much? Settle for a beer." He swayed, looked at faces bright with expectation and drink and good cheer. Winder ears, Dickey noses, others with neither, some both… old people and young, men, women and children, faces turned toward his. As the noise died, anyone walking in might see pale-skinned Wisconsinites beneath a tall, tanned figure like a Grecian ideal come to flesh, dispersing wisdom. Indeed, Mat saw something of that in their expectant faces… Mister Roper goes to Dickeyville.

He had no money, a couple of friends and almost no expectations other than to find pleasure, though that was no small thing, especially to others incapable of it. Even those few who came close to him had found not the man within, but a disinterested shell. Other than Daphne, if women wanted something of him they were disappointed. He had little to share. Now, seeing these faces, he understood that he still had nothing to share, naught to give. He didn't even want to give them anything. His inclination was to jump off the bench and walk through the crowd, these eighty or a hundred jammed into two rooms, and more pressing the doorway, faces happy, smiles broad and charged with the moment. It reminded Mat of a wedding, a best man's corny riff. A camera flashed and he saw Ma Dickey behind it.

"C'mon, Roper," came a yell. "Tell us what you think about the Dickeyville Grotto."

"Yeah, tell us about that work of unparalleled American folk art."

"Obsessed lunacy," someone else said.

"American art genius!"

"Gross excess! Makes our town a joke," shouted a woman.

"Folk art's pinnacle!" argued a weighty man in a suit.

"Sublime display of devotion!"

"Bullshit, crank crap!"

"Wait." Mat interrupted. "Wait for me to think. After a little drink, I gotta think. The Grotto? Grotto. I've said it before. It's... what can I say? It's the Grotto."

"Oh yeah!" one encouraged. "Go on, man!"

"That's what I'm talkin' about," another yelled. "You tell 'em, Mat!"

"It's the Grotto," he repeated, pleased with himself.

Mat disliked those moments at weddings. Sincerity bored him; it was tedious, fleeting. The same guys who delivered toasts usually hustled the ex-wife as soon as divorce papers were filed, often before.

He was too drunk to protest, even drunker than drunk. The alcohol on an empty stomach – two days empty – drowned restraint. With each passing minute, he was slipping deeper into... drinking to forget, the worst kind. He was spinning into incoherence and didn't care.

No, he didn't want to make a speech. There were important things that needed to be said, of course; maybe he'd better say them – that was true. These people needed to understand. They needed to know how influential films were. They needed to know about media, because media influenced their lives. They probably didn't know that. Yes, that was the thing. They needed to know.

"Tell us some more about the Grotto, Mat."

"Well, I'm a little drunk. But I got something else to tell you. I mean, you guys just don't know. I've gotta warn you, this might turn around your lives. It might scare you so badly you can't sleep at night. It could just plain freak you out, you hear?

"You know *logos*? I mean the real thing, the real word that's Greek? Where in some primitive societies people think you steal their souls if you take their pictures? Or what about where they don't tell you their private names, just their public ones? Then just their families know the private ones. You know how words have power? How much power do words have? An' if you don't think so, why there's those things... what're those things? *Lexicons.* Lexicons in professions where you can't speak their professional language. You guys can't talk – can't talk lawyer language. Legal language.

"You ever notice how muzak steals the culture of the young? It's not much culture, mind you. But oh man, do you know how they eat your voice when you're young? Damn. Oops, pardon me, Nels. You don't know, but I heard the Dead Kennedys on elevator music.

"That's something, though. As soon as the young like something, it gets packaged and sold. I've only got one thing to say to you: no disco, no fat chicks, no future. And what does that mean? Exactly. Give me a drink here, somebody." He teetered on the bench and several hands reached for him. "I'm okay. Don't worry."

Someone handed him a quarter-full glass of peppermint Schnapps and he tossed it down. Gagged, burped, then smiled.

"Thank you, thank you." He looked around. Everyone listening raptly. They probably sensed how important it was that they learned this, he thought. "In the movie *Eraserhead*, it was proved – proved beyond a shadow of a doubt – that everything will be wonderful in heaven. But then there was two of the great moments in cinema. And I'm here to tell you, indeed they was. Was what? I'm gonna tell you. But first, I need something. Hey, will somebody get me a drink or not? I asked for a drink, remember? I'm feeling thirsty up here."

"You tell us, Mat!" – They cheered again.

"Why did Buster Keaton do his own stunts? And on his wedding night, too? Courage. What makes the muskrat guard his musk?"

"Courage?"

"When the patrol boat passes under the cross, which is the tail section of that bomber like a cross, which after the 'smell of napalm in the morning', which is more famous yet not so succinct, but then there is the other horror, not just Dickeyville's, but Brando's 'Horror', he says, man, I got chills down my spine. Y'know why?"

"Courage?"

"Because the other one in *Amarcord* when the peacock fans in the snow when the boy looks for the beautiful lady. Don't you agree? Don't you? Oh, man, it just – just gets me."

A Leiney appeared in Mat's hand. "Y'know, these are pretty good." – He took a long pull. "I'll take some home wrapped up in celephant."

"Speech! More speech! Someone get a camcorder doodad!"

"Where was I? Yeah, the second great moment. In *Pee Wee's Big Adventure* he dances 'Tequila' on the biker bar. Shivvers up my spine. Where'd my beer go?"

"Get the camcorder doodad!"

"Old ads? Before my time? How 'bout this one: 'Girls are nice but oh, what ice-ing comes in O-re-os.' Hey? That right? So, I can't speech for everyone, no, of course not, but for me it was *The President's Analyst.* Man, I knew it, too. Especially in the *Playboy* interview and that actor, whoever it was you gotta love that guy, drove his Ferrari a hundred and fifty miles per hour across the desert stoned on peyote.

"Right now you're probably wondering, what did that *Blow Up* tennis game with no ball mean? Don't you see? Don't you get it? Man, it said it all. All of it. That's the whole enchilada. That's the point of that game. Hey, what was I saying?"

"We're all going down. No points.

"Did you know the planet's getting warmer? I bet you don't know that 'cause it's cold in Wisconsin. It's everywhere.

"Getting to no point, from then to here, is a bridge of faith, but we do it. That's how I got here, not falling off a white bridge on my way to Damascus. I flew here in a jet. I came to this town of mazes and we're all going to Damascus. Aren't we? Blow it up. That's the point.

"Where's that Daphne? It's her speech too; take time to listen to it.

"And speaking of Daphne, please take my fiancée. Ha! Nice little town. There's snow outside. Cold snow. It's white. And you're going, like, 'Zuzu's petals! Zuzu's petals! Can you hear me,' oh, watzisname? *Bert.* You know what you mean even if I don't. Get real.

"Why does everyone go to movies with angels? I don't know.

"About reality. Thing I like about reality is it's 3-D and you don't even need glasses. Thought you oughta know.

"What was it? *The Magnificent Ambersons.* Where he says at the end, 'Money is like quicksilver rolling across the cracks of a floor' or something like that. Can you remember? 'Cause it was that way for my family. Time slipped away and took everything. Little mercury balls falling into the cracks. My dad. Everything gone. I missed him when he was gone. And my mom, she lost everything, including me." Mat sighed. "Oh, well. Including me."

Mat shook his head, suddenly miserable. "I don't feel very good. I gotta get down. Thank you very much. But I still don't like the joke and I wanna go home. Can anyone drive me home? I gotta get home." Hands reached for his and guided him down from the bench. "I need a drink. Anyone got a drink?"

Mother Dickey handed Mat a glass of water. "I don't think you need that kind of drink, Mat, dear. Try this."

Mat sipped, set the glass down and lurched off to find something else to drink, stumbling through bodies that seemed to be laughing and full of good will for him. Stumbled through the smiles and hog calls again, right into chubby Brodie's arms.

"I know you're still mad, Mat," Brodie said. "But man, that was the best speech I ever heard."

Mat didn't know much about war, but Brodie's eyes looked like the slits in pillboxes with lurking machine-guns. "Thanks, Brode. I meant every word of it. Did you like it?"

"Best speech I ever heard."

"Didja like it?"

"It was the best."

"I put my soul out there for you guys." He focused, leaned in and looked closely at Brodie again. "Say, you don't look so good."

"My girlfriend, Babs, had a fight with me, so I drank a shot of Schnapps." He held aloft a tall tumbler.

"One?"

"After another."

"Fight with your girlfriend. At least you have one to fight with."

"You need a drink, Mat ol' buddy."

"I need a drink. What you got?"

Brodie yanked at his Dickey nose and glanced around. He pulled Mat close and held his glass under Mat's chin. "This," he murmured.

"Schnapps?"

"Hah. Shows what you know. This is it, man – the real muchacho."

Mat looked into the tumbler and saw something thick and white resembling milk of magnesia. "Whazzat?"

"That, my good man, is a Tom and Jerry. My uncle Boogie, the county coroner, found the recipe tattooed on the thigh of a cadaver. They say he was hunted for the recipe. Mafia after him."

"Hey, the Mafia's after me too. Fuck 'em. Fuck 'em all Mafioso."

"Try it." Brodie handed the tumbler to Mat, who took down the full thing, thick as a milkshake and tasting of egg whites and cinnamon and brandy and about a half-cup powdered sugar, and sludgy artery-clogging cream.

"Yuk!" he shuddered, wiping his chin with his sleeve to remove drips of the first food-like thing he'd had in days. "That stuff is great."

"Lemme get you another."

"I gotta go home." Mat draped over Brodie's shoulder. "Woozy."

"The Horror, man. Nobody's ever had that sucker come so close. It's like you're blessed."

"Yeah? Watch my bud Vinnie bestow blessings on me soon."

"I mean the boar, man." Brodie poked his nose into Mat's. "For some reason he came to you in daylight. That never happened before. Not any time to anyone."

"Shows how stupid is that smelly pig."

"Whoa. Speaking of the boar, you don't smell so hot either."

"I thought you liked this stuff." Mat raised a hand and smelled an armpit. "I smell sweet sort of, like your Tom and Jerry. Maybe better."

"I'm gonna get sick smelling you," Brodie complained and started to leave. "Future Cousin Mat, you smell like a urinal."

"Well, at least I don't have a nose like a – " Mat's words failed him. As drunk as he was, the light suddenly shined and he realized where he'd seen and smelled that soap cake and knew why it had pleasant connotations. "Did you say 'urinal', Brodie ol' bud?"

"You got it."

Mat flopped on a couch. "I gotta sit for a minute," he said to no one in particular. "I don't smell very good." He sniffed his underarm again.

"You don't smell good at all," Brodie confirmed.

"A urinal? There goes my fortune. All gone, like angel bones."

"All gone."

"Nobody tol' me. I gotta go home." He closed his eyes but the room spun, so he opened them again. Brodie's face was inches from his.

"I got a property, Mat."

"Now that's unusual."

"We're gonna be rich."

"Not you too, man."

"I gotta tell you."

"I thought you was my frien'. Most than everyone." Mat waved expansively across the room. "I thought you was."

Brodie looked pained. "I am. That's why I got to tell you."

"I thought you was my frien'. I got no home, no marriage."

"That's why I gotta tell you. So we'll both be rich."

"An' leave ol' Dickeyville."

"This is a sure thing."

"Always is."

"Don't tell anyone. When the money comes rolling, my girlfriend'll beg to come back."

"Not a word. Hey, I need a drink."

Brodie started. "I just thought of it tonight."

"A sudden inspiration."

"There's this young guy, picked-on weakling."

"Sounds good. He know karate by any chance?"

"But something happens to make him have a super power. He'll be like an animal or something. Snakeman, or how 'bout Weaselman?"

"Strength of the weasel. I like that."

"We'll let the power guys in Hollywood figure what happened. Maybe some radioactivity changes him."

"Right. Power guys with big ideas. Where've I heard that before?"

"And there's a superpower villain, wants to take over the world."

"Sounds logical. Say, you got anymore of that milkshake left?"

"So Snakeman meets this hot girl reporter…"

"Wait, don' tell me. You go to a lot of movies?"

23

Mat opened his eyes. "I use baking soda," he mumbled," attempting to stand and failing.

"That was the end." Brodie shrugged.

"Did you say chimpanzees and apes take over the world?"

"Said you wouldn't feel alone homeless and broken-up marriage."

"How old are you, Brodie?"

"Pretty old."

"Wha' finally happened?"

"The supervillain was banished."

"Jes' in time for a sequel. You have my sympathy."

There were hazy images of friendly handshakes and pats on the back and hugs. More hog calls. Then Mat had one of those lucid moments that sometimes occur inside the worst drunks, a picture window in the house of oblivion. He remembered Lana coming to sit beside him, remembered the couch sagging as she eased down. "I been looking all over for a month now. I'm getting hornier'n a three peckered-toad, Mat. I gotta find me a man."

"We gotta find you a man," Mat repeated with deep conviction.

"There's got to be a three-peckered one out there."

"You're a hooty-hoot, Mat. I sure wish you liked big girls. Do you?"

"I like 'em fine big."

"Don't tease me, Mat. You know what I mean."

"I been washing my face with a cake of urinal soap. Did you know?"

"Everyone knows. But nobody wanted to spoil it by telling you. Isn't this town a kick?"

Mat groaned. "Everyone knows?"

"You've smelled like hell. Couldn't you tell?"

"One blast of the stuff near my nose and I haven't been able to smell anything since."

"Big solid man," she said. "One with some thick meat on his bones. Wide-back man. I like a hairy, wide back." She sighed.

"How 'bout that Brodie guy?"

"Seriously? He's like nineteen. You trying to get me arrested?"

"I thought radiation got to him."

"What?"

"Doesn't it strike you odd that I didn't know I was scrubbing my face with a cake of urinal soap?"

"I tell you, Mat. Some people think you're a snob. They think I won't find me a wide-back man. You better find a way to earn their respect, that's all. Right now, as nice as they are, you're an outsider to them. The worst of it is, you'll always be outside unless you can make them respect you. Think about it."

"I can't drunk, I'm way too think. Anyway, I thought you wanted a friend. Not telling me about the urinal soap doesn't seem right between friends."

"I wanted to be your friend, not your fashion consultant. What do I look like, Vidal Sassoon?" She rose and left him. "I gotta find me a wide-back man."

I hate these people, Mat thought just before he nodded off, clinging momentarily to the back of the couch before slumping to the floor. I hate every one of them.

24

Often, a whole day takes its character at dawn, in the lingering, drowsy minutes between slumber and wake. Some days start with promise, awareness that something good will happen or has happened, an anticipation of holidays or Christmas morning or the first day of vacation or a significant birthday which has finally arrived. The sleeper recalls the good thing as he comes slowly conscious in daybreak. A day may begin like the tolling of distant bells, tinged with magic or pleasant discovery, of promise like a weighty skeleton key to the door of a house filled with antiques where no one has been for forty years; all inside will be yours. It may be a private day filled with what you desire, and you know it even as you rise. A spring breeze may billow the curtains as it comes up through an apple orchard, littering the cool earth with a fragrant confetti of white blossoms. There may be a chime of romance in the air, recall of a chance meeting the evening before which will lead to being invited into her Victorian home for dinner tonight, or of an opportunity to go with someone new to a science-fiction movie or director's cut of *Bladerunner* at the discount theater, stopping for brownie sundaes on the way to take into the show. A day might open like a gala affair, a Valentine's Day morning's surprise undressing and climbing into your bed or your children piling in to cuddle warm beneath the sheets, pressing between you and your lady, pushing cold feet and bony colt's legs and arms against you, sweet but sour child breath taken happily with morning kisses, recounting dreams.

Mat's morning was unlike any of those things.

His morning began an hour before dawn. A horrible growl woke him, a growl louder than any he had ever heard. When he jerked up, his head slammed hard into something. "Ow! Damn it!" His blurred eyes peeped open through tiny red slits and he saw only darkness and heard the deafening roar like a jet landing on his head and then saw its lights inches from his face and rolled over and ducked and his head, turned, was caught in a terrible vise that clacked shut his jaw. The roaring thing smashed into his forehead, retreated and smashed him again. Then the roar subsided and all went dark. He was freezing cold, laying on a hard, chilly floor.

"What in heaven's name?" came a voice. "Mat! We wondered what happened to you."

"Who's that? Where am I?"

"Let me help." Mother Dickey pulled his head from beneath the back of the couch.

He rolled over in a heap. "I don't feel so good. A train's been bumping my head." He was shivering from the chill.

"That was my vacuum cleaner. And you should see your eyes."

"Is everything red on your side too? I think Reverend Rantin's colored my world."

Mother Dickey chuckled and started to say something, but didn't.

"I gotta die," he added. "That would be nice. Yes, it would."

"Piffle. You're not going to die."

"Shows how much you know." If he'd had any bile, he'd be deadly sick now. Of course his bile system was tapped out from the day before and it had been so long since he'd eaten, it had probably petered out from waiting. Now the flapping of his eyelids pained him. Breathing pained his kidneys, which felt like dehydrated prune pits in his lower back. His eyeballs felt like ball bearings turning in sand. Had someone left an ice pick in the top of his head? Probably not; he felt worse than that. "What time is it?"

"Five-thirty a.m."

Mat glanced around the room. "I'm not seeing so well, but it looks clean in here." The effort of speaking made his head pound. Even his tongue throbbed.

"Nobody in town would leave a house the way ours was. They pitched in before they left the party."

"Oh." Mat had never heard of guests cleaning up before they left, unless it was cleaning out spare-change jars and liquor from cupboards. "Why're you up so early? And vacuuming?"

"You get up early with nothing to do and by night you're finished."

"I think I heard that one from Pa," Mat grumped.

"After the first forty years of marriage you've heard all the sayings and say 'em yourself. I could end every story Pa tells."

That was food for thought. "He up early too?"

"Five-thirty is not early. But even if it were, Daphne's supposed to get home today, remember? Your fiancée and my only daughter?"

"She is?"

"Phoned. Anyway, you need to be up for Verne. He called twenty minutes ago. Want some breakfast? I've got coffee and waffles and whipped cream with frozen blueberries."

Mat's stomach burped up a warning. "I don't think I better."

"Mat, you don't eat enough to keep a bird alive."

"I don't feel so good."

"I'm not used to so much frivolity either, and I've got to put a few more ornaments on the Christmas tree today. And Pa, he's dang near – pardon my French – done in. I pretty near had to drag him out of bed when the clock said four a.m."

That was some consolation. "What's he doing? Go back to bed?"

"You can hear him at the driveway. Been shoveling since five."

Sure enough, Mat heard a shovel on concrete out there. Although faint, the sound made his stomach cramp painfully and eyeballs ache. This morning made yesterday's killer hangover seem like pin-money. This morning was the lottery winner of hangovers. Looking toward the driveway side of the house, Mat saw it was dark still.

As soon as Mother Dickey bustled into the other room, he crawled on upstairs to the bath, the effort leaving him wheezy and gasping. He lay his cheek on the newly-mopped linoleum beside the toilet bowl and didn't care. His mouth tasted of dust swept from beneath a refrigerator, dust tinged with vile flavors from last night's drinks.

When he thought of the tall Tom-and-Jerry, of how it had tasted all sugary and thick, his stomach convulsed several times but there came only deep, empty rumbling. Tears ran down his cheeks. He lay panting and shivering from pain and cold.

He heard it even through the walls. An auto horn blast, once, twice. He heard the front door open and Mother Dickey yell something indeterminate, then the door slam and her shoes clomping up stairs into the hallway. Mat quickly stood; his head swam and pounded. He almost fainted. "Verne's here to pick you up. You ready?"

If it had been anyone else on the planet, even Daphne, Mat would have crawled into bed. He couldn't remember feeling so rotten. Although he'd spent much of his life's evening hours in bars, he didn't consider himself a big drinker. Typically he drank in moderation. Frequently, true; but moderately. Sometimes he drank only fruit juice. But this was beyond hangover. This was torture. Poisoning. Yet he couldn't avoid Verne, not after last night.

"I need some long underwear, please. Two pairs, okay? And I need a few minutes. Tell Verne to wait, would you?"

"Why, Mat, I thought you wouldn't wear long johns. I'll get you some." She bustled off while he pulled himself up to the basin and looked at himself in the mirror. He turned on the hot water, took up a washcloth and glanced down at the cake of urinal soap – the only "soap" – in the dish. Seeing it made him alternately angry and sad, as when he thought about his mother and father when he was a child. All of this, he thought, Daphne's family, my family, all of it's a bust for me. I've lost it all. No chance for respect with these people.

Not that he'd wanted it, or cared at first. And even if he had wanted their respect, he supposed his stupidity at falling for Heywood's asinine joke had taken care of that. Now it was gone and he felt sick and depressed, like he'd wasted an opportunity.

Taking the stupid soap in his hands, he rubbed it between his fingers. Hell with it, he thought. If I'm going to play the fool, I'll play it to the hilt. I'll give these damn hicks a fool to remember. I'll go out into the woods and fight Verne and stink up him and their stupid Mazy so badly that… Serendipity. Epiphany. It came to Mat as he looked at his haggard reflection – an inspiration. An idea so stupid and completely absurd that it could only have come to a dying man or one so hungover that he was near death. It was ridiculous. Absolutely ridiculous. Yet the brilliance of it pained his eyeballs.

Squeezing an inch of toothpaste onto his tongue, he swished his mouth with water and spit. Downstairs, stumbling slightly, he took the picnic basket Mother Dickey offered as he passed through the kitchen. The odors, appealing at another time, convulsed his stomach. He had no intention of eating: he knew he couldn't – not yet, anyway. He began pulling on a coat and gloves and the stupid flapped hat. He watched as Mother Dickey washed a coffee cup.

"Mother Dickey, that 'Hollywood' Heywood guy – they say he's a bit off the deep end."

She sighed. "I don't mean to bear bad news, Mat, but once at a party, he tricked Grandpa Winder into biting a sandwich with a slab of something he called Peruvian Fungo slug in it that he brought from the university. The slime on it leaves a rash and itches like crazy. Gramps' lips and chin were red as a strawberry for weeks. Looked like hell and wouldn't go outside. Heywood sneaked over and got a picture while the old fellow was asleep. He never let Grandpa or anybody else forget. Teased the old man right into the grave, if you ask me."

"Great." – Another reason for Mat to get out of Dickeyville. "Don't suppose there's any way to reverse such a stupid thing as believing in angel and devil dinosaur bones."

"Heywood's probably having breakfast at the diner and telling everyone about it right now. He pretty much drags around his retinue of adoring students to show everyone how important he is."

"Isn't he supposed to be teaching, or don't those kids go to classes? There's no branch college in Dickeyville, is there?"

"Tenure," Mother Dickey shrugged. "God knows what goes on in the university, but Heywood finagles a sabbatical every few years."

"So I'm the fool of Dickeyville for all time? Brand a big scarlet 'F' on my forehead. The only guy in the United States gullible enough to fall for Heywood's stupid trick."

"Gramps sure didn't escape Heywood's mean trick, and there's been others. Of course, it was pretty funny seeing the old guy's face purple as a plum. Darn near killed Granny Winder."

"Shock?"

"Laughter. Gramps said the only thing was to trick Heywood even worse, but he didn't live long enough or just wasn't clever enough. That Heywood's no slouch in the brain department. For years Winders have held against Heywood what he did to Gramps, but nobody's been able to pin a grand-slam joke on ol' Heywood like that.'

"Great. Simply great. I'm neck-deep in trouble."

"Well, that's what I always say."

"That Heywood is trouble?"

"That anything with tires or testicles is trouble."

Mat groaned.

"Of course you could be a hero somehow; that'd show everybody."

Mat poured a glass of water and drank it. "Hero positions aren't advertised. Anyway, I don't have the energy for it. One minute I'm a hero for 'facing the boar', then a couple hours later I'm the goat."

Mother Dickey dried her hands on her apron. "Honestly, Mat. I can't imagine how you fell for such a silly gag."

He felt too sick to care. Right now he had other things to worry about. "Just trusting, I guess. You think there'll be buses today?"

"Maybe they'll get the roads clear. But no buses yet."

"That Buster guy who's driving Daphne back – you say Father Dickey doesn't care for him?"

"Thinks he's as flaky as a fish scale pie. Never done a thing."

"Does Pa like me?"

"You don't know?"

"How could I? That first day here he barely spoke. Only talks to me now when we've been partying a bit."

"Believe me, Mat, if you don't know whether Pa likes you it's a pretty good sign he does."

Mat listened to the shovel scraping the drive. "Hard-working guy."

"Everybody works hard in farm life. During the harvest, Pa and the other men work sixteen hours a day, and we wives wake 'em in the morning and put 'em to bed at night. Seven days a week. Habit keeps farm people moving day in and day out, year after year, until we just drop dead. We don't know any other way."

Mat realized that the only time he'd seen Ma Dickey sitting was when she had showed him Daphne's high school picture. But something else nagged at him, and just before he went out he asked:

"Mother Dickey, what's 'piffle' mean?"

"If you don't know, just look in the dictionary."

"Can't see too well today."

"Well, enjoy your lunch. Since you boys spoiled my good basket yesterday, I packed the old courtin' basket from when I was a girl. Plenty of Winder and Dickey boys lost their hearts to deviled eggs and German potato salad lugged in this thing."

Mat started to protest about wrecking the basket, but felt too raw.

"For you vegetarian-types, I put in some of my pickled okra sandwiches, with basil dressing." She smiled, and he saw kindness in it, and pride. Friendly pride, not vanity. But his only answer to pickled okra and pesto was a burp. Apparently the bile supply wasn't depleted.

He thought about the airline's recent vegetarian meal: limp rubbery broccoli, squishy cucumber, radioactive pickle slices and an olive on a nest of soggy iceberg lettuce, served with two crackers and a packet of chemicals, probably toxic leftovers from the petroleum industry disguised as dressing. He hadn't eaten a bite.

Even in the half-light of early dawn, the glare off the snow hit his face like a laser blast as he stumbled out the door, nauseous, as if he'd been shoved. Everything earthly was white. He covered his eyes with his gloves and glanced upward into a cloudless dark sky. Weak orange glow tinged the horizon. The air was colder than the previous day, perhaps below zero – he couldn't tell. Of course there would be air traffic, he thought. Maybe air traffic from California to Des Moines. Maybe two stone-faced men and an old Italian in a dark suit. A big asthmatic guy with heavy lids and a lightweight cheap pistol.

He should be running. But he was too tired, hungover. Besides, where would he hide and how could he get there? Trouble would find him when he didn't expect it. It was better this way, better to die with a few people around than on some empty beach; at least he could expect burial. He sighed, full of self-pity. He'd done it all for love.

"Morning, Mat," Father Dickey called out cheerily. "Didn't take you for the early riser."

Mat lifted his eyes enough to take in the old man's smile as he leaned on his shovel. He was wearing a short-sleeved sweatshirt and didn't seem to be sweating. "Uhhh," Mat emitted.

"Yup, me too. Sure good to have you here. You California boys sure know how to have a fine time. I haven't had this much fun since a mouse fell in Ma's denture water."

"You gonna find a piece of string in the driveway today?" Mat fished in his pocket and pulled out a pair of sunglasses that still smelled of suntan lotion. When he opened the stems, fine white grains of Bahaman sand spilled out.

"Maybe I will, maybe I won't. Won't be long before I stop collecting string altogether because, if I don't find that end to tie onto, I'll have to throw away what I've saved since I lost it."

"Yeah? Sorry."

"Sure could use your help, Mat. I had a dream that you helped me find the end."

"You told me that last night."

"I dreamed it two times."

"Speaking of two, I've got two things I wanted to ask. Mind?"

"No, I don't mind. But Mat, you look terrible. You know that?" The old man's smile broadened, as if he'd paid a compliment.

"The first question is, why don't you like Buster."

"I like him okay. Question two?"

"No, I mean really like him. Say when he was with Daphne?"

Pa rubbed his balding head. "He's an idiot, and always took Daphne for granite."

"For 'granted'?'"

"That's what I said. Buster couldn't find his pocket in a snowstorm. Next question?"

"Why the soap, Mister Dickey. Joke?"

"Hell, no. That stuff lasts forever. Ma made me quit using it, though

– makes my skin redden up. We're pretty frugal around here, Mat. You'll get used to that."

Get used to it, he wondered as he trudged toward Verne's pickup, idling at the end of the driveway like some kind of rusty predator. He grabbed a handle and pulled a door open. Verne's smile spread like an accusation across his face. Today he also wore one of the idiotic quilt-checked green hats with earflaps.

"Nice shades, Mat. A bit early for sunglasses, isn't it?" Verne's breath steamed into the air. Apparently the heater hadn't been fixed since yesterday. "Ready to rumble?"

Mat didn't like Verne's smirk. "Give me time."

"Let me know when."

"You'll know. Where's your coonskin?"

"I only wear that old thing to offend California vegetarians."

"Why in hell are you here, Verne?"

He seemed dreadfully chipper. "Mainly because it adds to your misery. But also so you can't say I didn't show."

Mat grunted as he hefted himself and the lunch basket into the truck. "I feel too starved to fight this morning."

"But not too hungover? Too bad. I was looking forward to it."

"I haven't called anything off."

Mat let his head fall back against the bench seat. The view of a torn headliner would do nicely. "Second, I don't want to enhance my repu-tation as town fool." He set the picnic basket on the floorboards; inside the closed cab, its aroma filled the air. Pickled okra? At the thought, he felt sick and rolled down his window.

Verne sniffed the air. "Man, that picnic smells good. But what's this?" He sniffed again, leaning toward Mat. "Brodie spent the night on my couch. Said he told you about the soap you've been using. Since you obviously used it today, that must mean you've either developed a sense of humor or decided to get on with this 'fool' business."

Mat grimaced as Verne revved the engine and backed onto the street. Pa waved, then stooped back to his shoveling. "Man's gotta have a goal. Mine's king Dickeyville fool."

"So that's why you made that speech last night?" Verne slapped a knee. "I was wondering. As drunken rants go – and I've heard lots of them – it was a solid A-minus."

"Fuck you."

"That's articulate."

"Look. Our differences aside, I gotta get out of this town. Today."

"Why's that? To escape ball-breaker cousin Daphne?"

"Ball-breaker? Better watch your mouth, pal."

Verne ignored him. "Ma's not going to like your leaving much. Nor me, for that matter – I might miss my chance at you. Besides, Daphne's family." Verne shifted into second and simultaneously swiped the windshield with a shirt sleeve. "Take the wheel."

Mat grabbed it and steered with one hand. "It's not Daphne. I wouldn't ask if it wasn't important. I've got to get out of here."

Verne, sitting back, took the wheel again. "No can do, even if I wanted. The interstate's maybe fifty miles away. Between here and there it's two-lane country road and little of it plowed. Look at how much snow fell in the last couple days."

House roofs and yards were covered by deep fluff, snow blue-shadowed and clean at the pre-dawn hour. Yard pines and hedges and small conifers – everything was blanketed in heavy white drifts. "Buster's getting through. How come you can't?" Looking past the bowler on the hood, tiny gold ball poised to leave his fingertips, Mat saw that the streets had been plowed in the night. He added, "It's freezing in here. Why don't you fix your heater?"

"Streets are plowed by volunteers. Just guys helping out with their trucks. Same guys plow the road into the Mazy so the tourists can go huntin'. It's kind of a duty."

"Doesn't explain how Buster can drive and others can't."

"Old Scratchy here's just two-wheel drive, and even four-wheel doesn't work in eighteen inches of snow. Buster's borrowed a World War II-vintage Power Wagon, one of those big lorries about three feet off the ground. Pretty much go anywhere. It gets five miles to the gallon so Buster borrowed fifty bucks from Bascom for gas."

"Why in hell didn't he take me with him to Des Moines? I could've helped pay." The windshield on Mat's side was fogging. He wiped at it, but his gloves accomplished nothing.

"Don't you know?"

"Yeah, I know." He glanced at Verne's battered ears. "I feel worse than you look."

"That's saying a might. I could take you home so you could go back to bed."

"No. I want to go hunting."

"I thought you didn't like killing animals."

"It's a cretin's sport. So are you going?"

"That's the plan. You really want to? It's pretty cold today. Worse than yesterday."

"You think it could be colder than in your truck?" Mat shivered. "You got a gun for me?"

"We'll stop at the house and pick one up. Want a pistol again?"

"Why not? As long as it's got lots of firepower."

"If you're thinking about shooting me with it, you're as good as dead," Verne warned.

"If I was thinking about it, today the thought of dying wouldn't stop me."

25

They said little as they drove to Verne's place, an unlocked ranch house a few miles west of town in the middle of fields flat as tabletops. They picked up a huge-barreled thing called a .44 magnum. The pistol hung heavily as Mat strapped on a western-style holster with leg-tie and loops for slugs. The barrel diameter seemed huge; Mat imagined bullets splattering meat and bone.

Verne drove under the WELCOME TO DICKEYVILLE HORROR DAYS banner sagging over the street. "Told you before, it's all right there in the sign, Roper. Right there if you could see."

"I see plenty."

"All you see is California. And that's straight away a different life."

"Straight? Everything about you and this town is as crooked as a barrel of fish hooks."

Verne started to say something but didn't. At the plowed dirt road the truck turned, and Mat read the small plaque MAZY WOODS and in smaller letters: "No snowmobiles or motorized vehicles except on Mazy Road". The pickup jostled down into dense forest, passing under another drooping banner: WELCOME TO DICKEYVILLE HORROR DAYS HUNT! PARKING $10.00 ALL DAY, 8 MILES. GOOD LUCK! They rode through stands of snow-crowned conifers canopying dark caves of damp needles. Bushes and shrubs huddled, bent with the weight of deep snow, leaning into the road, and

Mat could see places where passing cars had swiped them, collapsing the drifts. Conifers, massive islands of snow-crowned, dark pine, grew patchwork within a skeletal hardwood forest. Dark silhouettes of crows rested like lost kites in spindly top branches of the great oaks, catching pale yellow rays as sun crested the horizon.

"Are these real bullets this time?" Mat asked, patting the object belted to his waist. "Or are you afraid I'll shoot up the Mazy."

"Be careful. That's the real thing. You hit a tree with a .44 and you'll knock it down. The slug is slow, relatively speaking, but it hits like a splitting wedge."

"Big hole?"

"Just about knock off someone's leg."

"Hey, what about Lana, the fat woman?"

"She's a bit the martyr, sort of wears misfortune like a fur coat."

"She told me she was shy, but didn't act that way last night."

"If Lana thinks she's shy, it shines light on delusion. She's just lonely right now. When she's happy, she's a good time. If you stick around long enough, you'll like Lana."

"She seems okay. She and a few others pitched scripts at me."

"I got one too. You'll get it soon enough. Too soon probably." Verne coughed. "What're *you* doing here?"

Mat's shrugged. "I don't know. But I'm not going to talk about why I have to leave Dickeyville." He toed the top of the picnic basket, wondering... but his stomach warned him off.

"Something you're scared of? You don't strike me as the type. Maybe Daphne's got you scared. You ought to be."

"I told you not to insult her. What're you saying?"

"Just making talk. No insult. I meant marriage in general."

Mat looked hard at Verne. "I'm not the scared type. Only getting old and being poor scares me. I already know about 'poor.'"

"If I were you, I'd be worrying about those two ministers who believe they're going to marry you."

"I didn't tell them that. You heard about it from Ma Dickey?"

"Everybody in town knows about it, except them. You ever seen a preacher fight over a stolen congregation? Worse are preachers fighting over marrying fees."

"Hair pulling and scripture-quoting?"

"Two kittens going *mano-a-mano*. Gives me the trembles to think."

The road smoothed a little and Verne shifted up to third; the truck drifted slightly, gliding though the road ran straight. It was obvious to Mat that Verne still wanted to talk, obvious from his furrowed brow that he was thinking something through. Clenching the wheel tightly, his big knuckles reddening, he said finally,

"It's funny in small towns. People laugh about us folks in the Midwest, everybody but Sinclair Lewis, I mean. But there's a lot that's honest. It's that 'heartland' thing. Bunch of hicks in suspenders, sitting on pickle barrels around the radio on Saturday night."

Mat said. "I see them getting drunk over at Pa Dickey's."

Verne replied, "They're religious folk. God wants us to have fun."

"I've met the comedy team of Rantin and Weems. Funnier than Jim and Tammy Bakker. Maybe we'll get married in the Catholic church. Holy Ghost. Have the ceremony inside the grotto."

"That would finish off Ma Dickey, for real."

"Shit." Mat added: "I'm freezing in here."

"It's a big deal, your deciding." Verne was amused. "You're about as close to celebrity as Dickeyville's got. Weems and Rantin are both after your eternal soul."

"Soul sweepstakes. Potential for reality TV… I'm not much for religion. I don't trust people who think everything will be fine once they're dead."

Verne shook his head. "I go once a year to each church just to keep Weems and Rantin guessing who'll bury me."

"Decent of you."

"There's lots of good people and I don't mean to belittle them. Work hard, save, be honest; take care of your own and still believe that the government mostly works for the common good. Sort of corny. Funny to outsiders because we seem simple. It's politically incorrect to admit that's what made this country what it is."

Mat didn't feel like talking, but he did. "Seems to me a small town's just like a big one, only smaller. Same problems, smaller scale."

"Not so."

He rubbed at his temples. "How about alcohol abuse?"

Verne shrugged. "I'll admit the winter drags on and people get a little wacky. They'd be better off spending a few weeks in the sun… So the kids smoke ditch weed and get headaches. Knock over a mailbox once in a while or get drunk and wreck their parents' pickup trucks.

Sometimes they're killed, but not most of 'em. Mostly they grow a little wild, but good, and know everyone in town. Usually say 'hello' when you pass in the street... You only get one first love. One first kiss. And especially one hometown. Get one first best friend?"

"Got you there. Never had a best friend."

"You're kidding."

"Never needed one. Had lots of buddies. They came and went. Mostly hung around for my spin-off girls."

"There were that many?"

"Friends?"

"Girls."

Mat yawned. "Only thing ever came easy."

"Shit, man. Never having a best buddy... Explains a lot about you."

Verne looked pensive as the truck slid over snow. Mat wiped at the glass again, gave up. "Crazed farm kids murder their parents and relatives out in the snowlands."

"Nothing like L.A., Chicago and New York killings."

Mat remembered Vinnie. "Give Dickeyville a chance. Maybe sooner than you think."

"A quarter million pioneers headed west from the Missouri Valley," Verne mused. "And kids still leave."

"Me too."

"But moving away, you take your hometown with you. New place, same you."

"I know. I've got to get home."

"Like that'll solve your problems?"

"What problems are you talking about? You're my problem."

"I lived in California, Roper. I know its gig. Golden Ego State."

"In basic training, like Heywood? Or flew over Disneyland?"

"Heywood wasn't in the army. He tell you that?"

Mat grunted.

"I was. But I was in California because I was a bit of a cocky jerk – not unlike you – and got myself into trouble here in Dickeyville."

Tired of the conversation, Mat sat forward and stabbed at the radio knobs. Nothing. A relic. "So how'd you get those ears, Verne? Ma told me to ask and now I'm asking. Did someone kick your ass? I'm willing to contribute." He burped. "Just not right now."

Verne's cheek muscles clenched as he chewed a thought. "My ass doesn't kick easily, Roper. You're the kind of guy who always had it made but had talent only for feeling sorry for yourself."

Mat nodded. "That, and women. I did have it easy. Then didn't."

"You know ring fighting? That's where the ears came from. That's why my ass doesn't kick so easily."

"Ring fighting. And you think *I'm* a fool."

"Every man has a talent. You think you choose, but you don't. You only choose friends, career and the place you call home."

"L.A.'s mine. I'd die of boredom in Dickeyville. Or lead poisoning."

"It's just two different ways, Roper, of looking at the same thing. Home. Now listen. I got a killer screenplay idea."

"Can't wait to hear."

"You're gonna love it."

"I bet. Watch a lot of movies?"

"How'd you know?"

"Lucky guess."

"It's about this guy from the ghetto. A white boxer, sort of a good-hearted guy, but pretty much a loser. The boxer's brother is in trouble with gamblers and needs money. Also the brothers' mother needs money for an operation."

"What a surprise."

"Sh. Listen. The boxer somehow lucks into this wise old trainer who starts to work him hard, hitting the heavy bag, jogging. See, the boxer's just some palooka but through a fluke he gets a title shot. Oh, there's also this woman…"

26

The truck bounced and slid over the rutted road.

"Supposedly, home's the place they have to take you when you go there. Worked for me. There was a lot of emotional stuff for me when I left here; the Horror, a broken romance, my father's passing… There were also some stunts I pulled, young guy stuff. Point is, they still opened their arms when I came back. You got someplace like that? You have a defining moment?"

Mat remembered the day of his father's death. But no place to go back to. "You mean *which* defining moment. There were plenty."

"I mean the one big one that changed everything."

"What was yours?"

"That's an irrelevant question since we're talking about you. The point is, so much turns on a little thing. Don't you get it?"

"What I'm getting is tired of your questions."

Verne snorted. "California guys piss-off pretty easily."

"Yeah, we're all alike. And you guys wear me out. Since I can't tell what's true anymore, tell me. Is there a moral to your story?"

"Sure. Don't go duck hunting with a guy whose wife you're having an affair with."

"I thought it was something like that."

"Or, 'Never go duck hunting with a guy with whom his wife you're having an affair'?"

Mat was overwhelmed by exhaustion and hunger. "I'm so fucking lost in life right now even you make sense."

"It was like water slapping the side of a pool... Migrated west and came back. Probably you had ancestors went west. You'll see. There'll come a time when people turn back."

"People leave the Midwest for California, not vice-versa. In case you hadn't noticed, the Midwest isn't exactly 'a destination'."

"It'll splash back. If you want it, you can find what you didn't know you were missing."

"Other than parts of your ears, you're missing something all right."

"I'm the last guy in the world to say where to find what's missing." Verne tugged at a ragged lobe. "End of sermon. Everything decent sounds corny anymore."

Mat had a thought. "You ever read any western writers? Before you went to California, I mean?"

"Are you nuts?"

"Never mind." For a while they rode in silence. "I don't know what to believe," Mat finally said. "It's all fucked up."

"Home?"

"I'm pretty clear on that. For me, summer morning, blue water, my surfboard rising and falling in the swells. Or drift fishing at sunset up by Point Conception. I make a trip every year with some guys."

"None of them your best friend."

"Drop it."

"Everyone wants to believe something. Like you believed in dinosaur angel fossils."

"Who says?" – The truck lurched; so did Mat's stomach.

Verne glanced over. "I'm not much on that religious stuff either, but I think faith only works when there's no proof."

Despite himself, Mat liked that. "Pretty philosophical."

"Everyone wants to believe something."

"Not me. I'm a cynical black hole."

"It's about believing in something," Verne insisted. "Even a boar, like a mythical beast."

"How'd we start talking about this stuff?" – Mat took off his stupid hat and briskly rubbed his hair, then stopped rubbing because even his hair hurt. "Believe in something, but it has to be something you feel and think. If you make yourself believe, it doesn't count."

"So why are you going hunting? You don't have to prove anything; way I figure, we'll never see you again as soon as you get away. You could spend the day in bed. Only an idiot would be out here in sub-zero hunting a killer boar, especially one he didn't want to shoot. I hope you're doing it for yourself. There's no one else to please."

But Mat wasn't sure. "You know this doesn't change anything between you and me."

"You got a green light from me. Right now, if you want."

Mat asked Verne to take him to the same spot as the day before. After five minutes Verne slowed near the small overgrown road where tire tracks disappeared into a tunnel of pine boughs.

"Yesterday was the first time in years I've seen the Horror's tracks near the old Mazy place. He'll be five miles from there today, which is about his normal cruising range. I've tracked him. He never sticks around anywhere, especially where hunters are, and yesterday probably scared the crap out of him. Let me take you somewhere better."

Mat was adamant. "I don't care. Drop me off. That's where I go."

"The boar won't even be close. You hunt there, and I'll spend all day worrying."

"That's a switch."

"You're a guest of my uncle and aunt's, Roper. And you're marrying my cousin. I won't be anywhere close. I'm into huntin' today since yesterday was for fun."

"Some fun. Take me by the old Mazy place."

"Ah, hell." Verne turned into the narrow evergreen cave, limbs snapping and bouncing off the windshield. There were no tire tracks;

snow had obliterated the ones from the day before. The truck slipped, tires spinning in light powder, but Verne didn't seem concerned about getting stuck. "Got chains," he explained, jerking a thumb toward the pickup bed as he bored on.

"Why didn't the other guys come out? Because of me?"

"Hell, no. My brother Brodie and Bacom think you're top cat. But they're already huntin'. Wanted to start early."

"How'd they get here?"

"Bascom's new Explorer."

"You mean we all crammed into this old jalopy when we could have been riding in a warm four-wheel drive?" Mat's arms were wrapped around his body. His teeth chattered uncontrollably.

"It's Horror Days tradition for first timers to go hunting in Old Scratchy." Verne's wicked smile broadened. "You wouldn't want to defy tradition, would you?"

"What a fucking pit. Dickeyville!"

Verne laughed and slapped the steering wheel.

Mat was too sick for anger. "How'd Bascom get a new car? work?"

"Your memory's short or you're still drunk. Either way, I shouldn't leave you here because later I want to kill you with my bare hands. That aside, didn't you hear me say we farm polliwogs in winter?"

Mat checked Verne's face for obvious signs. "Why would you think I'm dumb enough to believe that? Just because I thought there were angel and demon bones in Heywood's?"

"We sell them to distributors for walleye fishermen."

"What the hell's a walleye?"

Verne braked the truck. "We're here. This is the spot. Difference is, you'll be alone today. There won't be anybody at the old Mazy place. Get hurt, you could die."

"Been dying all morning. It'll be a relief."

"You still got my compass?"

Mat patted his coat pocket.

"You want to head southeast. You can't miss the estuary but you'll probably miss the clearing. Head one way or the other for a while and you'll hit it. Go too far east, you'll reach the Millawney near Big Bend Flats. If you get to the river, be damn sure you stay off the ice: it won't hold a teacup poodle out in the middle. Too far west, you'll be near the old lead mines. Where you want to be is right in the middle."

"I'll find it."

Verne rubbed his chin. "I'm pretty sure I don't give a rat's ass one way or the other about you. Folks' opinions seem to vary in town. But if you get lost and it snows, nobody'll find you till spring – if then. No tracks to follow. Snowmobiles aren't allowed in here unless it's life or death, and folks take that exclusionary rule to extremes. They'll hunt your corpse on foot, understand? So be damn careful."

"I'm not laughing but can't say I'm afraid." Mat climbed from the truck, surprised that the outside air could be colder than the cab. Much colder. "I'll take the lunch, since I'm the guest."

"Save me some, eh? Better yet, let me take some now. You can just keep it in the truck."

"Naw. The boys might get pissed."

Verne snorted. "Listen, if there's no wind and I really lay on the horn when I get back you'll hear me. Hump it back to the car. I'll be about four hours."

Before he slammed the door, Mat leaned in his head. "You never did say why you don't fix your heater."

"I usually drive my Land Cruiser in the winter. I just use Ol' Scratchy for having fun."

"You son of – " Mat's words were drowned by Verne's laughter and the revving motor as he yanked the steering wheel and plunged hood-deep into thick, snow-laden brush on the far side, wheels spinning as he backed up and headed around toward the main dirt road.

27

Mat pulled a handkerchief from his pocket and tied it across the bottom of his face. Only a couple days in Midwestern snow country and he already understood that the air was generally colder when it wasn't snowing. And it was cold today, wicked cold. He looked far down the road and watched Verne's truck disappear. After the engine sound receded, a deep silence filled the forest, silence that gave way to the sound of slow-moving breeze through the treetops. Listening to the quiet, Mat heard the distant caw of a crow, then an answer. A chickadee peeped up from somewhere in snow-covered brush, others peeped in answer. He was learning the Wisconsin deep forest.

He examined himself, the sensation of vulnerability, loneliness. He wished he could talk to Daphne; that was what he needed. He clapped his hand to his hip and the weighty thing there; the holstered pistol soothed one part of his anxiety. Another part he recognized from experience. When he was hungover, his moods were an antithesis to his drunk. Mat was usually a happy drunk, though he rarely drank to the point of oblivion; he was inclined toward moderation in everything, except women and the sea. And he hated being hungover.

He picked up the picnic basket and turned into the woods. Dry powdery snow dropped and filtered down from the limbs as he stepped under a tree canopy into muted blue light. Snow and earth crunched under foot as he walked, breath streaming through the handkerchief and freezing. Why was he doing this? to die? to live? because he had to without knowing why? Alone, the canopy seemed more ominous to him than on the previous day. He knew there was nothing to fear from the blue darkness, but when he passed under a hundred yard-wide stand of pines he felt oppression coming, thickening like fog settling over a beach. On toward the open meadow he staggered, between great deciduous trees. There sky would open like the mouth of heaven ready to gobble the world and the horizon be so wide out over great Midwest expanses that it would take your breath away. Here his footprints yawed. He was hyper-aware and so fixed in the temporal that his brain seemed to lift from his head. Consulting the compass, he took a bearing and pressed on toward where he expected the meadow to be. No tracks were there to follow but, holding the compass, he found that he had strayed to the west. No coincidence in that, he thought, and felt an urge to just go, to run west until he could no longer run or walk or move, then to throw himself to fate or freeze alone outside of somebody's locked, warm barn. When he'd been young, younger, he'd often hitchhiked; but this was different. Here, a man would die if he fell asleep beneath an overpass.

Of course here were no people. Just twenty feet from the road he'd felt an absence, a sensation of being alone. It was a thing he had conquered when young, fear of being alone. After his father had died, he'd mastered it, just as many of his peers who'd had fathers and mothers alive had had to master it. Maybe if Mat hadn't mastered it so well, he'd have been better; maybe not. He likened "alone" to sitting on his board as the last waves of afternoon leveled off and sun sank and the surfers, even off busy beaches, thinned away. Mat usually rode out the day and sunset, even if he simply sat on the swells. When he was completely alone, he would paddle in and strip off his fins and carry his board up the beach still strapped to an ankle. At his car, the old ragtop Karmann Ghia with dented-in nose and faded green paint, he'd towel his hair and peel down the top of his wetsuit and drink either a beer or, if the mood struck, Irish whisky, or swig a bottle of juice. He'd take his drink sitting on the hood, looking out to sea, sometimes turning to see the first stars, watch for a boat's running lights or just stare at the dark kinetic mass stretching halfway over a world, sea full of loneliness and mystery, death and life. For the ride home, his board would be wedged pointing skyward behind the front seat.

When he was younger than that, in his teens, with surfing companions or alone, Mat would light a joint and smoke it sitting on top of the bucket seats so that his head was high above the windshield and breeze would dry his hair and wet skin and he shiver. Sometimes he'd bring a girl surfing with him and they'd drink wine and walk down to the beach to have sex on a blanket he kept rolled under the Volksie hood-trunk or wrapped up in his lucky Bushmills towel; but in the last several years he'd stopped taking girls, because they made him lonely. He took the two things separately, the sea and girls, because it seemed right that they were appreciated for what they were, gifts from some indefinite God, an indifferent God but not one to be ignored. God's realm, for Mat, would be the sea and its eternal mystery. There was little of the modern God in him, the God that had been ferreted out of nature and enslaved in buildings by those who feared being alone; the perversity of their fear had on some level sickened him and made God even less. But here under the spires of great hickory and oak was His cathedral – Mat would admit it, if pressed, just as the roily sea was the bed of God, the God who gave life to earth or death. Sitting up in the bucket seats staring out to sea or watching the slowly-eroding cliffs, he, young and stoned, had had no trouble envisioning the passing of millennia as the coastline fell, molecule by molecule, grain by grain, stone by stone from clay into sea, all of it eroding slowly, inexorably, after billions of years, the sea swallowing the remaining grains of earth. That wasn't a horror to him. Not even his father's death was a horror, although it was pain, as was the loss of his mother, or rather loss of her desire to find him or not find him when, filled with despair in the belief that his father had died because of a wrongside-out baseball jersey, he had retreated to his room for days. She had not looked for him and, when he'd come out and sat across the table from her and they'd eaten a breakfast she'd made of cinnamon toast and strawberries, they both discovered they could not share their respective aches; and the distance across the table was farther than either was willing to go, she consumed with her own guilt, though what was grotesque to Mat was his indifference. He had closed that avenue immediately: he would be alone with himself, alone with his grief. He had understood then that one is always alone with grief. Eyeball to eyeball with solitude, he had stared across the length of his board drifting up and down the sides of swells while lights had winked on a darkening shore: he would wait for night before going in, night when the sea really came alive, the sounds of men gone. He would then belly down and paddle in, listening to the holy symphony of the waves lapping onshore and splash of his hands. He would hear in the distance a channel buoy clanging and see far down the coast the sweep of a lighthouse beam over the surface of water, of a sea that the more he knew it the more names he had for it and the more faces it had for him and, the more he thought about it, was the sole thing that truly mattered. Of all things, only the sea offered familiarity with indifference – at least until he had met Daphne. He knew that the shortcoming was his own, but it didn't matter and perhaps provided authenticity to his pleasure. His was no downstream respect; it wasn't subject to doubt. Not ever.

He sensed it in the Mazy: the majesty of the great body of land, the few yards around him, the geological district, the great breadth of glacial prairie, the Midwestern pan, the mass of a continent with three major north-south mountain ranges; its solidity; its mass of earth resistant to change... For a moment he knew that, of course, man was born as much of land as sea – this land anyway, this wild place, this great Mazy unchanged by man, virgin to his frequently heavy touch. This was an ocean of earth. Dazed by an unintentional fast, half-starved and alcohol poisoned, yet connected and hyper-aware, Mat sensed that, if he paused and listened, if he were patient – and now he was – he could feel the geological earth swollen and round below Mazy forest and beneath his feet and the snow; feel the land rise and ripple like a wave, a slow-running wave that would, after the passing of countless millennia, beach itself against the ancient cliffs of Big Bend Flats, collapsing the ancient shafts of lead mines. He could feel it, glimpse in his mind the passing of seasons, leaves falling and chilling north-westerly fronts hundreds of miles wide sweeping over the landmass, then snows turning to ice as the seasons progressed to false spring, more ice and snow and then the ice breaking on great lakes and rivers and scent of thawing earth and budding plants pushing through the cold ground, the days lengthening and warming and the buds sprouting, it seemed instantly, from sticks of bushes and trees. Insects hatching, then the quickening, thick forests of summer, green forests dampened by countless warm deluges, air teeming with bugs and their night sounds, fish splashing in shallows of water and fireflies glowing like phosphorescent magic in dark forests, and bats in pursuit, and giant velvet underwing moths dashing beneath streetlights and the air filled with swallows and martins by day, and the earth so alive that winter could never ever come again... until it did.

How did he know?

How could he not?

Mat sensed this slow passage of time, sensed it etched on the ancient stone bluffs rising over the river, sensed the little death of winter and rebirth of spring and, alone here for the first time in three days relaxed, felt the tension and fear and distrust slip off him, lift like some leaden yoke from his shoulders. Then he remembered the crazy old man on the bus that first night, and a momentary smile crossed his face. It isn't a matter of time to understand, he realized; it's a matter of perception, a matter of who does the perceiving. Maybe I'm beginning to *see*, he thought and felt better somehow, even if there were real things he should be worrying about. The solitude helped, though he wondered what he was doing in Mazy woods. But wonder later, he decided.

After walking a half hour, he hit the creek, a hundred yards away from but within sight of the clearing if he looked downstream, or what he imagined was downstream since the estuary was covered with ice, or what he believed was the clearing, because at first he couldn't be absolutely sure. Although he'd spent several hours there the previous day, heavy snow had changed the appearances. An examination of boughs along the high bank convinced him he was at the right place; convinced him not because he was adept at woodcraft but because, sitting on pine needles under a low bough, he came across a plastic fork that Bascom had obviously overlooked when cleaning up their mess. Besides, Mat reasoned, this must be the right place if what Verne had said was true, and Mat no reason to doubt it.

He slid down the bank overlooking the meadow and crossed the creek. Examining the clearing, he checked tracks that crossed the new snow but found none that he recognized as of a boar. The pressed snow and paths where animals had pushed through the accumulation onto ice covering the creek showed only small mammals, animals unfamiliar to Mat, who anyway had little experience in tracking. He was seeing fisher and deer traces along the creek; here and there birds, mainly crows, had congregated along a fissure to drink. Feeling woods-crafty, he looked for the best site to set his bait and finally settled on the middle of the clearing. What the hell, he thought.

He climbed back up the frozen bank to regain yesterday's vantage beneath drooping and somewhat sheltering boughs of a big pine where snow had barely accumulated. After scooping away needles and powdery drift that had filtered through, he sat back inside his blind and settled in. Pulling his stupid hat lower and tightening the earflaps, he sucked his head deep into his coat hood and pulled up the handkerchief covering his face. At last he slipped back the leather thong looped over the hammer of the huge pistol in his holster and pulled it out.

He thumbed back the hammer halfway just as Verne had showed him and turned the metal cylinder, which clicked solidly as it revolved. Thumbing aside the loading gate, he tipped the pistol barrel upward – a shell slipped smooth into his hand. Examining it, he decided as best he could that it was a real bullet, heavier than he'd imagined, bigger. He put it back into the cylinder.

Like most rational people Mat didn't particularly like guns. Especially pistols. He knew they did more harm than good as a whole and that the world could do without them. Yet he had to admit there was something more to a gun – this pistol – than merely machined steel for killing. That something was the compact potential for kinetic energy, energy now at rest. In even Mat's relatively tranquil bones, there was something unnerving about that energy potential, because something within him wanted to unleash it.

Mat wasn't afraid of the desire, though it was curious. First he smelled the pistol, and the smell was strong and fine, gun oil and maybe a little residual sulfur from a last firing. He hefted the .44 and sighted down the barrel toward the picnic basket in the clearing. The smell of oil reminded him of something – he couldn't recall what. It was a masculine odor, a nice smell.

Looking down that wavering barrel, lining the V-ramp with the sight, he realized that, at the distance he'd left the basket, a mere thirty yards, he probably couldn't hit a car. He felt a little drunk still. This wasn't like good guys shooting pistols out of bad guys' hands in the movies. He wondered what in hell he was doing, and the question immediately shifted... Absurd, his being there. Hunt for an ancient animal that, other than eating his lunch, had never harmed him in any way? He was really looking for approval. No, he was hunting for himself. Bullied by jokesters, a homicidal loan shark hunting him, separated from his fiancée, his inheritance such as it was spent on God knows what, federal police wanting to question him, much seemed chaos. A human perception – maybe he needed something to bully. Did he need to take out his frustrations on a pig? a wild boar that hadn't a chance in a million of showing, according to Verne, who'd pursued the creature since he was a kid over thirty years ago?

Mat thought about the physical aspects of shooting the animal. He hadn't even fired a pistol before, not one loaded with real bullets. He knew only the basics of shooting. He imagined the thing going off in his hands, the boar falling woodenly. But maybe not. Maybe the boar would stagger to its feet, blood pumping down a hairy chest, tusks popping (Mat had seen something like that in a film) as it charged, the pistol bellowing again and the beady-eyed thing spinning as bloody foam spewed from its black snout and bone chips flew as it charged up the bank on three legs, squealing like murder, snorting bloody mist over virgin snow while sighting Mat; charging, unstoppable, the beast like a hairy Volkswagen with angry red headlights and tusks like ivory sabers... Mat laughed off the vision. No, he wasn't afraid. Suddenly he understood: he didn't want to shoot anything. He wouldn't find himself in that – not even if it bought respect from these crazy hicks. But he'd had to carry it this far. He'd needed to see. It was okay for them: he didn't suppose they were wrong to hunt the Horror, great creature of Mazy woods; but it was wrong for him, because he did it for the wrong reasons. He'd hate himself if he shot it. He had doubts about himself – who didn't? – but pretty much liked himself for who he was, even if he didn't know who he was. He did know he didn't shoot animals or eat them. That he'd even considered hunting one was an indication of his addled condition, especially hunting one for the reason of impressing the hicks. Framed in that window of clarity, Mat realized what the scent of gun oil reminded him of: the perfume of *The Gordondale Gazette* reporter.

Everything would work out, he decided. His stomach growled and he thought about putting something in it. Eat, he decided. Clarity after a little more crisp air. He'd wait a minute; he had lots of time. Not pickled okra sandwiches; there were other things in there. Pretty soon he'd get up and look, when his stomach was more settled. Had to eat. He felt weak, fevered, almost like he didn't want the food, and that worried him. The life of a wino couldn't be worse, he guessed... Hadn't needed to come hunting. He was thankful for the two pairs of long johns Mother Dickey had given; other than his cheeks and forehead, he felt adequately dressed. Scooping piles of dry needles over his legs, he leaned back against a springy pine bough. He'd have to wait a while till his stomach settled and Verne came to get him. He could wait, alright. There was nowhere to go.

He thought about "nowhere" on a larger scale. Outside the woods, nowhere awaited. His thoughts drifted to Verne – what a strange guy he was, not unfriendly, still a sonuvabitch... not terribly bad, but the two were destined to mix it; just something about him... As he sat there, pine boughs gently brushing the back of his hat, Mat wondered about Verne being the last guy in the world to know what was missing in life. He looked across the clearing into dense foliage and the wall of the old cabin Verne had pointed out. A good site for a cabin, Mat decided. He wondered what a whole winter here might be like.

28

Steam puffing through fungus and age-mottled nostrils, the beast had risen slowly when the sun hit the thicket under pine boughs. For the past three weeks he had been sleeping there, despite seventy-yard proximity to rutted Mazy Meadow road. Rays of sunlight slanted through shaded limbs and sparkled on the stiff black and gray hairs bristling from his thick hide, two inches thick at his neck but now sagging from a massive frame.

He had lain motionless in the bed of needles as a pickup had passed before dawn, his good eye widening, discerning only dim shapes of gray and white. He had raised his withers, rear legs quivering with effort; he weighed a hundred pounds less than two years before. Haunches raised, he now brought the bulk of his shoulder weight over one front hoof, then the other, and straightened his legs until arthritic knees locked. His body heaved with the effort of standing. His head drooped, muscles slow to respond in the piercing cold. Diminished body mass increased the cold's effect. The animal's body required more calories than its diet provided.

He had slumbered in the thicket because the deep bed of pine needles stayed dry beneath the canopy and held warmth. Loamy earth cushioned his trichinosis-riddled muscles; this stand of pines provided for his needs. A small spring several hundred yards to the south served him, among other animals. Nestled in a thick berry glen, the spring gurgled into a stone depression filled with dead leaves, flowed twenty feet on to freeze or seep back into the ground. It seeped year-around undetected by humans.

For several minutes the beast stood with his sides heaving and muscles quivering, parasite-tunneled lungs filling and emptying like wheezy bellows. His wormy heart beat rapidly. He raised his snout to take in air currents, but did so only out of animal habit: he could barely scent anything. This morning, again, faint but discernible, the scents of food and man… He opened his mouth to scent more closely, rolling his eyes back, the one that barely worked and the one that didn't work at all, shot by Milt Thackery years before. He chopped his remaining outward-curving nine-inch tusk into upward tusks, honing both. From the scent of human, the brute's neck muscles stiffened; twin sensations of anger and danger arose, sensations stemming from a fighting spirit and the desire to survive. Highly intelligent, an atavistic response of hatred pumped through his blood. In younger years this process had sometimes set him rampaging through the Mazy, uprooting brush and saplings, stripping them with knife-sharp tusks and trampling hooves. The hated scents of humans and dogs… he had run from them until his panic subsided and evolved into frenzied anger as the packs closed. Furied, man and dog scent in his snout, he would turn in mid-stride to slash through trailing boar hounds in tight underbrush, plunging and ripping side to side, hooking with those caramel-colored tusks, squealing, chopping and slashing as they came. Boar dogs snarling, baying, yelping, launching at him, teeth and jaws worrying his thick hide, trying to pull him off of his feet, hounds bred for ferocity and power... Tail lifted and head lowered, driven by fury and powerful legs, the boar would collide into the angered dogs with leathered and buckshot-riddled chest, fighting, squealing, blood-slicked sides heaving... fighting until no dogs came any longer.

This morning the huge animal merely stood, head down, swaying slightly as he snuffed the air. Needing food, but with small desire for it, his was a timorous disdain more feline than porcine.

He was near his end.

Two years had passed since he'd scented a domestic sow in estrus.

He would not eat what he could not smell, so he starved slowly. What hounds and bears and shotguns and rifles had not destroyed, time had. But he detected a strong scent from the previous day and began walking into the breeze. The scent meant life, human scent mingled with creamy egg yolk spiced with homemade brown mustard, dill, onion slivers, salt and a dash of curry. The previous day he hadn't heard the trucks until they were almost upon his glen; he had done little more than raise his head and roll his eyes. Almost three decades had passed since Milt Thackery had blinded that left eye, but nearsighted his eyes mattered little. Life had depended on his ears and especially his sense of smell. Now he relied on memory to find food, mainly acorns rooted from beneath fallen layers of oak leaves. His olfactory organs had deteriorated equal to the parasites in his brain. Forty years, a Methuselah-lifespan, accounted for the rest.

No longer dictated by nocturnal instincts, he followed the scent into daylight. Without food, he would perish soon. Without the previous day's nourishment, the deviled eggs, aching joints and shriveled stomach and all, the previous night might have been his last.

He ambled stiffly over springy needles, his left hock unbending with rheumatism, pain stabbing through his sacrum into fused lower vertebrae. He stayed under the pines until he had reached the road. There he crossed, oblivious to his tracks bisecting deep ruts of Verne's tires in the unplowed snow. Occasionally snuffing the air, his shrunken stomach growling pitifully, he followed a downwind current from Mazy Meadow. His porcine brain centered on deviled eggs and another good scent drifting up from there. He moved slowly but with purpose. In human terms he might have been diagnosed as senile.

For the second time in two days he followed the only odors in the air currents strong enough to detect. To the great beast, urinal soap smelled good enough to eat.

29

Mat felt foolish with needles mounded over his legs but found comfort leaning against a springy bough. Head rested in the inverted V of the sagging limb, he stared across toward the old basket sitting conspicuously in the meadow. He imagined Verne coming back early, finding the basket and realizing that Mat had set a stupid trap – worse, telling everyone how Mat baited his trap with pickled okra sandwiches. Mat didn't like the idea of priming Verne's ridicule machine, but he didn't want to get up. If and when he felt like eating, it would be another matter. The fresh air had helped, but he was still too poisoned to stick his head in that basket. Soon, but not quite yet.

Again he got the idea that this Dickeyville Horror thing was an elaborate hoax with hundreds of players, like God's snipe hunt or a cosmic short-sheet. It was a sudden paranoia, resulting from the same vanity that led schizophrenics to believe the universe existed solely because they imagined it. Shell-shocked as he was, psychically battered, Mat realized that even these warped hicks couldn't pull off the boar stunt – Heywood, maybe, but not the rest of them. And yet... couldn't it be a hoax? And he, innocent that he was (he sniffed back self-pity), a trusting soul, exemplified the gullibility of a five year old by bumbling into the trap again. Step right up and see the Incredible Moronic Man, folks. Tell him anything and he'll believe it. Tell him again and he'll still believe it. A mental condition. Only a dime and you can't go wrong... But no. All those out-of-state truck licenses – it couldn't be. No way was it a hoax. Though, after all, Heywood had gutted a house to create a film set. Insanity!

Then came a worse thought... Maybe Verne wouldn't be back for him. Maybe Mat was supposed to wait until it became intolerable and he was forced to walk out. Didn't that beat all? The yokels were nuts, the result of long winters. And Mat didn't show a lick of sense falling for it; by comparison, Buster looked like a college professor. Probably everyone was whooping it up at some bar, waiting for Mat to trudge in sometime later that night.

The hell with walking out, Mat decided. If that was the game, he was too sick to play. Better to freeze to death with dignity than die of humiliation. Anyway, another day in Dickeyville and he'd starve. A sobering thought... better die in the forest than have Vinnie find him.

Distracted and bored, Mat pulled out the compass. He turned it until the arm aligned with magnetic North, then put it back and buttoned his pocket so it wouldn't get lost. A flock of birds, juncos, lit in a tree above and flitted to the ground to dig busily in the needles. As one, they rose into the boughs before flying to a next tree. Two crows settled in the snow beside the picnic basket, cawing noisily, heads bobbing as they examined the foreign object. One pecked at the wicker. The pair then flew off to the tops of nearby trees to begin a vocal argument, the avian equivalent of *Deliverance*'s dueling banjos.

Cold peeked around the bottom and top of Mat's bandanna. A breeze came up – not much, but enough to make his eyes tear. His fingers began to chill; he opened and closed them rapidly. How much time had passed? A half hour? maybe. Four hours would be hard. Weakened by hunger, alcohol and indecision, Mat's resolve wavered.

I've gone insane, he thought. How did I let myself wind up here? Breeze rattled the bare limbs and twigs of nearby oaks and rustled through the dense boughs of pine. It sounded like water, swish of an ebb tide tickling over sand. Mat listened. Time passed. His eyes grew heavy, but it was too cold for sleep. He straightened his back, suddenly afraid of dozing off. He might freeze if he slept. Under mounded loam his legs felt warm enough, but cramped. Situated with the direct sunlight to his back, even in sunglasses Mat's eyes were dazzled from the brightness of the snow fallen over the meadow.

Time... God's contrivance so that everything in the universe didn't occur at once. So why was everything happening at once to Mat? Not ten feet from him, to the side, a motion caught his eyes. He saw a rodent, a meadow vole, push up through the needles. Its miniscule snout wriggled as it sniffed the air, then it scampered away. When Mat ticked his head to see better, it dashed back to its hole and disappeared.

On impulse Mat snubbed back the leather thong over the hammer and pulled the big pistol from his holster. It sat weighty in his glove, barrel pointed away. He slipped off one glove and hefted the .44, pointing it toward the picnic basket in the field. Extending his arm, he found the pistol too icy and heavy to steady. Propping his left arm under his right hand, he said, "Ka-blooey! Blam! Blam!"

Pulling in the pistol, he thumbed the hammer back to catch on the safety. He liked the solid click as the cylinder half-revolved and hammer caught. Again he tipped a shell from the cylinder to examine it. The shell was brass and lead. Mat knew it was real. A bullet. The small yet weighty capsule possessed potential for death. Though the weapon was ice-cold, he liked the heft of the steel and checkered wooden grip. I don't like guns at all, he thought, but I kind of like this one.

He heard a limb jostle behind him but had listened to snow packs falling from the pines all day. He sighted the basket again. A guy couldn't hit a damn thing with one of these, he thought. He thumbed back the hammer until it cocked, the cylinder smoothly revolving a final half-turn. *Cli-ck!* just like in the movies. Something in him wanted to fire the pistol to free the energy, energy waiting for fulfillment (he imagined), for release.

He heard something scrape bark a few feet behind him, but ignored it as he sighted across the meadow to the crumbled Mazy wall. He tried to imagine how different the meadow must have looked once, but could not. So wild, the place must have always been this way.

Then he heard the heavy breathing, a deep asthmatic huffing close behind his head. He froze. Mat's breath caught in his throat.

30

In the instant Mat's muscles involuntarily contracted and released, he was already prepared to face Verne's prank. But then he turned to find his face sixteen inches from that of the enormous boar; and five thousand units of adrenaline couldn't have jolted him harder.

Only the briefest moment of disbelief... The beast's scarred snout writhed, an alien prehensile membrane stretching from a hideous head the size of a watermelon. Ribbons of slobber hung from its mouth. A single tusk curved upward from the left side of its jaw; ragged ears stood out from the sides of its head. Its one beady eye, ringed with white, bulged with hatred. No mask could look this unreal.

The monster snorted, recognizing its enemy. Massive, over four feet at its shoulders, it loosed a terrible squeal that exploded Mat into motion. Screaming in terror, he leaped over the embankment and swung the .44 barrel toward the head of the beast. The pistol roared, jerking hard in his hand. He dove forward, somersaulting down the bank and thumbing the hammer, firing another shot. In a continuous roll, he flopped onto the creek, firing a third shot behind as his head and shoulders collided with earth and ice. Dimly aware of the ridiculousness of this film maneuver, Mat hammered off three more shots in the direction of the bank while rolling over the snow. The hammer fell on two of the spent shells before the weapon slipped out of his hand.

For several moments he lay stunned, head halfway buried in powdery fluff, ears pounding from the roar of the big bore pistol. Then he stood, groggily, raising his hands to ward off the slavering monster. Realizing the pistol was lost and his sunglasses gone, Mat clawed at the snow powdering his eyes. He dug into drift until his hand touched something solid and loose: the .44. He backed away from the bank. "HEY-YA! GET OUT OF HERE! HEY!" he screamed.

Nothing happened. Nothing moved up the bank. Wired with adrenaline, Mat expected the boar to launch itself over and slice him up like a tomato with that immense tusk stuck from his jaw. Nothing could have prepared him for the size of the creature, ugly and horrible. His shaky fingers broke open the cylinder and tipped the brass cases into the snow. His unsteady fingers dropped half the shells he pushed out of the holster belt. Finally he was reloaded and, pistol leveled in two hands, breathing in gulps, he backed across the creek.

Something, a dark shape, up under the bower of limbs... he knew it was the boar. The idea that he had wounded it and it was readying itself to charge in bloodied fury occurred to him. Teeth chattering from fear and adrenaline, cold and hangover, Mat turned and ran to the far edge of the meadow. Pressing his back against an ancient trunk, he watched the bank. He was afraid to enter the forest, where the beast would have an advantage.

He waited, ears still ringing from the .44, head pounding from alcohol poisoning, shoulder throbbing from collision with frozen earth, stomach rumbling weakly. Eyeballs and bones and muscles ached from the cold, teeth ground from adrenaline. Trembling shook him as he stared, eyes squinting against snow-reflected light, and waited for the boar to rise. He no longer felt anxious to release the .44's power.

31

That's the way Verne and cousin Bascom found him thirty minutes later. They had followed the trail he had plowed across the snow clearings almost to the pines overlooking the meadow. Mat heard Verne yell, "Mat! We're coming to the clearing. Can you hear? I don't want my head blown off."

"Here," Mat shouted weakly. Then, alarmed, he shouted louder: "Look out for the boar! I think I shot him and he might be wounded."

"What? We're coming!" Pine boughs bounced wildly, brush snapped, then Bascom burst onto the edge of the bank, right on top of where the boar lay. A second later Verne was standing there too. They were silent above the shape and, for a terrible second, Mat had a fearful image of having shot a human being.

"My God!" he heard one of them whisper loudly enough to carry. "It's him. Mat's killed the Horror."

"I can't believe it! After all these years!"

Then the air filled with hoots and yahoos. "He got 'im! Mat killed the Horror! Yee-ha! He got 'im! Sonuvabitch, he got 'im!"

Mat stepped cautiously across the frozen stream, and Bascom and Verne pulled him up the bank and swept him into a circle dance.

"He got 'im! Mat killed the Horror!"

He told the story twice of how the Horror had come up behind him and he'd blasted it from two feet away.

Verne and Bascom listened with their mouths open.

It was huge but moth-eaten, sure as hell worthy of the designation "horror". It lay in a heap of wilted flesh and bone and muscle, flatter in death than it had ever been in life, its wiry hair missing in patches of fibrous, fungus-mottled skin, its one good eye nearly covered by a cataract, the other nothing but a glazed-over sunken scar. Its right tusk had rotted above the gums, broken off, and grown no further. Even the left tusk was rooted loose and wobbled when Bascom grabbed it. The boar's body was a mass of scars, including a long white one on its shoulder that Verne supposed was where Bailey Thatcher had hit him with his .30-30 years back, before the Horror had shivved him.

Verne, most interested in the missing eye, stooped reverently to feel the knotted scar tissue where Thackery's shotgun had blasted the creature. "Guess old Thackery wasn't bullshittin'," he said at last. "I'll be goddam, it really is the Horror." He turned to Mat, who leaned against a tree looking at the beast, and rose to put out his hand. "I don't know how you did it, but put 'er there, Mat. I just don't know what to say, other than I'm sorry I underestimated you."

A few minutes later Brodie and Nels had crashed through the brush. "We heard the shots! Sounded like a war – "

"What the...?" Nels wondered, falling to his knees before the dead animal. "Merciful heavens, is mighty Satan's hench-beast vanquished at last? Can it really be?"

"Mat, you did it? You did? You sonuvabitch! Ya-hoooo!" Brodie howled. "Mighty Mat!"

"No way! I don't believe it. I still don't believe it!" Nels said, shaking his head. "I detect the Lord's hand in this. Yes I do!"

While Verne, Nels, and Bascom stood talking excitedly, then retrieved the picnic basket and sat down, Brodie gathered himself "to get help", as he said. They could hear his shrieks as he disappeared into the forest. "Help with what?" Mat wondered, noting ruefully that it hadn't taken them a minute to migrate to the picnic basket, while he still felt too crappy to eat.

"Getting the boar out of here, of course."

They found the glove Mat had removed before he'd dived over the bank, then offered him some of the okra sandwiches as they munched happily; but just the sight of the little pickled cylinders between the bread slices nauseated Mat. And he felt badly about shooting the animal, even if their excitement was contagious. Glory of course felt good – yes, I am sort of incredible, aren't I? – and his mood picked up. Then he added ruefully: I shot a poor old pig that was just looking for dinner. Poor goddam old thing.

Mat wrapped his arms around himself and settled away from the others against the gnarled trunk of the big pine. Overhead, sun had climbed higher in a thin blue sky and he guessed the time to be around ten-thirty. A jet left a wispy trail across the blue; he was bored and cold, and his hangover needled at him, and he decidedly didn't want to take the poor old boar back to town. He envisioned everyone crowding around with congratulations, maybe hog-calling, and just the thought of that noise and the excessive distraction hurt his head worse. Verne, Nels and Bascom sat eating a little ways off, occasionally laughing and gesturing and setting down their sandwiches or fried chicken or deviled eggs to examine the fallen boar, which with its scarred sides and head reminded Mat of *Moby Dick* at the film's climax, when the pocked and riddled leviathan rose out of the sea trailing harpoon lines. Both elated and deflated, Mat felt the aftermath of the successful hunt. He'd be like Ahab, forever enmeshed in the history of a mythic beast; at which thought, deflation turned for the worse, to depression.

Mat emptied shells from the .44 and dropped it back in its holster. Idly listening to a crow cawing, he wondered at the duality of aftermath: being spent and elated. Not thirty minutes later, he heard in the still air distant tootling of horns and yelling. Fifteen minutes after that Brodie and three others had brought rope, a tarpaulin and hatchet and were standing over the boar. Mat recognized the ridiculous top hat, then features of the stooped Mayor emerging through pine; he seemed somewhat less excited than the others. The clearing filled with joyous exultation and happy swearing. Everyone pulled off their stocking caps and orange-lined quilted caps and top hat and threw them into the air. Then they gathered them up and pulled them on again.

One of the newcomers, name of Tabor, was a lanky fellow of late middle age whose leathery, lined face suggested he'd spent a good deal of his life out of doors. Tabor grabbed Mat's hand and pumped at it furiously. "Been after that boar near thirty-some years, Mister Roper. Longer'n Verne. And you just sashay in here and blow him away. Yee-hawww!" he reb-yelled across the clearing. "You must be the best damn hunter I ever saw, Mister Roper." Then he added for good measure, "You're the damn best man ever was!"

"Pleased to meet you," Mat responded. "I haven't had the pleasure, have I? It's kind of hard to keep track in Dickeyville."

"Some boys go a-partying. You an' I go huntin'."

Mat glanced at another man who stood back from the group and started toward him. "That's Calico," Tabor said. "He never ever talks, never does. He'll be just fine, Mister Roper."

Calico nodded, and Mat nodded back. Calico was rail-thin and ferret-faced. His most notable feature was that he seemed to have no lips, just a narrow slice of shadow where a mouth should have been. Small dark eyes burned under a quilted green hat.

Mat watched as Verne and Nels traipsed over the meadow and hatcheted two tall saplings near the old Mazy homestead, saplings about twelve feet long and uniform in diameter. They stripped the limbs of branches and twigs and carried them back naked to lay parallel in the snow beside the boar to use as handles, lashing the tarpaulin to them to form a travois. All the men working together rolled the animal onto the tarp. It was already stiff with cold and death. "So what're we doing here?" Mat asked as they squatted in snow.

"What're we doing? Why we're going to bring this trophy back to town," the Mayor said. But then he paused, standing and straightening as much as his stooped back allowed. "That is a good question. Look at this noble beast. Magnificent."

Noble beast. Mat stared at the flea-bitten carcass, sunken, patchy, scarred, one-eyed and ragged-eared, more resembling the hybrid offspring of a science-fiction wasp and a burned-down tent. It could audition for the role of a lazored four-legged giant cockroach.

The men piled their rifles and the picnic basket beside the boar, then tossed in the hatchet. "Let's go. Four on one side, three on the other. Hoist on three," Verne ordered. "One, two..."

They grunted, lifting the thicker front ends of the travois off the ground, and dragged the dead weight over rough ground. Before he'd gone ten feet, head pounding with exertion, breaking into a sweat, Mat's regret at having shot the animal had increased. They had to skirt fallen trees that they'd simply stepped over before. Powdery snow plowed like water ahead of the travois and began to fill it. After what Mat guessed was halfway to the road, the men sat down to rest and empty snow from inside the travois.

The Mayor pulled an unopened pint of Canadian whiskey from inside his coat pocket and twisted the cap. "I think this calls for a toast. Never thought I'd live to see this day." He took a pull at the bottle and handed it to Brodie, who sat nearest to him, and turned to Mat. "I suppose you're thinking about the prizes."

"Prizes? For what?"

"My store's got a .300 Weatherby in the front window," the Mayor explained, sounding somewhat regretful.

"I'll never hunt again. What's a rifle to me?"

"About eight hundred dollars," Verne said.

"Of course, a guy can always use a new rifle," Mat admitted.

"And a new pocket warmer from Humphrey's Hardware and Sports Supplies, and dinner for two and membership at the Dickeyville Diner and Rifle Club," Brodie added.

"Not to mention a weekend for two at the Dickeyville Motel and Ammo store," Bascom said. "And a twenty dollar spree at Graybow's Grocery and Hunt Shoppe."

"Woo-woo. Must be my lucky..." Mat's voice tapered away.

"You might also be interested in the cash prize," Verne said. "A thousand dollars, right, Mayor?"

"Something like that," the Mayor mumbled without enthusiasm.

Mat mulled it over. Maybe he wasn't sorry about the boar after all.

Tabor interrupted his musings. "I'll be ding-danged. You must be some kind of a hunter, Mister Roper." Lighting a pipe full of aromatic tobacco, Tabor sat in the snow and reclined against a deadfall.

"Not really. Only my first time," Mat said, then added, "Second, if you count yesterday."

Tabor glanced up, figuring something. "That so? Then how'd you get him, Mat? If you don't mind my calling you Mat. Jump shooting or still hunting? Tree blind? I see you don't have a dog pack."

"I was just sitting there." Mat shrugged, hot breath billowing from his nose. He didn't know if he'd been 'still hunting' or 'tree blind,' so he said nothing more. 'Jump shooting' conjured images of Reverend Rantin; too ludicrous to consider.

"After we get the boar back to town, then what?" Brodie wondered. "Bascom and me was thinking maybe we could put 'im in a water trough and freeze him in a block of ice; then we could float him in the punch at Mat's wedding and, when all the punch was gone, boom! there he is – the Horror floating in the punch bowl."

"Gads," Mat said, shuddering.

"By rights he belongs to Mister Roper, so whatever he wants to do with the Horror is his decision," the Mayor said.

All eyes turned to Mat. "What would I want a dead pig for? You know I don't eat meat."

"*Eat it!*" Tabor exclaimed. "You kidding?"

Mat shrugged. He was anxious to get back to town, but would be hard pressed to say why. There was nothing for him there. "Let's just leave it here, for the coyotes, and the scavengers – "

The Mayor interrupted. "Um, Mister Roper, I don't think you quite understand what the Horror means – meant – to Dickeyville."

Mat's mind worked as hard as possible, but he couldn't think of any reason to keep the boar if it couldn't be eaten.

Verne bent over the dead thing, a solemn expression replacing earlier excitement. "It's funny. I've been waiting so long for this ol' boar to get shot. Seems like a whole way of life just died, doesn't it? Kind of sad. I mean, me and Brodie's dad hunted this boar, and so did Uncle

Monk and Uncle Bud. Nothing will be the same around here."

The Mayor nodded his hunched neck. "This boar has been the center to most of my life, the important parts of it. Hell, Maggie and I were married the first day of the Dickeyville Horror season back in sixty-two. My gross receipts for that weekend were, if I remember right, damn near twelve hundred and sixty-three dollars, even if the money was lost on one of my many unsuccessful bids for the Assembly seat."

"That's what I mean," Verne said. "With her own money, Dead Alice put this wild boar in the Mazy for all of us. Somehow I never thought it'd come to this."

"To Mat," Brodie said, taking a deep drink off the pint.

Nels took it from his hand. "To Mat."

They passed the bottle, and silence ensued. Mat's sip was tentative.

"I feel like a bit of the sand's gone out of me," Verne said. "Damn me, but I've always suspected I'd feel this way."

"An outsider kills him," the Mayor said. "More o' them than us locals, so it stands to reason." He shrugged.

"God's will," Nels said.

"End of an era," Verne said.

"I mean, how'd you figure him in this meadow after yesterday?" Tabor asked, talking around his pipe stem. "By his habits, today you wouldn't find him within miles of here."

The others listened intently, though they were as anxious as Mat to get back to town, if for different reasons. This was a story they'd tell their grandchildren: death of a legend, the end of something.

"I had a hunch while I was washing my face this morning. Thought he'd be hungry," Mat explained. "Then I thought he'd want some of that damn pickled okra." He laughed.

"Pickled okra?" Tabor wondered, pulling his pipe from his lips.

"But it wasn't the picnic basket he wanted," Mat said. "It was Pa Dickey's cake soap he came for. Came right to it, just like yesterday."

"Cake soap? What's he mean?" Tabor asked nobody in particular.

"Urinal soap," Nels explained. "Mat washed with urinal soap."

Tabor leaned forward. "*What?*"

"I used it for a joke this morning," Mat said, slapping his knees.

"A cake of that urinal soap?"

Mat chuckled. "One and the same."

"Let me get this straight," Tabor said, standing to strip his stocking cap. "An outsider, only your second time hunting, and you lure in the Dickeyville Horror, a majestic European wild boar that's been loose in the Mazy for near forty years, with urinal soap?"

"That's about it," Mat said, rolling onto his belly where he lay in the snow. "A cake of urinal soap."

Tabor started pacing. "Something's wrong here." He pulled on his stocking cap, then jerked it down low with no roll to the brim. He flapped his arms. "I don't like it. No sir, I don't. You come in here and shoot our boar after attracting him with urinal soap." He began to rub at his forehead. "A goddam cake of urinal soap."

Bascom sat up. "Doesn't seem too sporting, does it?"

Verne said, "I don't know. Others tried baiting the boar before."

"Yeah, but not with no urinal cake," Tabor said.

"Not much dignity in that, for sure," Nels said.

"It was an accident," Mat explained. "I didn't know."

"That's another thing," Tabor said. "You don't even know anything about hunting. We've been after that boar for forty years and you just march in here as if you owned the place."

The Mayor nodded. "Doesn't seem right, does it?"

Tabor turned and fixed Mat with a beady stare. "You California movie stars just march in here and take what you want and march right back to L.A. as if you owned the world."

"I'm no movie star."

"Yeah," Nels said. "With your pretty face and all. Just like you stole ol' Daphne from Buster."

"Poor Buster," Bascom said. "Bastard never had a chance, did he?"

"Now everybody'll go to Gordondale. Won't be any reason to come to Dickeyville," the Mayor said sadly. "And Mat's going to get money and all the prizes."

Then Calico, who never ever never spoke, pointed a skinny chicken-bone finger at Mat and said, "Ye-ye-ye-ye-ye – oo-oo-oo-oo-oo – "

"Huh?" Mat wondered.

"Ye-ye-ye-ye-ye-ye-ye-ye-oo-oo-oo-oo – "

Tabor interrupted. "He says, 'You march right in here like you owned the place and take what your want, Mister California surfer boy.'"

"Ye-ye-ye-ye-ye-ye." Calico agreed.

"Calico, you say a lot with few words." Mat said. "I think I'm having a bad bio-rhythm week."

"We better get going," Verne decided.

They began dragging again, the townsmen occasionally darting glances at Mat. "Jeeze. Give it a rest," he said.

"Ain't right," Tabor grumbled ominously.

At the narrow road three trucks other than Verne's waited for the men dragging the huge thing, the boar now as stiff as a burnt turkey. Brodie and Bascom had a new idea and, instead of putting the Horror in a punch bowl, wanted to tie it to a hood and ride into Dickeyville with horn blaring. But the Mayor had other plans.

"We've got to sneak up on this thing," he explained. "We don't want to do anything hasty until we've had time to think."

"There's nothing to think about, Mayor. Roper's already slaughtered our boar," Tabor pointed out bitterly.

"Now you listen, buddy," Mat warned, his stomach rumbling noticeably. "I've heard enough of this – "

"Hold it, hold it," Verne interrupted, sticking his arm in front of Mat. "The Mayor's right. Let's take a day or two to figure this thing out. I think we can count on everyone to keep their big yappers closed, can't we?" He looked at Tabor and Calico.

"You don't scare me, Verne," Tabor growled.

"No?" the Mayor asked. "How about that jack-light deer you hung in your garage this fall? I bet Henshaw at the Game Department would like to know what you're up to."

Mat looked at the hunched, mild-mannered old man. He was a politician, all right. "That still don't scare me," Tabor said.

"How about Wanda Lee Skeeter?" Brodie asked, picking at the end of his big Dickey nose. "Runs the Chop Shop Hairdressery in Gordondale? Real hussy, that one. Reg'lar firecracker of a gal. Sure hate for any false rumors about Wanda and you to get home to your Leticia, who I hear is a bit of a firecracker herself."

Tabor's eyes widened and he swallowed, Adam's apple bobbing, like he was engorging an unpitted martini olive. He glanced at the Mayor. "On second thought warden Henshaw could make my life a living hell. Won't say a word, promise. And Calico, he can't."

Lifting together, they hefted the boar overhead and walked to each side of the Mayor's pickup bed and laid it where it would stay until, as he said, he had time to mull it over, especially after next week's tourist influx for the hunt. After everyone took a last long look at the creature, they covered him with the tarp.

"I'll park outside and freeze him solid," the Mayor explained.

"We could put him in Ma Dickey's freezer," Bascom suggested.

Brodie agreed. "She could reach in the freezer for some frozen peaches, and grab a handful of boar scrotum."

Mat started to get into the Explorer with Brodie, Bascom and Nels, but Verne stopped him. "You ride with me."

"It's cold," Mat said, shivering. "I got to freeze my ass off in your entertainment vehicle again?"

"One more ride isn't going to kill you."

In the truck, Verne explained: "Those are good boys, Mat. Even a crusty fart like Tabor isn't too bad. But all of them, they'll need a few hours to straighten things in their heads. Fact is, he was our goddam boar and now you killed him. Don't much like it myself."

They sat in silence, then Verne figured what else he wanted to say.

"You're family now. Or will be soon. I'd do anything for a Dickey or Winder. But you're going to have to pull yourself out of this mess, Mat." He started the truck and turned around before the other trucks could and headed down the road.

"An hour ago I'm a fucking godling. Sixty minutes later I'm the pariah of Dickeyville," Mat complained.

"In small towns, change hits people hard. We need time to get used to things. Some never do adjust. Like I said, I just wish to hell you didn't shoot our goddam boar."

Mat resisted the urge to remind Verne that he'd been shanghaied to hunt the "goddam pig" and resisted the urge to remind him that he hadn't wanted to kill an animal. His thoughts were interrupted by a funny buzzing sound behind them, and he turned to see a pickup following closely, Tabor half hanging out the window with his arm and fist pumping the air; behind Tabor's truck came Brodie's and the Mayor's. Mat resisted the urge to flip the finger at Tabor. He felt so mad his stomach rumbled and he forgot to be hung over.

"I'm hungry, Verne. Did that picnic basket get in the back?"

"Huh-uh. Bascom and Brodie got it. And the way those two young pups eat, especially Brodie, I wouldn't count too heavily on leftovers."

"The hell with it. The hell with you all." Mat watched the rearview.

32

He stewed about it the whole way back into town. When the pickup passed under the DICKEYVILLE HORROR DAYS banner at the turn-off for Mazy woods, he glanced at Verne, who glanced back but said nothing. They passed through snowy streets where families were decorating front lawns with snowmen and plywood Nativity scenes or stringing strands of lights over porches and shrubbery. "Doesn't anybody work Mondays around here?" Mat wondered, unbuckling the holster and laying it on the seat.

"Not in this kind of weather. Except at the new mall in Gordondale."

When they turned off for Ma and Pa Dickey's, only Brodie's rig honked a farewell. Verne slowed the old truck to let Mat out.

"It's a damn amazing thing you did today, man. I've been hunting that old boar for, like Tabor said, thirty-odd years, and now it's dead, it sure looks small. I guess it's like most things in life: the wanting is always bigger than the getting. Sorry it turned out this way."

Mat studied Verne a moment. Then he slammed the truck door and headed up the drive, its length of forty yards now clear of snow. Several cars were parked at the street end while at the far end, his face rosy, Pa Dickey's rear rested in the scoop of his shovel. He was twisting the stem of an apple; as Mat approached, he looked up.

"Hey, Mat. Didja shoot the Horror today?"

Mat gave him a glance that would have chilled a snowman, but the old man beamed. "Smoked 'im, all right," Mat shrugged.

"I'll bet you did. Want to grab a shovel with me?"

"Thanks. But I need something to eat. My stomach's killing me."

Pa shook his head in consolation and continued twisting the stem off the fruit. "Mother's in there cooking with the ladies from the Christ Church auxiliary. Putting up a little something for a party tonight. Did I tell you how glad I am to have you around? Haven't had so much fun since Sam Bushwhisker's dick froze to his outside toilet lid."

"Another party?"

"Yessireebob. Another wing-ding."

Mat nodded toward the apple. "You know, that stem's twisted off."

"I know that."

"So why're you still pulling at it?"

"Don't you know?"

"No."

"Because each twist of an apple stem stands for the alphabet. It's the first letter of the girl's name you'll marry. Ma's real name is Petunia, so I gotta twist an apple stem sixteen times."

Mat figured Pa and Ma must have been married forty years, but said nothing. He started to go in, then thought of something else and paused. "You spend all your time shoveling snow?"

"In winter, pretty much seems like it."

"Why don't you get a power snow blower? You heard of them?"

"There's lots of companies makes 'em. But how'm I gonna get any winter exercise unless I shovel snow?"

"And Ma? She works hard."

"You don't know the half of it."

"I got a question for you. Did Verne ever live in California?"

"Not that I know of. Other than the army, he ain't lived nowhere but here. Why?"

"Never mind."

"Listen Mat. I'm pretty sorry about the friend thing."

"What 'friend thing'?"

"That you never had a best friend. I feel bad about that."

"What the hell…"

Determined to snatch a bite of something, Mat stripped off his quilted hat, boots and oily coat on the porch and went to the kitchen. There he was enveloped in a maelstrom of a dozen older women preparing food. An odor of warm, fresh-made cinnamon bread mingled with that of other spicy-sweet baked goods almost brought him to his knees. His mouth began salivating uncontrollably. "Look who's here, girls," a large-chested matron exclaimed. "It's Matty."

In his whole life, nobody had ever called him Matty. He started to protest but got nowhere.

"Oh, my God, he *is* the gorgeous one, isn't he?" a white-haired grandmother exclaimed. "Would you look at this boy?"

"Lord, honey, where were you when I was eighteen?"

In a gesture Mat was still unprepared for, despite recent frequency, several fleshy, wrinkled hands snatched at and pinched his cheeks.

"Isn't he just a cream puff?"

"Didn't I see you in *The Sting*?"

"No, honey. That was whatsisname."

"Gladys, you're right. Matty was in… oh, what was that?"

"Butch Castaway and the Sunshine Kid."

"Matty, I saw that picture of you in *The Gordondale Gazette*. Cutest thing I ever saw."

"Are we out of vanilla?"

"I thought I saw a bottle over the stove. There it is."

"Where?"

"By the dill. What's the matter with you, Emma. You have boy eyes? Can't see a milk carton in front of your face?"

"Can't hit a toilet with a fire hose," someone added.

"*Louise!* I'm shocked!" They laughed.

"Something's sticky on the floor. Could you get me that mop, Hilda? There's a girl."

"We're going to need another bun pan. Better start calling around."

"Another? How many do we have already?"

"Butter. That's what we should have told Ma to get. More butter."

"Speaking of Ma, where is she?" Mat asked. But now that their focus had been diverted back to cooking tasks, nobody paid attention to him. He faced a wall of wide backsides over which ankle-length cotton dresses and embroidered aprons hung.

The smells drove him crazy. He'd never smelled such cooking. He tried to peek at the counter by crowding beside one of the white-haired gals who'd smiled so nicely. He spied before her a cookie sheet piled high with flat brown cookies, still warm and aromatic from the oven, stamped into reindeer patterns, Santas, angels, Christmas trees, candy canes. A pile of tin cookie cutters were strewn across the counter, right to the invisible line where the next woman rolled out a strand of thick yellowish dough dusted with brown sugar and cinnamon. Mat watched the woman in front of him squeeze a baker's bag and dribble white frosting buttons on a gingerbread man. His stomach rumbled and he reached and grabbed a Christmas tree festooned with frosting ribbons and dusted with red and green sprinkles. With a nimble motion the woman snatched a wooden spoon and brought it with a sharp crack! across his knuckles. "*Nein, nein*. Not to touch *mein pepparkakor!*" Mat froze, unsure, until she smacked his hand again. "Girls! Girls! A *pepparkakor* snatcher!" The "girls" roared happily and Mat dropped the cookie. "You just wait 'til tonight, honey. That's the rule."

"We must say, Matty, how sorry we are you never had a best friend."

He growled under his breath and left the kitchen for his room. Storming upstairs, he threw back the window curtains. As far as he could see over a flat horizon, the sky was clear and blue. Starve or go crazy, he thought: it's a toss-up which will come first. Or wait for a blood-crazed loan shark to appear. He cupped a hand under the faucet in the bathroom and drank the equivalent of a pint of water, contemplating with each sip a tube of Pepsodent toothpaste sitting on the windowsill. He unscrewed the cap, squeezed out a dollop and tasted it. Better than nothing: a vintage toothpaste, not a great one.

Going back downstairs, he dialed his mother's phone in California. After several rings a man's voice answered and said he'd get "the lady of the house". A few minutes the receiver clonked loudly upon something and a voice responded, "Hello?"

"Who was that?"

"Mat, honey? Is that you?"

"It's me. Who was that?"

"That? That was Peck. He's staying a few days while his screentests run." She whispered: "Peck, as in pectoids? Honey, this man is the next Stallone."

"Aren't they all?"

"Oh. We're going to be that way, are we?"

"So mother, there any chance at all to get any money?"

"I told you, dear. I spent it all on your party. Wasn't it divine? Did you make any contacts?"

"I wasn't there, remember? I'm in Wisconsin."

"Are you on location, dear?" Something covered the receiver. "Stop that, you silly boy," a muffled voice protested; then: "I do remember hearing something like that. Isn't your girlfriend in a film back there?"

"My fiancée. We're going to be married. I think."

"As long as she's connected, dear. I'd hate to see you throw away your career by marrying for love." Then she whispered confidentially: "It's getting to be quite the common thing to do."

"I've got to go, mother."

"Mat, all kinds of people have been looking for you. Some image men from the Film Engineering Turpitude Investigation Division – "

"FETID? They're worried about Hollywood's reputation?"

"Also some men from BATF."

"Bureau of Alcohol, Tobacco, and Firearms. Now what?"

"I meant DEA. Mat, honey, have you been smoking pot again?"

"I've really got to go. I've got a headache. I've got a terrible head-ache and it won't go away."

He hung up and tried to dial Daphne's cell but got no tone. He swore and went back upstairs to take three aspirin. Then he dropped onto the bed and began to drift into an uneasy sleep, once again under the eyes of ever vigilant Dickey and Winder ancestors.

33

He hadn't fallen asleep before he heard noisy footsteps pounding upstairs. His door caved in under rapid blows, and he lifted his head to see two jacketed girls he vaguely remembered from the night before – or the night before that – standing side by side in the doorway. The shapely twins were chewing strands of flaxen hair dangling over their stick-out ears. Their bulb noses were red from cold. Both wore idiotic pink knit caps with puffs on top. "We're out four-wheeling, Mr. Roper. We thought you might like to go for a spin."

He avoided their faces and lay back his head. "Thanks, but I've had a terrible day. What were your names again?"

"Twila and Cabella. I'm Cabella."

"Yeah, Cabella and Twila. I'm just a little tuckered from – hey, you said four-wheel drive? In this snow?"

"Sure thing. We can go anywhere in our Ford truck."

He sat up. "You two wait downstairs and I'll be right with you, okay? I'll just put on something warm."

Ignoring his swimsuit, still damp with Caribbean salt water, and the bottles of Coco Tan lotion, Mat pulled on two shirts and two pairs of slacks and stuffed his credit cards and wallet and passport into his pants pocket. The imitation leather duffel was nice, but what the hell, next time he was in Tijuana he could pick one up for ten bucks. In the bottom of it lay his wadded Hugo Boss linen jacket and the "lucky" Bushmill's Irish Whiskey beach towel gifted to him by his father. He looked at it for a moment. Then he didn't look at it anymore.

He slipped on his watch and tucked his custom-fitted diving mask under the shirts. Nothing else mattered enough. He tossed the duffel behind the bed and, patting his new bulk, glanced at himself in the mirror. He looked like the Pillsbury surferboy.

The way Mother Dickey fluttered, it was plain she didn't like him out with Twila and Cabella. "It doesn't look right, does it?"

"No problem," he called as they breezed through the door. "These girls aren't allowed to view *Sea Watch*."

Mat wasn't big on trucks or customizing, but he knew a great professional paint job when he saw it. This Ford was old, '50s, with a high chassis riding on big mag wheels. Yellow and red flames blazed from wells across midnight-blue panels. "Ain't she a beaut?" one twin asked. Mat wondered briefly what a job like this cost.

Father Dickey, leaning on his shovel, yelled as Mat climbed in. "Looks like that beer last night bloated you up a bit, Mat."

The girls got in on either side of him, one grabbing a welded chain steering wheel in one hand and the stick shift with the other. Mat saw that the shift knob was covered with hair.

"What's that?"

"White-tail buck's ballsack."

"How appealing," he murmured.

Frank Sinatra crooned Christmas carols from a tube radio as the truck rolled over plowed streets. The cab warmed and Mat could smell the scent of the young women: clove, ginger, shampoo. He supposed they'd been baking earlier. As the truck jostled, their hips rubbed his, pinning him loosely between them on the bench seat. They passed a party of couples wearing what appeared to be black tights; they were skiing beside the street in what Mat guessed was a park. This was the first time he had seen cross-country skiers and he had to laugh. He could appreciate hard work but the sport looked silly. He commented on it; the twins didn't reply; the truck passed houses decorated with wreaths and Christmas trees, some highlighted by light strands though it was daytime. Mat saw that they weren't steering toward the two-lane highway and was just about to say something when a black sedan with three huge men in front passed slowly in the other direction, then braked. Mat looked out the rear window and saw the automobile pull U-turn. He recognized the driver and passengers.

"Oh shit! Cabella! Hit it! We gotta get outta here," he said.

"No, I'm Twila."

"Dammit, who cares. Get going!" He jerked a thumb toward the rear. "Those guys want to kill me!"

Twila glanced in the mirror and saw the sedan come up fast. She whooped, and Cabella turned to look while Mat attempted to duck. "A car chase? Man, you Hollywood guys really know how to live," Twila said. "Waddya think, sis? Race?"

"I dunno," Cabella answered as the sedan pulled almost to their bumper and an arm came out of a window gesturing to pull over. "If we put any dings in the truck, daddy'll have a shit-hemorrhage."

"Come on!' Mat yelled, leaning under the dashboard. 'These guys are going to put dings in *me*!"

"If they want to kill you, I guess we have an all-clear, don't we, sis? It's life and death!"

"Death is one thing. But you know how daddy is."

"Ladies, will you get the fuck going?"

"The hell with daddy. You don't get many chances in life for a car chase," Twila said, gritting her teeth and stomping her foot on the gas. "Hit it, snow daddy!"

The Ford's four-barrel carburetor slurped a slug of supreme, sucked oxygen, and 289 cubic inches roared through a tuned exhaust. The wide rear snow-and-mud tires spun in the slush, and the truck's rear-end fishtailed a hundred yards down the street. Mat's stomach spasmed as he grabbed the dashboard. The twins whooped. The big rubber knobs caught the asphalt and the truck careened onward, leaving the other car behind.

"Here they come again," Cabella said, and Mat turned to see the big sedan not two hundred yards behind coming up fast on the residential street. An elderly woman on the sidewalk paused and shook a cane as truck and car passed her. "Hoodlums," she yelled, but they picked up speed and were gone.

The street curved, twisting around the spreading rise of Dickeyville, above the wide farmlands. The truck's rear slipped on the corners but held, careening, occasional bare boughs swiping its side mirrors.

"Yee-hawww!" Twila yelled.

"Daddy'll have a shit fit, if you wreck his truck!" Cabella shrieked.

Twila jerked the wheel and slid across a snowy lawn, sped down an icy street back into the heart of town and flashed through the intersection. Mat glanced to see the car that would crash into and kill them. He saw something else a block away. "A bus! There's a bus!"

"You don't have buses in California?" Cabella wondered through gritted teeth.

"But the snow. When'd they get through?"

"Run every day. Haven't missed a day in twenty years."

"But I thought – "

"Don't think. Be quiet!" Cabella yelled over the racing engine.

The sedan came up within twenty feet of the tailgate and Mat turned. Vinnie-the-Tide, one huge fist pumping behind the windshield, sat between the two goons hunched by the dash and steering wheel. "Oh, Christ," he mumbled, knowing what these stone men intended.

Roostertails of syrupy snow flew behind the pickup, splattering the sedan's windshield. The driver tried to pull even, swerving toward the pickup's rear, not colliding, and Twila floored it again. The sedan hung on, coming alongside in the other lane. Mat waited for them to bump it, but that was the stuff of movies. The two vehicles dropped down a slight incline and burst through the last of the town's houses onto a plowed road, straight and marked only by fence posts and trees and odd tracks that must have been cut by other tires.

A sudden thought: Mat glanced at the truck's gas gauge – plenty.

Both vehicles hit eighty, the sedan still hanging on slightly behind, its nose and hood bobbing as it plowed through occasional drifts, neither vehicle inclined to pull close enough to collide at speed. Looking back, Mat's eyes were met by Vinnie's, intent. Vinnie drew a finger across his throat. "They're hanging in," Twila warned, the truck's rearend suddenly drifting dangerously close to the automobile. "Use the CB, Cabella," she ordered.

Cabella jerked open the glove box and grabbed a mike. "This is Bobbsy Twin One. Can anybody read me? Whoa!" The truck slipped again, swerving close and clipping the sedan's bumper. "We need some help out on Clover Road. Now! Anybody read me?"

Something indecipherable crackled back. "What is it?" Mat asked.

Cabella dropped the mike and shrugged. "Someone, at least. Can't you go any faster, Twila?"

"I wish to hell I had something in the rifle rack," Twila cursed. She wrenched the wheel close to the sedan, then pulled back. "We're getting pretty far out of town. Bad if they catch us here." She feathered the pedal, then tromped it again. The truck bucked and surged onward.

Mat grabbed his head with both hands. "Jesus Christ."

"Mat, your language," Cabella warned.

"This looks a hell of a lot more fun in the movies," Twila complained, tromping again. They swept through a grove of bare-limbed oaks, and the road ahead ran straight to the horizon. Only outlines of farmhouses and fences and craggly-armed trees off to the side broke the vistas. They were in big trouble if they slowed or collided.

Then the road dropped into a hollow, the truck's bumper spewing up a cloud of powdery snow that swept over the windshield. "Don't let up!" Cabella yelled, reaching across Mat for the wiper knob.

"You better stop," he said. "It's not worth you two getting killed!"

But that wasn't necessary.

"You're getting him!" Cabella yelled, and yes the sedan began to swerve and spin out; it fell back, its momentum broken by axle-deep drifts across the hollow's pit. The pickup slowed too, tires spinning furiously as they fought to grip up the incline of the hollow's rim, rear end drifting dangerously to one side, momentum easing, then they were hanging at the top of it, free of heavier drifts. The tires dug in and they had rubber on asphalt. They slowed, turning to watch, and for a moment the sedan's grill and hood seemed slowly to clear the rise, but the vehicle's rear drifted to the side and lost momentum. The auto tilted slightly over the road shoulder and stopped. Somewhat deflated, Twila feathered the gas and the truck inched ahead.

Behind, a hundred, two hundred yards, three figures got out of the sedan. "Holy Christ, that was close!" Mat wiped his forehead.

The twins laughed. "Whoo-eee! Some fun!" Cabella exhaled. Three hundred yards ahead of the sedan Twila pulled to a stop.

"What're you doing? Are you crazy?"

"Going out for some air, Mat Roper. I need fresh air." She climbed from the cab and bent beside a front wheel.

Mat turned and looked back. The three men beside the big sedan had noticed. They gestured excitedly and began slogging down the road toward the truck. The biggest figure, Vinnie, fell back.

"Hey!" Mat yelled through the windshield at Twila, who had meandered to the other side of the truck. He glanced at the ignition below the dash. "Dammit!" She had pulled the key out. "What in hell's she doing?" he asked Cabella.

"Just corral your horses, Mat. She's putting 'er in four-wheel, is all. Clutch's pretty shot in the old buggy and she grinds like hell if she's idling when you switch over."

The three men walked confidently toward them as Twila squatted beside the truck's rear wheels. "Old-style hubs," she explained, opening the door to climb in. The two men, still a hundred yards behind, yelled and burst into a trot again, closing on them.

"Better get it on, honey," Cabella said.

"Go," Mat ordered, both hands clamped to the dash and knuckles white. "Go, go, go!"

Twila turned the key, but nothing happened. "Uh-oh."

"We're fucked," Mat said. In the rearview he saw the set of the men's red faces as they jogged heavily through snow in their loafers. Frostbite, he thought. At least as they killed him he'd have the satisfaction of their toes having to be amputated.

"Knock it off, sis," Cabella warned. "It's a bit close."

"Just kidding," Twila twisted the key. The engine turned over and caught. She pulled a shift stick practically under the seat and gears grinded until the truck lurched to a crawl in low. She pushed the stick forward and gained momentum into second.

The glass in the rear window suddenly popped and a bullet passed Mat's head and punched through the windshield.

"Duck!" he cried and leaned forward.

Cabella rolled down her window. "Those sonsabitches shot daddy's truck!" She leaned halfway out and yelled. "My daddy's going to be pissed, you sonsabitches! He'll twist your friggin' heads off!" Mat pulled her back in as another bullet struck the tailgate.

Twila pulled the stick into third, then fourth, and then the men were far behind. "Assholes. We oughta go back and run them over," she said. Mat turned and saw specks receding, small spots, insignificant in the white forever horizon. *Vanishing Point.*

"Some fun, huh?" Cabella leaned forward and looked past Mat to her twin. "Did you see that one fat one run after us?"

"God almighty," answered the one Mat supposed was Twila. "You sure know how to live, Mat. What a riot."

"More fun than the night we put that badass banty rooster under Uncle Monty's toilet lid."

"This is the life, sis. Life should be like a movie."

Mat gradually eased back. The chase had been too thrilling. Were these girls nuts? He had a happy thought. "I'm not hungry anymore!"

The truck continued west, away from town, slowly plowing through occasional drifts covering the road. In various places fences and skeletal black oak or other hardwoods bordered it; lonely farm-houses and, beyond, the plains, sometimes broken by stands of farm woods or frozen ponds or creeks... Out here there were no other tire tracks to blemish the snow. "Some country," Mat said, feeling adrena-line's grip subside. The cab was warm and he felt himself sinking into the bench seat. "These people all farmers?"

"Most," answered the twin he believed was Cabella.

"What do they do in winter? Can't work, can they?"

"Mostly stay home and fornicate. They have lots of time to kill."

"There's lots to do," Twila added. "Equipment repair alone keeps you busy all winter."

"I suppose they can go to town and watch movies," Mat suggested.

"When they can get out. Plow the road yourself here," Twila said.

"This is *North by Northwest* country," the other explained.

The passenger, Cabella – wasn't she Cabella? – leaned over and pulled a whisky pint from beneath the seat. "Dad doesn't like us to drink," she said, tipping it back. "He'd just about kill us if he caught us out here drinking. But I suppose this is a special circumstance."

Mat laughed uneasily, thinking the girls might be underage. But with Dickey noses and Winder ears, they were as safe as chimpanzees for all he cared. "You mean us alone out here?"

Cabella unzipped her jacket. "He'd be afraid we'd wreck the truck." She passed the bottle past Mat to Twila. "These bullet holes are gonna cause us grief, sis."

"Think they kinda add something. But you're right; daddy won't see it that way."

All the more reason to get the hell out, Mat thought. "Any chance we could drive to Des Moines? I bet you girls would like to do a little shopping, huh?"

Twila rolled her eyes and rubbed one leg of her jeans with her stick-shift hand. "Sure thing. Us hayseed chicks just love to shop in the big city, don't we, Cabella?"

"Shucks, sis, I'm wet in my panties for thinkin' the fun of it. Maybe I can find me some suspenders for my milkin' bib."

"Some rubber boots for muckin' stalls. I go all soft for rubber boots." The girls laughed.

Mat ignored them. "How do you think those guys got to Dickeyville from Des Moines? Isn't the highway snowed in?"

"I suppose they got a tow."

"A tow company?"

"A pity about your never having a best friend, Mat," Twila said. "Maybe we can help."

"I can't believe it. Where'd you hear...?"

The young women didn't answer. Mat looked at the countryside. It all looked the same. "Where are we? I don't even know."

Twila downshifted to second, the truck slowed to a crawl. "Daddy owns this land. You own anything, Mr. Roper?" Cabella slid her hand over Mat's thigh, right to his balls, and began to rub. "Oh, jeeze," she said, "I feel so... so warm after all that excitement. Don't you, Twila?"

Mat looked down at Cabella's hand. If it had been a tarantula he couldn't have been more horrified. "Hey! I'm a married guy. I mean I will be." He chuckled uncomfortably and grabbed for her fingers.

"Made me hot, too," Twila replied. "That was more fun than a tunafish sandwich at a blind lesbian convention."

Mat's eyebrows rose. "You – you can't say that. That's indecent!"

"I'll show you wrong, Mister Matthew movie star," Cabella said.

"God, he's so damn reluctant," added Twila. "It just turns me on." She glanced into the mirror and fluffed her hair. Twila's free hand also landed in his lap and began to rub. "Right here, Mister Surfer Guy? This how the beach girls usually do it?"

"Hey, I don't even do that," he protested, grabbing their wrists and lifting the hands. "I mean, only once in a while. Or a little more often."

"Pull off, Twila," Cabella ordered, and her sister turned the wheel to one side and the truck bumped over a ditch and steered into a rutted field of remnant corn stalks sticking up scraggly over the snow. "Keep going, sis!"

Mat struggled to climb over Cabella. "I'm out of here," he yelled above a sound of winding gears. "Open that door!"

But there was, of course, nowhere to go. Even before the Ford stopped, Cabella and Twila were out of their sweaters and working on his. He tried to fight them, but there were after all two of them. He devised a legal defense as his second shirt came off. And their bodies were warm and smooth and white as ivory, and their breasts shapely with pink rosebud nipples, and there were after all four breasts to look at, and two hands were no match for four and he was, anyway, weak from hunger and sinking fast into a kind of erotic stupor in the warming cab and he hadn't been with a woman the whole week. There were also the some-odd millions of years of evolution working against his resistance, though there were plenty of reasons to resist.

"How old are you two, anyway?"

"Old enough daddy let's us watch horses do it," Cabella said.

"Christ! I got to go. Does the death penalty apply in Wisconsin statutory cases?"

"She's kidding, surfer boy. We know what we're doing," said Twila.

Mat glanced at the ears and noses of the half-dressed pair, thinking, as so many have before him, fantasies rarely work out the way a guy imagines them. Twila meanwhile pulled Mat's pants to his knees and hooked a finger in his underwear. "These gotta go." Her breath felt warm as she bent, her tongue flicking underneath the elastic.

"I'm all about fucked if we do this," he said.

"You're all about fucked, all right."

"Twila, save some of that for me," Cabella ordered as she pulled down her panties. Mat looked down her smooth belly to the Y of pubic hair, and all fight went out of him.

Twila sat up, her hand gripping Mat's penis. "You California guys sure wear a lot of clothes," she panted as the windows began to fog. "You got a pair of britches for each of us to take off. Downright thoughtful of you." She rolled down her window and tossed out her bra and an armful of Mat's clothing.

"Check it out, a diving mask," Cabella giggled. "Watch this!" And then the windows fogged completely as they did things to him that no beach babes ever had – not, at least, two at the same time.

34

When they started back, a crisp black night had fallen, and stars blinked in the cold sky. Mat's stomach growled as noisily as the Ford's four-wheel gears. Not only hunger, but a stone of guilt occupied his empty gut. How could he face Daphne? He'd betrayed her. They'd barely been apart and he'd cheated. He knew it was mostly the twins' fault, or reasoned it that way. Yet he'd loved every second of it. He'd gone back for more, humping Twila a second time on the crowded bench seat as Cabella rubbed his bare back and buttocks, then squeezed his balls. My god, my god. All the while reasoning, what the fuck. He was lost anyway. What the fuck, what the fuck.

After a half hour they carefully closed on the rise where the black sedan had been bogged, but it was gone. The pickup's headlights swept over the road, revealing tire tracks and footprints where the car had been. They pulled up, got out and adjusted snow-damp clothes.

"You have a good time, mister surfer-boy?" asked one twin, he couldn't tell which.

"Yeah, was that fun, mister little-bitty nose?" asked the other.

Mat giggled nervously, rationalizing that he was good to go on with this marriage thing now. Tonight had pretty much iced the last reason to stay single. Sure, he thought – a last fling to get it out of his system. Sort of like a bachelor party, he reasoned. Never again, that's for certain. He brightened momentarily, thinking Daphne would never find out. Then guilt swept over again and he felt panic at the thought of facing his fiancée, even if she never found out; of seeing her beautiful face, a face that had never turned toward him with anything other than trust and open love; of the enormity of betrayal. He would have to make it up to her; love her more. He brightened, but depression returned immediately. He realized the impossibility of self-deception, how it wasn't in him anyway. He'd never cheated before because he'd never been committed; regret was the weakest of emotions, and he'd scoffed at it his entire life. How had he doubted for a moment his love for Daphne? It was absurd. He loved her more than he'd ever loved before, more than himself – more than life. That sweet beautiful woman, more kind and decent than any woman he'd ever known...

What had he done?

Twenty minutes later the truck climbed the rise to Dickeyville and passed the houses at the edge of town, houses with bright Christmas lights hung along rafter-tails and on yard trees and shrubs and inside uncurtained front windows. Mat wasn't focused on Christmas lights, though. He thought about Mafia-type goons. He thought about constricting guilt and physical pains in the chest. He looked at the two young women riding beside him and noticed how their smooth skin was green-lit from the dashboard lights. Those inscrutable faces... What were they thinking? He wondered how old they were. He hoped to live to look back on this night, yet he hoped never to look back on this night. He dreaded going into Mother Dickey's house.

I'll tell her, he thought. I would never keep a secret from Daphne.

When the truck drew close, they discovered another party in progress, more riotous and bigger than before, cars and trucks parked for blocks. As the twins' slowed in front of Pa and Ma's house, young Dickey boys in the yard started hooting hog calls, burping lewdly and pelting the truck with snow. "Gonna be trouble," they warned.

Mat leaned across Cabella and rolled down a window. "Did Daphne get here?" A kid laughed and warned again, "Gonna be trouble" and waved his finger, "Naughty, naughty." The teens laughed, and so did the twins. "A secret all over the world," Mat mumbled. He scanned the immediate cars for a black sedan but didn't see it.

They four-wheeled through a snowbank onto the neighbor's lawn. Mat pushed past a twin out the truck door and through the mobbed front porch toward the riot. The moment he passed under the porch cove and opened the front door, the boisterous party fell flat.

Bodies were squeezed like crayons in a box, fit together in violation of laws governing matter and space. Faces turned his way. The twins tapped his back, whispered something unintelligible, and melted off into the crowd. A half-head taller than most everyone in the room, Mat looked across and immediately spotted Daphne, beautiful Daphne in a diaphanous white dress. He pressed through hushed revelers. "Daphne! Honey! I was so worried."

A face turned toward him. Mat saw a garland of tiny white flowers, baby's breath, encircling her blond hair. The finest woman. The house had been full to bursting last night; now it overflowed onto porches and down halls and outside, many of the faces familiar to Mat, many not. He pushed through packed bodies.

"Daphne, I'm coming. I missed you so much..." To be in her loving arms, he thought, I'm coming, baby.

She met him with cold eyes. "That so? You certainly found a funny way to show it, humiliating me like this."

She was beautiful. The most beautiful woman in the world. Mat took her arms but she remained rigid as frozen cordwood. He tried to explain. "Nothing happened," he lied, in the face of this steely reception losing desire to confess, resolve for truth dissipating on the instant. "We just went out in the snow." He let his arms fall. "Aren't you happy to see me?"

"Happy to see, all right."

"Daphne?"

"Don't give me that 'innocent' crap."

"But Daphne – "

Mother Dickey interrupted, opening one of Mat's hands and slapping a frosty-wet Leiney into it. "I'm sorry things worked out this way, Mat." She tsk-tsked. "The flap Uncle Abe's in, those goons, and now this with Daphne – I don't see how your day could be tougher."

"You know about the goons?"

"Why sure. Didn't the twins – " Ma paused. "Didn't you hear how the goons got to town? And got out?"

"No. How?"

"You better ask Daphne."

"Buses been running this whole time," he complained.

Ma shrugged. "Fancy."

"And who's Uncle Abe?"

"He's the one dead set on making your day worse. And by the way, Reverend Rantin called to pass on his regards. Says he's mightily thankful for you jumping into his congregation."

"Thanks for the message." Mat turned to Daphne. "Can't we talk somewhere quiet?"

He reached for her again but she held him away. "Mat, your head's so far up your ass you could talk out your own mouth."

"You're kidding. *Darling.*"

Dickeys and Winders surrounding Mat and Daphne moved aside as Buster Hieman edged up to them. He wore a too-big suit and his hair reeked of pomade. Something – Mat swore it was shoe polish – glistened in his wire-thin mustache. He squinted ominously at Mat.

"Don't just stare at him, moron," Daphne said. "Punch him out."

Mat gaped. "I must be on drugs."

Buster's small jaw twitched. "I suppose you and me got to go outside like gentlemen, Mr. Roper. There's honor to be done."

Daphne's face was screwed up in a rage. "I told you, Buster – enough jawing around. If you really love me, prove it. Kick his ass."

"What?" Mat stammered. He couldn't take his eyes off Buster's ridiculous pencil moustache. "You mean me and the twins – ?"

Buster snorted. "Don't play us dumb, Mr. Roper. I know you suave California fellows like to string along country folk, but I reckon you know why we got our showdown."

Mat laughed. "Just like seventh grade, only not as sophisticated."

"So you don't care about me and Daphne?"

"You and Daphne?" Mat's mouth fell open. "What in hell did you and Daphne do?" He struggled toward small, wiry Buster, but several hands grabbed his arms.

Buster reddened. "Don't go getting personal, Mr. Roper. We just did what any other married couple does."

"Why, you... Married?!"

"Didn't anybody tell you? Last night I drove down to Des Moines and spent all night sparking Daphne. In the end she broke down and said she'd be mine. We got hitched come dawn by a preacher."

"Buster, you dumb hick. I told you to start swinging," Daphne warned. "You want to sleep alone tonight?"

"No, dear. I'm sorry." Buster readied himself.

"Married. By God, you did, didn't you? You went down there and married my Daphne!" Mat laughed. Then he roared, lifting his beer above his head. He shouted so the partiers could hear. "Here's to a good man and his lovely bride! Long life and love!" Mat pumped Buster's hand. "Congratulations, Mr. Hieman. May I kiss your bride?"

He leaned to kiss Daphne's cheek but she pulled away. "I'd rather kiss a poison toadstool," she replied. "I'd slap you silly even if my twit of a husband is afraid to."

Mat lowered his voice. "Excuse us for a moment, will you, Buster? I need to talk to Daphne a minute."

Buster shrugged. "Should I, honey?"

"I don't give a good goddam one way or the other what you do."

Buster gulped, nodding. "Okay, dear. I'll be by the keg."

Mat turned to Daphne. "Honey. Daphne. I don't have the right to say this, but – "

"No doubt you're going to anyway."

"You can afford to take care of someone like Buster, I guess, but my god! The guy's a pump-jockey. How're you going to get by if something happens?"

She laughed bitterly. "The big financial lecture from a surfer beach bum. Thanks for the advice, and do you still wear the clothes I bought you? Model them for the twins?"

"Listen, take this in the spirit it's intended. I'm just saying, because of what we were..." His voice dropped to a whisper. "Daphne, I hate to tell you, but this poor guy's got the IQ of a cabbage. Maybe less.

Think what your kids will be like. If you have any kids, I mean, since his chromosomes are probably defective."

"You still don't get it. It was a joke. His dad owns the station."

"Daphne, you're not listening. The only thing this guy could get on an IQ test is drool."

"You're saying Buster's stupid? He's got problems but he's also got a Masters from the University of Wisconsin."

"A Masters? No way. You think he's smart?"

"I didn't say that. He's brilliant. Look at him. He wrote his thesis on Alexander the Great. *Reading Digest* published the book."

"I saw that book. The one with big print."

"It sold like one hundred and three copies."

"Jeeze. What'll you do with all the money."

"We have mine. You of all people ought to know."

He ignored her. "Does he have a real job?"

"You mean like yours? big-time actor? Hardly. But he can teach at the community college in Madison. Something a little more regular than part-time station attendant."

"You are bullshitting me. A teacher? Do I look as dumb as Buster?"

"You *are* as dumb – more. He's not much to look at, but it was an act. The boys were just spoofing."

"What in hell... *Spoofing*, you say? If you haven't noticed, there are more goddam liars in this town than dogs."

Daphne's eyebrows rose. "Are you so blind you haven't figured their fun?" She giggled. "You idiot. What did I get you into."

"Spoofing."

'People in a small town like to have fun. What else would they do?" Mat rubbed his temple. "You call it *spoofing*. I call it – "

"Just local custom," she interrupted. "Christ, what did you think?"

"I don't know. That there's collective insanity from inbreeding."

She shook her head. "You're a *bigger* moron than Buster."

"Lies... Snowbound mental disease."

"Come on. Everyone lies. Every time you said you loved me you stumbled over the word, so don't give me this 'lies' crap. My money didn't hurt your love spiel."

"You aren't the woman I thought you were."

"Well, don't worry. The twins are loaded too."

"The whole fucking town... Who can you trust? It's sick."

"Give me a break. What could be more human than lying? If a town's got little else, there's always a surplus. What a Pollyanna you are. It's funny, but you're leagues dumber than Buster."

"I'm getting tired of you saying that."

"That you're dumb? Or that Buster is."

"The same Buster you said was practically a genius."

"In some ways," she snapped back. "Anyway spoofing's been around since Dead Alice's funeral; since all the big lovers in town claimed to have screwed her."

"That's a little indecent."

"No, brain bank, that's fun."

"A mean little town. Everyone lied to me."

"We usually lie to people we like."

"I feel sick."

"For some reason they all like you. To me you're just arrogant."

Mat glanced at the faces around them. "I don't think I'm all that popular," he whispered.

"Imbecile. It's all in the banner. The word."

A light switched on. "*Welcome.* Verne and the boys kept saying the answer was in front of me."

"Welcome."

"*Welcome?!* Well, I've got one for you. Your father thinks Buster's an idiot, to quote him. Doesn't he know about Buster's education?"

"Sure, he knows. Pa never liked Buster. He hates Buster because he would never be a farmer. That's why we didn't marry."

Mat felt mean. "Speaking of liars, how about your pancake ears and a corn cob nose in your high school picture."

Daphne's jaw clenched.

He continued: "If Buster's so smart, why in hell doesn't he shave off that stupid moustache?"

"I'm going to make like a bird and fly away now," Daphne said.

"Good idea."

"I'll add one thing. I am sorry Buster and I gave the tow to those guys. They offered too much money to refuse and Buster had a borrowed Power Wagon."

"You towed the goons from Des Moines?"

"Not from Des Moines. They were out of gas, about froze to death, stuck in a rental car on the unplowed road, halfway to Dickeyville.

There was no other traffic, except the buses. When we stopped to help, Vinnie remembered seeing me with you in California. Sharp old buzzard. He said you owed him money and we figured what was going on. You borrowed the money for that pitiful ring, idiot, even if it was sweet of you. We towed them the rest of the way. Pretty much everyone heard about it, including the twins you didn't do anything with. But before we could talk sense to Vinnie he took off after you. Wanted to tell you he didn't want the money. Wants to return to the church."

"His goons aren't going to church."

"No. They got an act on the Disney channel. Puppets."

"Vinnie told you all this?"

"He did. Just wanted to rough you up for old time's sake. For his reputation. Say in person the loan is forgiven. But you screwed up."

"I didn't screw up. I ran."

"Right. So he got pissed and decided to kill you after all."

"Short fuse. I hope you didn't invite him here."

"It's done. After they chased you, and the guys towed them to town a second time, Buster and Verne took up a collection from everybody and we paid Vinnie the money."

"Come on. People wouldn't put up that kind of money for me."

"It wasn't much, spread out between everyone in town. It wasn't that much of a ring."

"They wanted to kill me."

"Not at first. Just beat you up."

"I suppose you know they shot at us? The twins and me?"

"Piddling twenty-two pistol. Barely kill you. As far as the collected money, I don't know why everyone seems to like you."

Mat cleared his throat. "We've partied."

"Except a few guys who are mad at you," she continued. "The Mayor, for one. Know why? He said about hunting. You shoot off somebody's dick?"

"About the Horror. About what happened."

"What happened?"

"You haven't heard."

"Heard what? That they made a fool of you? that Heywood jerked you off too and is not even close to clever?"

"Clever enough to be a college professor."

"Heywood? He's a salesman at Mengel's Shoes and Shotshells. I doubt he got past sixth grade."

"I gotta get out of here." – Mat thumped his head. "What's with you? You were never like this."

"The goody two-shoes you fell for… God, am I glad to shed that skin. It was fun while it lasted, though. You are the looker. A little vain but fun in bed. But not that fun. Wormie was better."

"Wormie? at the Wet Stork? and the jewelery store?"

"Just for grins. Don't even know why. And you, maybe for your looks. After you got to know me, you'd never have put up with my shit. Now Tweedlebeans over there," she jerked her thumb toward Buster who pretended not to be watching, "since he finally got into my pants, will do just about anything I say to get there again."

"I don't believe this."

"Who cares what you believe? Buster's not a sentimental guy, and he doesn't mind that you gave me the ring." She held up her hand and displayed it. "It's not much but will always remind me of a good time."

"I thought we had something."

"Measles." – She laughed.

"This is a trick. You don't mean it."

Daphne's face softened; her shoulders drooped. She searched his face, then her eyes dropped. "No, this isn't true, Mat. How could you believe it for a moment, after all we've been to each other? I thought you trusted me. Of course I didn't marry Buster. I've been dying every day just to see you." She reached for his neck.

He breathed hard. "Hey, baby. I knew it was an act. God, I missed you." He spread his arms, laughing. Another spoof from the hicks.

Daphne stepped away. "Wow. You really eat it up. Sorry, Mat. Just wanted to see if I could web you in one more time."

"What?"

"*What?* What if I told you I loved you more than life?"

"I'd know that was the real you."

"Unbelievable. You aren't even worth the game."

Mat shook his head. "You're crazy. What about Buster?"

"Whatever."

Mat tried to shake it off, all of it. "I don't know. It's all a big joke. You, that pig – "

"*Boar.* It's a boar," Daphne interrupted.

"Boar, then. Heywood's bones, the Grotto – "

"Not the Grotto. Don't even say the Grotto's a joke."

"The joke is my stomach. I almost starved in Dickeyville and all this time you didn't care."

"Now you're trying to bullshit me. Ma never let anyone go hungry."

"And that ring. It almost got me killed. Vinnie's known for his revenge diet – take a pound off here or there. A hand or kneecap."

"Not now. When Verne and Bascom and Brodie and the Sheriff and some boys showed in pickups to tow Vinnie and his buddies out of the snow, the boys sported rifles and wore huntin' hats. After that the fat man seemed relieved to get his money and out of town." She paused. "But I'd think twice about showing your face in L.A."

"They're gone?"

"For good. Like me."

"I can't believe what you really are."

"Well, I can't believe someone never had a best friend."

"Now how did – "

"But I do believe I said this conversation is over."

"Sonuvabitch hicks!" Mat looked around and saw Verne, one man in the room as tall as himself. Mat nodded; Verne winked back. "Verne said he'd do anything for a Dickey or a Winder, but not a Roper. Even if I'm not going to be a Dickey after all."

"I'm not so sure about that."

"You're not bullshitting me about being married."

"Not what I mean but forget it," Daphne shrugged. "Tell me something. It's important."

"First tell me: why didn't you say about the nose and ear job?"

"I wasn't going to marry you; didn't matter to tell. For me it's games every day. I didn't care. That's why I wanted you to meet my family. You were so fucking full of yourself. I wanted you to see what small-town Dickeyville was like. I wanted you off your high-horse."

"Because?"

"Told you, for fun. I take it you know Ma and Pa were in on the whole thing from the start. Knew you were coming."

"I figured. What kind of fool do you think I am?"

"No hicks could pull one over a California surfer boy."

"So what was your question?"

"Did you wonder why I never married before you came along?"

"Yeah. So why was it?"

"You *are* dumb. No wonder I hung you out like a shitty diaper."

Something passed behind his eyes. He remembered what Verne had said: *ball breaker*. Daphne was a poison vine that had worked its way into his heart. "You've crushed me, Daphne. But I swear I forgive you." The bus... If he packed tonight and caught a late Greyhound to Des Moines, or anywhere but Dickeyville... Probably had just enough credit left on his Visa for a ticket to Hawaii, to Maui or Kauai. No cash, but what the hell. He was free and safe as long as he didn't go back to L.A. Religion or not, Vinnie would never forget. But Vinnie was overdue for a heart attack. Matter of time.

Somewhere there was a worldly woman, a nice leather lady with a bottomless heart and purse who'd like a black t-shirt and white shorts kind of guy, a lonely woman who'd help him drown heartache in margaritas beside a white sandy beach. He would go cheerfully for her drinks with little umbrellas and they would love in that cheerless little way, that happy-sad lonely way that was better than nothing but not so good as it had been with Daphne... because they *had* been good. But what the hell. Bring on the gilded cage. He downed his beer and asked – yelled – to Mother Dickey for another. She handed it from ten feet away and several hands grabbed and passed it. The noisy celebration of Buster and Daphne's nuptials quickly amplified a few hundred decibels to fill the room. There were toasts and cheers and it seemed that Mat had never been so popular. Funny, he thought, but I think I'm going to miss these hicks.

He smiled. Miss them? I already got the swing of spoofing.

"Tell you what," Father Dickey said as he draped an arm over Mat's. "I sure as hell wish you *was* my son-in-law instead of that damn no-good. I know that someday you'd find my string end for me. I tell you I had a dream about that? I'm nervous as a horn worm on a hotplate, Mat, that you're going to go away."

"Who, me?"

"It's written in the Bible that a Winder's got to marry a Dickey."

"Is Buster a Winder or Dickey?"

"Not either. You know, that lazy bastard doesn't have a real job. Just plunks around in his daddy's gas station; ain't even paid to be there."

"Worthless."

"Right. I think the sonuvabitch is after my money. Have a drink."

"I never gave a goddam about your money, I want you to know."

"You're all right, Mat."

"Everyone said there weren't any buses."

"They wanted Buster to have a chance."

"You've been the most helpful. I appreciate that."

"They wanted to help that piece of shit get my Daphne."

"Where did you say it was written about Dickeys marry Winders? In case I ever want to look it up?"

"*Deuteronomy*. Old Testament."

"You're a good guy, Pa."

"Only stupid people think stupidity's a virtue. Remember that."

Mat patted Pa's back and slipped away as soon as he could. Visions of tropical vistas flew through his head, a life away from crazy Midwest farm people. How close he'd come to becoming a part of it! Close to a way of life that could never make him happy, especially now that he'd killed their stupid boar. He bumped into the Mayor's arms.

"I had plans for you, son. Then you killed our boar. You've ruined all of us. I hope you know that." Drunk, the bent old man swept off his top hat and, with his free hand, tried to smooth hair as frizzled as Einstein's. "Ruined us, don't you see?" He began to push past Mat.

"I didn't want to shoot any animals in the first place." Mat snorted. "If you guys hadn't done all that crap to me for... spoofing, I wouldn't have gone hunting. I can't change that now, but how about you keep your Weatherby rifle?"

The Mayor turned. His smile was weary, but he nodded. "Damn square of you, Roper. I suppose you'll be leaving us now."

Mat nodded, hardly able to conceal his glee.

The Mayor pursed lips. "Shame. With Buster marrying Daphne the population gains no one. Nine hundred and ninety-nine. One citizen shy of receiving this year's Wisconsin State Community Development funds. First the boar, now the population. You've really done for us."

"I'm outta here, Mayor. By the way, you have a cell phone?"

"Who the hell doesn't? How'd you think we knew to come out to the Mazy after you killed our Horror?"

Time to pack, Mat thought. Pushing through the densest part of the throng, he reached the hallway at the foot of the stairs. Someone's hands caught him from behind.

"Jump!" a voice thundered.

Mat's feet lifted off the floor. "Reverend Rantin!" He turned to face a body as thick as a blue-ribbon hog's, a pair of eyes heavy-lidded and dark under a pile of dark bluish-black hair sprinkled with gray, a block of hair so thick it seemed to be made of varnished wood. Standing under the hair was just one more person he wished not to see. "Reverend Weems. What a surprise. I guess you heard the news. I'm afraid there won't be a marriage ceremony after all."

"No, I'm sorry there will not. The table of marital bliss is not set for you, Mat Roper. The succulent fleshy feast of love is for another."

"I suppose." Mat was distracted, focusing elsewhere, but glanced back when he realized Weems expected a response. "I've got to go."

"What I want to say is, if you did stay in Dickeyville, you'd want to worship at your church of choice. And your choice would undoubtedly be the New Reform Church. We're elevating our cross by sixteen inches this summer. We'll be the tallest church in town by five inches."

"Wowsers."

"It'll be constructed from recycled plastic milk cartons. Indestructible and non-conductive; no worshipper will be at risk from lightning."

"They'll pray easier knowing that."

The Reverend shifted his weight from one foot to the other. "Saying 'jump' was just a joke."

"I kind of figured."

"Well, no joke for Reverend Rantin. But it sort of seems you haven't figured out very much."

"Now listen here – "

"Because Rantin and I never attend parties together. We suspect the proximity of differing faiths might cause a theological schism that could ignite a celestial conflagration. Like ether and flame. There's potential to ignite the eternal heavens."

"Sorry?"

"Another joke. A spoof, a secularly sanctioned suspension of veracity. So speaking of truth, I should mention that at the Lord's banquet there are toastmasters and there are partakers of the divine feast. You are a dog of poverty, one of the Alsatians who get only scraps."

"So now I'm a dog, huh?"

"I too am doomed to be among the hungry," Weems went on. "Salivating for the souls of man, that mankind might exist forever at the Lord's bounteous table, which is set before all but partaken by few."

Mat glanced over the room to where a hungry fat woman leaned over the dining table. "Reverend, there is a soul you may know, a soul longing for the feast."

"Of whom do you speak? Say, that I might escort said soul toward the celestial tureen to slurp with He whose table overfloweth."

"Not 'he'. It's a woman, a gourmet cook missing the blessing of church-sanctioned matrimony. You could say there are no mashed potato pancakes with garlic, sour cream and smoked-cheddar chips upon the smorgasbord table of her heart. No heaping stacks of deviled – beg your pardon – eggs with dill and Dijon mustard under smoked salmon strips. No country-fried catfish with buttermilk batter and smoked red pepper smothered in sweet corn and onion rings. No – "

"Excuse me, but where would I find such a starved soul? Where in this world of want, so far from the heavenly feast and smorgasbord of His table, would I find such hunger? Nowhere, I think."

"She's right over there." – Mat pointed.

"Where? The... that big one, standing alone?"

"That's her."

"That's Lana Winder."

"An honorably divorced woman of culinary talent."

"Lana's never been married."

"Fuckin' rats," Mat mumbled.

"Beg your pardon?"

"Suckling fats," he corrected.

"What does that mean?"

Mat shrugged. "Just look at Lana."

"A fallen woman. Divorced."

"*Divorced*? You just said she's never... never mind."

"Rather, a woman of virtue and culinary discrimination. You know she wrote a cookbook of divine recipes and dishes?"

"Nonetheless I understand she's not regular in church attendance."

"How could she be? She's too busy preparing enormous Sunday brunches of glazed baby hams and sweet potato soufflés and home-baked buttermilk biscuits and fresh-churned homemade strawberry ice cream dribbled with baba-au-rum sauce."

"Baba-au-rum sauce?"

"Tough to do a fine one. How that buffoon stole all her recipes..."

"Who stole her recipes?"

"The husband. The one she doesn't have. I'm confused."

"Buttermilk biscuits. Good ones are like celestial clouds."

"Light as a croissant still hot from the oven. With homemade black-berry jam."

The Reverend smacked his rubbery lips. "Never can it be said the Reverend Weems passed by an opportunity to deliver a soul to God's sacred banquet. Perhaps I'll just stroll over."

Mat set course through the throng for the stairs so he could pack. Hands slapped his back. Through the living room, at the foot of the stairs, a man waited, an oak of a man. Though Mat stood tall, his eyes rose only to the other's nose. He guessed this was Uncle Abe even before the lantern jaw, stubbled with a day's growth of black whiskers stiff as finishing nails, pressed near his face.

"Son, I guess you know who I am."

Mat stuck out his hand. He had never before seen a wool shirt filled near to bursting from biceps. "Ah, sir. I suppose you're the uncle of the bride? And, umm…the father of…?"

"That would be me. Uncle Abe, the twins' father. I wanted to talk to you in private."

There was in the voice something that sounded like a door closing. "Sir. In the kitchen?"

"I think we'll be needing a more private venue, son."

Epilogue: Summer

So what does a man do when faced with the immovable and has lost half the wealth of Dickeyville? What can he do? The right thing, of course. Become cousin to his ex-fiancée by marrying one of her floppy-eared, bulb-schnozzed cousins in a ceremony performed by the Reverend Weems, himself married only one month before to the witty Lana Winder, said to set the finest table in Dickey County even though she's reached a svelte one hundred and fifty pounds. The Reverend and Lana are remarkably well-suited.

Best Man Verne raises a laugh when he presents Mat and Twila with the prescribed something "old", a slab of polished and brown-stained ivory, curved and honed on one side, nine inches long. Twila looks puzzled but doesn't question. Later guests at the Roper residence will be pleased to see the object on a stand over the mantle. A few will recognize what it is. Those happy few will know why it's Mat's.

Mat's and Twila's wedding feast, prepared by good friend Lana Winder-Weems, becomes a culinary legend in Dickeyville, and Mat avails himself to all manner of good things, none of which is meat. His prodigious appetite gladdens the hearts of Winder-Dickey matrons. The good Reverend Weems joins in the repast and demonstrates a healthy respect for both celebrants and cuisine: he and Mat sit shoulder to shoulder plowing through plates until sweat drips down their cheeks and their shirts glue to sweaty backs. Mat finally surrenders.

Then the other twin is married – also to Mat – in a ceremony performed by the Reverend Rantin, a ceremony proclaimed as legal and obligatory by the Mayor of Dickeyville by virtue of his own authority. At this event, Best Man Ed "Buster" Hieman drinks too much California champagne and burns half of his mustache when he lights a gift cigar from the Mayor. This infuriates Buster's wife Daphne, who calls him an imbecile, especially when he insists on wearing the remaining half-mustache for the duration of the celebration.

Mat enjoys the conflict.

The ceremonial first dance strikes a lively chord, and Mat and Twila and Cabella dance for the guests, initiating a half-hour bunny-hop performed by even the oldest and youngest of guests. The Reverend Rantin joins in and is a lively bunny-hopper. It is the stuff of legend in the annals of Dickeyville matrimony.

Matrimony and spoofing are Dickeyville customs. Lovely, lonely Dead Alice, condemned to consort with liars, her portrait hanging in the foyer of the courthouse, a veritable hotbed of lies; patroness of Mazy Woods, feared and never loved... Marriage, because Mat has learned that the twins are inseparable, have been since birth, always will be. Whatever one does, so does the other.

Mat learns they are a fun-loving and inventive pair. He cannot imagine life before them. He finds the routine of marriage breeds not boredom but something as deep and quiet as the murky depths of the Millawney where it flows into the Mississippi. Not a thing to understand, a thing to be. Like the rivers, the twins and Mat merge into a thing greater than each, inseparable as the mingling waters. In love he finds contentment. In contentment is peace.

He also learns that the father of those twins owns all the rich southern Wisconsin farmland to the west of Dickeyville, black loamy soil stretching as far as the eye can see, land worth something in the neighborhood of ten million, give or take. So a husband knows who he's talking to, sweet Cabella gets a nose-job. Lovely Twila gets an ear-job, because that's way twins are.

The father-in-law is a pretty good guy once a fellow learns to appreciate the Packers and Badgers and that it's practical to wear a stupid quilted cap with earflaps and make Uncle Abe a granddad. A guy learns to read, really read, and does so in his old Dickey farmhouse before a roaring fire. He sits back in an oaken rocking chair under a bare, swaying bulb during the worst blizzards, Alaskan ice storms sweeping down the Great Plains. Sometimes his son or daughter climbs into his lap to suck a thumb and listen to the wind howl.

Once in a while he closes his eyes and imagines the old boar's early years, the beast so far away from Europe, an outsider, who in his brute stupidity found life within the great Mazy forest with unlimited food and room, living like a king. Mat likes to think how every spring when time was ripe, the boar would find his way to the penned sows of a few luckless farmers. He likes to think that the boar, an ancient loner, would have liked how it ended, have appreciated that the last one to see him alive was a tall Californian with no inclination to hurt.

Time passes, a couple years, and routine comes to Mat. He learns the seasons and the sweet odor of thawed earth. Every year after harvest he leaves Dickeyville for a couple months with his father-in-law and twin wives and children with slightly-big noses and floppy ears to stay in their beachfront condo in Maui. It's a big place and usually thirty or forty Dickey and Winder relatives, old and young, show up. This takes care of Mat's need for ocean. He never minds the company. Hog calls still sound like fog horns squeaked through garden hoses, and the sound still sends unpleasant chills down his spine, but what the hell. Mat has hogs of his own even if he won't eat them. He's been known to unlimber a hog call once in a while, which doesn't please his mother and her various beaus during their annual visits. She's comes to accept the Dickey-Winder clan since they're the only ones who'll listen to her Tinseltown lore.

A fellow becomes protégé to an aging, hunched Mayor when he becomes citizen number one thousand and telephones an industry acquaintance who specializes in production of mechanical monsters. Mat asks: "Could you stretch an old boar skin over a frame and animate it a bit? Hydraulic system of some sort? Remote control? Would it cost too much to make it look half-assed convincing, like a monster wild boar with nine-inch fangs?"

"Those are called tusks, Roper. Christ."

"Whatever. *Tusks.*"

"What happened to you? I heard some big Mafia don took a hundred-G contract on you."

"Me? I snack on those guys."

"Then I heard the studio police and DEA went for you. Some big coke deal in Colombia."

"Rumor. Not a bit to it."

"So what'd you do with the money?"

"Broads, booze, fast cars, gambling. Then I spent the rest foolishly."

"George Raft. Christ, then I heard – "

"So can you do the monster or not? It's a hush deal; has to be done outside the studio. And this is important: it has to be bulletproof."

"You mean flawless?"

"No, as in bullets bouncing off. *Bulletproof.*"

"That'll cost. But I sure as hell wouldn't use old boarskin. That would look phony as hell. I'll do it in my garage. I got some Mexican guys do real good work. Twenty-five, maybe thirty thousand bucks, tops. You making a low-budget?"

"Something like that."

The crate eventually arrives in Chicago and Mat, Brodie, the Mayor and Verne pick it up. Mat is happy after the preserved Horror's real carcass is thawed and examined in secret by Dr. Wilma Winder at the University of Wisconsin School of Veterinary Medicine in Madison. Her expertise is in animal physiology and she specializes in large mammals. Swine are her passion. She's a discreet individual who understands the confidential nature of the job. She finds no fatal bullet holes in the beast, but autopsy reveals something else. Seems as how Mat did kill the Horror: he frightened the beast to death. It died of a heart attack. Source of hilarity for Verne and Bascom. Mat feels better knowing his part in the boar's demise was indirect.

With a Wisconsin State Community Development fund of $30,000, Cousin Buster gets a prestigious job. His position as Dickeyville Horror Days Commissioner often takes him into the woods during the annual winter boar hunt. Only a few can figure exactly what Buster does, but as boar sightings increase, the hunts seem to prosper and, with them, the town.

It's noted Buster spends a lot of time away from home. Mat now understands why no one before Buster married beautiful Daphne.

One year during a sighting of the Dickeyville Horror, a near-sighted fellow from New York manages to get off a few shots as the snorting beast charges into a clearing. There, fortunately, at the behest of The Dickeyville Horror Days Commissioner, a cameraman from the KBIB Channel 7 NBC affiliate in Madison just happens to be waiting. That the shot is well-directed and a dead-ringer for a scene from *Jurassic Park* escapes everybody except Mat. That night the Dickeyville Horror Days celebration, along with footage of the Horror, is featured on CBS, NBC, ABC, FOX and CNN, not to mention over 2,000,000 You Tube hits by day three.

Tabor and Calico are a "trifle hornswaggled" but happier'n hell that numb-nuts greenhorn Roper didn't shoot the real boar. Hell, that little bitty thing Roper shot didn't amount to a pile of pig poop. Given a few days and a couple cases of Leineys, and some prodding from the Mayor, they barely remember the little hirsute squealer Roper killed. Imagine thinking that bitty oinker had been the Horror.

The following year is projected the best hunt ever. The Dickeyville Chamber of Commerce treasury swells.

There is more talk about Roper for Assemblyman. The rumor

won't be quashed that the modest man will indeed run, and frequently he's seen having breakfast at the Dickeyville Diner and Rifle Club with the Mayor. Both wear camouflage top hats. Mat supposes his candidacy is the stupidest thing he's ever heard. Rumor has Mat getting rich breeding polliwogs with his buddies, Verne and Brodie. They have indoor ponds in a couple barns.

When he first saw the set-up, Mat had thought Verne was crazy. "I don't know much about raising things, but I do know you can't make frogs breed in the winter. Can you?"

"Pretty savvy for a layman," Verne replied.

The barn was warmed by an overhead system of grow lights and heat lamps. Mat guessed they took plenty of energy. He stood beside one of the filtered pools. Six inches of water filled half of it, and from the water rose a sandy slope with some sort of beach grass. Dozens of ten-inch, yellow-mottled frogs leaped into the water from the grass when Mat bent over. He saw their bodies glide along the pool's bottom. In the water were hundreds of two-inch polliwogs.

"Incredible. I've never seen bullfrogs like these."

"That's because they're Australian gold-backs. Like all things 'down-under', their summer is our winter. These puppies breed like crazy in the wintertime."

"So how'd you think of something so crazy? It's amazing."

"My post-Vietnam legacy. These Aussie frogs are pretty much all I brought back."

"You weren't in Vietnam."

Verne scratched his nose. "Who the hell says?"

"Pa Dickey."

"He's a liar."

"What do you feed frogs?"

"They're particularly fond of pickled okra sandwiches."

Once in a while a guy goes walleye pike fishing through the ice. A guy uses polliwogs for bait. Mat discovers that polliwog breeders make salaries of around forty thousand a year. The income helps to supplement a guy's other profession, as organic farmer. Corn-raising, Mat discovers, is in his blood, and he pioneers a market for organic corn in Madison.

He especially likes July when a late-afternoon breeze sweeps across the fields and the cornstalks rustle and glisten in lowering light. From where he sits on the back verandah after a day's work, sipping a cold Leiney with Twila and Cabella and a friend, the wind's whispering reminds him of a distant surf break.

"Used to be an ocean right here, Verne. About two million years ago and it sounded like this."

Best friend Verne nods: "I know that." He tips his beer.

"So do we," Cabella adds. "You say it often enough.".

"You want to hear my story, Verne?" Mat asks.

"What's it about?"

"Good-looking guy on a bus. Going to Wisconsin."

"Uh-huh."

"He's from California."

"So? What happens?"

"Hunts this giant killer pig."

"Boar."

"*Boar.* Jeeze. Who's story is this? He meets unique people. Gets drunk a lot and starves. Finds contentment."

Twila leans over to kiss Mat on the cheek.

"Bullshit. Who'd believe a story like that."

The phone rings a week after he marries the second twin. Mat takes time to lift the receiver. "Mat? Ike Russ here. How ya hangin', babe?"

"Ike. Nice of you to call. I guess mother told you I got married."

"Hell, I won't hold that against you. Heh-heh."

"What's up?"

"Mat, babe, I can't get a handle on what's going on. You coming home soon? I got a smoker here, a real smoker."

"Home. Nice ring to it, Ike."

"Listen, I'm flying near the sun. You and me, we're going flying."

"Ike, way I hear it I'm not too welcome with the studio."

"All in the past, pal. You've been flying low these past few months and the heat's off. There's been confessions. You're clear."

"A job?"

"It's so hot I'm melting. Really. It's scorching."

"Tell me about it, Ike. I was just going to bed."

"At eight?"

"It's eleven here." Mat hears cloth rustle as Twila pulls back the sheets. Then he hears the springs of the king-size bed stretch as Cabella sits down. "I got to go, Ike."

"No, listen. Beetleman stepped on an urchin and pin-cushioned his foot. The *Sea Watch* gig is yours. Less my commission, of course."

"Beetleman stepped on a sea urchin? Didn't that happen to the other guy too?"

"Tragic."

"Why me? There's a hundred cinema divers in L.A.. Dime-a-dozen." Mat heard the silky rustle of delicates lifting off two bodies.

"Not now. Spielberg's got practically every diver on the coast under ink for his remake of *Twenty Thousand Leagues*. You can practically call your shot, babe. This is a major-league contract, the kind guys kill for. And it's all yours, good for two years minimum."

"I don't know, Ike. It's kind of far away."

"Mat, it's right here, right now. Ninety G's a year. Warm-water dives with the babes. I know you're married and all, but what do you want? If this isn't it, what have you been looking for all these years?"

Mat smiles, but Ike Russ can't see that. "Good question. I guess I was looking for a home better than the one I lost. Looking for people who didn't want anything from me."

"You're flying too low, Mat. This is the chance of a lifetime."

"It's like when I was a kid and at night I'd swim out in the water. I'd look back over the waves to beach fires with people standing around."

"Yeah, yeah, very poetic. You're a regular Longfellow."

"Just me and the stars and the sea. The little fires looking like back-lit holes ripped out of a black curtain."

"One year ago or a hundred, it's still the past."

"It's like water slapping off the sides of a pool, coming back here."

"What, you joined some kind of cult?"

"No. Just realized how much the thread unraveled in California."

"What are you talking about? Follow the thread back? *This* is home, babe. Waiting. Find your way to the good life. It's all here for you."

"I won't go back, Ike. I found what I didn't know I was looking for."

"Man, you're in the boonies! Have you lost your fuckin' mind? Listen, maybe I can get you ninety-five. I'm sure I can – with a studio contract; everything you've ever wanted. Come out from the mildew, babe. Fly in the rarefied air. You're a great-looking guy and the sky's the limit, if you get a little exposure. No telling what could happen."

"Oh, I know what could happen."

"Spread your wings and let go!"

"You know what, Ike? These people think my nose and ears are too small. Isn't that a hoot?"

"You are fucking out of your mind. What the hell are you talking about? This is the chance of a lifetime!"

So something ended as something begins. A fellow knows he'll be forgotten in the babe battles at beachside bars. The Jimmy Buffet crowd will change, the bars fill like tip jars and what is charming will grow wearisome, what is eccentric debauched. The dramas will play out with big irony but small tragedy. Hedonism will go on, timeless and appealing as ever. There will be new players; there will be black t-shirts and Hawaiian shirts with white slacks and sandals, sweet-hearted leather ladies and desperate leather men, laugh-lines botox-ed from corners of eyes that laugh less every year, ladies (and gentlemen) with deep purses and a tolerance for drifters... The young and fresh will roll away the old ones like tires off a rack. But Mat won't think about it. The family will close around him, not like a corral but like a quilt, an old hand-sewn quilt made by a pioneer ancestor.

He realizes what it means to be family. He is happy as a king and possesses a kingly smile. He knows the twins were right: life should be like a movie, with a car chase, a monster, a loan shark, a hero – and love. Because every story is a love story.

There should also be a fool.

Mat, Verne, Bascom, Brodie and Buster sneak outside "Hollywood" Heywood's outhouse one moonless night in December. Heywood has no inside bathroom because his place is completely gutted. Just as Heywood opens the door of his shitter to head back inside, a huge boar, the Dickeyville Horror, snorts and rushes at him. Heywood slams the door, narrowly avoiding certain death. Nine-inch tusks rattle and scratch on the wooden shack – the snorting beast looking for meat. It almost tips the outhouse; tusks rip holes in the walls; Heywood cowers back, screaming for help as boards splinter. He takes refuge. All night, temperature in the low teens, Heywood stands shivering with head stuck out of a stinking hole while the boar snuffles outside the door. When Heywood yells for help the Horror starts to scratch at the walls, so he waits quietly in waist-deep shit... Not a pleasant night for "Hollywood" Heywood.

Mat and Verne and Bascom and Brodie and Buster share a quart of Irish whiskey. Dawn brings a crowd, but the boar has vanished. When

Heywood gathers courage to exit the outhouse, there it sits in front of the door: a pink ceramic piggie-bank from the Dickeyville Savings and Reloads. "Hollywood" Heywood yells it wasn't a six-inch piggy that attacked his outhouse, but the evidence is clear.

Mat and his friends witness humiliation but don't stand close to it. "Heywood, you're a funny guy," says Ma Dickey, part of the crowd. "Sorry Grandpa Winder's missing this."

Later a guy stows the mechanical Horror in its storeroom. Dickeyville tradition has become enjoyable.

These are not the most sincere people Mat has ever known, but they do have fun. A guy can say he modeled for Sauron's eye in Jackson's *The Lord of the Rings* – can say pretty much anything: he played a fencepost in *Giant*. But the day "Hollywood" Heywood stands in shit is a good day for Mat and the town. Still laughing, Ma Dickey goes out to the family plot in the Dickeyville Cemetery and Rifle Range and puts a rose on Grandpa Winder's headstone.

A guy's good friend Lana Winder-Weems bakes a pie even if she's pretty preoccupied with her new wide-back husband who seems to have found an earthly feast to precede the celestial one. Lana has abandoned the profession of screenwriting. She's down to one-thirty.

A guy decides that, even though he eats alone at the existential feast, for the rest of it, it's not so much about hunger as about wanting. Not so much about eating as about feasting. Not so much the set of the table as the company.

A guy learns to appreciate the Dickeyville Grotto for what it is, inspiration born of faith in what cannot be proved, and if a guy cannot believe he can at least appreciate. The distance between the grotesque and the sublime is sometimes more a matter of choice than of taste.

A guy has an idea that convinces the whole family that a Californian is the bee's knees. Good buddy Buster Hieman agrees. Best friend Verne and Brodie and Bascom say so too. It's just a matter of pushing into the maze of small-town relationships, finding a common thread to follow and knotting family ties.

Mat says you take some flypaper. And then you take it to Ma and Pa Dickey's old farmhouse, the place you've come to think of as home even if you live a mile away. You walk back in the maze of rooms where something incomplete awaits you. Then you press the flypaper all over that big unwholesome blob of knotted strings. You just keep it up and press all over. And there you go. Pa Dickey was right. Sooner or later you're bound to pull out... the end.

Made in the USA
Lexington, KY
26 July 2012